ST. MARTIN'S
MINOTAUR
MYSTERIES

GET A CLUE!

Be the first to hear the latest mystery book news...

With the St. Martin's Minotaur monthly newsletter, you'll learn about the hottest new Minotaur books, receive advance excerpts from newly published works, read exclusive original material from featured mystery writers, and be able to enter to win free books!

Sign up on the Minotaur Web site at:
www.minotaurbooks.com

More...

"Spooky séances, ouija boards, nights spent cavorting in Mount Auburn Cemetery, and mourning jewelry made of human hair take center stage in *Mansions of the Dead* . . . a story of grief and remembrance, and its pleasures include the explication of the 'cult of mourning' that overtook America in the wake of the Civil War, and grief as we experience it today."

—*Boston Sunday Globe*

"With three possible love interests for Sweeney and strong secondary characters, this is very compelling reading. The graveyards, antique shops and historical societies of Boston and Newport are artfully sketched, and the invisible social boundaries of both cities are well drawn."

—*Romantic Times*

"Sarah Stewart Taylor has written an exciting mystery featuring characters that are so easy to like. . . . The heroine . . . is spunky, sweet, and sparkling, and readers will want to read more books featuring this dynamic character."

—*Midwest Book Review*

"An intelligent tale, leaving readers begging to know more."

—*Booklist*

"This moody, atmospheric novel will appeal to fans of darker cozies."
—*Publishers Weekly*

O' ARTFUL DEATH

"Taylor does a lovely job of setting an atmospheric scene and luring us inside."

—Marilyn Stasio, *The New York Times Book Review*

"[*O'Artful Death*] rings subtle—and enormously satisfying—changes on the venerable tried-and-true."

—*Newsday*

"A strikingly atmospheric debut. The writing is crisp and the characters all quite forcefully alive, especially Sweeney."

—*Denver Post*

"An elegantly wrought first mystery with layers within layers like carved ivory balls . . . rich and rewarding reading."

—*Booklist*

JUDGMENT
of the GRAVE

SARAH STEWART TAYLOR

St. Martin's Paperbacks

JUDGMENT OF THE GRAVE

Copyright © 2005 by Sarah Stewart Taylor.
Excerpt from *Still as Death* © 2006 by Sarah Stewart Taylor.

Cover photo of church © Monserrate J. Schwartz / Alamy.
Photo of landscape © Elvele Images / Alamy.

Library of Congress Catalog Card Number: 2005042960

ISBN: 0-312-94016-5
EAN: 9780312-94016-4

Printed in the United States of America

St. Martin's Press hardcover edition / July 2005
St. Martin's Paperbacks edition / August 2006

St. Martin's Paperbacks are published by St. Martin's Press, 175 Fifth Avenue, New York, NY 10010.

10 9 8 7 6 5 4 3 2 1

APRIL 19, 1775

JOHN WHITING SAT IN HIS FATHER'S WORKSHOP, LOOKING UP
at the night sky through the open door. It was a clear night,
the blue-blackness filled with stars, and he looked for the
ones his father had taught him to recognize, the pinpricks of
light making out patterns in the night as surely as his father's
chisels etched patterns on stone.

His father liked stars, liked carving them on his grave-
stones, and one of John's favorite border designs was the
one with the little starbursts along the edge. His father used
stars in various ways as ornaments, and John remembered
when he'd realized that his father found inspiration for his
work everywhere around him—the leaves he brought back
from his walks in the woods, the summer flowers John's
mother collected from the fields and placed in pots around
the house. Even seashells and the very waves of the ocean,
which his father remembered from his childhood in Ply-
mouth. All of these things ended up on the grave markers
made in the workshop of Josiah Whiting of Concord.

John knew that his father was one of the best stonecutters
in the area. He knew this because of the way people talked
about his work and because his father was always busy.
Lately, it seemed he'd hardly had time to complete one order
before another came in. He'd joked to John that people must
be dying in greater numbers than usual, for he never seemed
to have a moment to spare.

"Once I have you trained, once the sign on the shop reads, 'Josiah Whiting and Son,' then we'll be able to take on even more work," he'd said only a few days before. Josiah had been training John, but John knew it was only wishful thinking that they'd be able to take on much more work. It was true that there were things he could do in the shop, the fine carving work and some of the lettering, but stonecutting was hard, backbreaking labor, and with his bad leg, there was no way John could be much help. There were days when the pain was so bad that he could barely stand.

He shifted in his father's chair, feeling the leg talk back to him. He'd learned to handle this kind of discomfort. The best thing was to keep moving, so he lifted himself out of the chair, found the cane his father had carved for him leaning up against the wall, and hobbled out into the night air.

As he passed the stable, he heard Monteroy whinnying nervously in his stall, and the anxiety he'd been feeling ever since the horse had come barreling into the yard that afternoon, still wearing his saddle and saddlebags, the reins trailing and muddy, returned in force.

Where was he? He should be back by now. It must be nearly midnight and his father had been gone since almost this time the night before. The alarm had been raised that the Redcoats were on the march and all of the men from the Minuteman companies were to meet at the tavern to take orders. John had watched his father as he'd dressed by the fire. By all rights, he should have gone too. He was sixteen, more than old enough, but he wasn't able to fight any more than his six-year-old sister was.

"You take care of things, John. I'm depending on you," Josiah had said as he'd slipped out into the night. He'd taken John's hand and held it for a moment, a strange, sentimental gesture, and then he was gone.

They'd heard news of the shooting on the green in Lexington, and then had heard the shots fired at the bridge. John's brother Daniel had run down through the woods and seen shots being fired. He said he'd even seen a dead Redcoat lying on the ground and the Minutemen chasing the regulars out of town, shooting at them from behind trees and stone walls. But he hadn't seen Josiah, he said.

John tried to calm himself. His father was an excellent marksman, one of the best in Concord, and he was surely with John Baker, his closest friend, whom John himself had been named for. Nothing bad could happen to Josiah if John Baker was there. But then, where was he?

John heard a rustle in the trees and he hobbled out onto the path. "Father?" he called into the darkness. There was only silence and then a short yip as Jack, the family's spaniel, came hurrying up, his tail wagging and his tongue lolling.

Beyond him, there was only the black and empty night.

BOOK ONE

ONE

SUNDAY, OCTOBER 10

SWEENEY ST. GEORGE HAD JUST FOUND ANOTHER EXAMPLE of a gravestone by the elusive round-skull carver when the late-afternoon peace of the cemetery was broken by the sound of gunfire.

Crack! Crack! Crack!

Without looking to see where it was coming from, she hit the ground, her arms covering her head, her heart slamming against her rib cage, all of her nerves going nuts as she heard another series of shots come quick and fast.

Crack! Crack! Crack!

"Don't worry. It's just pretend," said a voice behind her, and Sweeney got to her feet and turned to find herself looking down at someone who at first appeared to be a short man with a high, girlish voice. His bald head glinted in the sun and he looked up at her with huge eyes in a pale face.

But he wasn't a man. He was a boy, a completely bald boy of about eleven or twelve and as Sweeney looked into his intense brown eyes, which gave him the look of a young Ben Kingsley, the boy flushed and looked away. He reached down quickly for a baseball hat lying on the ground and put it on his head. "It's a demonstration. Up at the Old North Bridge."

"You mean, like Civil War reenactors and all that?"

"Yeah. Except it's not the Civil War. It's the Revolutionary War." She almost expected him to finish up with a "duh."

"Oh yeah, we're in Concord, aren't we?"

She had come out to Concord in order to find some more examples of the work of the eighteenth-century stonecutter Sweeney had come to think of as the round-skull carver. Sweeney, who studied gravestones and other funerary art, had been after the round-skull carver for months now, ever since she'd seen one of his stones in a Lexington cemetery and been intrigued by his unusual border designs and his oddly shaped death's-heads. They were very human death's-heads, she thought. That was the best way to describe them, with their round skulls and almost cheery expressions. She had found five stones she was positive had been made by the same carver and, after a doing a bit of asking around, discovered that no one knew who he was. So she had done what she normally did when looking for a carver's identity and checked the Middlesex County probate records for the names of the people buried beneath the round-skull carver's stones. The records often stipulated payment to this or that gravestone carver for the deceased's stone and it was one of the only ways of finding a particularly elusive carver. She hadn't had any luck yet, but now that she had found one of the stones in Concord, she could try again. And Edward Martin's stone boded well because it was a large one, with elaborate carving on the side borders. It had cost a nice sum when it had been made in 1740, and since Edward Martin seemed to be a man of means, there was a good likelihood that he would have a probate record stipulating where his worldly possessions would go after death.

And here, in the South Burying Ground in Concord, it hadn't taken her long to find another one. It was all there, the distinctive shape of the skull, the delicate wings at its side, the odd, unnaturally twining plants in the border design, the cramped lettering the carver had used to write, "Here Lyes the Body of Edward Martin."

The boy looked down at her notes. "What are you doing?"

"I'm taking notes on this gravestone. I'm trying to figure out who made it."

The boy sat down next to her and looked at the stone. "You don't know who made it?"

"No, it's not signed, but I've found a whole bunch of stones around here that I'm almost positive he made, and now that I have Edward Martin's name, I can see if his estate paid the person who made his stone. It's kind of like being a detective." Another shot sounded and Sweeney started. "That didn't sound pretend," she said.

"Well, they don't put any bullets in the guns," the boy said. "They're not allowed to. And the ones up at the Old North Bridge, they're not even allowed to point the guns at each other. So it's kind of stupid. They just, like, shoot them up in the air. My grandfather has reenactments up in his field, though, and up there they can pretend they're really fighting because it's not National Park property. They did Battle Road at the last one, which is also stupid because it's not even the right time of year."

Sweeney didn't say anything, but clearly more explanation was needed and he went on.

"Well, you know, the Old North Bridge and the shot heard round the world, that whole thing, that was in April." He looked around at the orange, red, and yellow trees and, as though he were breaking something to her, said gently, "This is October."

"That was when we finally shot back at the British, right? I kind of forget my Revolutionary War history."

He looked up at her, his face swollen and puffy, then said condescendingly, "The British regulars were on their way out to Concord because they were going to take all the guns and stuff from the provincials. So the Minutemen and everybody stood on the green in Lexington and the British shot at them and killed a bunch of them. No one thought they would actually do it. Then they came to Concord and we thought they were burning houses down. So the provincials decided they'd had enough and they went up to the North Bridge. No one really knows who fired the first shot, but we got a bunch of them. The Redcoats had to run away back to Charlestown, and the Minutemen hid in the fields and behind walls.

They never knew what hit 'em. That was called Battle Road."

Sweeney remembered a bit of Longfellow, something her father used to recite. She quoted, " 'You know the rest. In the books you have read, / How the British Regulars fired and fled . . .' Do you know that one?"

The boy picked it up. " 'How the farmers gave them ball for ball, / From behind each fence and farm-yard wall, / Chasing the red-coats down the lane, / Then crossing the field to emerge again.' " Here Sweeney remembered the rest and she joined in again. " 'Under the trees at the turn of the road, / And only pausing to fire and load.' "

He smiled up at her. "Of course, Longfellow kind of added stuff. You know, like, to make it sound better. But that's how we won the war," the boy said in an authoritative way. "The British liked to fight in the open field and we knew how to fight guerrilla-style."

"So, what, did you write a book or something?" Sweeney sat down on the ground and leaned her back against the gravestone, wrapping her arms around her knees. The boy had been right. It was October, and though they'd had a few nice days the week before, there was no denying it was getting cold.

"No. I just read a lot. My mom is director of the Minuteman Museum, so she knows about all this stuff. And my dad knows about it too."

"Yeah? What does he do?"

"Oh," he said uninterestedly, reaching up to scratch his scalp under the baseball hat. "He makes gravestones."

Sweeney studied him for a moment. The puffiness of his face made him seem younger than he must be. Studying his eyes, she decided he was closer to twelve than ten.

"That's a coincidence," she said. "I study gravestones."

"I figured that," he said.

"Yeah. I'm an art historian. Do you know what that is?" A nod. "So, I study gravestone carving over time, the different art that was used. That's why I'm out here, actually. I'm working on a paper about eighteenth-century gravestones."

"You mean like for school?"

"Kind of. I don't have to hand it in to a teacher, though. It's going to be published in a journal."

He didn't say anything for a moment and she was anticipating the usual bewildered response to her odd livelihood when he stood up and, gesturing her to follow, led her over to a stone near the back of the cemetery. "That was made by one of our ancestors," he said.

She studied the stone. It was a tall slate headstone with elaborately carved shoulders and a rounded tympanum, giving the stone the "bedboard" shape that had become common among early New England stonecutters.

The strange death's-head at the top of the stone was about the size of an actual human face. The skull was shaped like a lightbulb, with wide-set, rounded eyes, complete with pinpoint pupils. The mouth was a crude box, filled with lines that approximated skeletal teeth. But what its creator had carved above the figure's head was the remarkable thing. The skull had a Medusa-like head of hair, thick tendrils that rose above it in an electrified halo. In contrast to its hair, the skeletal face stared out blandly from the stone, seemingly unperturbed. She read the name on the stone, Abner Fall, and the dates of his life and death, 1721 to 1760. In the thin light, it was impossible to make out the very faint epitaph at the bottom.

"So, what was this ancestor's name?" Sweeney had seen some similar stones near Plymouth, but the Medusa heads were unusual for the Concord area. She was intrigued.

"Josiah Whiting. He was, like, my great-great-great-great-great-grandfather or something. A lot of greats."

"How much do you know about him?"

"Well, he made gravestones. And he fought in the war." He clarified. "The Revolution. He was some kind of hero or something. My grandpa's always talking about it. He's a member of the Concord Minutemen. Josiah was a member of them too."

"Is your dad a reenactor too?"

"No. He was in Vietnam and he says that he doesn't like

war, even pretend ones. He won't even go to them. But I like the ones where you can see people die, or pretend to die. It's interesting. It's like a play, kind of; it's like you can see what it might be like."

"You said your dad makes gravestones. Does he own a monument company?"

"Yeah. Well, I guess the family really owns it. My grandfather."

"What's it called?"

"Whiting Monuments."

It was one of the big ones in the Boston area. "I'm Sweeney St. George, by the way." She offered her hand.

"Pres Whiting." He shook her hand seriously, looking up at her for a minute with those huge dark eyes and then looking away. "I never heard of anybody studying gravestones before."

"Well, I spend a lot of time in cemeteries, taking pictures, tracing the work of different stonecarvers and sculptors. I usually teach too, so, you know, I spend a lot of time with my students, helping them and stuff, though I'm not teaching right now." She hoped she didn't sound bitter about it. A lowly assistant professor, Sweeney hadn't been assigned any classes for the fall, so she was using the time to work on some of her own research.

Pres reached up to scratch his head again, then gave up and took off the hat. Through the thin skin stretched over his skull, Sweeney could see snaking blue veins, a few burst blood vessels. She saw a vein twitch on his temple, and he seemed a shade or two paler. But maybe it was just the light.

"Yeah, I like cemeteries too. I like to sit in them and read the stones. A lot of the kids at school think I'm weird because of it. But then, they pretty much just think I'm weird. Even before this." He pointed to his head. "Now it's even worse. It's because of chemotherapy," he explained suddenly, as though he was afraid she would think it was something else.

"I'm sorry." She didn't ask why he had to have chemotherapy, even though she wanted to know.

He looked sad for a minute. "Did people ever, like, think you were weird because you liked to go to cemeteries?"

She smiled. "Oh, yeah. I was *so* weird when I was a kid. Weirder than you, probably. How old are you?" Sweeney asked him. What she really wanted to ask was how sick he was and if he was going to be okay.

"Twelve." He pulled a fleece jacket out of his backpack and put it on, zipping it up to his chin. "How old are you?" But she could see he was just asking to be polite. Anyone over twenty probably seemed ancient to him.

"I just turned twenty-nine, last week."

"Oh. What did you get?"

"Nothing much. It's different when you get older. Too bad, really."

"Yeah." He looked off into the distance, then closed his eyes for a moment, and Sweeney felt a flash of concern. He *was* pale. She could see it now. He looked the way people looked before they threw up. When he took a deep breath, she could hear the air in his lungs.

"Are you okay?" she asked him.

"Yeah. I'm just tired. I'm going to walk home."

"Can I give you a ride?"

He looked horrified. "I'm not supposed to get in cars with strangers." He stood up and waited for a minute before hoisting his backpack onto his shoulder.

"How far do you have to go?"

"Just up to my grandparents' house. They live up by the North Bridge." Sweeney had walked past the Old North Bridge the day before. It was a good three quarters of a mile up Monument Street.

"Do you want me to walk with you?"

"No."

She hesitated, not sure what to do. "Okay, well, it was nice to meet you. Maybe I'll see you around."

He studied her for a minute. "Yeah, I like to go to cemeteries."

"Okay, then. Bye." She watched him walk off, making his way slowly along Main Street. He walked like an old man,

his steps slow and cautious as though each one hurt him.
Sweeney gathered up her notes and slung her bag over her
shoulder. And before she knew what she was doing, she was
walking along, keeping the top of his head in view. She
could follow him for a little bit, just to make sure that he got
there okay. She'd be able to stay out of sight and that way, if
something happened, if he collapsed or got sick, she could
call and get him some help. If he caught her, she could just
say she was walking up to the Old North Bridge.

Up ahead of her, Pres Whiting walked slowly along Main
Street, then turned left and walked across Monument
Square. She thought about how there were certain people
people you met in life, people who stuck with you, whom
you were willing to take care of, and how once you had
taken responsibility for them, it was hard to give it up. It was
dangerous to take that responsibility at all. You never knew
where it was going to lead. I'm just making sure he gets
home okay, she told herself. That's all. And Sweeney, who
did not pray, found herself saying a prayer for him, a prayer
that he would be okay.

TWO

THE WOODS WERE LOVELY, DARK AND DEEP.

He'd heard that somewhere before. In a book or something. But it was true, it was almost as though he'd thought it up himself. The woods were lovely, dark and deep. Pres Whiting could hear his shoes crunching on the ground, and when he stopped and breathed deeply, he felt that he was the only person in Concord. The trees seemed to go on forever. He breathed again. That was good. He felt better now.

Usually, he didn't like going out there when it was almost dark, but he didn't really have any choice. If he walked along the road, there was a chance that Gramma would see him, or if not her, one of her friends who would tell her. She'd dropped him off at the school that morning, to play basketball with some of the boys in his class. He'd promised her that one of their mothers would drive him home and had managed to stop her from waiting around to be sure.

"Mom said I should try to keep a sense of normalcy. Well, this is something normal. You all have to let me be a kid," he'd argued. She hadn't been able to say anything to that, so she had given him her cell phone and let him go.

The thing about letting him be a kid he'd gotten from a book he'd found in the drawer of his mother's bedside table. The book was called *It's Just Not Fair: Caring for Terminally Ill Children*, and it had a picture of a bald kid on the front. Pres had been nervous as he looked through it, in case his mother came in, but she hadn't and he'd read a whole chapter about how you were supposed to let your kid do regular things, even if you were worried about his health. She must have read the book, he decided, because lately she'd been letting him do a lot more stuff, though she always looked scared when he left.

It had been okay at first, at the basketball court. There had just been a couple of kids there, Jeremy and Keegan and a kid from another class who was pretty nice. They had played horse and he had gotten a couple of baskets. But then, just when he'd been thinking about going home, Rachel Martino and a couple of other girls from their class had walked across the soccer fields and sat down to watch them play. Pres had talked to Rachel only once, when they'd been sitting next to each other at a stupid assembly about going for your dreams, and he'd whispered to her that probably the only thing the stupid guy onstage had ever gone for was a pizza. She'd laughed and they'd almost gotten in trouble, but ever since then he watched for her in the halls, hoping to talk to her again.

He hadn't been able to leave the basketball court once Rachel showed up, even though knowing she was there made him feel sick and unhappy. Then Mike Farmer and a couple of other older kids showed up and they wanted to play three-on-three. Pres was starting to feel tired and during the first game he'd stumbled and tripped over Keegan's foot. His baseball hat had fallen off and he'd felt them all staring at his head.

"If you can't keep up, you should get off the court," Mike Farmer had said. Everyone had been looking at Pres and he'd said the first thing that came into his mind, something he remembered his mom saying to his dad just before his dad left.

"Screw you!" he'd shouted. Then he'd picked up his hat and his backpack and taken off across the soccer fields. Once he was out of sight, he'd sat down behind a tree, trying not to cry. It hadn't worked very well, but after a little while he'd felt better and he'd taken off for town, where he thought he could kill an hour looking around the cemetery and then walk back to Gramma's. But then he'd met Sweeney in the cemetery. He'd never met a lady who looked like that before. She was almost as tall as his dad and her hair was so red that it looked like a Popsicle. And she had been nice. She had talked to him as if he were her age, rather than just a kid who didn't know anything. He liked Sweeney, he realized, though it wasn't the way he liked Rachel Martino, it was the way he liked Lindy Harris, who had been his babysitter until she'd gone away to college. It was the way he had liked Mr. Babyak, who had been his fourth-grade teacher.

He was almost to the clubhouse. He always knew because of the big maples that grew together in a circle along the path. They made a kind of bowl in the middle, and in the summer and the early fall, when the leaves were still on the trees, you could go in there and lie on the ground and look up at the leaves, and it felt good there, like it would be a nice place to live.

Passing the maples, he kept walking into the darkening woods. Most of the houses in Concord were right up next to someone else's, but his grandparents had owned their house forever, so they didn't have any other houses next to theirs, just the woods, which was where the clubhouse was.

The clubhouse had been built by his dad and some of his friends when they were in high school. It wasn't very big— just one room that had a couch and a table and a few other chairs in it. The furniture was old and it reminded Pres of the kind of furniture you saw on old TV shows, and the one window had these funny curtains made out of brown material that was the same as what they made towels out of. Someone had sewn green pom-poms all around the edges. It was pretty ugly, but Pres realized that he wouldn't want to change it. It was how the clubhouse was. It was special.

Pres's dad had once told him that they built it as a place to have parties, but Pres didn't see what was so great about having parties—his mother had parties and they weren't a lot of fun, just a lot of her friends standing around. He did like the idea of a secret place to go where nobody could find you. You could have a club there and let in only the people you liked and wanted to have in your club.

He rested for a minute and then kept going, and pretty soon he could see it up ahead, just a little bit of brown and a flash of silver through the trees.

Pres had once asked his mother if Gramma and Grampa were rich because they had a big house and the woods behind it, but she said that they weren't rich, it was just that they had owned their house for a very long time and that was why and that if they wanted, they could sell it for a lot of money, but they were probably never going to do that because they liked their house and it was close to Pres and his mother's house and also to Daddy and Lauren and Noah and Rory. "Your grampa likes having all that land behind him," she'd said. "There are people in town who'd pay millions for it, but he's too stubborn to do anything but what he wants to do."

As he got closer to the clubhouse, Pres stopped and listened. A breeze rustled through the trees, making a soft, whispering sound. Even though he knew what it was, Pres shivered. It sounded like voices talking to him, scolding him. "Liar, liar, liar," it seemed to say.

The breeze was what made him notice the smell. It was coming from the direction of the clubhouse, but Pres was confused for a moment, thinking that he'd stepped in something, or something had spilled on his shirt. He checked and found nothing. When the breeze died down, it was fainter, but it was still there, a rotten kind of smell, like when his mom left chicken in the garbage, or the time a rat had died in their wall and Grampa had had to come with his saw and cut a hole in the living room wall to get it out.

It was almost dark now. The light seemed to have been squeezed out of the woods, with just a little line of deep blue sky showing somewhere beyond the trees. The breeze picked up again and he started walking faster.

He'd never been in the woods when it was completely dark before, and where they had seemed lovely and private only a few minutes ago, they now seemed a little scary. That smell, for one thing. And the breeze was blowing louder; the voices were more urgent now. He'd just quickly check at the clubhouse, make sure everything was okay, and then he'd go right home.

He was fifty or so yards from the clubhouse when he heard the noise. Pres stopped and listened, his back rigid underneath the backpack. At first he thought he'd imagined it, but then it came again, *tap-tap-tap*. It wasn't a sound he could identify, like footsteps or someone opening or shutting a door. And it was coming from the clubhouse.

He was frozen now. The air was murky and the night was coming on fast. He could just see the clubhouse up ahead of him, but when he turned around, the woods behind were a blur of reaching, skeleton branches, of spindly trunks and shadowy shapes. Something made him walk forward, his heart thudding so hard in his chest, he thought it might jump out.

There was a sudden movement, a quick rustling of the leaves and then someone was jumping out from behind the clubhouse, slamming against him, knocking him down. He screamed and shut his eyes, feeling the strong arms pinning him to the ground, the hot, wet breath on his face. It seemed to go on forever. He could hear breathing and feel the weight of the body on him, scratching at his face and neck.

And then came a bark. Pres opened his eyes and looked up into the brown eyes of the McClintocks' golden retriever, Buster. He had jumped off Pres and was standing there, watching him and wagging his tail.

"Buster!" Pres dragged himself up and brushed the leaves and dirt off his pants and jacket. His backpack had fallen off and he retrieved it and put it back on. "Bad dog! Naughty dog!" It was what he had heard Mr. McClintock yelling at Buster before when he came to get him in the woods.

But Buster didn't respond. He wagged his tail again and turned around, trotting around the far corner of the clubhouse. The sound came again, *tap-tap-tap*, and Pres realized what it had been: Buster's tail wagging against the boards on the side of the building.

Pres followed him, worried about what Buster might be

doing. Could he have gotten into the clubhouse . . . ? No, the doors and windows were all closed. It must be something else.

He came around the corner and saw Buster rooting about in the dirt. Or maybe it was garbage, because there seemed to be some kind of cloth there. As the fact registered, he realized too that the smell was stronger than ever. And as he stepped closer, he realized what it was and he felt the sourness rise in his throat until he could no longer keep it down and he turned away, knowing he was going to be sick.

Pres knew about vomiting. He had done so much vomiting so far in his young life that he knew exactly how many times he was going to be sick. He knew that this sickness was caused by what he had seen, not by something in him, and he knew that after he threw up once, he'd probably be okay. He let the sour liquid go and stood up, wiping the sleeve of his jacket across his mouth and taking a deep breath.

He was terrified, his heart pounding, his head racked by a dull throbbing he thought was going to make it explode. But he turned around to look at the body.

The man was dead. There was no doubt about that. He lay on his back, one arm splayed out, the other curled toward the stomach, as though it were clutching at the wound.

In fact, the whole middle of the man was a mess of dried blood and leaves, as though he'd rolled around in the dirt after he'd gotten hurt. Parts of the cloth had been torn away. Pres forced himself to look at the face. It too seemed torn, but he could see a nose, oddly bent, and a bushy brown beard. Somehow, he couldn't find the eyes. There was a lot of dark mess where they should have been.

And, he realized slowly—everything sluggish, taking its own time—the man was wearing a soldier's uniform, a Revolutionary War soldier's uniform, just like the ones he'd seen at reenactments. Pres turned away and sank down to the ground. He should run, he should call Gramma on the cell phone and tell her to get an ambulance. Except he knew that an ambulance wasn't going to help the man, whoever he was. And thinking about Gramma reminded him that he had done something bad. He had lied to her and he had walked through the woods by himself. She would be mad. And if they came, if the police came, they might think the man had something to do with the clubhouse. He couldn't let them go in the clubhouse. *He couldn't.* He turned around again to look at the body. Maybe he could move the man away, then call the police. But as soon as he leaned down, he knew he couldn't touch the body. The smell was too strong, for one thing, and the body looked a little mushy, like it might not stay together if he tried to drag it. Besides, he thought he remembered seeing something on TV about there being laws to stop people from moving bodies. He didn't want to get arrested. There were laws about telling if you saw a dead body too. He was pretty sure about that.

No, he had to tell someone. But first he could look and make sure that everything was okay. Then maybe they wouldn't go in there. He forced himself to look away from the man and walked very slowly around the side of the building. He looked under the rock for the key, but it wasn't there. As he walked closer he realized that the door of the clubhouse was open very slightly, the key still in the padlock. He looked inside. It was empty.

Pres locked the door again and instead of replacing the key under the rock, he put it in his pocket. He was about to turn and run to his grandparents' house when he looked up to find Sweeney walking toward him. He blinked, not sure if it was her. But then she said, "I'm sorry, Pres. I was worried about you," and kept walking. He didn't know what else to do, so he put a hand up, the way the crossing guards at school did to stop cars.

"No, don't go there," he said quickly. "There's a dead man there." He pointed to the side of the clubhouse.

"What do you mean?" She looked at the clubhouse and then back at him. She sniffed the air, and he saw her eyes get very big.

"There's a dead man there. I just found him. I was just walking home." She blurred in front of his eyes, as though she'd melted. He took a step back.

"Pres," Sweeney said, taking a step toward him. "Are you okay? We should call someone. We should get help."

"I don't think anyone can help him," he said, watching her green eyes watch him as he felt the woods pitch and the trees ran together, and then everything went dark.

THREE

IT WAS TWO IN THE MORNING WHEN DETECTIVE TIM QUINN realized something was wrong with his ten-month-old daughter, Megan. She'd been fussy the night before and he'd had trouble getting her down. He'd just dropped off to sleep himself when he heard her crying, not her typical getting-his-attention-in-the-middle-of-the-night crying but an anguished howling that made him feel suddenly nauseous with fear.

He sat up in bed, disoriented, then raced to her room. When he opened the door, she was standing up in her crib, gripping the top bar and looking at him as though she had been crying for hours. In the dim light from the hallway, he could see her flushed face, the wet eyes and running nose.

She had a cold.

"Poor baby," he murmured to her as he walked back and forth across the hallway, holding her hot little body to his bare chest. "Poor baby. Do you have a cold?" Megan's crying was now ragged, hiccuppy, as though she'd exhausted all of her resources just getting him to come to her. She looked up at him, admonishing. *What took you so long?* she seemed to be asking him. *I needed you!*

He walked her up and down the hallway for ten minutes and then took her into the bathroom, where he wiped her nose and started a lukewarm bath. Maybe that would make her feel better. His mother had always run him baths when he was sick, as though getting clean would chase away the germs. When the bath was full, he got in with Megan, sitting her on his stomach and letting her splash around a little in the water.

At first, after Maura died, he had felt funny about getting in the bath with her. But not for long. It was so much easier to give her a bath when he took his own, and he'd even taken her in the shower with him a couple of times. She'd been scared at first, but now she laughed when the water hit her face. He'd never seen his own mother without her clothes, seen his father nude only a couple of times by accident. In his house you weren't supposed to see adults in the nude. But at some point it had started to seem silly to him. Megan was just a baby. She didn't care.

And maybe it was because of the way he'd felt since Maura's death, like a . . . like a . . . eunuch. That was the word. He was no longer a sexual being. He was just a father, that's all he was. He couldn't imagine ever being with a woman in that way again. He thought back on all the people he had known who had lost wives or husbands and then gotten remarried, sometimes only months later. How was it possible? He couldn't see it.

He lay back in the water, holding her up under her arms and letting her paddle at the water with her feet. It was weird how it had never bothered him being in the bathtub where his wife had died. He had thought it would, even considered ripping out the tub unit and putting in a shower stall or something, but it was just a bathtub now, with its pink tiles and peeling grout, the edges covered now with Megan's bath toys, rubber duckies and *Sesame Street* characters. If he closed his eyes and forced himself to remember, he could see her again, lying in the warm, pink water, still wearing her pajamas and bathrobe, her wrists with the wounds like ribbons lying face up on her stomach, as though she were displaying them with pride. But he didn't like to think about that and so he didn't, most of the time.

"Okay, Button," he said, standing up and lifting Megan out of the water. "You ready to go to bed?" She laughed.

"You're feeling better, aren't you?" he murmured as he tow-eled her off and replaced her diaper and sleeper.

She smiled up at him, a gorgeous, angelic smile that said, *Yes. Thank you. You made me better.* His heart contracted. He couldn't bear to put her down in her crib, so he brought her into bed with him and curled up next to the warm little body lying in the place where her mother used to sleep.

She was fussy the next morning but seemed better, and he gambled that she was well enough for day care. Still, it seemed to take longer to do everything—to get her dressed and into the car and out of the car again—and by the time he was at his desk at Cambridge police headquarters in Central Square, he was a good forty-five minutes late for work.

He thought he'd gotten away with it, but just as he lifted his phone to check his voice mail, Havrilek walked in and said, "Nice of you to join us, Quinn."

"Sorry, sorry. I know. Megan was sick last night and it was hard to get her ready this morning." He tried to keep his voice even, not resort to complaining about his kid.

Havrilek didn't say anything for a moment, and when he spoke it was in a low, sympathetic voice Quinn wasn't used to hearing. "Quinny, I feel for you, I really do. I think it's a great thing you're doing, taking care of your kid. But this is the fourth time this month you've been late and it's gotta stop."

"I know, I know. I think she's fine now and I'll make a real effort to be here on time. Sorry."

"All right." Havrilek studied him for a minute as though he was deciding something. "Listen, I got something for you. Missing persons."

Quinn looked up quickly. He was a homicide detective, for Christ's sake. He didn't do runaway teenagers anymore. "But I thought I was on this gang thing."

"Yeah, but with Marino on his back, you're without a partner. I want you to do this."

Quinn watched Havrilek's pale blue eyes, trying to figure out if he was being punished. "Look, I know I've been preoccupied, but I'm trying, I really am. I've already done some legwork on the gang thing, I've got—"

"This is what I want you to do." His voice was final and he reached across Quinn's desk and offered up the message. "I don't know why she waited so long to call. It's been a week now that she hasn't heard from him. Go figure. Some people are funny that way."

Quinn looked down at the little slip of paper. *Beverly Churchill. Husband Kenneth, age 46, missing since a week ago Friday.* There was a phone number and an address in an expensive part of Cambridge. He folded it in half and put it in his pocket. "Okay," he said. "You got it."

Havrilek nodded. "Good. I need you to go out to the house and get a statement." He picked up the picture frame on Quinn's desk, looked at the picture of Megan for a second, and then replaced it. Quinn saw him glance over at the picture Marino had on his desk, his wife in a bikini on a Florida vacation that must have been twenty years ago now. Quinn had put his picture of Maura away, mostly because it made the other guys uncomfortable. "We could make her come in, but in case it turns out to be anything, it might be good to kind of check out the house, see what's what."

Quinn knew exactly what he meant. When these missing-persons cases turned out to be murder, you could pretty much count on it being the spouse.

"Just outta curiosity, why does she say she waited so long to call us?"

"She said he was away for the weekend or something. Supposed to come home last Wednesday. She waited all the way through the next weekend to see if he'd decided to stay. When he didn't come home by last night, she was worried, so she called us this morning. I don't know. You never know about people's home lives, huh? Pretty crazy shit that goes on." It took him only a second to realize what he'd said, and he colored, then cast his eyes down at Quinn's desk.

Quinn was embarrassed for him and hurried to cover it up. "Okay, I'll get right on it," he said quickly. "I'll give her a call."

* * *

IF MARINO HAD BEEN WITH HIM WHEN HE PULLED UP IN front of Beverly and Kenneth Churchill's house, he would have made some kind of a joke about latte-drinking liberals.

The Churchills lived in a magazine-perfect Cambridge house, a big white Victorian with a row of rocking chairs on the wraparound porch and a huge wreath made of autumn leaves on the front door. There was even a Volvo parked in the driveway. Quinn knocked on the front door and waited a few minutes. Nothing. He tried once more and, again getting no answer, went around back. A dark-haired woman was kneeling by some flower beds along the side of the house, using a pair of hedge shears to trim a neat row of tall green plants. A big gray cat rubbed against her, switching its tail among the greenery.

"Mrs. Churchill?" Quinn called out.

She looked up and waved. "I'm sorry, I lost track of time. It always happens in the garden. Hold on, I'll be right there." She made one last trim and then lay down the shears.

In the moment that she stood up, brushed off her jeans, and started toward him, two things struck Quinn. One was that Beverly Churchill was very, very beautiful. The other was that she had not been lying when she said she had lost track of time. However much she was missing her husband, it hadn't stopped her from getting completely wrapped up in her gardening.

"When did you realize that he might be missing?" Quinn asked her once they were sitting at the dining room table, she with a mug of Earl Grey and Quinn—who didn't like taking food or drink on the job—a glass of ice water.

"Wednesday," she said. "He had gone out to Concord on Friday for the encampment and he was going to stay for a couple of days to do some research." She had light blue eyes, sled-dog eyes, that reminded him of Havrilek's, and perfectly black hair to her shoulders. Her well-placed cheekbones gave her face a sharp, exotic look that made her seem very aloof and very calm. But her hands worried on the table, and drawn by the movement, he looked down at them. They were raw and red, the skin peeling and cracking along her knuckles. "Hands like chopped meat," his mother would've said. Despite a lifetime of cleaning houses, she had kept her own hands as soft and young-looking as a girl's, slathering them with thick cream she got through the mail and wearing a pair of white cotton gloves to bed every night. After she'd died, he'd found pairs and pairs of them in her bathroom.

Quinn looked up. "Wait. Encampment. What's that?"

"What's that?" She stood up abruptly and led the way into a sort of family room off the kitchen. The walls were covered with rifles and muskets equipped with bayonets, and a huge gun case against one wall held another twenty or so weapons. Quinn looked around in amazement. The place was an arsenal.

"That," Beverly Churchill said, pointing to a black-and-white photograph framed and hung below a large machete, "is an encampment." Quinn leaned over and looked into the depths of what seemed to be a very old photograph of a bunch of soldiers sitting around a campfire, a grouping of primitive tents behind them. They were wearing Revolutionary War–era uniforms he remembered from school history books and had strangely long hair or ponytails. "And that's Kenneth." Quinn followed her finger and saw a tall, dark-haired man standing behind a seated group. "It sounds silly to anyone who doesn't do reenactments, but he's part of a Minuteman company that re-creates famous battles from the Revolutionary War. On the weekends that they don't have battles, they do these encampments. They dress up and cook their food over campfires and sing old songs. I always thought it was just an excuse to act like twelve-year-olds again, but he loved it." He saw a look of horror come over her face. But she didn't say, "Loves, I mean. Loves," or try to cover up for her use of the past tense.

Quinn looked at the rest of the pictures on the wall. His eyes rested on one of Kenneth Churchill, wearing tan khaki fatigues and standing in front of a tank.

Beverly Churchill noticed him looking at the photo and said, "Kenneth was in Desert Storm. I know it seems, well . . ." She gestured around at the house, and Quinn knew she'd read his mind. "I mean, there aren't a lot of college professors who joined the Marines. But it was important to him. He'd had his education paid for by the Corps and he felt it was important to go back in when his country needed him." There was a note of annoyance in her voice, as though she'd explained this so many times to herself that she was tired of the words.

She stepped away from the wall and went back into the dining room. He followed her and they sat down at the table again. Her hands, resting on a woven place mat, were active, the nails scratching and picking at the skin.

"So, he went out to Concord on Friday the first—this is a little over a week ago—and then . . . ?"

"And then . . . nothing. He was supposed to be home that next Wednesday night and he didn't come home. I thought he might call to say that he was staying another day, but . . ."

"Wait, so you didn't talk to him all weekend? Was that unusual?"

"Well, you see, he couldn't. I mean, they weren't supposed to use modern inventions of any kind."

"What about after the encampment?"

"No." She picked up the corner of the place mat, twisting it between her fingers. "I guess I should explain. Kenneth is an American history professor. He's writing a book. About a Minuteman from Concord who disappeared in 1775. His name was Josiah Whiting and he was a stonecutter, a gravestone maker, in Concord. Kenneth was . . . well, he was kind of obsessed with Whiting. It had turned into a . . . *obsession* is the only word for it."

She looked at him as though she expected him to understand, but when he didn't say anything, she went on. "He was gone almost every weekend over the summer. If he wasn't at reenactments, he was doing research. He'd been spending a lot of time in cemeteries, doing research on Whiting's stones. He always used to call when he was away, to check in, but this summer he stopped doing that, because of the book, I think. He was so wrapped up in it."

"So, he didn't come home Wednesday and . . . then what?"

"I just thought maybe he'd decided to stay. There was another reenactment this past weekend. I thought maybe he hung around for that, but when he didn't come home last night, I started to get worried."

Quinn waited for a minute, in case she was going to go on and say it for him. "I hate to have to ask this, but was your husband involved with anyone else, another woman?" He asked the question in what he hoped was a nonchalant way. No big deal if he is, he wanted his voice to imply, happens every day.

She hesitated for a moment and he had the sense that she was about to confide in him when they heard the front door slam. Beverly Churchill stood up—gratefully, Quinn thought—and went to the door of the dining room, saying, "In here, Marcus."

A boy of about fifteen or sixteen, his dark hair cut into a spiky almost-Mohawk, came into the dining room, looking warily at Quinn. He had the half-grown, too-skinny body that Quinn remembered despairing about when he was that age. A neon green backpack sagged from his shoulders as though it were full of rocks. He had one pierced ear, Quinn saw. A little blue penguin rested on his pale right earlobe.

"This is Detective Quinn," Beverly Churchill said. "My son, Marcus." He noticed that she said "my son," not "our son." He made a note to himself to check that out. Might have made it easier for Churchill to leave if the kid was a stepson.

"Hi, Marcus," Quinn said, standing up and shaking the boy's hand.

The boy shook it unenthusiastically and didn't say anything.

"Why don't you go upstairs while we talk," she said, sitting down at the table again. "You can watch TV in my room if you want."

Marcus nodded and headed up the staircase. They both watched him go.

"You were saying . . ." Quinn was hoping that she would pick up whatever she had been about to say.

But she just smiled nervously and said, "My husband was very devoted to us. Even though he was obsessed with his research. No, there was nothing . . . like that."

He made a note on the legal pad. "Have you looked through his things, to see if he took a lot of clothes with him?"

She blanched. "It was supposed to be a five-day trip, anyway. So, yes, he took a lot of things with him."

"What about business-related things? Laptop, research materials?"

She thought for a moment. "He would have taken all that kind of stuff with him."

"How about money? Have you checked your bank account? Have any unusual amounts of money come out of it in the last week? Any credit card charges?"

She looked panicked. "I hadn't thought of that. I don't know. I'll check this afternoon. Do I just call them?"

"Yes. I can call if you want. You'll need to authorize them to release your account information."

"That's all right. I'll do it."

Quinn thought of something. "Where was he staying out there?"

"Well, he was camping. I mean, that was the point."

"But what about after the encampment was over? He was going to be doing research, wasn't he?"

"I don't know. A couple of times he'd stayed at the Minuteman Inn, but I called and he wasn't there. I don't know where he was going to stay." As though she'd read his mind, she said, "I have his cell phone number in case of emergencies. And, yes, I've been calling it, but he doesn't pick up."

Quinn put the legal pad down and looked steadily into her eyes. "Mrs. Churchill. Have you considered that your husband may have gone away voluntarily?" He felt like a hypocrite even as he said it. If Kenneth Churchill were a fourteen-year-old girl, no one would be asking if he went off voluntarily. And even if they were, they'd be doing everything they could to find her right now. But that was the point, wasn't it? Kenneth Churchill wasn't a fourteen-year-old girl. And when it came right down to it, there wasn't a whole lot he could do until some evidence of foul play showed up. He couldn't subpoena phone records, and it was going to be hard to get the Concord cops to make much of a stink about a guy who was probably off balling a student.

Tears came into her eyes, and he found he was almost relieved to discover that she wasn't as calm as she'd seemed at first, that she did in fact appear to miss her husband.

"Maybe he did! Maybe he did!" she choked out. "But if that's the case, shouldn't there be someone who can *do* something? It doesn't seem right that he should be able to just . . . go off."

He told her he'd be in touch and left her with her anger. She was right. There should have been something he could do for her but, of course, there wasn't.

FOUR

THEY BROUGHT SWEENEY IN FOR THE THIRD TIME ON MON-
day.

"Tell us again what you were doing in the woods," Chief
Tyler said. He was the local cop, the one who had arrived on
Sunday after she'd stumbled out of the woods to the road
and flagged down a passing car. The second time, later that
night, there had been a couple of state homicide investigators there too. She had told them them whole thing from the
beginning, and Detective Lynch, a cocky young guy with
copper-penny hair and a boxer's crooked nose who now
seemed to be in charge of the investigation, had seemed suspicious when she'd said she'd met Pres for the first time only
that day.

"And you followed him into the woods?" he'd asked, as
though she were a child molester planning to ambush him
like Little Red Riding Hood and the wolf.

"He seemed weak. He had already told me that he was
undergoing chemotherapy. He wouldn't let me drive him
home, but I felt funny about letting him go without making
sure that he got there okay, so I thought I would just follow
him, to make sure."

"Even though he had already said he didn't feel comfortable having you drive him?" Detective Lynch had looked at
Sweeney with his small, ironic eyes and she had wanted to
punch him for his insinuation.

And now, sitting in the dingy, claustrophobic room at the Concord police station on a bright, lovely Monday morning, Sweeney went through the story again of meeting Pres in the cemetery, trying not to let her exasperation creep into her voice. "He seemed very weak. He had already told me he was undergoing chemotherapy. He didn't want me driving him home because he didn't know me, but I thought that I could follow him and at least make sure that he got home okay."

"All right," Detective Lynch said as though he was giving her a pass. "So he had already found the body when you arrived."

"Yes. I told you. He found the neighbor's dog and then he found the body. I walked up and he was kind of standing there, looking strange, and as I walked toward him, he told me. It was like he wanted to stop me from seeing the body or something. And then he fainted. It was getting dark. So I carried him back to the road and I flagged down a car for help." She leaned back in the hard plastic chair, trying to get comfortable. It was very warm in the room and she wished she hadn't worn a wool sweater. For some reason, she didn't want to take it off in front of them. She fixed her gaze on a poster on the opposite wall picturing an ice castle and a man dressed as a maple leaf. "SEE QUEBEC," it read in bright red script.

"And neither of you touched the crime scene? Do you know what he did between the time he found the body and the time that you saw him?"

Sweeney hesitated. Did she know? It had all been a strange kind of dream, her impressions of what had happened infused with her confusion when she'd come upon him standing there, and the adrenaline that had run through her blood when he'd said those words: "No, don't go there. There's a dead man there." But she was sure that there was a shadow of something there, a memory of walking up and seeing him first through the trees. She thought maybe she'd seen him coming out of the clubhouse. Not around the side where the body had been, but out through the door. She couldn't be sure, though, and she had the feeling she'd had in the cemetery, that she wanted to protect Pres, wanted to do anything she could to keep him from harm.

"It wasn't very long," she said. "I was following pretty closely. I don't think he would have had time to do much of anything."

Lynch had noticed her hesitation, and she saw him study her for a minute. "Okay, Ms. St. George, can you tell us what you were doing earlier that day? Up until the time you started talking to the boy."

"I drove out to Concord around two and then I was in the graveyard, looking at gravestones."

"That's right," Lynch said, looking over at one of the other state cops. "You study 'em or something, right?" She could see what he was thinking. Some kind of freak, spending all her time in cemeteries. She probably *is* a child molester.

"Yes. I'm an art historian and I specialize in gravestones and other funerary art."

"Funerary art," Lynch said, pronouncing it "foo-ner-ary." "How do ya like that? I didn't even know they had a name for it like that."

"Look, I'm sure you realized this too, but there isn't any way either of us could have had anything to do with the guy's death," Sweeney said. "He had been dead quite awhile before we got there."

"How do you know? I thought you said the boy found the body and you just carried him out of there and went and got help."

"No, I said that I went over to make sure that the man really was dead before I went and got help."

"You said you didn't get a good look at him," Lynch said, as though he'd caught her in a lie.

"I didn't. His face was . . . all eaten away. And there wasn't much light. So I couldn't get a look at his face, but it was clear that he had been dead for a while."

She was afraid he was going to ask her how she knew that, but instead he scrawled something in his notebook and looked up at her again.

"So, you didn't know who he was? You'd never seen him before?" Chief Tyler asked in a more kindly voice. She shook her head. "But what did you think about the . . . uh . . . the costume he was wearing? It must have seemed strange to you?"

"It did at first but then I remembered that Pres told me about the reenactments and that his grandfather sometimes holds them on his land. So I think I just figured it was somehow related to that. The woods . . . where the body was found . . . is pretty close to his grandparents' place."

"Do you have any connection to these reenactments?" Tyler asked. "Do you ever go to them?"

"No. I've heard about them. I think my father once took me to one out here when I was about ten. But beyond that, no." She raised her eyebrows and held her hands out as if to say, "Sorry. Nothing else I can do for you."

Lynch looked annoyed. "Okay, Ms. St. George, you can go now, but we'll probably need to speak to you again. So don't go too far."

When she walked out into the hallway, Sweeney stopped for a minute and blinked to be sure she wasn't seeing things. Sitting in folding metal chairs along one wall were a trio of Colonial Minutemen completely outfitted in breeches, blue vests, and tricorner hats. They even, Sweeney noticed as she walked past them, smelled like Colonial Minutemen, or what she imagined Colonial Minutemen smelled like.

"Well, of course we had to check our firearms, Jack," one of them was saying. "This is a police station."

At the other end of the hallway, Pres Whiting was standing with a slight dark-haired woman who had an arm around his shoulder. He was speaking to her in low tones and she was looking down at him with a concerned expression on her face. When he caught sight of Sweeney, he broke into a broad grin and said something to the woman, who looked up and smiled.

"Hey, Pres," Sweeney said. "How are you feeling?" She

hadn't seen him since they'd taken him away in the ambulance while she waited for the police.

"Okay," he said, bashful suddenly, looking down at his shoes. "This is my mom."

"Cecily Whiting," the woman said, shaking Sweeney's hand. "Pres told me all about you. And the police told me what you did. I wanted to thank you yesterday, but in any case, we really appreciate your concern." She was a slim, angular woman who knew how to dress for her body type, realizing that anything more than the simplest, most beautifully tailored clothes would look garish on her boyish frame. She was wearing simple black pants and an eggplant-colored cashmere sweater that hugged her small waist and nearly flat chest. Her auburny brown hair was cut short and close to her head—the only possible hair style for her small, sharply boned face—and her eyes were Pres's eyes, large, dark, haunted.

Sweeney smiled and said it was no problem. Ha. Take that, Lynch. Pres's mother didn't think following him was creepy.

"So, you study gravestones?" Cecily Whiting asked her. "Pres told you about Josiah Whiting, didn't he?"

"Yes, the one stone I've seen is really interesting. I'm thinking about looking into him some more."

There was something overly eager in her voice. "Well, let me know if you need any information. I have quite a bit on him at the museum. Just stop by sometime."

"I'll do that," Sweeney said. "It was nice to meet you. Pres, I hope I'll see you around."

"Yeah," he said. "Okay. Oh, there's Dad." He seemed nervous all of a sudden, and Sweeney followed his gaze to the front door, where a tall dark-haired man and a much shorter young woman with curly blond hair were walking hand in hand toward them. Sweeney could feel the tension in the little hallway, and she saw Pres glance at his mother. Cecily Whiting pressed her lips together and turned away as the man hugged Pres and the blond woman reached over to rub his shoulder.

"Hi," the man said, reaching over to shake Sweeney's hand. "I'm Bruce Whiting." She looked up into a rugged, sunburned face, well lined and pleasant, and remembered what Pres had said about his father having gone to Vietnam. He had to be a good fifteen years older than Cecily Whiting and another ten years older than the woman he was standing next to.

"Sweeney St. George," Sweeney said.

"Sweeney was with Pres when he . . . in the woods," Cecily Whiting said, glancing very quickly at Pres's father and then away.

"That's right. Thanks for taking care of him," Bruce Whiting said, looking at Sweeney curiously. "Oh, this is my wife, Lauren."

They shook hands, Lauren Whiting saying that it was wonderful to meet Sweeney and flashing her small, perfectly white teeth in a friendly smile. Sweeney heard a small, almost silent exclamation of annoyance slip from Cecily Whiting's lips. Cecily turned away from them and fumbled desperately in her purse for a moment, but came up empty-handed, letting the purse fall back against her hip.

"Well, I'm going to get going," Sweeney said. "Bye, Pres. I'll see you soon."

"Don't forget to stop by the museum," Cecily said, falsely bright.

"Right, thank you. I will."

As Sweeney walked away, she heard Bruce Whiting say, "Why does she want to stop by the museum?"

"Why do you care?"

"I don't. I just—"

"She's interested in Josiah Whiting, if you want to know. Other people can be interested in your family members, Bruce."

As the door closed behind her, Sweeney turned to find Pres staring after her. She heard Bruce Whiting say, "For God's sake, Cecily . . ." And she shivered as she stepped out into the cold.

* * *

SHE WAS DRIVING BACK THROUGH TOWN WHEN SHE SAW THE inn. She'd seen it on her way in, a large, well-kept Colonial on Lexington Road, painted a dark blue accented with shiny black shutters and trim that matched the black-and-gold sign out front reading, THE MINUTEMAN INN. FOUNDED BY JOHN BAKER 1762.

She turned impulsively into the drive, parking her old Volkswagen Rabbit next to a gleaming Land Rover, and sat there for a minute, thinking. The police had said that she shouldn't go far and she did have research to do in Concord. She thought of her apartment in Somerville. It had been a while since she'd cleaned it and, as she hadn't been teaching this fall, she spent virtually all of her time in her four modest rooms. She pictured a pristine rented room, cleaned daily by someone else. It wasn't that far out to Concord, it was true, but maybe a little vacation would be good for the soul. Besides, there wasn't anyone counting on her. She lived alone, didn't have any pets. Actually, she didn't even have any live houseplants, just an aloe vera in the kitchen that appeared impossible to kill, no matter her level of neglect.

That was it, then. She would just see if they had any rooms. She got out and gave the Rabbit an affectionate pat. The lime green paint job, dull in some places and pocked with large patches of rust and a sampling of other cars' paint jobs in others, seemed somehow sad. Sweeney had bought the car almost two years ago from the woman whose apartment she moved into when she came back from England. The woman, a psychology graduate student who had fallen suddenly in love with a Turkish physicist who lived in San Diego and was leaving town, had offered Sweeney the car for $400, an offer that had seemed too good to pass up. The car was over twenty years old, but the engine had held up fairly well and Sweeney didn't worry much about security. No one wanted to steal it. Still, the time was approaching when she was going to have to start thinking about replacing it.

The lobby of the Minuteman Inn perfectly re-created the feel of a 1770s lodging house, the foyer and guest lounge painted a burnished orange and furnished with Colonial antiques. A glass cabinet near the reception desk held a collection of Revolutionary War–era silver, including, Sweeney noticed, a piece by Paul Revere. A wide fireplace blazed in the library, and a few guests were taking advantage of the shelves of books and games that lined the walls. The room smelled of woodsmoke and applesauce.

"Can I help you with something?" A tall man with thinning blond hair, beautiful hazel eyes, large behind thick glasses, and a prominent Adam's apple stood behind a high desk. He was wearing, Sweeney noticed, a vaguely anachronistic ensemble, woolen trousers and a white collarless shirt. He smiled eagerly.

"Yes. I was wondering if you might have a room for about a week."

"Let me see. This is our busy time, what with foliage, but I had a couple of cancellations, so you just may have lucked out. Let's see, yes. How long did you say?"

"I think about a week," Sweeney said, taking a deep breath. "But I'm not really sure. I'm doing some research here in Concord, so it kind of depends on how things go."

"Okay, good." He tapped away on a keyboard discreetly tucked into a drawer in the desk, and Sweeney watched his eyes move across the slim computer monitor. "Here we go." She handed over her driver's license and credit card and he noted them down and handed her a printed receipt and a key card. "My name's Will Baker. I own the inn and I'd be glad to help you with anything you might need while you're here. Breakfast is served in the dining room from seven to ten A.M. and dinner is served starting at five. We have a very good dining room and there's the tavern for more casual dining. If you'd like to eat in your room, we'd be glad to bring it up to you. May I help you with your luggage?"

"Actually," Sweeney said, suddenly embarrassed. "I'll bring my luggage in later." In fact, she had to go back to Somerville to pack her luggage. But he didn't seem to care.

"Great, I'll just show you to your room." She followed him up a narrow flight of stairs. "Sorry about the stairs. We wanted to keep everything authentic, but it means it's a bit tricky sometimes. What kind of research are you doing?"

"Oh, gravestones," Sweeney said. "I study them and I'm working on a paper about eighteenth-century stonecarvers from this area. I have one in mind who I'm going to try to identify. And I just discovered the work of a carver named Josiah Whiting, who I'm really interested in."

"Josiah Whiting?" He turned to look at her, and in the dim light of the stairway, his eyes were intent.

"Yes, I'm really intrigued by his work. I understand he was kind of a Revolutionary hero too."

"That's right. My great-great-great-great-great-grandfather was a fellow member of the Concord Minute-men. He built the inn."

"Really? And it's been in the family all this time?"

"No." He led the way along a narrow hallway lit with old-fashioned wall sconces. The wallpaper had a small pineapple pattern, and wooden floors were covered with threadbare Oriental rugs. There was a strong and pleasant smell of lemon oil. "It was owned by another family for a long time," he went on. "But a couple of years ago it came back on the market and I was able to buy it. It had been a longtime dream of mine. Here we are." He used the key card to open the door of room seven and held it so Sweeney could walk past him into the room. "Is this okay?"

"It's beautiful. Thank you." Sweeney's room was furnished with simple Colonial pieces, and the walls were painted a pale salmon color that was picked up in the stenciled salmon-and-green curtains.

He smiled. "If there's anything you need, please let us know."

When he had gone, Sweeney sat down on the bed and took a deep breath. The week would take a chunk out of her savings, but she would be able to write it off her income tax since it was a research trip, and besides, her coffers were a bit more padded than usual after the sale of one of her father's paintings last month. Sweeney's father, a well-known American painter who had committed suicide when she was thirteen, had left her the weighty legacy of almost a hundred canvases. They'd been in storage for years, but she had decided to put a few on the market and was working with a dealer to find museums that would really appreciate them. In any case, she would think of her vacation as coming courtesy of *Brown House #12.*

Sweeney had a thing for nice hotels. She had inherited this from her mother, a once successful actress who had continued to insist on staying at the best hotels even when the work had dried up and she could no longer afford them. But then hotels, unlike apartments or schools, could be put on credit cards. Sweeney remembered a winter soon after her parents split up when they had gotten evicted from an apartment in Boston and her mother had checked them into the Copley Plaza for two months. She supposed her father had ended up footing the bill. She still remembered the easy luxury of her room, the satiny sheets and little bottles of delicious-smelling shampoos and lotions that were replenished every day by the silent, smiling maids.

She lay back on her bed and smiled. She had done the right thing in staying. She was sure of it.

FIVE

CECILY WHITING OPENED THE STORM DOOR AND TOOK HER coffee through to the picnic table on the back patio. It was just a little too cold to sit outside, the autumn sun not strong enough to warm the earth anymore. She wrapped her dressing gown more tightly around herself and caught her reflection in the sliding glass door, a long, too-thin wraith in blue silk, her short dark hair gleaming in the early light. She had always been too thin, too sharp, her breasts and hips just barely rounding beneath her clothes. It was only one of the reasons she'd loved being pregnant with Pres, the way her body had finally seemed to look the way it was supposed to.

She turned away and looked out at the little stand of glowing maple trees behind the house. It was a nice enough house, in a good neighborhood, an easy walk to town, but still she hated it, had hated it from the moment they'd moved in. She remembered the mother of one of Pres's friends telling her how much she loved the little house she'd moved into after her divorce. "It was the first house I'd ever lived in that was just mine," she'd said. "I ended up selling it when I got remarried, and it almost killed me. That house was independence; it was where I became a person again."

For Cecily, the little ranch house behind the Hill cemetery represented her new life after the divorce too, but it wasn't a life she'd ever wanted, and the house—which Bruce had found and bought for them like some kind of consolation prize—seemed to hold her very disappointment. When they had told her about Pres, about how sick he was, she had even wondered if it had been the house that had poisoned him, as if the sick sadness of her grief had seeped into the walls and ceilings like that mold you were always reading about.

She'd said so to Bruce. They'd been at the hospital and the doctor had said that jumble of words . . . acute myeloid leukemia . . . chemotherapy and bone marrow transplant . . . progresses quickly . . . good results from treatment . . . and she had turned to Bruce and said, "It's your fault. His heart was broken over the divorce and we had to live in a house that wasn't even his own and this happened. It's because of you."

Bruce had stared at her dumbly, and the doctor had coughed uncomfortably and told them that it was normal to experience anger and to want to blame someone for a child's sickness. He'd handed her a card with the name of a therapist on it and said that it might be helpful for her to talk to someone about her anger. But she didn't need to talk to anyone, she knew who was at fault and she knew that Bruce knew it, too. He'd looked away, his shoulders slumped, exactly the way he'd looked when he'd finally admitted that he was having an affair with Lauren, that he was in love with her, that in fact she was already pregnant with his child.

She almost gasped, remembering the extent of her fury. She'd hit him—she was ashamed of it now—and screamed that he was destroying his son's life. He had started to cry and said that he knew it and that at least Pres had her, that she was a good mother, that if she wasn't a good mother, he might not have done what he'd done. That had made it worse somehow, that her own love for Pres had allowed Bruce to leave them.

She wiped the sleeve of her sweatshirt across her eyes, trying to get a grip on her emotions. She had to get Pres to school and be at the museum by nine. There was a school group coming in and there would be tons of tourists in town for foliage season.

She looked out at the trees beginning their autumn show

and tried to calm herself down. The childhood cancers coordinator at the hospital had given her a book about guided imagery and she had worked with Pres on it every night at bedtime. The idea was to give him a way to deal with the pain when they were putting in IVs or catheters or when he was sick from the chemo. She had had him lie in bed and asked him to picture himself in the most peaceful place he could think of. He had told her he was picturing himself lying on the ground in the woods behind Gramma and Grampa's house. "What does it smell like, Pres?" she'd asked him, the way the book told her to. "What does the air feel like? Is it warm or cool?"

"It's warm," he'd told her, "and I'm lying between the maples, looking up at the leaves."

"Okay, now picture everything about the woods; picture the trees and the sky. The idea is that you create a place inside your head, a place you can go to whenever you need to."

It had actually worked. The next time he'd had to have a catheter put in, he'd done his visualization and he said that it was better, that he hadn't felt it as much, that he'd just thought about being in the woods. He'd seemed calmer after that, she'd thought, though he'd been sad, or maybe scared since Sunday. He still hadn't told her what he was doing in the woods when it was nearly dark, why he'd walked back to George and Lillian's that way instead of along the road. The police had called and asked her to come to the hospital, and at first she thought he'd done something wrong, shoplifted or something. It would have been out of character, but the psychologist had told her to be prepared for Pres to act out in reaction to his illness.

But he hadn't shoplifted.

"He fainted," Chief Tyler told her. "There was a woman who found him and she carried him out to the road and flagged down a car. But before he fainted, he told her he'd found a dead body. She said it was very strange, the way he just stood there, not wanting her to get any closer."

"You don't think he . . . ?" she'd gasped suddenly, and Chief Tyler had known exactly what she meant.

"Oh, no. The body had been there a week or more. But you might want to talk to him. Make sure he's okay. He wouldn't tell us why he was in the woods, wouldn't say anything about the body."

After the police station yesterday, she'd asked him about it, but he hadn't wanted to talk. He'd just looked up at her with something like accusation in his eyes and said that he'd wanted to go for a walk in the woods. "I'm not the only one who likes to go for walks in the woods," he'd said.

For a few minutes there, she'd almost worried that he'd found out about her. But she couldn't imagine how, and besides, it was over now. It was over for good and she was glad. She'd have to try to talk to him again, or maybe get Bruce to do it. That was the thing, get Bruce to take some time out of his precious family life to talk to his son.

She got up and took one last look at the trees behind the house. There were so many different colors, golds and yellows and greens, it almost seemed that they were shimmering. For a second, she thought she saw someone standing there, but it was only a trick of the light.

SIX

BY THE NEXT MORNING MEGAN'S COLD HAD REAPPEARED, HER
eyes dull and rheumy, her nose streaming greenish phlegm.
And despite his casual comment that she seemed to have a
little bit of a "sniffle" but seemed fine otherwise, the middle-
aged woman who ran the day care on Mass. Ave. seemed to
see right through him.

"Mr. Quinn, your daughter is very sick. She has a fever
and she could pass it on to the other children. We can't take
her today. I'm sorry." Her name was Mrs. Richardson and
she was a tall, no-nonsense woman with short gray hair who
reminded Quinn of an elementary-school teacher he'd once
had. When he'd visited the day-care center, he remembered
being impressed when she'd told him that she didn't take
children who were obviously sick. "Little ones belong with
their parents when they're not feeling well," she'd said. "Any
day-care center that takes sick kids does so for the conve-
nience of the parents and not the children." Now he was re-
gretting how impressed she'd been.

"But she's doing much better. I don't think she's conta-
gious anymore." He was grasping at straws, and he knew it.

"Mr. Quinn, I'm sorry. You need to take Megan home and
let her get better."

Now he felt guilty. "Okay, you're right," he said. "I'll
bring her back in a couple of days."

When he'd got her into her car seat again, he sat there for

a minute and tried to decide what to do. He was supposed to be working on the Kenneth Churchill thing. He had planned on calling all of Churchill's colleagues to see if they might have any idea of where he'd gone. And he wanted to put out a trace on the car, see if the Concord cops had found anything. That was the weirdest thing about this whole case—if something had happened to the guy, then where had the car gone? No, it was more likely that the guy had taken off with some Betsy Ross impersonator or something. But Quinn remembered Beverly Churchill's face and decided that he owed her the truth at least.

He turned around to check on Megan and found that she was fast asleep in her car seat. Maybe he could just take her into work with him. He had avoided doing it before because you couldn't take a baby out on police work, but it wasn't as if talking on the phone was particularly dangerous. He could bring her inside in the stroller and maybe she would just sleep all morning. Then, after he'd made all his phone calls, he could take her home a little bit early.

He was feeling confident about the plan until he actually walked through the front door of headquarters and the young woman on duty behind the front desk looked up and smiled and said, "Who's this?"

"Oh, this is my daughter, Megan," Quinn whispered, trying not to wake her up. A homeless guy sitting in the waiting room looked up and leered, making Quinn lean a bit more protectively over the stroller.

"She's so cute," the young sergeant said too loudly, reaching down to look at her and pat her hand.

"Thanks," Quinn whispered. "She's sleeping, so I'm going to . . ." But at that moment, Megan opened her eyes, saw the strange face looming over her, and began to howl.

The girl looked surprised, as though she hadn't known babies could cry quite that loudly. Quinn hurried inside and went up to the homicide division, checking to make sure that Havrilek wasn't around. At the sound of Megan's plaintive screaming, though, every head on the floor looked up to see who it was. He put the stroller next to his desk and took her into the men's room to check her diaper. All was well and he held her and walked up and down the bathroom, letting her crying run its course. When she finally hiccupped and sighed, her eyes sliding shut against her will, Quinn took her back out to his desk, easing her into the stroller. She was already asleep again.

His first phone call was to the Concord police. The chief wasn't in, so Quinn left his number and the dispatcher said she'd have him get right back to Quinn. His next call was to the history department at BU. He asked to be connected to the department chairperson and was getting a new notebook out of his desk when a female voice said, "Delia Harmon."

"Oh, yes, Ms. Harmon, I'm a detective with the Cambridge Police Department and as you may know, one of your professors, Kenneth Churchill, seems to have . . . um . . . disappeared. His wife asked us to look around, and I was thinking you could answer some questions."

"Disappeared? Is that how you describe it? 'Run off' is more how I'd say it. We've had to cancel his classes this week. After the way he's been behaving this year. And now he just—"

"Yes, that's why we're looking into it," Quinn broke in. "That's why I'm calling you. We want to find out what happened. You know, there is the possibility that he's been in an accident. Have you considered that?"

She was silent for a minute. "Is that what you think happened?" she asked finally.

"We don't know. Now, do you have any idea where he could be?"

"No, of course not. He was going out to Concord for one of his reenactment things." She said "reenactment" with a hint of sarcasm. "And he was supposed to be back Thursday to teach. He just didn't show up. The students were all waiting. When I called Beverly, she said she didn't know where he was either, but that she thought he'd probably decided to stay a little bit longer. I assumed he was just blowing us off."

"What did you mean when you said 'the way he's been behaving this year'? How has he been behaving?"

"Flaky. He's been missing meetings, canceling classes. All because he said he was working on his book. I was all in favor of the book. If it's as groundbreaking as he says it is, it'll be good for the department when it's published, but he can't just forget about his students whenever he feels like it."

"How much did you know about the book he was working on?"

"Not much. It was about Josiah Whiting. Do you know who he is?"

"A bit. Apparently he was a big shot during the Revolution."

"Right. He had been a top man in the Massachusetts militia. One of Colonel Barrett's most important men. A real American hero. Kenneth had discovered something big, but he wouldn't say what it was. I think he felt that some of his claims were so explosive that he wanted to wait until the book was out."

"Explosive?"

She laughed. "Well, something that contradicted the way Whiting's role has been understood by historians up until now. I dare say you wouldn't find it very explosive."

"Where was he doing the research? I mean, was he talking to people out there or going to the library, or what?"

"He was doing interviews, as far as I know, with people around Concord who knew about Whiting. I know he'd spent a lot of time at the Minuteman Museum. It has quite a nice little collection, and I think he said that the woman who runs it is somehow related to Whiting."

Quinn made a note of that, thanked her for her help, and asked for the names of other department members who had been friendly with Churchill. She gave him three names and then said, "Call me if you hear anything, will you? As negative as I sound about Kenneth, he is a friend, and a damn good scholar. I'd hate to think that anything's happened to him."

Quinn told her that he would and said good-bye.

Megan was still sleeping, so he called each of the three names that Delia Harmon had given him. All three expressed their concern for Churchill, but none had anything to add to what Quinn had already learned. Then he moved on to the list of friends that Beverly Churchill had given him. Most of Kenneth Churchill's friends didn't know that he was missing and, though they expressed their surprise, couldn't shed any light on where he'd gone.

When he was done, he tried the Concord P.D. again, and this time the dispatcher put him through to Chief John Tyler.

"What can I do for you, Detective Quinn?" Tyler asked. "Sorry I didn't get back to you. Things are a little nutty around here."

"No problem." Quinn explained about Kenneth Churchill's disappearance. "He was a Revolutionary War reenactor. That's why he was out there. I was going to see if you could put out something about the car. Make sure it's not abandoned in some lot somewhere. Then, I was thinking—"

Tyler interrupted him. "Actually, I think we may be able to do better than that. We've got a body." Quinn heard him call out to someone else in the room, "I've got something here. Get Lynch."

Quinn leaned back in his chair. "No shit?" An image of Beverly Churchill's hands flashed into his mind.

"No shit. A kid was out walking in the woods Sunday. Found this body. It's a man, six feet. Dressed in some kind of soldier's costume. Revolutionary War, I think, so that fits. Partially decomposed. Been in the woods a week or so. You know, it's been pretty warm during the days. This is a lucky break for us, let me tell you. The guy didn't have any identification on him and we've been calling these guys who do reenactments, asking if anybody's noticed that someone's missing, et cetera, et cetera. I'll tell ya, it's not exactly model detective work."

"Sounds like him. Right down to the costume. Any idea on cause of death?"

"Stabbing, it looks like. Something sharp entered his chest cavity. We'll know soon enough. We've turned it over to the state police already, so they'll get the crime scene guys in." Suburban police departments such as Concord's turned major murder cases over to the state investigators connected with the county D.A.'s Office.

"You might want to try something like a bayonet," Quinn said. "This guy had a whole arsenal of Revolutionary War weaponry in his living room."

"Yeah, that's a good idea. Thanks. We should know more after the P.M. anyway."

"Wait, so you find the car?"

"No. But we weren't looking. Give me the plates and all that and I'll check it out."

"Sure." Quinn read off the numbers. "And I already interviewed the wife. I can get the dentist from her so you can compare dental records."

"Great. I'm sure they'll try for an ID as soon as they can. Hey, assuming it's him, would you mind telling the wife? Since you know her already?"

"No, no, of course. It's gotta be him. The uniform and everything. Listen, I'll send some photos." Megan started crying and Quinn pulled her up into his lap, bouncing her up and down as he talked.

"Well, that's the thing. The face is mostly gone. Pretty woodsy out where they found it. Lot of weasels and stuff, and it looks like one of the neighborhood dogs had been at it."

Quinn swallowed. He didn't like to think about that. "Okay, well, I'll talk to the wife and get the dentals. I'll get them out to you as soon as I can."

"Thanks. That's great."

Quinn had put the phone down and was checking Megan's diaper when a voice said, "Hey, Quinny, I don't think I've had the pleasure." It was Havrilek and he was standing in the doorway, looking amused.

"Hey, I'm sorry about this, boss. She's got a cold and they wouldn't take her at day care. I'm making phone calls on this missing professor thing, so I thought I'd just . . . Hey, listen, they've got a body out in Concord. Wearing a Revolutionary War outfit and everything."

"Really? They know how he died yet?"

"Doesn't sound natural. I'm going to get dentals through the wife and see if I can help with that."

"Great. When'd they find the body?"

"Oh, uh, Sunday."

"Shouldn't we have known about it yesterday?"

Quinn blushed. He should have called Concord already or checked the online databases. "Yeah, maybe. I was just . . . I talked to the wife and I was just gonna see if . . ." He was fumbling, and Havrilek knew it.

"Why don't you take the rest of the day off?"

"You sure? I can . . ."

"No, no. You got a sick kid. You take her home and put her to bed."

Havrilek stopped to tickle Megan under her chin. She smiled a little. "Cute kid," he said. But somehow he managed to make Quinn feel bad.

SEVEN

"WELL, YOU'VE GOT YOUR BARRE GRAY. THAT'S A NICE CLAS-
sic granite," Bruce Whiting was saying. "And then if you
like something a little darker, there are some nice granites
out of Minnesota: St. Cloud Gray, Autumn Brown. Most of
the real black ones come out of Africa: Flash Black, Nero
Black." He handed over the little blocks of granite to the
woman. She was the one who'd be making the decision. He
had known right away. Someone always took charge, came
right out and said what he or she wanted. It was like death
erased the need for the regular stuff couples did—all the
"What do you want, honey?" "No, what do you want?"

It was their fifteen-year-old daughter they were buying
the stone for. A car accident. The boyfriend, who had lived,
hadn't even been drinking. It had been a rainy night and he'd
lost control on a well-traveled suburban road. Bruce remembered reading about the accident in the paper and wondering
if he would see the parents. He always wondered about that
when he read about a death in the paper. Would they scatter
the ashes? Would there be a funeral? Would they even get a
monument?

The mother was the one making the decisions here, despite being so distraught that she could barely speak.

"Did you have something in mind?" he asked finally after
she had turned the granite samples over and over in her
hands as though she couldn't remember what they were for.

"She liked pink," the mother said. "It was her favorite color." A tear rolled from her eye to her cheek. Bruce watched it. Once, he had been able to feel a real sense of sympathy for the bereaved. Now, since Pres had been sick, he found that he was threatened by shows of emotion. He wanted to turn away from her, to leave her crying in the showroom. But with some effort, he was able to look her in the eye and say, "I'm sorry, I know this is hard. What about this one? It's called Colonial Rose. I've always liked it. Very feminine, don't you think? And you can do a rose or a lily on the face. What was her favorite flower?"

When they had gone, he went into the office and sat down at the desk to go through the mail. His father had been in already. The mail was spread out all over Bruce's desk, a few bills opened and then discarded. It drove Bruce crazy, but he'd tried talking to George about it and George had just said he was too old to change his ways.

"I'll be out of here soon enough," he'd said in his fatalistic manner. "When I retire, you can do all the mail your own way and no one can stop you." He'd looked at Bruce with his gray eyes that almost disappeared against his gray hair and grayish skin, then turned away, a slumped figure dressed in his usual uniform of baggy tweed trousers and a charcoal wool sweater.

Ever since George had announced that he was going to retire, he had seemed to shrink into himself. Over the summer he had spent more time in his vegetable garden than in the showroom, and Bruce wondered if the end of the growing season wasn't the source of George's recent depression.

There wasn't much in the mail, a few bills that he put aside to pay and various advertisements that he threw out. He leaned back and looked at the mess on his desk. There were catalogs everywhere, his own sketches, scraps of paper with notes on them arranged in precise piles. Lauren was always trying to get him to clean it off, but he liked it the way it was. "This way, I know where everything is," he always told her.

He was looking through a catalog of new laser-carved designs for monuments when she came into the office. His wife had her own desk on the other side of the showroom, where she answered the phone and did the accounts. She was wearing a pink wool skirt and a pink sweater and her curly blond hair looked shiny and clean. There was something about her that had always reminded him of Shirley Temple, something perky and sexy and young. Next to her, he was a shaggy, middle-aged giant, and on the rare occasions that he was forced to look at a picture of the two of them, he was always struck by how incongruous they were, Lauren's tiny blond figure and his dark, overly tall one. And he was always struck by how lucky he was, which made him feel desperate and uneasy.

"Hi, hon," she said, putting her hands on his shoulders and rubbing them. "Whatcha doin'?"

"Just looking at some new stuff. What do you think of this one?"

She leaned over him and studied the design. "Tacky," she said. "How did it go with the car accident?"

"Okay. The mother was the one. I think I got 'em squared away."

"Poor people." It always amazed him that Lauren was still capable of sympathy after dealing with as many grieving families as she had over the years. She sat down in the chair across from him and leveled her blue eyes at him. "Did you talk to Cecily?"

He closed the catalog and swiveled his chair away. "I couldn't. Pres has a doctor's appointment tomorrow and this thing with the body in the woods . . . She was really upset when I called. I just couldn't do it."

"Pres told you what he was doing up there yet?"

"I don't know. Just walking." But he hadn't answered her question. Pres hadn't told him anything, hadn't wanted to talk about it at all.

She got up, smoothed the front of her skirt, and leaned over to kiss his forehead. "Bruce, I love you and I know this is really hard with Pres and everything, but we've got to get this settled. Especially with . . . well, if we're right, it could just be a really bad situation for everyone. And if we want to start branching out when your dad retires, she could make trouble about it. We've got to get those shares back."

Bruce looked down at the desk. It was the fourth time they'd had this conversation that week and he repressed the desire to snap at her. She was right, of course. The stupidest thing he'd ever done had been to allow Cecily to claim a third of the shares of the monument company during the divorce. He'd been so guilty, willing to do anything to make her go away so he could be with Lauren, and she had been so angry, she'd wanted to do anything to hurt him. Asking for the shares had been her way of exerting her power, though she'd said it was because of Pres. And he supposed it was fair on some level. When they'd first gotten married, the monument company had been deeply in debt, two or three years from shutting down if he and George had continued on the path they'd been following. But Cecily had some money her father had invested for her, and she had put it all into the company. They'd expanded, gotten better lines, improved the whole look of the place. She had deserved something, but he knew he should have just bought her out.

"He won't have anything else," she'd said when she'd told him what she wanted. Bruce remembered feeling like he was going to cry and telling her that of course he would always provide for his son.

"But we don't know that," she'd countered. "You say that now, but when *she*"—she couldn't say Lauren's name—"has the baby, you may feel differently. This is the only way to make sure that Pres will be taken care of."

He'd felt so guilty that he'd been more than happy to agree.

But Lauren was right. It had to be taken care of, sooner rather than later. They'd been to the bank and had talked about taking out a loan to buy her out. It would be difficult, but it could be done.

If she agreed, he reminded himself. If she agreed.

"Okay," he said finally. "I'll talk to her tomorrow."

She caressed his cheek. "Where's your dad?"

"I don't know." He shut down the computer and swiveled his chair around to face her. She gave him a sexy little grin and sat down on his lap. "You got any appointments?"

"Uh-uh," he said, already kissing her neck. Her hair smelled of strawberries and vanilla.

"Good." She opened her mouth a little to him and placed her right breast in his hand. They were practiced and it took only a few moments before he was unzipped, before her pink wool skirt was up around her waist. The desk chair creaked and in a few minutes it was all over. It was the way they always did it in the office, quickly, focused on him, worried that George would come in. If they thought about it, they both knew that that was part of the turn-on, that it reminded them of those early days when they could be together only at the office.

Bruce had known the first time he'd seen her. Not that he was going to fall in love with her, marry her, have two children with her. But he had known that he was going to sleep with her. It had surprised him, sitting across from her in the office during her interview, hearing about all the computer programs she knew, all the responsibilities she'd had at her previous jobs. He'd never cheated on Cecily before, though he'd thought about it, but somehow when he'd seen Lauren, he'd just known.

Now he lay his hot face against her neck, breathing hard. He loved her so fiercely, he sometimes felt guilty about Noah and Rory. Of course he loved his son and daughter too, but it was an easy kind of love, fun love, sweet love. The way he felt about Lauren, still after all this time, made him feel ashamed and scared sometimes. It was the way he felt about Pres, he realized with a start. If he was honest with himself, they were the two people he loved the most in the world.

EIGHT

THE HILL CEMETERY WAS LOCATED ACROSS FROM MONUMENT Square, climbing away from Lexington Road, the headstones perched along the rise like trees hanging on by their roots. The story went that the reason for its existence, only steps from the South Burying Ground on the other side of Main Street, was the superstitions of Concord's earliest settlers. Believing that carrying a corpse across running water caused the soul to be carried away, the townspeople living on the far side of the Mill Dam that had run under Main Street refused to carry their dead to the South Burying Ground. So they had built their own.

There were a few well-known stones that Sweeney had seen before, but she didn't stop to look at them again. Today she was looking for further evidence of the round-skull carver.

She started at the bottom of the hill, moving across the rows of stones and looking for the distinctive death's-head. If she could find another stone that the round-skull carver had made for a prominent Concord resident, then she'd have a good chance of finding at least one of the names. This was always her favorite part. As she looked out across the stones, she saw only promise, only the stories that these stones had to tell. Once she waded in among them, she would confront the realities of her field, broken stones, stones that would never yield up a clue to their maker no matter how hard she tried, stones made long after the death date on the stone that hopelessly confused a time line. But for now she looked out across the little city of stone and smiled.

As she searched, she had fun browsing through them again, finding typical seventeenth- and eighteenth-century stones, a few wonderful death's-heads complete with skulls and crossbones, and some winged death's-heads. The classic death's-head—a primitive, often grinning skull—was a common sight in seventeenth-century graveyards, and to contemporary minds it presented a macabre image of the consequences of the grave. But it was by no means a simple symbol, and Sweeney was interested in the various ways it had been used over the centuries.

Sweeney's specialty was the funerary art of the Victorian world, and she thought it must be difficult to find a culture as obsessed with death as the Victorians had been. But there was no denying that the Puritans had also spent a lot of time and energy contemplating their final demise. Children were brought up on pithy little rhymes such as "Time cuts down all / Both Great and small" and "Youth forward slips / Death soonest nips."

Puritan stonecutters had made good use of the skull or death's-head on their stones, and it was a common sight in cemeteries filled during the eighteenth century. Over time, the death's-head had evolved into the soul's head, the moon-shaped faces, often winged, that were a common sight on eighteenth- and early-nineteenth-century stones. And in the late 1700s, stonecutters had even started to carve actual portraits on their memorials.

But as time went on, she felt her hopes flag. She had climbed to the top of the hill and had finished with the stones from the 1740s and '50s, when the round-skull carver seemed to have done most of his work, and still she'd found nothing.

She was looking along one of the back corner rows when she saw the distinctive death's-head. It wasn't one of the round-skull carver's, but immediately she recognized the shape of the skull and the strange Medusa hair. She knelt down in front of it and cleared some dead grass away from the base. The stone wasn't signed, but it had to be by Josiah Whiting. She knew it as certainly as if he had signed his name. Sweeney felt a little buzz of excitement as she checked the date on the stone. The Abner Fall stone in the South Burying Ground had been dated 1760. This one had been made sometime about 1773, when John Stiles, buried beneath it, had breathed his last.

In her notebook, Sweeney found the quick sketches she'd made of the Abner Fall stone and compared them with this one. The differences were startling. Between 1760 and 1773, Josiah Whiting had radically altered his distinctive Medusa head. This mask was elongated and the hair had a different feel to it. It rose above the head in a more frantic way, the strands thinner and longer. The skeletal face seemed more haunted and desperate, the eyes wild. Sweeney looked closely and found that the circles were smaller and the pinpoint pupils larger, which accounted for the look. Whereas the death's-head on the Abner Fall stone had seemed peaceful and bland, this one looked to be in torment.

She studied the lettering and took measurements. Her initial instinct that the letters were precisely centered on the stone was borne out by her tape measure. Josiah Whiting had been a singularly exact stonecutter during a time when many gravestone makers had made up for their lack of planning by squeezing extra letters in at the end of a line or above the other letters. She felt a sense of respect for this craftsman who had worked so long ago.

Sweeney took a series of pictures of the stone in the midday light, made some notes, and was starting her search for more of Whiting's work when she looked up to find Pres Whiting watching her from the back of the cemetery.

"Hi," she called out. He was wearing the Red Sox cap and a woolen sweater that looked a little too hot for the day. "What a coincidence."

He came closer, clutching his backpack and looking a bit afraid. "No," he said nervously. "It's not a coincidence. You said you were going to come to the cemetery, so I was checking for you."

"Oh. Well, I'm glad you found me. How are you?"

"All right." He stood awkwardly, looking around him at the stones.

"So, what have you been up to since yesterday?" she asked.

"Oh, just, like, school." He blushed a little.

"Yeah? Isn't today Tuesday? It's been a while since I was in school, but I remember we usually went on Tuesdays."

"Well . . ." He looked around the cemetery as though he was looking for someone. "I don't know. It's just that I get so bored there. I would rather learn stuff out here."

Sweeney, who remembered feeling the same way, had to refrain from telling him that he probably was learning more out here than he was in there.

"I found another Josiah Whiting stone. I was just about to start looking around for more. Do you want to help me?"

He brightened up at that and followed her up and down the rows of stones as she looked for something that reminded her of the carver.

"Here we go," she said as she stopped in front of a smaller stone with the characteristically skinny shoulders and a variation of the Medusa death mask.

"Annie Gooding," Pres read out loud. "She was born in 1761 and she died in 1774."

"It's later," Sweeney said after a moment, trying to figure out if he'd realized she was only thirteen. "His style has evolved over time."

"That man looks crazy," Pres said.

"He does. He looks really crazy." She took some photographs and made a few notes.

"Why do they put them on gravestones?" Pres asked. "Those skulls."

"It started out as a pretty straightforward Puritan symbol for death," Sweeney told him. "The Puritans used gravestones as a way of warning the living about the horrors of the grave. The idea was that you should live a saintly life, or you'd end up nothing more than a bag of bones. Of course, there was kind of a theological problem there, because they also believed that whether or not you were saved was preordained and you actually had nothing to do with it."

"I feel like that's how all religions are," Pres said. "My gramma makes me go to church with her sometimes. They're always talking about stuff that doesn't make any sense to me. Like, you should do certain things because it's the right thing to do, but then if you don't do them, God will always forgive you. I don't get that. Why would you do good things if God will always forgive you if you don't?" He reached up to take off the hat and scratched his head. He looked rounder today, like someone had blown him up like a balloon.

"You're not the only one," Sweeney said. "The Puritans did change, though, because of people like you who asked questions and pointed out things that didn't make sense. By the time Josiah Whiting was making his stones, the church had loosened up a little, started opening up to the idea that everyone could be saved. A lot of carvers started using different symbols, more human-looking heads and more angels. They started putting wings on the death's-head, to signify the idea of life after death." She watched him. "What's a stone you really like here?"

He led her over to a big 1740s headstone featuring a little portrait of a woman at the top. She was surrounded by twining vines of ivy and flowers. Her name, according to the carved letters beneath the portrait, was Anne Thomas. Beneath her name and the dates of her life were the words "Piety and love she gave / To all who knew her / The judgment of the grave She'll face / and find her true reward."

"What do you like about it?" Sweeney asked him.

He traced a finger over the carved lines of the woman's face, the primitive likeness nonetheless suggesting femininity. "It's pretty sophisticated," he said. "For 1740. Look at her hair. And it's cool that you can see what she looked like. A lot of stones, it's just the name, you know. But you don't really know what they were like. My dad makes a lot of stones that have pictures on them. It's pretty cool. They use lasers, or you can put, like, a real picture behind a piece of Plexiglas. I'd like to have my picture on my gravestone. So people can see who I was, you know?"

"I'm impressed. I don't think I knew the difference between a sophisticated 1740 stone and a not-so-sophisticated one until I was in graduate school," Sweeney told him. But that wasn't strictly true. Part of the reason she'd gotten interested in gravestones as an adolescent was that she had liked comparing them, seeing how they were different in different eras.

"Yeah, well, I told you. I like hanging around cemeteries."

Sweeney took out her camera and handed it over to him. "Take a picture of it for me?" He nodded and carefully focused the camera on the stone, pressing the shutter with intense concentration and then handing the camera back to her.

"This is great," she told Pres, going back to the second Whiting stone. "I want to get some photos before the light changes. I think I'm going to try to find out more about your ancestor. Maybe write my paper about him. I'm not finding that much about the other guy I was working on, and I think there might be something really interesting here. The death's-heads change so much. You said he was a Revolutionary War hero? Right?"

"I guess so. My grampa thinks so, anyway. When he dresses up at reenactments, he's always pretending he's Josiah."

"Is there anyone in town who knows about him? Anyone I could interview?"

"My mom," he said. "She knows about all that kind of historical stuff. She has a bunch of letters in her museum that my grampa gave her. And my dad and my grampa know about him. My grampa especially."

"I'll have to talk to them."

Pres thought for a minute. Then he said, "Kids used to say there was a ghost. In the woods near my grandparents' house." He colored suddenly and Sweeney wondered why the association embarrassed him. "They said maybe it was Josiah Whiting."

"Really?"

"Yeah, I don't really believe in ghosts, but kids said they heard things sometimes. At night." He took a little notebook and pen out of his backpack and tapped the pen nervously against the spiral binding.

"What did they hear?"

"A guy screaming. Like he was in pain."

He opened up the notebook and jotted something down in it.

"What's that?" Sweeney asked him. "Your journal?"

He closed it and put it back in the backpack as though he was afraid she was going to take it. "No. Just a kind of record book. I write down when things happen."

Sweeney asked, "Why?"

"Just so, you know. People will know what I did."

He had used the past tense and it took her a minute to re-alize what he meant. It was to be a posthumous legacy, that little book. She felt her throat constrict and she had to stand up and pretend to inspect a gravestone behind him so that he wouldn't see her face.

He read over something he'd written, then shut the book and looked up at her. "Are your parents married still?"

Sweeney sat down, trying to figure out how to explain it to him. "No," she said finally. "Actually they never got married. But we all lived together until I was five and then they split up. My dad died when I was thirteen, but my mom's still alive, although I don't see her a lot. How old were you when your parents got divorced?"

"Eight," he said. "I knew they were going to, though. They used to fight a lot and it seemed like my dad didn't like being around her anyway. He decided to live with Lauren in-stead."

"Do you get along with her? My dad never got remarried, but he had this one girlfriend I hated. She was always telling me to go to my room and leave them alone. I was so happy when my dad broke up with her."

"Lauren's nice. And I like Rory and Noah. That's my sister and brother. But my mom hates her, and I can't really talk about her at home."

"Adults can be real pains in the neck," Sweeney said, but he didn't smile.

They sat in companionable silence, looking out across the stones.

"What did the police want to know from you?" she asked after a few minutes.

He seemed surprised she would ask. "I don't know. They just kept asking the same questions over and over and over. Did I touch him? What did he look like when I got there? I kept telling them, but it was like they didn't even listen."

"Me too," Sweeney said. "I got tired of saying the same thing over and over. They asked me if you went into the clubhouse before I got there."

Pres leaned back and stared up at the canopy of trees and didn't say anything.

Above them, the trees blazed.

"Pres," Sweeney said, "did you go into the clubhouse? When you found the guy?"

He turned to look at her.

"I didn't tell the police that I saw you. I'm not even sure I did see you. If you tell me, I promise I won't tell them unless it's really important."

"Maybe I did. I might tell you later," he said, looking up earnestly at her. "I don't know. I don't want to tell you now."

"You're like Scheherezade," she said. "Keeping me on the hook."

"Who's that?"

"*The Arabian Nights*? Don't you know about Scherezade? She married a sultan who said he would kill her, so she started telling him a story, except that every night, she said she had to tell him more the next day. That's like you."

"That man," Pres said after a minute. "He smelled pretty bad, but other than that, it wasn't that gross. He was like a big pile of rags or something. You could tell he was just . . . dead. Do you think that's what being dead is? Just being a

pile of rags and not moving or smiling or talking or anything? Not even knowing?"

"It may be." Sweeney wanted to touch him, to put an arm
around him or pull him into her lap or something, but she
knew she shouldn't. "I don't know."

He nodded, then said, "I was thinking. I know a lot about
gravestones. I could help you maybe, kind of be your assistant, you know? I can take pictures and maybe you could
give me assignments, like, to go and find a certain gravestone." He looked up at her, afraid she was going to say no,
and added, "You wouldn't even have to pay me. I could do it
for free."

Sweeney picked up his hat from the ground and put it on
his head. "Okay," she said. "You've got yourself a deal."

SWEENEY HAD DINNER IN TOWN AND WAS BACK AT THE INN
by eight. Tired from her long day outside, she put on her pajamas, got into bed, and took out the stack of books she'd
brought with her about Massachusetts stonecarvers.

Gravestone making in Colonial New England had
evolved from a necessary function for public health into a
sophisticated art. The earliest grave markers most likely had
been made of wood. They had long ago disintegrated, but
references to these gravestones as "rayles" in some probate
documents led historians to believe they resembled fence
rails or crosses.

As the early settlers of Massachusetts started using lo-
cally mined slate to mark the graves of their dead, the stonecutter became an important person in the community.

He was very often a farmer or housewright who also
carved hearthstones and other stone products, and he was
usually chosen for his profession because he had a rudimen-
tary education that allowed him to carve names and dates
and compose epitaphs. Sometimes a minister or teacher
might be the only literate member of the community and
would learn to carve.

The first chapter of one study detailed the lives and times

of the Woodbury family of carvers. The first Woodbury had
come over from Kent in the 1660s and settled in the Concord
area, finding work as a stonemason. In the 1750s, a descendant named John Woodbury began carving gravestones for
his neighbors, and the book detailed a series of probate pay-
ments made to Woodbury for amounts between £1 and £5.

There were a series of photographs of stones that had
definitely been carved by John Woodbury, and Sweeney
noted the unusual style of his lettering, the serifs scrolled
and curlicued, the top ones to the left and the bottom ones to
the right. She also began to see a pattern in the way he
carved his numbers, the 5s oddly formed, with a straight
spine, and the spine of the 7s extending far below the line.
She had always been interested in the way that gravestone
carvers tried to put their personal stamp on their pieces. The
particular pattern of shapes and figures that a carver made
when he put chisel to stone reflected the carver's background, training, and developing aesthetic.

Most of Woodbury's earlier epitaphs began with the
words "Here Lyeth the Remains of . . . ," the use of "*lyeth*"
rather than "*lies*" being common until the later 1750s. After
that, Woodbury began employing the new usage, and most
of the stones had the rather unimaginative epitaph "Here lies
the body of . . . who departed this life . . ."

The Woodbury family was distinguished by its simple tri-
angular faces that reminded Sweeney of African masks.
There were actually a surprising number of these mask-like
faces on early New England stones. It had always been a
puzzle to her, and she remembered wondering, when she
first encountered them in college, if there had somehow been
contact between these early stonecutters and the African
artists who made their famous ceremonial masks.

She was reading along when a particular line of text
caught her eye. "Woodbury's death's-heads are somewhat
similar to the early work of another Massachusetts stonecutter, Josiah Whiting, who worked in the Concord area in the
1760s and 1770s. Whiting's work shows signs of sophistica-
tion and remarkable potential, but it has not been determined

whether he finished any gravestones after 1775." Not been determined? Sweeney looked through the rest of the chapter for another mention of him, but there wasn't one.

She read on. "Whiting's sons continued in the stonecutting business and there are a series of later Whiting family stones in Concord-area cemeteries." Sweeney took some notes and checked the index for other references to the family. But there weren't any.

She wrote Josiah Whiting's name down in her notebook. In a lot of ways, he was just what she was looking for. Someone obscure who hadn't been written about a lot, yet someone who had a lot of work in the Concord area. The Woodburys had already been done, but Whiting was hers to discover. And she was fascinated by the three stones she'd seen already. Why had Whiting's style changed so dramatically between the 1760s and 1770s?

There was also the fact that she now had a connection to the family. There was a lot she could find out from Pres and his father and grandfather. Did they see themselves as continuing the family tradition, or had they fallen into the mass-produced monument industry?

So, Josiah Whiting it was. She had chosen. Though it was almost, Sweeney thought, as though he had chosen her.

She checked the clock next to her bed. It was only a little after eight, but in London it was past midnight. Sure enough, her cell phone rang and she picked it up, saying, "You're up late."

"I am," Ian Ball said, his precise English pronunciation familiar to her now. "Late night at the office and then an interminable client dinner. Really awful."

"I'm sorry." Sweeney put the books aside and leaned back against the pillows. She had met Ian Ball in Vermont nearly a year ago and they had had a short . . . she didn't know what they had had in Vermont. It hadn't been a fling exactly. It was more than that, but she hadn't been able to figure out yet what it had meant to her and what she might want it to mean in the future. She had resisted getting in touch with him for some months, but ever since she had bro-

ken down and called him back in the spring, the late-night
transatlantic phone conversations had become a part of her
routine. At first it had been maybe once a week, then twice a
week, and then every other night. Lately it had been almost
every night, and Sweeney felt that they had reached some
kind of crossroads. They talked about their childhoods,
about his daughter, about books and movies and music and
traffic and food and money. They did not talk about their
feelings for each other, about the fact that they talked so often and had not seen each other since that Christmas in Vermont, when they had been thrown together.

Every once in a while, there would be a long silence and
one of them hurried to fill it. But somehow they had word-
lessly agreed to talk more frequently, and Sweeney now
thought of their relationship—or whatever it was—as a series of infinitesimal gestures that moved things inexorably
forward. It was like that game where you built a tower of little blocks of wood and then removed one at a time, hoping
not to topple the whole thing.

But where was it all leading? She was conscious that Ian
deliberately held back with her, afraid to spook her by getting too serious, by suggesting that they see each other, by
telling her how he felt.

"I'm sorry I haven't called you back," she said. "I've had
quite an eventful couple of days." She told him about meeting Pres and finding the body in the woods, and about her
decision to spend some time in Concord. "So, anyway, I ran
into Pres again today. He's offered to be my assistant. He's
such a funny kid. At times he seems younger than twelve and
other times he might as well be forty. He was so matter-of-
fact when he told me about his parents' divorce, like he
could understand why it's better that they're not together
anymore, but I couldn't help being mad at them. Why do
people have kids with people they're not sure they want to
be with?" It took her only a minute to realize what she had
said. Ian was divorced from his daughter's mother. "Oh God,
I'm sorry, Ian. I didn't mean that."

"It's okay," he said. And his voice sounded like it was. "If I could choose a life for my daughter, it wouldn't be this one, but we manage. And I can't really think about what-ifs, because this is what our reality is."

"God, that sounds so *healthy*."

He laughed. "Well, that's on a good day. Then she calls me and says she hates Mummy's new boyfriend and she's miserable, when are we going to get back together, and I want to die."

She pictured him holding the phone, his dark hair and the aristocratic lines of his face. Those dark blue eyes that she had found too probing, too eager to see into her.

They chatted about his work for a few minutes and then she said she'd better let him get to bed.

He hesitated as though he was going to say something else. She could hear him breathing. "Sweeney?" he said suddenly.

Sweeney took a deep breath. "What?"

Again, she could hear him hesitate. "Good night," he said finally, a note of discouragement in his voice.

She switched off her phone and checked the clock next to her bed. It was only nine. She read halfheartedly for another couple of minutes, then turned out the light and slid down between the freshly laundered sheets. There was a particular pleasure to clean sheets. When she and Colm had lived together, she had never been able to get him to launder the bed linens, despite all of his socialist ranting about men and women sharing household chores equally. She had a sudden memory of their bed in the Oxford flat, a huge king-size futon, the sheets rumpled and wrinkled and stained. Colm had liked to sleep right up against her at night and he had a way of pulling out even the most carefully tucked sheets, leaving them worn-looking the morning after they'd been washed. One of the worst things about going back to their flat after his death had been facing the sheets that still smelled of him.

She inhaled the faint scent of lavender from the cotton and tried to imagine the room with someone else in it, a pair of men's shoes marring the empty floor, a dark sweater thrown across the end of the bed, another suitcase lying next to hers.

And then, because the vision disturbed her too much, she pulled the covers over her head and tried for lavender-scented oblivion.

NINE

THE FIRE WAS REALLY GOING NOW, THE STICKS AND NEWS-
papers she'd used to start it nearly crumbled away and the
three birch logs blackened all around with orange embers
glowing away in their center.

Beverly Churchill sat back and enjoyed the heat from the
fire for a moment. It had been ages since they'd made one.
When they had bought the house, she remembered telling
Kenneth that she wanted to have a fire every night. It had
seemed such a luxury, the wide, old fireplace with the ornately carved Victorian mantel and the stack of pristine
birch logs that the previous owners had left behind. But
somehow they hadn't used it much. A few times at Christmas or when they had company, and that had been it. For the
past few years, Kenneth hadn't been home much in the eve-
nings, and it seemed sad somehow for her to make a fire just
for herself.

But it hadn't stopped her tonight. She hadn't been able to
find the matches and she'd finally rolled up a piece of newspaper and held it to the gas burner on the stove, then carried
it, flaming, into the living room.

Now, for the tenth time in as many minutes, she checked
the clock over the doorway. It was eleven. Where the hell
was Marcus? He'd promised her that he'd be home by ten, if
you could call his muttered "yeah" on the way out the door a
promise, but Marcus's promises didn't mean a lot these

days. He had turned fifteen and become someone else. His grades had dipped, and he had started going out at night, shrugging and disappearing upstairs when she asked him where he'd gone. She had bought some parenting books to try and figure out how to set limits for him, but it sounded so much easier than it was. "Let your child know what is expected of him or her and things will go much more smoothly." Yeah, right. She had let Marcus know she expected him to be home by ten over and over and over again, but it didn't make any difference. He just stared at her and mumbled words she couldn't understand, and by the time she had said, "What did you say?" he was gone, out the door in a cloud of cigarette smoke and acne soap.

She threw more paper onto the fire, strangely satisfied by the way each sheet shivered for a moment when it hit the heat, the way the flames licked at the corners and then whisked it away altogether. It was amazing how quickly the paper was gone, turned to ash. In five minutes, she was done. She sat for a moment watching the charred wood glow, the wispy bits of black paper fluttering around them, then got up and went to the kitchen to pour herself a glass of wine. There was a bottle of Syrah that she had opened the night before and she was surprised to find it nearly gone. She'd had only a glass. It must have been Marcus. She checked the microwave clock. He was now more than an hour late.

She took her wine back into the living room and watched as the fire burned hotly. For the past few days, she had been trying to keep as busy as she could, but suddenly she found she had nothing to do and she was terrified. She and Kenneth didn't have a lot of friends in Cambridge. When they had moved into the house, she'd imagined herself having tea with women in the neighborhood, becoming best friends with the mothers of Marcus's friends. But it hadn't ever happened. For one thing, none of their neighbors ever seemed to be around, and the few she had met at neighborhood parties or out walking their dogs seemed too busy for friendship.

She heard a car on the street, then an idling engine. A car door slammed and she jumped up, trying to get a glimpse of it. But by the time she got to the window, the car was disappearing around the corner and all she saw was a silvery bumper. A key turned in the lock and Marcus came through the front door.

She didn't know what to say, so she just watched him as he shrugged off his denim jacket and draped it over the chair next to the front door. She wasn't even sure he'd seen her until he said, "Hey," in such a soft voice that she could barely hear him.

"You're over an hour late," she said.

He kept his eyes on the floor and murmured, "Yeah, sorry."

Beverly strode over to him and lifted the brim of his hat so she could see his eyes. He refused to look at her, though, and she couldn't tell whether they were red or not. After a moment, he turned away, leaving the baseball hat in her hand, then started up the stairs.

"I don't know what to do, Marcus," she said finally, hanging the hat on the hat rack and going to sit on the couch. Marcus inched a foot up to the first stair, staring ahead, as though there were someone up on the landing. Beverly could hear her voice getting high and tight. "We're going through a tough time right now and I need you to be a little more thoughtful. I thought something had happened to you. Don't you see? I can't lose both of you!" And suddenly she was crying. She didn't want to cry, didn't want Marcus to see her crying, but there was nothing she could do. She wiped her eyes on the back of her bathrobe. She stared at the side of his face, the tears running down her face. How could he just look up the stairs like that without saying anything? It was like he wasn't even human.

She turned away and sat down on the couch, using a tissue from the box on the side table to wipe her face. Marcus looked even more uncomfortable, inching another foot up the stairs as though she wouldn't notice if he disappeared.

"Marcus!" she said, her composure back now. "This is ridiculous. Did you take some of the wine that was in kitchen?" He inched a foot up to the next step. "Well, did you?"

"Sorry," he said, still staring straight ahead.

"Sorry? Why did you take it? Do you have a drinking problem? What is going on?"

"I just wanted to try some. What's the big deal? In France kids my age drink wine all the time. It's practically required." It was funny, she thought, how he always seemed younger when he opened his mouth. Surly, silent, she hardly knew him. But making his argument, she remembered him as a little boy, the stubborn way he always made her do exactly what he wanted.

"Go to bed. I'm too tired to talk about this. We'll talk more in the morning."

Silently, he climbed the stairs and vanished, as though he'd never been there at all.

She lay back on the couch. Damn Kenneth. Damn him! Why should she have to do this all by herself? It wasn't as though he'd been much help with Marcus over the past year, but at least she'd been able to use him as leverage. She took a photograph of Kenneth and herself off the side table and studied it. It had been in New York, three years ago. They had been to see a play, and on impulse she had asked a passerby to take a photo of them. It was November and they had been wearing coats and scarves. Behind them, Broadway glowed red and green. They were grinning and Kenneth's arm was wrapped around her shoulders. You could see his gloved hand gripping her upper arm. She had always liked the picture because it brought back what she remembered of the trip, their breath in the cold air, taking a taxi back to their hotel at midnight.

She held the picture high above the stone hearth in front of the fireplace, then dropped it and watched the glass shatter, the tiny fragments so broken as to be hardly recognizable as glass.

TEN

IT HAD BEEN A CRAPPY DAY SO FAR.

To start with, Quinn had woken up to find that there was something wrong with the seal on the dishwasher and it had leaked all over the kitchen floor. Racing across to mop it up before it ran through onto the living room carpet, his socks—the last clean pair—had gotten soaked.

Megan had woken up feeling better, but her nose was still running a little, and when he'd dropped her at day care, he'd felt like the worst father in the world. He could still see her little face watching him as he walked away.

Now he was sitting at his desk, going over the notes he'd taken on the Kenneth Churchill case. "Josiah Whiting," he read to himself. "Militiaman. Stonecutter." The guy had been doing research on this stonecutter—Josiah Whiting, his name was. Beverly Churchill had said that's why he'd stayed in Concord. So, how had he ended up rotting in the woods? If it was him, he reminded himself, if it was him.

It was funny, this thing involving gravestones. Not directly, but still . . . If it turned out that the gravestone maker guy had anything to do with it, he could call Sweeney and see what she thought. He hadn't seen her since the morning they'd found Maura together, but he'd been certain that seeing her would bring back the awful rush of horror, grief, and relief he'd felt standing at the top of the stairs and knowing that his wife lay dead on the other side of the bathroom door.

But still, if it was Churchill and he needed some advice about this gravestone thing, maybe he could just call her, just kind of run it by her. Maybe that would be okay.

He put the file aside and went to call Beverly Churchill.

AS QUINN PULLED UP TO THE HOUSE AT NINE THAT NIGHT, he took a deep breath and steeled himself for his sister-in-law's assault. He ran through everything he thought she might say, just so it wouldn't be a surprise. "You're irresponsible. You have to put your daughter first. Why couldn't you just tell them you needed to leave?"

At four o'clock, it had become apparent that there was no way in hell he was going to pick Megan up at day care by six. He'd already gotten yelled at a couple of times for being late, so he'd called Debbie at work and asked if she could pick Megan up and take her back to the house and watch her until he got home. She'd sighed loudly but agreed. He'd been waiting on the results of the dental-records comparison on the Concord body and he'd known that if it turned out to be Kenneth Churchill, as Quinn was sure that it would, he would be at it most of the night, notifying Beverly Churchill, starting to liaise with the state homicide guys assigned to the Middlesex County D.A.'s Office. They'd take over responsibility for the murder investigation, but there would be a lot to do.

As it turned out, though, the forensic dental specialist that the state police used had been running late and finally they told him they probably wouldn't have the results tonight. The Concord cops had Quinn's cell number, they told him. They'd let him know when they knew anything.

"Hi," he called out, coming in the door and tripping over a stuffed animal. "I'm home." He heard Debbie's voice upstairs, along with Megan's laugh, and he followed the voices up to Megan's bedroom at the top of the stairs. Megan was on the changing table, and Debbie was getting her into her sleeper.

"Hi," she said over her shoulder. "I thought it was going to be late tonight."

Christ. Now she was mad that he was early. "Well, we didn't get back the results I was waiting for, so they sent me on home."

"Oh." She leaned over Megan and cooed at her. "Yes, we've got you all nice and clean, don't we?" Quinn smelled the strong tang of diaper rash ointment, the soft scent of Megan's bubble bath. Megan waved her legs on the changing table and grinned at him.

"I can take over, Debbie. You go on home now. I really appreciate your helping out tonight. Thanks. Really."

But she ignored him and went on cooing at Megan. He stood there dumbly and finally she said, "That's okay. I'll put her to bed. Since I'm here."

He didn't know what else to do. He couldn't force her out of the house, so he just kissed Megan good night and went downstairs, where he sat on the couch and waited for Debbie to come down. He felt the way he remembered feeling as a teenager, when his mother would make him sweat it out before she let him have it for coming in late or forgetting to do something around the house she'd asked him to do.

Finally he heard her footsteps on the stairs. "She's asleep," she said. "She always goes right down for me."

"Thanks, Deb. Really. I appreciate it." He couldn't look her in the eye while he said it. "I hope you didn't have plans or anything."

"No. Not really." She picked up her white sneakers from the bottom of the stairs and sat down across from him, easing her feet in and carefully lacing them up. For as long as he'd known her, Debbie had always worn these exact white sneakers. She had foot problems—he'd never quite understood what they were—and when she had to wear shoes other than the sneakers, she complained loudly about the pain. If he was honest, Quinn had to admit that he'd always thought she was a bit of a hypochondriac, but now as he watched her face twist into discomfort as she tightened the laces, he felt guilty. He'd never liked Debbie. Poor Debbie, with her too-long, overpermed hair and her tight little face. Someone had once told her that her slightly bugged blue eyes were her best feature and she covered them with eye shadow and mascara, only calling attention to their bugginess. She'd always been so much Maura's kid sister, wanting to come along on their dates, never leaving them alone. He remembered sitting in Debbie and Maura's grandmother's living room the night after the first time he and Maura had slept together. They had both been virgins and he had been in a fever of desire that night, terrified that he would have to go home without doing it again. They had been watching TV and he remembered hating Debbie for not going to bed and finally he had asked Maura if she wanted to go for a walk. They had made love the second time leaning up against the back wall of the corner deli on the next block.

"Timmy," Debbie said, and he looked up with surprise to find that she was nervous. She folded her skinny little legs into her chair and twisted a piece of hair so tightly that he thought she might pull it out by the root. "I was thinking and I don't know if it's, well, I don't know what you . . . Anyway, I was thinking that you need someone to take care of Megan and I was thinking that maybe I could do it. I mean, I could be like her nanny. Instead of paying for day care, you could pay me and I wouldn't mind if you were late or whatever."

Quinn forced himself to sit back in his chair and study her before saying anything. She seemed serious. After getting out her suggestion, she was leaning expectantly forward, fiddling with the perfectly tied shoelaces.

"But what about your job?"

"I never really liked it. I mean, it's just something to do for a living, like. You know? But I really like taking care of Megan. It just makes me happy. Nothing else makes me that happy, you know?"

"Well, wow. I . . . thanks, Debbie, I really appreciate the offer. Let me think about it, okay. I kind of have to, you know, just think about my schedule and what would work the best."

She looked a little hurt. "Okay, yeah, definitely. Thanks," she said, getting up and putting on her leather jacket.

"And, hey, thanks again for tonight. I really appreciate it."

When she had gone, Quinn lay back on the couch and covered his face with his hands. Now she was mad at him. Why hadn't he just said yes? It was, in many ways, the perfect solution. He wouldn't have to worry about working late, and Megan loved Debbie. She knew her, was happy with her. So, what was his problem?

It was that he couldn't stand the thought of coming home to her silent accusations every night. He couldn't stand the thought of her neediness. So, what was he going to do? Well, he supposed he'd have to find another babysitter.

He thought of Maura, wondered what she would do, though he supposed that wasn't really the way to think about it, since Maura hadn't shown herself to be the model of parental responsibility. Damn it! What had she been thinking? Goddamnit! Then he felt guilty for even thinking it and he felt his eyes fill with warm tears. He wiped them with the back of his shirt and took a deep breath, trying not to lose it. When it came down to it, it wasn't any grand self-control on his part that kept him from breaking down. He was just too tired.

He cleaned up a little, putting away Megan's toys and emptying the dishwasher, and tried to get his mind back on the Kenneth Churchill case. When he'd called Beverly Churchill to get her permission to release the dental records, he had tried to sound casual about the body. "We don't know anything," he'd said. "I want you to be prepared for the worst, but I have to tell you that it very well may not be him."

"But it's in Concord. And the uniform. How could it not be him?" She had seemed oddly calm and he had realized that perhaps the not knowing was worse than the knowing. He almost had the sense that she was relieved something had happened at last, but he told himself to reserve judgment.

People did strange things when informed of a loved one's death. It didn't necessarily mean anything.

Well, he thought, checking the wall clock, it was eleven, so he probably wouldn't know tonight. He should get to bed. Megan would be up at six and he had to get her to day care, get to the station, deal with whatever the day brought. Intense and unrelenting fatigue washed over him, and for a moment he leaned against the kitchen counter. "Get to bed, old man," he said aloud in the silent house.

He had just dozed off when his cell phone rang. In the dark, he scrambled for it on the bedside table and caught it on the seventh ring.

"Detective Quinn? John Tyler out in Concord. I wanted to let you know. They've got an answer for us on this Concord body. It's definitely not Kenneth Churchill."

Quinn sat up in bed, wide-awake now. "What? What do you mean?"

"It's not him. Different set of choppers."

"Jeez. I really thought this was gonna be it. The uniform and everything."

"Hey, I know. That was a funny thing, actually. Your guy was a Minuteman. This guy was a Redcoat."

"What?" Quinn's sleepy brain struggled with the unfamiliar words.

"We've been talking to some of these reenactor guys about it. Apparently, your guy was one of ours, a Minuteman. This guy we found in the woods, he was wearing a British soldier's uniform. He was on the other side. I'm sorry, you're going to have to look for your guy somewhere else."

ELEVEN

THURSDAY, OCTOBER 14

THE MINUTEMAN MUSEUM WAS LOCATED ON LEXINGTON Road, across from Orchard House in a low Colonial building painted white and trimmed in green. The sign out front was calligraphed in gold, and the whole place had a classy, well-cared-for look that appealed to Sweeney's sense of aesthetics.

She pushed through the glass doors on the side of the building to find herself in a well-decorated eighteenth-century American home. The main room served as a kitchen, with a wide hearth and a sort of sitting room, and as her eyes adjusted to the lower light, she noticed display cases around the room.

"Hello," said a white-haired, grandmotherly woman sitting behind the ticket desk and wearing a nametag that read, "Phyllis. Volunteer."

"Hello. Oh, one please," Sweeney said, noticing the sign that informed her that she, as an adult, would have to pay $5 for the pleasure of looking around the museum. She handed over the bill and the woman handed her a little aluminum button with intertwined M's.

"I was wondering," Sweeney said, once she had tucked away the receipt, "if Cecily Whiting is here today."

"Cecily's with a group," the volunteer said. "But if you want to look around, I'll send her out to see you when she's done."

Sweeney said that would be fine and spent the next forty minutes looking around the museum.

She loved small historical museums, and this one was as good as any she'd seen. Its focus was the Minutemen, the average citizens—farmers, wheelwrights, and housewrights—who had formed a ready army in order to protect their rights, rights increasingly under assault from the British crown in those tense years leading up to the Revolution. The museum explored the Minutemen from every angle, the typical Colonial home, the community lives of the towns that provided the men who would defeat an empire, the women behind them.

Cecily Whiting, if that was who had authored the informative panels around the various rooms, had not presented only the red, white, and blue version of the Revolution. The point was made that for many years the colonists had enjoyed far greater autonomy than most other British subjects and that the standard of living in America was higher than it was for most men, women, and children living in the British Isles at the time. The Revolution, the point was made, was in many ways a civil war, between those loyal to the crown and the upstart nouveau-riche craftsmen and men of business.

Sweeney moved onto an exhibit called "Spy Letters of the American Revolution," featuring biographies of Benedict Arnold as well as a handful of lesser-known spies—British and American ones—who had operated during the Revolution. There was even a little exhibit on women spies, which told about women such as Sarah Bradlee Fulton, the "mother of the Boston Tea Party," and the group of women in Philadelphia who passed information about the British to General Washington.

The exhibit featured facsimiles of the ingenious letters that the spies had used, some in invisible ink, others cut into thin strips that could be hidden in quills and then reassembled, and yet others made so they could be read for their true meaning only when viewed through a "mask," or a piece of paper into which an oddly shaped window had been cut. She was reading about crude, early codes involving the replacement of a number for a letter when a voice behind her said, "Hi, Sweeney."

Sweeney turned around. "Hi." Cecily Whiting was wearing an elegant dark brown suit, an orange and russet scarf at her neck, and against the backdrop of autumn leaves showing in the window behind her, she looked like a catalog model. "I thought maybe I'd come and find out some more about Josiah Whiting. I don't know if Pres told you, but we found a few more stones yesterday and the more I see of them, the more interested I am."

"Pres did tell me. He said he's going to be your assistant. I hope he's not pestering you. He wasn't feeling well in the morning, so I let him stay home from school, but I think it was all a ruse to go find you in the cemetery."

"No, he's a great kid. If you feel okay about him hanging out with someone you barely know, I'm having fun."

Cecily smiled again. "It's funny," she said. "With Pres being sick, I've kind of let some of that old maternal protectiveness go. You'd think it would be the other way around. But I want him to have any experience he can have. And he's a good judge of character. If he likes you, you must be all right. So, what do you want to know about Josiah Whiting?" Again, her voice was just a little too eager and Sweeney found herself wondering about Cecily's motivation. Was she trying to get back at her ex-husband by helping Sweeney with her research?

"Well, I've gotten interested in his carving, his death masks in particular, and I'm hoping to write a paper about him. From what I can tell, there hasn't been much done on him."

Cecily raised her eyes and seemed about to say something, then stopped herself and turned away from Sweeney to adjust a picture on the wall that did not need adjusting.

"My ex-husband is a descendant of Whiting's, so a lot of what I know is family lore." She turned and smiled. "Not always reliable. The family was from Plymouth and his father moved to Concord in the 1750s and set up shop as a stonecutter. He did masonry too. Josiah Whiting apprenticed with the father and then took over the family business. He made stones for people in Concord and Lexington and the surrounding towns. I don't know much more about his gravestones, but I can tell you about his life. Let's go sit in my office." She led the way through the galleries and into a back office decorated with lithographs and paintings of Revolutionary War battles and framed copies of the Declaration of Independence and the Constitution.

There were a series of file cabinets against one wall, and Cecily flipped through the hanging file folders and took out a manila folder. "My ex-husband's family donated a collection of family letters to the museum. I had a special exhibition about Josiah Whiting last year and displayed some of them. These are copies, but you're welcome to look through them if you want. Anyway, what can I tell you about him? Josiah Whiting married a girl from Concord named Rebecca Abel. They had five children, one who died as a toddler. Their stones are in the Hill Cemetery if you want to see them. The oldest son, John, had health problems and died young. The second son, Daniel, became a stonecutter and carried on the family tradition. My husband's family is descended from Daniel's line.

"Anyway, Josiah got interested in the Revolutionary cause early on. He was educated and he wrote some pamphlets about the Stamp Act. And he was a principal member of a local underground group that was agitating for war. As things heated up, he became even more deeply involved in the cause and joined one of the Concord Minuteman companies.

"As you probably know, he was killed after the fighting at the North Bridge here in Concord. There's a good bit of information about what happened that day, mostly through the depositions of the Minutemen and British soldiers after the fact. There are letters too, written by townspeople who witnessed the events or the men who fought. You have to take a lot of this stuff with a grain of salt, though, because misinformation was rampant and rumors spread very quickly. Many of the accounts are blatantly romanticized. But they still offer us a pretty good look at what people were doing that day.

"Josiah Whiting's Minuteman company was warned by Dr. Prescott around one A.M. The bell in the church tower would have been rung and the men woke and gathered at Wright's Tavern. We have accounts from other men in the company who say he was there. They knew that the British regulars were coming out to confiscate ammunition and stores of flour and other staples, so they arranged a signal and went off to help the townspeople hide anything that hadn't already been put away. We don't know what Josiah Whiting was doing, but we can assume that he was helping with this task. At dawn, the word came that there had been shooting at Lexington and the Minutemen gathered again, joined by a company from Lincoln. There would have been about two hundred and fifty men there. Am I boring you?"

"No, not at all. My Revolutionary history isn't the best. Pres had to remind me what Battle Road was the other day."

Cecily smiled and went on. "Anyway, the three companies started marching to meet the British, but as they went along the Lexington Road, they met the British who were coming in the opposite direction. The Minutemen turned around and started marching back toward Concord, with the regulars following. You have to remember that all this time, the alarm had been going out all over the countryside and companies of Minutemen were arriving from every direction."

She got up and took an old-fashioned-looking map down from a bulletin board on the wall. "The British light infantry were sent up on this ridge, where the Minutemen had gathered," she said, pointing to the map. "And so the Minutemen retreated back to the center of town, but they kept men on all of the ridges, where they could observe what was going on and plan their attack. They were always one step ahead. People say that we won the Revolutionary War because we knew the land, and that was largely true. The Minutemen watched from the ridges as the light infantry and the rest of the regulars met up on their way into town."

Sweeney felt goose bumps on her arms. Cecily Whiting told a good story, and looking at the map, she could almost imagine the men marching over the land, the drums beating and the fifes sounding.

"John Baker was a member of the Concord militia company that Josiah Whiting was a member of, and the two men were good friends. Anyway," Cecily went on, "everything we know about where Josiah Whiting was and what he was doing on April nineteenth comes from an account given by John Baker ten years later. He said that he and Whiting were sent up to a spot on one of the ridgelines, where they watched the regulars make their way across the town to search the townspeople's homes for stores meant for the militia. A group of them were sent to the North Bridge in order to search Colonel Barrett's farm, where a lot of the supplies had been hidden. Meanwhile, it was decided that the provincials would retreat across the North Bridge and wait until more Minuteman companies had come from the surrounding towns. Whiting and Baker came down and joined the men at the bridge, just as the British commander Colonel Smith sent a group of his men over the bridge. The Minutemen were just waiting there, to see what the British were going to do. That was when they saw the smoke. I've always thought this was one of the best misunderstandings in American history, that as they waited, the provincials saw smoke rising over the town. They thought that the town was being burned, but in fact the regulars had just set fire to some of the provisions they'd taken. The amazing thing about that day is that the provincials were outnumbered by the British to the tune of two to one. But Captain Parker still made the decision that he did, to march across the bridge. We know from Baker's account that he and Whiting were among the men who marched back across the bridge, driving the regulars back across as they went. They had left their horses tied to nearby trees and went with the rest of the men on foot.

"We don't know who it was who fired the first shot, though it was probably a regular, but once the firing started, the scene was chaotic. Baker said later that he only remembers firing and reloading three times and that he saw Whiting shooting with a calm hand. In a few minutes it was over. And that's when Battle Road began. It's hard for us to imagine what a nightmare Battle Road must have been for the British. After the North Bridge, all they wanted to do was get back to Boston and safety. But they were literally surrounded by militiamen who were opening fire on them at every turn. The provincials knew the land, they were everywhere. There was no way the regulars could compete. Of course, all of the British generals considered that the provincials had fought dirty. They were used to a very formal fighting style. Everybody stands out in a field and fires politely at one another."

"And Whiting was there? He was shooting at them too?"

"Yes. Again, everything we know about this is from Baker's account. They rode off together and Baker claims that they each killed a few Redcoats. That may just be boasting, but it's also very possible. They were both experienced marksmen. Anyway, Baker says that he and Whiting saw two young Redcoats go into a house by the side of the road. They followed them in and found them threatening to shoot the old woman of the house if she didn't feed them. Whiting confronted them and killed one of the Redcoats. The other one chased him down and stabbed him through the heart. Those were Baker's words."

"Wow." Sweeney made a few notes in her notebook. "Where's his gravestone? Is it in the Hill Cemetery too? I'd love to see it."

"Actually," Cecily Whiting said, "he doesn't have one. His body was never found."

"But I thought you said he was killed?"

"Well, he was. But the body wasn't found. It actually wasn't as strange as it might seem. On April nineteenth, there were men on both sides who were listed as missing. Who knows why? It's possible that some of them were wounded and dragged themselves off into the woods, where they died. Or it's possible that in the chaos of that day, there were men who were simply . . . lost."

"There wasn't any question about whether he had actually died?"

"Well, where else would he have gone? His family was in Concord, his business. Besides, Baker's account doesn't leave a lot of room for doubt. It may be that the British hauled him off somewhere. It's . . ." She trailed off and Sweeney had the feeling that she was going to say something more. But then she glanced away and said vaguely, "It's a mystery."

"Well, thanks so much. It's a great story. I was wondering if you have a list of all of the Whiting gravestones in Concord and the surrounding area. Sometimes people do little surveys or whatever." Sweeney tried not to hope too fervently. It would save her a lot of work.

"No," Cecily said. "But my father-in-law . . . I mean, my ex-father-in-law, George, has a complete list, I think. He loves it when people get interested in Josiah Whiting. Once you get him going, you'll have a hard time getting him to stop, actually."

"Great. Well, thanks again for your time. I really appreciate it."

"No problem. It sounds like an interesting project. And thanks again for your concern about Pres."

"How's he doing?"

"He seems okay. Actually, he doesn't want to talk about it at all. I still can't figure out what he was doing in the woods, why he decided to walk home that way. He hasn't told you, has he?"

Sweeney shook her head.

"It's hard to know what's going on with him. He's twelve and he doesn't want to tell me anything. I've tried to let him have as much freedom as possible, but it's been hard with him being sick. I don't know. This is what's hard about being a parent. You don't know if you've done the right thing until after the fact."

Sweeney stood up. "Well, as I said, he's a great kid. Where would I find your . . . George?"

"He's usually at the shop. Whiting Monuments on Lowell

Road. If he's not there, Bruce can probably tell you where he is." As she said her ex-husband's name, Cecily Whiting's face changed, her eyes suddenly angry, her mouth turning up in a little sneer.

Sweeney suddenly felt that she wouldn't want to cross Cecily Whiting.

Whiting Monuments was a squat brick building located at the end of a short driveway just off Lowell Road. A low stone wall flanked the driveway and an odd little garden, featuring perennials and various shrubbery interspersed with examples of the monuments on sale inside, sat next to the part of the building labeled "Office." The other side was more industrial, with a wide driveway housing a truck with a flatbed and an attachment for lifting heavy stones into place.

The walls of the waiting room were covered with tasteful French impressionist paintings and embroidered Bible verses. The sun had come up high in the October sky and the room was stuffy and overwarm. A bell on the front door rang as she came in and after a few seconds French doors at one end of the waiting room opened and Lauren Whiting entered, already pasting a sympathetic look onto her face.

"Hi," she said softly, a soothing half smile on her face. "I'm Lauren Whiting. Can I help you?"

Sweeney studied Pres's stepmother, seized with a sick desire to pretend she was actually looking for a gravestone, then said, "Actually, we met the other day, at the police station. Sweeney St. George. I'm here to talk to your husband and your father-in-law too, if he's available. I'm doing some historical research and I was told they might be able to tell me about their ancestor Josiah Whiting."

"Oh," Lauren Whiting said. "You're the one who . . . you're Pres's friend. Hang on. Bruce is here, but I don't think George is." She flashed Sweeney a warm smile as she went back out through the French doors. "Just as well, probably. Once he gets going on Josiah Whiting, it's hard to get him to stop."

A couple of minutes later, Bruce Whiting came out and sat down in a chair across from the couch.

"You're Pres's friend," he said.

"That's right. We met at the station. I was talking to Cecily about Josiah Whiting and she thought your father might be able to tell me a little bit about him."

He studied her for a moment, then said, "Can I ask you why you're interested in him?"

Sweeney wasn't taken aback as much by the question as by his tone. He seemed suspicious, almost hostile.

"Well, I was out here because I'm trying to track down a stone carver I call the round-skull carver. No one knows who he is, so I'm trying to figure it out. Anyway, I was looking for more round-skull stones when I met Pres and he told me about Josiah Whiting. I've kind of come to a standstill with this other guy and I got really interested in the way that Whiting's stones change over time. They start out kind of typical and then get really, really strange. I have this theory about him reacting to political developments."

That seemed to relax him. "Leave it to my Pres to pick up a pretty girl talking about gravestones." He smiled and then his eyes seemed very sad. "Yeah, the death's-heads are amazing, aren't they?" He motioned for her to sit. "His parents were Puritans, you know. I always thought that was why. But he takes them in some pretty unusual directions, doesn't he? It's actually kind of a thrill to talk to a real expert. I make the things, but I don't really understand them."

"That's not true," Lauren Whiting said, coming back into the waiting room. "Don't believe a word he says. He's always studying, looking for ways to make his work better." She walked past her husband, hesitating for a minute in front of him, and he put a hand on her rear end before she sat down. It had been an overtly sexual gesture and the room was suddenly charged with a tension that hadn't been there before.

"Are you inspired by his work?" Sweeney asked Bruce Whiting, embarrassed.

"Well, as I'm sure you know, it's a completely different world now. Most of our customers come in and choose something that's already been made. I do the text, I help them choose a cross or a Star of David or whatever, but I'm not creating much original art. I started doing custom stones a few years ago, though, and that part of the business is actually really growing. I hadn't thought much about it, but I suppose he does inspire me. Here, let me show you some of the things I've been doing lately." He took a small photograph album from a drawer in the coffee table and handed it over.

Sweeney flipped through the pages, looking at his work. The shapes of the stones reminded her of the three Josiah Whiting stones she'd seen.

"Your shoulders look like his shoulders," Sweeney said, tracing the design of a stone decorated with a classic willow-tree-and-urn design. "Look at them. You've taken the idea of them—the skinny shoulders and the sharply rounded tympana—and you've kind of modernized it, but they still have the same feeling."

Bruce Whiting grinned and said, "Yeah, although this is going to sound crazy, but I hadn't thought of it until just now. I must have internalized those stones somehow."

"Anybody ever asked you to do a death's-head?" Sweeney asked him.

"Not yet. Actually, I think I'd be a bit concerned if they did."

"Hon," Lauren said. "There was that guy who wanted you to make a gravestone with his tattoo on it."

"That's right. It was a hula girl or something." He laughed, a deep, husky laugh that made him suddenly handsome. "I told him it was too hard to do and he got really pissed off at me."

"I once saw this biker guy on the T who had a huge tattoo of a skull and crossbones and the words 'memento mori' underneath," Sweeney told them. "I thought I might get a paper out of it or something, but the guy looked at me like I was insane when I started asking him about it." She handed the album back. "Thanks for your help."

"Let me know how you make out."

"I will. It was really fun seeing your work. Oh, I was hoping to talk to your father sometime. Your ex-wife said he had a complete listing of the Josiah Whiting gravestones."

"Yeah. He'd probably be a big help, actually. He and my mom aren't around today, but they should be tomorrow. Just stop by. I'll tell him you're coming." He gave her the address on Monument Street.

"Thanks for your help. I really appreciate it."

"Hey, if Pres has you as a friend, that's good enough for me."

And again, she saw something sad in his eyes.

"HOW'S TOBY?" IAN ASKED HER THAT NIGHT DURING THEIR phone call. He hadn't asked about Sweeney's best friend, Toby DiMarco, in a while and Sweeney wondered what had brought on the sudden interest. She was sitting, talking to him, curled up in the armchair in her room, the quilt from her bed wrapped around her shoulders.

"He's fine," Sweeney said. "He's decided that he's going to finish his novel by the beginning of Lent."

"Lent? I didn't know he was . . ."

"He's not. He's half WASP and half Italian Jew. He chooses these days. He's so weird."

"Have you ever read the novel?"

"Just parts. He's pretty secretive about the whole thing, but from what I can tell, it's a loosely veiled autobiographical account of the year he lived in Italy, trying to establish a relationship with his dad. The main character is staying in this villa out in Tuscany somewhere, and his father, who lives with his family about an hour away, keeps coming up with excuses for why he can't come stay with him. There's a kind of *Waiting for Godot* thing going on, and in the meantime he starts sleeping with this girl who lives down the road from the villa. Her name is Isabella and she is eighteen and gorgeous and naive and all that. But she . . . well, she likes"—Sweeney lowered her voice—"she likes domination or something. And Toby—or the main character, I think his name is Tad or something—finds out later that she's been abused, by her brother or her cousin. And after that he refuses to sleep with her anymore. But he loves her."

"Is this all true?"

"Basically. Toby is one of those people who strange things just *happen* to. This is when I was living in Oxford and he would send me these long letters. They were so entertaining."

Suddenly Sweeney had a flashback to the sight of those long air-mail envelopes sitting on the kitchen table of the flat she and Colm had shared. He had been jealous of Toby and when she came home to find those letters on the table, her enjoyment of Toby's adventures. She was suddenly flooded with images: Colm's tight face as he drank alone in the tub while she read the letters. The way Toby's face had looked when he'd left for Italy. She had been thinking of those letters as fun, informative missives from a friend, but now that she thought back, she realized they had been obsessive, an attempt to make her jealous, maybe. No wonder Colm had been suspicious. He had been good at picking up on things like that.

"Are you in the book?"

"God, yes. There's a character named Susan who comes to visit him and ends up OD'ing in this seedy apartment in Rome. I've never quite forgiven him for that. She's beautiful, though, so that part I liked."

"And is he dating anyone?"

"No. He was dating this woman I really liked back in the spring. But it just kind of fizzled. Now he's making himself a monk for his art. He actually said that. He's sworn off women."

"Well, I'm glad he's well."

"Yes, he said to say hello, actually. Well, he said to say hello weeks ago, but I forgot."

There was a long silence and Sweeney listened to the faint static that came across the air. "Sweeney?" Ian said softly.

She panicked, but he rushed ahead. "So, I was thinking

that you've never told me much about Colm. Other than that time . . . in Vermont, when you told me how he died. But you've never told me what he was like. I'm sorry. If it's hard, I don't want you to. I was just thinking that he was an important part of your life, is all, and I don't really know very much about him." She could hear the fear in his voice and she knew that he was asking because he wanted to know if she was over Colm. She could hear it. He wanted to know if he would always be competing with the dead fiancé. He had asked her if Toby was seeing anyone because he wanted to know what was going on with her and Toby. He was trying to figure out where he stood.

She forced herself to say something, her heart slowing. "No, no. You're right. He was, he is, an important part of my life. He, uh, he was one of those larger-than-life people, you know? Everybody knew him. He played the Irish flute and you would walk into any pub in Oxford or Dublin or anywhere and people would remember him and say hi. He was the kind of person who you would agree to meet for a cup of coffee and three days later you'd be coming back from a weekend in Scotland."

He was silent, so she went on. "It was fun, you know, being with someone like that, but there were times when it was awful. I used to get left alone a lot and you couldn't count on him. He was always late and he would get bored easily. We were working on that when he died. We were planning the wedding and everything, and he was trying to be better about showing up for things. I don't know. Sometimes I wonder if I wouldn't have gotten tired of it."

But as she said it, she remembered Colm holding her after one of their fights. "We have to make it work," he'd said. "It's you and me. This is the real thing." And it had been the real thing. That was about the only thing she knew.

"Thank you," Ian said softly.

"No, no. It's okay." But she was shaken and even after she'd hung up the phone, she couldn't get rid of the image of Colm, holding her as though his very life depended on it.

TWELVE

BEVERLY CHURCHILL STARED AT QUINN AS THOUGH HE HAD blood dripping down the front of his shirt.

"What do you mean, it's not him? How can it not be him?" She had answered the door in a bathrobe, her dark hair wet and glossy from the shower, and before he had even been able to make it in the door, she had started crying. "It's him, isn't it? I know it's him," she'd demanded. He'd noticed that while her voice broke as though she was about to cry, her eyes were only slightly moist.

"No, Mrs. Churchill. It's not him. It's someone else. We didn't get a match." He didn't touch her, because of the bathrobe, because it was gaping open in front and he could see the full swell of one breast, a hint of pinkish nipple.

She didn't seem to notice. "Who is it, then? What do you mean, it's not him?"

"Here, let's go sit down and I'll tell you what we know. Is that okay?"

She seemed to realize that her bathrobe was open then and she tied the belt tight around her waist.

"Okay, Mrs. Churchill? Come on, let's go sit down."

He took her arm and led her over to the living room couch. The room was subtly different and it took him a moment to realize what it was—it was messier. She had let the place go since the last time he'd been there.

"Who is it?" she screamed at him. "If it's not my husband, then who is it?"

"We don't know. The Concord police and the state investigators haven't been able to make an identification. They don't know who it is, but it's not your husband."

That seemed to satisfy her because she leaned back on the couch and closed her eyes and was quiet for a moment.

"We're still looking for your husband, Mrs. Churchill. Is there anything else you've thought of since we talked the last time? Did you check with your bank?"

"Yes, there haven't been any withdrawals or anything. Just what I've taken out of the ATM."

"Okay, good. No strange phone calls? Hang-ups?"

She shook her head.

"Okay. The next thing is to look a little more deeply into what your husband was doing out in Concord. Do you know who he was talking to, that sort of thing? I'd like to be able to trace his movements the last few days before he disappeared."

"He didn't tell me anything. All I know is that he was researching this guy Josiah Whiting and he kept saying the book was going to be explosive."

"That's the word his department chairwoman used too. What do you think that meant?"

"I don't know. Kenneth wrote a book a few years ago about the socioeconomic demographics of the Minutemen and how it impacted the development of the modern American military. Something like that. He said that was explosive too, but I doubt you'd think it was if you read it."

"I'd like to look at his office. See if there are any references to his research among his things."

She looked exasperated and then said, "Fine. If you have to. It's the second door at the top of the stairs." She sat down at the table again, her hands worrying in her lap.

There was a large landing at the top of the stairs, and hearing the sounds of a television, Quinn glanced into the first room on his left, a large master bedroom painted dark blue. Marcus Churchill, who was sprawled on his stomach on the bed, glanced at Quinn, didn't acknowledge him, and went back to watching television. Quinn checked his watch. It was 10 A.M. What was he doing home?

Kenneth Churchill's office was painted a brick red that almost matched the leather couch and armchair sitting across from the wide, dark wooden desk. A matching coffee table was cluttered with books and old newspapers. One of the newspapers was stained with brown, as though someone had spilled a cup of coffee on it. The desk, on the other hand, was very neat, dust-free, with piles of papers decorated with Post-its in precise piles. Quinn shut the door and went over to study the framed diplomas hanging on the wall behind the desk. There was one from the University of Missouri and another from the University of Illinois. There were a couple of Marine Corps citations as well, and another framed picture of Kenneth standing next to a tank in the desert.

Quinn started looking through the piles of papers, scanning for "Josiah Whiting" or "Concord," but all he found were student papers in various states of being graded and a few bills and letters from other professors. He opened the drawers of the desk and found paper clips, pens, stacks of canceled checks, and, in the bottom drawer, hidden underneath a red bandana, an older-looking Colt Diamondback .38 Special. He took the handgun out and checked to make sure it wasn't loaded, then left it on top of the desk.

Next he moved on to the coffee table, but as long as it took Quinn to look through the mess, it yielded only a variety of books on American history and a good three weeks' worth of *Boston Globe*s. Quinn browsed through the bookshelves, pulling out the volumes to make sure there wasn't anything hidden behind them, then shut the door behind him and went back downstairs. This time, Marcus Churchill didn't look up from the TV.

She was still sitting at the dining room table, and he dropped the gun in front of her. It thudded against the wood. "This should be in a locked gun case," Quinn said. "You have a teenage son and it's really dangerous to have it lying around the house."

She looked surprised for a minute, then said, "You can take it if you want. I'd like to get it out of here. I hate his guns and weapons."

"Why did he have it?"

"What do you mean?"

"Was he afraid of someone? Sometimes people obtain weapons after being threatened or having some kind of an experience that makes them feel as though they're in danger."

She was surprised at that. "He never told me about anything like that. He just liked guns."

"Okay," Quinn said. "There isn't anything related to your husband's work in his office. Would he have taken everything with him?"

"I don't know. He must have." She looked very tired. "Do you think Kenneth had something to do with this man's death? Is that why you're trying to find out what he was doing in Concord?"

Quinn waited a beat, then said, "Do you have some reason to believe that that's the case? Was he violent? Was there anybody he was angry at?"

Beverly Churchill blinked and looked away. "No, of course not. I just thought since you were . . . Sorry."

"Is there anything else you can tell me? Had he done anything unusual in the last few months? Gone on any trips, other than the ones out to Concord?"

She looked up at him. "He went to London. In May."

"For vacation?"

"No, for business. Something about his book. I don't know why. He didn't tell me anything about it."

"How long was he gone?"

"Four days, not long."

He waited, but she didn't say anything else. "Okay. I'm going to get out of your hair. Let me know if you hear anything. I'll be in touch. Oh, and I'd like to check his office at BU. See if there's anything there that would help us. Is that okay with you?" She nodded. As he reached past her to pick up the gun, his hand grazed her shoulder and she jumped, as though he'd burned her. She turned very slightly in her chair and looked up at him. Her eyes were very slightly turned, catlike. She watched him. "Good-bye," Quinn said, his heart pounding. And holding the gun, he fled.

After searching Churchill's office at BU and finding nothing more exciting than what he'd found at the guy's home, Quinn headed back to the station and checked in with Havrilek, telling him about Beverly Churchill's reaction.

"So, you think she knows something?"

Quinn sat down and ran a hand over the top of his head. Christ, he was tired. "I don't know, boss, she was pretty torn up about him not being dead. It's weird. I can see how she might be almost, I don't know, sad that she didn't have the closure or something. But this was different. It was like she was surprised he wasn't dead, or something like that. I don't know."

"Well, let's keep an eye on her. Stay in touch."

"I just can't help thinking that this body out in Concord's got to be connected somehow."

"You think Churchill did it and took off?"

"I don't know what I think. I guess we'll know more once the state guys get all the evidence back from the scene. I could get DNA from the house and we can compare. It's just weird that it's been over a week now and there isn't a trace of him, not his car, not his fucking bank account, nothing."

"The state guys have taken over, right?"

"Yeah. I can get in touch and see who's working on it. See what they can tell me." Quinn closed his eyes and leaned back in his chair. When he opened them again, Havrilek was watching him.

"You okay? You look a little tired."

"Yeah, yeah. The baby was up last night. She's had that cold for about a week. I'm fine. I'll get a good night tonight."

"Yeah? You sure you're handling all this okay? You've got some time off coming to you, you know. You didn't take very much after . . . after Maura. And if you need more, we can arrange it."

"No, no. I'm fine. Look, why don't I get on the phone to whoever's working on things out there and see if there's anything new."

John Tyler didn't sound all that happy to hear from Quinn. "You have anything on your missing guy?"

"Not yet. I'm beginning to wonder, though, if he might not be connected to your body in the woods. It just seems like a little bit too much of a coincidence that my guy disappears right around the time your guy got his lights put out permanently, you know?"

"Well, you better talk to the state guys. They seem to be going off on some scent or another. They've been out in the woods all day."

"Who's the detective in charge?"

"Guy by the name of Andy Lynch."

"No shit. Andy Lynch? Tall guy? Red hair?"

"That's him. You know him?"

"Yeah, we grew up together."

"Well, I'll tell him you called. Hey, there's another one of those whaddyacallit, encampments, this weekend. You might want to check it out, ask around about your guy. And I was thinking that it might be a good idea to get in touch with our local paper here, say you're looking for information about the whereabouts of this man, et cetera, et cetera. It's pretty well read and it might turn up something."

Quinn said he'd do that, thanked him, and hung up the phone, then sat back in his chair, thinking about Andy Lynch.

Andy Lynch. From the time they were old enough to play cops and robbers, Quinn and Andy Lynch had been best friends. Andy had been a scrappy little red-haired kid with a saddened, always-sick mother and a father who liked to give Andy a hiding if he looked at him the wrong way when the father came home late from the bars. As they'd gotten older, Andy had spent more and more time over at Quinn's house until Quinn's mother had started setting a fourth place setting for supper without asking if Andy was staying. But then in high school they'd kind of lost touch. Quinn had never been sure why, but Andy had dropped him. After high school, Andy had joined the Marines, gone to the Gulf in 1991, then gone to the academy, and when Quinn ran into him on the street, there was something in Andy's eyes that made Quinn think Andy didn't like being reminded of what Quinn knew about him, about his father's belt, his mother's sad forays down from her bedroom. It had been years now since Quinn had seen him.

But somehow Quinn was glad it was Andy.

He was thinking about the time that he and Andy got drunk off his mother's Bailey's Irish Cream and puked all over her new sofa, when his cell phone rang.

"Quinn," he said.

"Mr. Quinn, this is Lindsey at Megan's day care. I'm sorry to bother you, but she's running a fever again and we'd like you to come pick her up."

"But . . . she was doing much better this morning."

"Well." She sounded a little exasperated. "She's got a fever now."

"Look, couldn't you just . . . I'm at work and I can't really leave."

There was a long silence and then she said, "According to the agreement you signed when you enrolled Megan at Little Treasures Day Care, you are responsible for picking her up when she's sick. It isn't good for her and she could infect the other children."

"Okay, okay. I'll be there soon. Thirty minutes at the most."

"We'll be here." He tried to remember which one Lindsey was and couldn't.

"Shit!" He took a deep breath and went to knock on Havrilek's door.

When he heard "Come in," he pushed the door open and stood there awkwardly for a moment, watching Havrilek signing one paper after another, methodically turning them over in a pile.

"You talk to the guys in Concord?"

"Yeah. State guy in charge is an old friend of mine, actually."

"Great, that'll smooth things along. So, what do you think about this thing? What's next?"

"Well, there's one of these encampments out in Concord this weekend. I could go out and interview some of the people who knew him. They may have an ID on the body by then. The state police are taking over this thing. Course, if it turns out that Churchill had something to do with this guy's death and that's why he took off, then they'll have jurisdiction, but if Churchill's still missing, I may need to liaise with them, anyway."

"Yup. Sounds good." He kept signing, his pen scratching along the paper. "Anything else?"

"Look, boss. I hate to ask. But my daughter's day care just called. She has a fever—I thought she was better when I dropped her off this morning, but I guess she's . . . anyway, I have to go pick her up. I'll come right back, though. She'll sleep this afternoon and I can make some more phone calls. I've got paperwork to do too, so I can—"

But Havrilek cut in. "Quinn, I got five kids, I love kids, but I'm not really so into turning my station into a nursery, you know? If she's sick, she should be at home. Look, you got yourself some child-care issues, Quinny."

"But, it's just the . . . the . . . ," Quinn stammered.

"No, no. I want you to get your situation sorted out, go out to Concord, and interview some people at this reenactment thing. Stay at the hotel the guy stayed at on our dime so you don't have to drive back and forth with the kid. Follow his tracks. See if you can find anyone who knew this guy. Trace his last couple of days, so to speak. I'm willing to be patient for another week, but if you haven't got things taken care of by the time you're back, we're going to have to talk about your job."

As Quinn walked out the door, he realized that Havrilek had been signing papers the whole time. He hadn't missed a beat.

THIRTEEN

WILL BAKER LIKED ROUTINE. EVER SINCE HE'D BOUGHT THE inn, he had existed in a happy state of perfect predictability, rising at five for an early-morning walk, usually up to the Old North Bridge and back, then into the kitchen to make sure that the breakfast chef had arrived and was starting the meal preparations. He had a cup of coffee and a croissant in the kitchen while they talked about the day, then went upstairs to shower and change. By seven, he was at the front desk, making a list of which guests were staying and which were checking out so he could give the housekeepers their orders for the day.

He spent much of the morning greeting guests as they came down for breakfast, then oversaw the housekeepers and helped arrange flowers and set things right in the lobby and the lounge. Then it was time for lunch, after which he did errands and spent a couple of hours on accounting and bookkeeping. Then the new check-ins started arriving and he helped them until it was time for dinner. He liked to visit each table for a few moments, then have his own meal alone in his apartment at the back of the inn. In bed about ten and then it was time to get up and do it all over again. Perfect.

The only time he deviated from this schedule was on weekends when he had a reenactment. Then he was able to let his head housekeeper handle a lot of the room details and his assistant manager was able to take care of the guests.

But it was now 11:30 and he wasn't in bed and didn't think he was anywhere near being able to go to sleep. Somewhere in the past couple of days, his routine had been disrupted and he didn't like it one bit. The first thing that had happened was that his head housekeeper, a capable, grandmotherly woman who knew how to clean a bedroom better than anyone he'd ever had on his payroll had informed him that she was too old to be "crawling around on the floor with a vacuum cleaner." Her husband, she said, had forbidden her from working anymore. She was going to retire. He supposed she had the right to retire if she wanted to, but it was damned inconvenient for him and he was going to have to hire someone to replace her before the holidays, which were a busy time of year.

Then there was this whole thing with the body. Will had heard it had been found from one of the local boys who helped in the kitchen. "There are police everywhere up by Whitings'," he'd said, coming into the kitchen twenty minutes late for his shift. "Someone said there's a body up there." Later Will had heard all the details, how it had been Pres Whiting who had found it, about how the police were baffled by the British uniform, how nobody knew who it was. The police had even called him in to look at a drawing, to see if he recognized the uniform, but of course it was impossible to tell. They said they were going to ask around at the encampment coming up on the weekend, and this bothered Will somehow, that one of the encampments, which he loved, would be marred by this . . . this awful thing that had happened.

And then there was that woman looking into Josiah Whiting. That, he realized, was what bothered him most of all. It was just too much of a coincidence. Why Josiah Whiting? Why now? He had thought that that whole thing was finished, but here she was, asking questions about him and saying she was interested in his gravestones. It might be true, but he wasn't sure he bought it.

He got up and put on the teakettle. Outside, it was dark and he couldn't make out any of the details of the wooded hill behind the inn, or the buildings he could sometimes see above the trees. It was just blackness out there. His mind couldn't help going to the woods, to the clubhouse and the place where he had spent so much time that one year, that sweet year he couldn't stop thinking about, no matter how hard he tried.

The water boiled and he made his tea and sat down in the chair again. He wasn't sure what he was going to do, but he knew he had to do something.

FOURTEEN

FRIDAY, OCTOBER 15

SWEENEY HAD ALREADY DRIVEN BY THE WHITINGS' HOUSE
and seen the modest white Colonial just barely showing behind the high hedgerow next to the road, but she was unpre-
pared for how driving down the short driveway and into a
small gravel-lined parking area would send her back in time.
The house looked as though it had barely been changed
since it was built by Josiah Whiting's father in 1756, and the
woods that provided the backdrop to the house made her feel
that she was much farther away from town than she really
was. It was hard to tell exactly where the clubhouse was, but
you entered the woods a few hundred yards down Monument Street and walked parallel to the house. It was somewhere back there in the dark trees that the man, whoever he
was, had been killed.

It was a beautiful old house, but the peeling paint on the
clapboards and the shutters, and the withered vegetable garden on one side of the house, the tall, drooping tomato
plants and a witchy-looking scarecrow, gave the place a sinister feeling. Sweeney looked at the woods and shivered.

She knocked on the door, and it was answered almost immediately by a tall woman dressed in a pink sweatsuit and a
flowered apron, her white hair piled on top of her head in an
elaborate bun. When Sweeney introduced herself and explained what she wanted, the woman said, "Oh, for heaven's
sake, the last thing he needs is to get going on Josiah Whit-

ing again," but she held the door open and led the way through a cluttered, darkened living room stuffed with old furniture and cardboard boxes into a large Colonial kitchen. A fat orange cat jumped off the counter and glared at Sweeney. At the table was a thin gray-haired man, eating what looked like a bowl of tomato soup.

"I'm Sweeney St. George," Sweeney said nervously. "Your son was going to tell you I might stop by today. Is this a good time? I'm happy to come back if not."

George Whiting waved her away. "No, no, no," he said through a mouthful of tomato soup. "Sit down, sit down, tell me what you want."

Sweeney shrugged off her tweed jacket and sat down across from him at the table. "I'm an art historian. I study gravestones. And I want to know more about Josiah Whiting," she said.

"He was a hero," George Whiting said. "He was an American hero, is what he was. What did my son tell you about him?"

"We talked a little bit about his gravestones," Sweeney said, not sure what the right answer would be. "He showed me some of his work."

"He's good at what he does, Bruce, but he doesn't know anything about Josiah Whiting. He's lost his sense of patriotism. That's the problem, and he doesn't have the proper respect for what our forefathers accomplished here in Concord." He took a spoonful of soup, dribbling a bit of the red liquid onto his chin. "He went to Vietnam, you know. Didn't like what he found there. And so he thinks that anyone else who fought in any war feels the same way he does. I can tell you, when I was putting my life on the line in old Italia, I wasn't thinking about whether my government was justified in sending me over there. I just did what I had to do."

"George, she doesn't want to know about you," the woman said. "She wants to know about Josiah Whiting." She turned to Sweeney. "Do you want some coffee?"

Sweeney said she was fine and turned back to George, "Cecily said he was killed on April nineteenth, but they

never found his body. What do you think happened to
him?"

George Whiting pushed his soup bowl aside and stood up.
"Come with me," he said. Sweeney followed him out
through the back door onto a little stone patio. A peeling
metal table held a couple of anemic-looking begonias in
clay pots. They stood for a moment, and Sweeney smelled
the woods, the dark, wet, leafy scent of them, and remembered what Pres had said about people hearing a man crying
out in pain sometimes.

"Back in those days," George said. "This was all fields or
woods. You've gotta imagine what it was like for those men.
Josiah was awakened around one in the morning on the nineteenth. The alarm would have spread across the countryside
by then and he would have gotten his horse from the stable,
which was over there." He pointed to a low garage on the
other side of the vegetable garden. "And he took off through
the woods for town. They waited most of the night and then,
when the word came from Lexington, they started assem-
bling. Josiah was sent up as a scout, to watch the approach of
the British from the ridge, and when it was clear what the
Redcoats were up to, he came down and gathered with the
rest of the men at the bridge. We know that he fought bravely
at the bridge. We have a couple of accounts of that, and we
know that as the Redcoats hightailed it back to Boston,
Josiah and his company chased them. A number of the regulars were going into houses along the route back and ran-
sacking them, even killing the people who lived there, by
some accounts. Josiah and his friend John Baker were chasing down a couple of Redcoats when Baker saw Whiting get
bayoneted by a young regular. He gave an account of it ten
years later. He tried to help Josiah, but he got caught up in
the fighting again and lost track of him. The next day they
searched for his body.

"I've always thought," George Whiting continued, "that
he must have dragged himself into the woods. He could have
been somewhere not too far and maybe he just wanted to go
home to his wife, you know? Have her take care of him. But

maybe he didn't make it and he died in the woods and no one ever found him."

He looked upset for a minute, then said, "This guy they found out there, last weekend. You know about that?"

Sweeney nodded.

"It just about gave me a heart attack, when they told me. It was like . . . I don't know, I thought somehow they'd found Josiah. But that's ridiculous, of course. And this guy, they say he was wearing a Redcoat's uniform." Sweeney had the sense that he was going to say something else, but he didn't. Instead, he just kept looking out at the trees.

They stood there for another few moments and then he turned and walked back inside. Sweeney followed him.

"Who else in town might be able to tell me about him?" she asked.

"Will Baker, who owns the inn, he's quite a historian. He's a member of the Concord Minuteman company with me and he's done a lot of research on his ancestor John Baker. You could ask him."

"That's great," Sweeney said. "I'm staying at the inn, so that will work out well. Oh, and Cecily said that you might have a list of all of Josiah Whiting's gravestones."

"Yeah, I've got it here somewhere. I have an extra copy from when I made one for Kenneth, the other guy who's looking into Josiah. Where did I . . . ?" He searched through the piles, turning pieces of paper over and stacking them back up again in a seemingly random order.

"I'm sorry, did you say that there's someone else who's studying Josiah Whiting's gravestones?" Sweeney felt her heart sink. That was all she needed. She thought she had found someone who hadn't been written about.

"Yeah, Kenneth. He's a reenactor. He joined the Concord Minutemen this year. Teaches at BU, I think. He's writing a book about him. I helped him a lot, but I'm not going to help him anymore."

"Why not?"

"Well, he started asking funny questions. I didn't like where he was going with it. Oh, here it is."

"What do you mean? What kind of questions?" She took the three pieces of paper that George handed over.

"He asked me if I'd ever heard anything about Josiah or John Baker being a spy. Ridiculous. I don't know where he got an idea like that. He didn't have anything to back it up. I told him I wouldn't help him anymore if he was going to be talking like that."

Spies? Why spies? Maybe he'd seen the exhibit at the Minuteman Museum.

She looked down at the pieces of paper. There were hand drawn maps of various graveyards, with stones presumably by Josiah Whiting circled in dark pen. "This is terrific. Thank you for all your help," she said.

George Whiting walked her to the door and stood with her for a moment.

"Getting cold," he said. "Always gives me the blues when it starts getting cold." And then he smiled at her and went back inside.

On her way back to the inn, Sweeney decided to visit the Old North Bridge. She told herself that it made sense to try to get a feel for the place before she got seriously into her research about Josiah Whiting's heroism at the bridge in April of 1775, but in truth, she just liked the idea of strolling along the river in the crisp October air.

She parked in the designated parking area and crossed Monument Street, headed toward the bridge on a little path flanked by trees. Since it was a weekday, the site was nearly deserted and she wandered past the monument to the British soldiers who had died at the Old North Bridge. The modest plaque, set into a low wall, read, "They came three thousand miles, and died / To keep the past upon its throne: / Unheard beyond the ocean tide / Their English mother made her moan."

She crossed the bridge and stood beneath the Minuteman statue. This was where Josiah Whiting and the other men of the Concord militia had gathered before the first shot was fired.

She felt an odd surge of pride. Sweeney was not a particularly patriotic American. She had spent much of her adult life living outside of the United States and had gotten used to preempting her British friends' comments about American imperialism and cultural vapidness with cuts of her own. Though she didn't like paying them, she rather believed there ought to be more taxes than there were, more government control. But when it came right down to it, she believed in the values that Josiah Whiting had spilled his blood for: democracy, self-determination, freedom.

She looked up at the woods. "Where are you, Josiah Whiting?" she said softly before she turned back for the parking lot.

It was five as she walked into the lobby of the Minuteman, and she decided that she'd see if Will Baker was free to talk. She could ask him about Josiah Whiting and see if he had anything to add to what George Whiting had told her. She also wanted to call BU and see if she could track down this Kenneth Churchill.

But as she walked into the lobby, she saw a man standing there, talking to the woman behind the registration desk. He was holding a baby and trying to balance a stroller, two suitcases, and a large diaper bag, and as Sweeney watched, he dropped one of the suitcases and the baby began to cry.

She crossed the lobby and stood there, not sure what to say. "Hey," she said finally.

He looked up, and the expression she saw on his face was not mere surprise but something more like shock. He stared at her as though she were the very last person he would ever have expected to see in the lobby of the Minuteman Inn.

"Sweeney?" His blue eyes looked dark in the low light.

It was Quinn.

FIFTEEN

HIS FACE WAS DIFFERENT. AS SWEENEY LISTENED TO HIM TALK about Kenneth Churchill, she studied him, trying to figure out what it was. She remembered the first time she'd seen him, at the police station, when she'd been called in to look at the jewelry found on Brad Putnam's body, and she'd disliked him at first, because he had the kind of cocky, athletic good looks that she'd always found off-putting in a man. But as she looked at him now, she saw lines around his blue eyes and his mouth that made his face seem longer and older. He had let his dirty blond hair grow out from the military crew cut she remembered and she saw that his hair was slightly wavy—and shot through with gray. There was something about him that made her sad, and made her remember the last time they'd seen each other.

He was telling her about the investigation. "So, anyway, when we heard that a body had been found, we thought it had to be Churchill, but it's not and now I'm right back where I started, trying to figure out what happened to the guy, trying to figure out if he had anything to do with this death. I can't believe you were there when the kid found him."

"They still don't know who he is?"

"Apparently not. I'll get in touch tomorrow and get an update, but they've talked to a lot of these reenactment people and no one knows who he is."

Sweeney sat down in the armchair in his room and watched him unpack Megan's diaper bag. "How can they not know? There was a reenactment the weekend before up near where the body was found. He must have come from there."

"You'd think so." He lay Megan down on the bed and changed her into a red fuzzy sleeper.

"So, you think that his research into Josiah Whiting may have had something to do with his disappearance?" she asked. She'd already told him about her own interest in Josiah Whiting's gravestones and what she'd learned about his disappearance on April 19.

"Not necessarily. But I'm feeling like if I can retrace his steps down here, I might be able to figure out when he disappeared. He was down here to do research and to participate in the reenactment, so I think it makes sense to figure out what he was looking into. What got you interested in Whiting, anyway?"

Sweeney took her notebook out of her bag and opened it to the page where she'd made sketches of the Josiah Whiting stones. "His death's-heads are really interesting," she said, pointing to the pictures. "He's got this Medusa hair thing going on, for one thing, and so the question is: What did it mean for him? Why did he choose to do it like that? And then if you look at the way they change over time, you have to ask why. Carvers' work would get better over time, more skilled, but this goes beyond that. His work gets angrier, more tormented. I'm fascinated by that."

"You would be," Quinn said.

He'd been holding Megan, who had quietly observed the conversation, but now she squirmed in his arms. Sweeney leaned over and took one of her hands. "Hello, Megan," she said. "You're so much bigger than the last time I saw you." Megan, who now had a head of fine blond hair and a broad, gummy smile, grinned at her accomplishment.

"How old is she now?" Sweeney asked. "I'm terrible at guessing babies' ages. She could be three or three months, for all I know."

Quinn grinned and put her down on the throw rug on the

wooden floor, where she stood, hanging on to the side of the
stroller. "Ten months. She'll be walking soon. She's almost
there. See how she uses her heels." Sweeney watched as
Megan flexed up and down on her feet, taking little steps
while she held on to the stroller.

"That's really cool," she said. "I see what you mean. It's
like she's testing different ways of walking, to see which one
works best."

"Yeah, it's pretty amazing, watching how they pick things
up, sounds and little mannerisms and stuff." Quinn looked
embarrassed for a moment, then smiled down at Megan and
smoothed her hair.

"So, how are you doing?" Sweeney asked him. She wandered over to the desk and flipped through the tourist pamphlets on top, trying to seem nonchalant in case he didn't
want to talk about it.

Quinn cleared his throat. "We're doing . . . we're doing
okay. Having Megan, I kind of had to get it together. That
was probably good."

"Yeah, I can see that." And she could. If she had had
someone else to worry about in those awful weeks after
Colm's death, she might have had to pull it together too. She
said impulsively, "I should have called or something, after.
I'm really sorry. I don't know why I didn't."

"It's okay. It's hard."

"Yeah, well . . . Anyway," she said, "I don't know if you
knew that there's a reenactment tomorrow. I was thinking
about going. Seems like it might be interesting."

He looked at her suspiciously. "Yeah, I'm going too. I'm
going to ask around to see if anybody remembers seeing
Churchill that weekend."

"Hey, maybe we could kind of go together. You'll need
someone else there to help you with Megan. I could take her
while you interview people."

She could see him contemplate that. He glanced at
Megan.

"Okay," he said finally. "What time does it start?"

* * *

"HE'S THE COP I TOLD YOU ABOUT, THE ONE WHOSE WIFE killed herself," Sweeney told Ian on the phone that night. She was sitting up in bed with a glass of wine poured from the bottle she'd bought down at the tavern. It wasn't very good—she hadn't been willing to go for the $40 bottle—but seeing Quinn had unsettled her somehow and she needed to relax.

"Oh, yes," Ian said. "Poor man. What an awful thing. How is he doing?"

"It's hard to tell. He didn't seem to want to talk about it. He had tried to help her, but I think he felt like he should have done more."

"Well, you would, wouldn't you?"

"But how much can you help someone? I mean, is it possible to help someone if they're really in that bad a way?"

"I don't know," he said simply. "There are probably some people who you can't help. Some people who are determined and, well, I don't imagine it's anybody's fault."

He was quiet and she knew he was thinking about her father, wondering if he should say any more.

"So, anyway, I'm going to help him with the baby tomorrow, so he can question people at this encampment." She wasn't sure why she felt she needed to tell him about it.

"Oh, right. Sounds like fun." Was that an edge in his voice? She wasn't sure.

"I went to the Old North Bridge today," she said, changing the subject. "That's where our guys vanquished your guys."

He laughed and she thought how much she liked his laugh. It was because it was so surprising. She pictured him, his dark, neatly cut hair and nobly shaped head, his eyes, which were serious behind his glasses, and then that laugh. "Yes, we're very good at getting vanquished by uppity colonials."

"They have a little memorial to the Redcoats, though. A little plaque that says, 'They came three thousand miles, and died / To keep the past upon its throne: / Unheard beyond the ocean tide / Their English mother made her moan.' "

"That's a backhanded tribute if I ever heard one," Ian said with a little snort.

"I know. It's true, though."

"How so?"

"Well, it is kind of sad when you think about it. These young guys who came all the way over here to fight for an outmoded system. Defending a tyrannical regime whose days were numbered, anyway."

He hesitated. "Well, now. That's a bit harsh."

"No, it's not."

"Oh, come on, Sweeney. That's just a kind of patriotic fairy tale. The truth is that the American colonists were getting rich in the New World and they just didn't want to share the wealth with the Old World. It was all about taxes. If a bunch of rich landowners decided they didn't want to pay taxes to the government, we wouldn't call them patriots, we'd call them greedy. Now, I will admit that we were outfoxed by your Minutemen. They knew how to fight. Our men were used to a different kind of war. Should have given themselves more practical uniforms, for one thing." He said it lightly and Sweeney knew she had the choice of letting it go or following through.

She wanted to let it go, but instead she felt a return of the uncharacteristic national pride she'd felt at the bridge. "That's ridiculous. It was about much more than taxes. It was about self-determination and freedom. It wasn't the taxes they objected to, it was that they were taxed and had nothing to say about how their taxes were spent. It was about representation. And about unreasonable invasions of privacy."

"Sweeney, I'm as cool-eyed about the British empire as the next person. Throughout history we've been awful bullies, and colonialism has caused most of the terrible problems in the world, but I'm just saying that you can't pretend the Revolutionary War wasn't about the same things all wars are about: money and land, those who have them protecting what they've got and those who don't wanting them."

Sweeney was fuming, but she didn't know what to say to him. "Maybe so," she said. "I'm going to bed."

"Are you mad? I thought we were just . . ."

"No, I'm just tired. Anyway, I'll talk to you tomorrow."

"Sweeney . . ."

"Good night, Ian."

She hung up and got ready for bed, still angry but not exactly sure why. She was hardly a blindly passionate patriot. Politically liberal, decidedly pacifist, she was usually among the first to bash American foreign policy overseas. But this had mattered to her. Why? It had to be Concord, she decided. There had been something deeply affecting about being at the bridge today, about seeing the spot where men had died for an idea. Of course Ian was right; it was much more complicated than that. But it was true that men had spilled their blood for an idea.

Life, liberty, and the pursuit of happiness. She lay in bed, thinking of Colm, and was transported back to one of the only moments of her life when she was sure she had really been happy. She and Colm had only known each other for four months or so, but she had already fallen hard. She remembered the sense of anticipation when she knew they were going to see each other, the way she could listen to him talk for hours. It was early spring and they were on their midterm holidays and he had suggested, one night on the way home from a pub, that they go up to the Lake District for a week. "We'll hike and see the daffodils," he said. They had driven up the next day and checked into a youth hostel in Windermere that was full of German teenagers.

Sweeney had loved the Lake District. It had been a warm, sunny spring. The weather was glorious and the lambs had all just been born. They were everywhere, the snowy tiny creatures, in singles or in pairs. When they had returned from the holiday, Sweeney had developed her film, only to find three rolls of identical pictures of lambs. Days, they hiked all around the lakes. They visited Wordsworth's cottage and Beatrix Potter's and in a little shop near Windermere, Colm had bought her a silver bracelet that had

"William Wordsworth" written in script on the inside. Nights, Colm played music and sang, and they cooked odd and incomplete meals in the hostel kitchen.

It had been in the Lake District that they had fallen in love. Hiking high above Lake Windermere, they had stopped for a picnic off the trail, and they had found, finally, a field of daffodils and had stopped to have their picnic among the greens and yellows, then made love as the sweet scent of grass and sun rose up around them. Afterward, she had looked up to find that Colm was crying. At first she had panicked, but then he had grasped her arms as though he were trying to stop her from falling, and he had looked into her eyes and said, "Sweeney, I love you," in his rough brogue, and then she had been crying and she had said that she loved him too.

In the middle of the night, Sweeney got up to go to the bathroom. Her head was still full of the Lake District and the green-and-yellow fields of daffodils, but when she looked out the window, she remembered that it was fall. It seemed impossible that she'd find those daffodils again. She got into the empty bed and lay down in the place where someone else would sleep, if someone else had been there.

SIXTEEN

GEORGE WHITING LIKED GOING INTO THE SHOWROOM ON
the weekends. It was quiet and he could look through the
mail without Bruce hanging over his shoulder and telling
him not to get it messed up. He could sit at the big desk and
flip through the catalogs and check things he liked without
Bruce saying, "No one's going to take that. Too big."

The showroom was dark when he went in, and he left the
lights off and stood for a minute in the doorway, his keys in
his hand. They hadn't set a day for his retirement yet, but he
found himself wondering if they were going to do something
to mark it, if he would hand the keys over to Bruce or something like that. When he'd taken over the business, it had
been because his father had died suddenly, in his sleep of a
heart attack at fifty-eight. George had been thirty, just married to Lillian, and he remembered going in that next morning and thinking, "It's mine. The business is mine." That had
been over in the other building, and he had stood in the door
and looked around and realized that every little piece of paper, every pen, every tool and file and block of granite now
belonged to him.

Bruce wouldn't feel that way, of course. He'd felt that the
place belonged to him for a long time now. Too long a time
now. That had been George's fault, maybe. Bruce had always been so good at dealing with clients that George had
kind of let him take over that part of things years ago. And

then when Lauren had come along, Bruce had wanted to turn all the bookkeeping over to her. "She's trained to do it," he told George. "She can do it on the computer, and everything will be really easy to figure out."

Somehow, George had persuaded him to leave the book-keeping as it was, but he knew that as soon as he retired, Lauren was going to love putting everything in the computer and printing out all her little checks. She'd shown him how it worked once, how she wrote the check on the computer and it automatically deducted from the accounts, then printed out on the little blue checks she ordered from a mail-order stationery company. Maybe her way was faster, but he liked the way he'd always done it. He kept everything in a big notebook and he could turn to any page and know what he was looking at.

He sat down at the big desk and used his key to open the bottom drawer of the desk. He supposed he'd have to give it to Bruce eventually. But for now, he was the only one who could get in there.

He took out the notebooks and lay them out on the desk, checking and rechecking the numbers, then got the stack of receipts from the box where Lauren put them and laid them out, entering the numbers carefully with his black pen. It was something he loved to do and usually it made every-thing seem okay, the numbers adding up and making sense right there on the page.

But today they didn't. He went over them again to be sure. There was something wrong. He tried again, but they wouldn't add up. What was it? There was money missing. Quite a lot. He sat back in his chair. There had to be an expla-nation, but he was damned if he could figure out what it was.

He would just have to try again. Tomorrow, when his mind was fresh. That was what he'd do. That was what he'd done with the tomatoes this year. He'd been battling tomato worms and he hadn't known what to do. In two nights they'd nearly cleaned him out. He'd gone to bed one night not knowing what to do and then when he'd woken up in the morning, he'd known. Just like that. As though he'd been visited in the night by the garden fairy, he'd known that he needed to use both of the powders, one right after the other, and that was what he had done and it had worked. Look at how his tomatoes had turned out. He had picked a bowlful, probably the final crop, just last week.

He was thinking about his tomatoes when he heard a car engine outside and stood up to look through the plate-glass window. It was Bruce. George gathered up all the notebooks, shoved them in the drawer and locked it, then restacked the receipts in the box and pretended to be flipping through the mail.

"Hey," Bruce said, coming in the door. "What are you doing here?"

"Just wanted to go over a couple of things." George didn't look up at him. "How 'bout you?"

"Oh, I've got a family coming in. Ninety-three-year-old mother. She already told them what she wants, so it's just a matter of putting it all together."

"Well, good, then. That's that."

Bruce studied him. "You okay?"

George didn't feel the need to dignify that with a response. "Did you see these?" He opened one of the catalogs and pointed to a series of laser-cut memorials made for members of the military. You could add on various symbols and there was some very nice art. George particularly liked one of a lone soldier staring out at a horizon dotted with what looked like fireworks. "We should start carrying these, especially with everything going on over in the Mideast."

Bruce looked over his shoulder and gave a little snort. "You mean, so we'll be prepared when the local boys start coming home in body bags?"

George stood up and looked his son in the eye. "Don't talk to me like that. You know that's what I mean. What's wrong with honoring the young men and women who are putting their lives on the line for you and me? What's wrong with that?"

Normally, Bruce was up for an argument about war, but today he backed off and said, "Nothing. Nothing's wrong with it," picking up the mail George had been looking at and flipping through it, taking out some more catalogs and opening an envelope in his signature way, by tearing off one end.

George wasn't sure why it made him so mad, but he would have been happier if Bruce had stood up to him. "Then, why do you talk to me like that?" It suddenly occurred to him that he wasn't just talking about this conversation, he was talking about all the conversations he'd had with Bruce lately.

"Why do I talk to you like what?"

"Like you think I'm pathetic."

"I don't think you're pathetic. I think it's pathetic that there are kids coming home in body bags, that's all."

"They're not just coming home in body bags. They gave their lives for their country." George was mad now. "They gave their lives for their country. And you don't have any right—"

"Any right to what?" Bruce cut in, his fists clenched at his side. George stepped back. He found he was a little afraid of his son all of a sudden. "I have every right." He stared George down, his face red and angry. "It was just luck I didn't 'give my life' for my country, and you know what? I wasn't happy to give it, Dad. I wasn't."

SEVENTEEN

IT WAS A BRILLIANTLY SUNNY FALL MORNING, THE KIND OF day that Quinn always wanted to squander, use to go fishing or to sit on the beach with a beer and a radio. It had been a long time since he'd done anything like that, and he had a moment of guilt for the thought that had flashed into his mind. If he didn't have Megan, he could do it. He could do a few interviews and then take off, maybe even drive to the Berkshires. He hadn't done that in years, since before he and Maura had gotten married. He remembered the smell of pine needles, the way the light had filtered through the trees.

But if he didn't have Megan, he wouldn't even be there. He'd be working, he'd be . . . Maura would be . . . He panicked suddenly, feeling awful for having wished Megan away, even for a second. He leaned down and kissed the top of her head as she sat in her stroller.

The three of them had left the inn about nine and driven out to the field on the outskirts of town where they were holding the battle reenactment and encampment. As they'd walked with the tide of people from the parking lot, he'd started to notice that nearly half of them were dressed up in Colonial costumes, the men dressed as Minutemen or in dark blue uniforms, the women in long dresses and bonnets, even the kids wearing little skirts and knickers. It was weird, he thought to himself, all these people wanting to pretend that they lived in a time when there were no bathrooms, no

medicine, no electricity. It was because they got to go back
to their real houses at the end of the weekend, he decided.
That was the only reason they liked it.

He looked over at Sweeney. It had been so strange, seeing
her again last night. If he was honest, he had felt a sudden
urge to turn away, walk out of the inn, and stay somewhere
else. It was ridiculous, of course. He had to stay there. It was
where Kenneth Churchill had stayed. It was where he would
follow Churchill's steps on the last weekend he'd been seen.
But when he'd seen Sweeney, he'd had the urge to run, because it had brought him back to the last time he'd seen her
and her bright red hair and those strange green eyes, with
their flecks of dark brown and amber, those eyes that seemed
to look right into you and see you somewhere you hadn't
thought anyone could see, seeing her had almost made him
throw up, remembering racing up the stairs to get Megan,
knowing what was behind the bathroom door.

She was wearing khaki pants and a green sweater that
made her hair look even brighter than usual. And over the
sweater, she had put on a tweed jacket that reminded Quinn
of something from an old movie. It made her look like she
was going hunting or something and he didn't get why she'd
wear something like that. He realized he had forgotten how
tall she was, nearly his height, which made him feel shorter
by comparison. He wasn't used to feeling short. It had been
a fact of his life since he had had his first growth spurt at
fourteen that he usually had a good few inches on most of
the people he knew, especially women. But Sweeney made
him feel not that tall after all, and he didn't like it.

Now, looking at her smiling around at the day, at the people dressed in Colonial outfits, he was annoyed at her for
forcing him to bring her along. It was just like on the Putnam
thing. She would force her way into the investigation and he
wouldn't be able to do anything about it.

She broke his train of thought. "I'll take Megan. You go
and talk to whoever you need to talk to."

He hesitated, but Megan seemed happy and he'd be
nearby if anything happened. He felt his annoyance shift a

bit. It was nice of her to offer. "It would be faster," he said. "You sure you don't mind?"

"Not at all."

"And you'll be okay?"

"Yeah. I'm good with babies." She grinned. "I didn't date much in high school. Did a lot of babysitting instead. A lot."

He smiled. "Okay. I've got my cell phone if you need me. Just give a call."

"We'll be fine." She smiled confidently and Quinn felt much better.

"Thanks. Let's meet up around one. Over by those tents." He pointed, and she said that was fine.

He had decided to start by casually asking the participants if any of them knew Kenneth Churchill. There had been an article in the newspaper that morning asking for any information about his whereabouts the weekend of October 2 and 3, so some of the people at the reenactment were going to know that he was missing, but Quinn was betting that there were quite a few who didn't.

The field was the width of a good-size football field, with the food at the end near the entrance. A local Boy Scout troop was setting up to sell hot dogs and hamburgers out of one tent and another one offered pancakes and eggs. Quinn ignored the pangs of hunger in his stomach—he'd completely skipped breakfast, what with getting Megan up and ready to go—and headed across the field toward a sea of white canvas tents. There were three neat rows of smaller tents—where the reenactors slept, he assumed—and then a line of larger, open tents displaying Colonial clothes and fake wooden rifles and toys. Other tents had signs out front that proclaimed the owner was a "Toymaker" or "Surgeon." He decided to start with the first tent, which had a sign reading, JESS HARROW. GUNSMITH.

The tall bearded man behind the counter was showing a long musket to a young guy in militia clothes. Quinn wandered around, looking at his wares—various muskets and rifles, a whole wall of hunting knives, a table of leather bags. When the other guy had gone, he went up to the proprietor. "I'm Detective Tim Quinn, Cambridge police." He forced himself to say "police" rather than "homicide" so as not to scare the guy off. "I'm investigating—"

"The guy found in the woods, I know. The Concord police have been here all morning. I'll tell you what I told them. I don't have any idea who it could be."

Quinn watched his face. He was obviously annoyed.

"Actually," he said. "I just wanted to ask you if you know someone named Kenneth Churchill."

"Kenneth? A bit. He's in the Concord Minutemen. Professor or something, right? He's not from around here. I think he lives in Cambridge. Oh."

"Yeah. When was the last time you saw him?"

"Why are you asking questions about Kenneth?" the guy asked, suddenly suspicious.

Quinn did a quick assessment. This guy wasn't going to tell him much if he didn't level with him about what had happened. He'd keep it simple. See what he could get.

"His wife reported him missing earlier this week. He never came home after the last encampment the weekend of October second. She thought he was down here doing research for his book, so she didn't get in touch with us immediately. But it seems now that he's disappeared."

That wiped the annoyed look off of Jess Harrow's face. "God. That body they found in the woods near the Old North Bridge . . . No, but that was a British uniform."

"Wasn't him," Quinn said. "So he's still missing. Do you remember seeing him that weekend. Of the second?"

"I do. On Saturday."

"Why?"

"Excuse me?"

"Why do you remember seeing him that weekend? How do you know it was Saturday?"

Jess Harrow smiled in a self-satisfied way. "Because he bought a musket from me. He wrote me a check for eight hundred dollars. That I remember."

Quinn sat up at that. There hadn't been a weapon found with the body in the woods, but if the wounds were identi-

fied as bayonet wounds, he might have found the weapon.
"Yeah? What did it look like?"

"It was a reproduction of the Brown Bess flintlock mus-
ket. That was the gun most of our guys carried against the
Redcoats. I'd done some special little things for him, though.
Etched his initials on the plates, stuff like that."

"Did it have a bayonet on it?"

"Yeah. I can draw you a sketch if you want."

"Okay, that'd be great. Can you give me the exact measurements too?" They ought to be able to match the specs on
the bayonet with the wounds on the John Doe.

"Sure." He jotted some figures down on a piece of paper
and handed it over.

"Do you remember what time that was? That you saw
him."

"It was later in the day. They'd done a weapons demonstration and I'd gone up to look at that. He caught up with
me up in the field and asked if he could come down and get
the musket. He was really excited about it. Couldn't wait to
try it out."

"And that was the last time you saw him that weekend?"

"Yeah."

"That seems odd to me. I mean, there aren't that many
people here, really. Wouldn't you be likely to see him if he
was around Saturday night or Sunday?"

"This is a small encampment. The one that weekend was
much bigger. There were regiments from all over the North-
east."

Quinn thought for a moment. "You said you don't have
any idea who the body might be. Is that because it was wearing a British uniform?"

"Maybe, if he was a newer guy. But the thing is, we all
pretty much know each other. On the battlefield, it's all Brits
and Yanks, but as soon as the shooting stops, we're all pretty
buddy-buddy. Most of us, anyway. There are a couple of
guys I know who don't like consorting with the enemy. But
they're in the minority."

Quinn took down a dark wood and silver musket that was

hanging on the wall. The barrel felt smooth and warm in his hands. The bright bayonet glinted in the sun. "This is beautiful," he said. "Did you make this?"

"Yup. That's another Brown Bess. Pretty similar to the one I made for Kenneth, actually."

"So, they just used muskets in the Revolution?"

"For the most part. They used rifles too, but the thing is, rifles took longer to load. On the battlefield, that made a big difference. But rifles had longer range."

Jess Harrow warmed to his subject. "Those over there are the cartridge boxes." He crossed the tent and opened up one of the leather bags, showing Quinn the wooden compartments inside. "This is where you kept your cartridges. They were made by girls, you know. It was very dangerous work, and girls were expendable. You needed boys to farm or to play the fifes and drums—that was how they communicated on the battlefield—and you needed women to cook and men to fight. So they let the girls work with the gunpowder."

"Interesting. Well, thanks for your help. I really appreciate it."

"No problem. Hope they figure out who that guy is in the woods. It's kind of awful to think of him being out there and no one knowing who he is. And I hope you find Kenneth too."

Quinn was about to go when he turned around and asked, "What was he like? As a, you know, as a person?"

"He was an okay guy," Harrow said after a moment. "The thing about him was, he really believed in all this stuff. Really believed in the importance of keeping the history alive. He liked war too. I mean . . . he'd been in Desert Storm and sometimes I got the feeling that it was his way of keeping things alive, if you know what I mean. He still got to be a soldier when he was here. There are other guys like that too. Or guys who wanted to serve and couldn't."

"Thanks."

Quinn wandered around the tent next door, which had been set up as a kind of old-fashioned mercantile shop, looking at Colonial clothes and tin cups and lanterns. He bought

Megan a little Colonial bonnet that would be good for keeping the sun off her face, and as he paid, he casually asked the teenage girl behind the counter if she knew Kenneth Churchill. She didn't, but she explained that she only helped her mother out sometimes and didn't come to most of the encampments. At the next tent, where a group of women were sitting around, sewing and talking, the story was much the same. The women knew Churchill's name, but they didn't remember seeing him the weekend of the encampment on Whiting's land.

Outside, he thought about what to do next. There were a couple more tents, including one that seemed to have more clothes, and ones belonging to the toymaker and the surgeon, but he had the feeling he'd be similarly unlucky there.

At the other end of the field, a line of militiamen, dressed in white leggings, dark-colored coats, and dark hats, were standing in a row and practicing what looked like military maneuvers. It couldn't hurt. . . . They might be more likely to remember seeing Churchill than the people who had the shops.

He crossed the field and stood watching them for a few minutes. They held their muskets at their sides, barrels pointed in the air, as a man dressed in the formal uniform of a general called out commands. The men dropped their weapons, then raised them again, ready to fire.

When they'd finished, Quinn approached a small group of them and introduced himself.

"Is this about that body up in Whiting's woods?" one of them asked. "We've been talking to the cops about that all morning. Nobody knows who the guy is. It's like he just dropped out of the sky."

"No," Quinn said. "It's about Kenneth Churchill." He decided to go for it. "We don't know where he is. I was wondering if you might be able to help."

"Kenneth?" one of the men said. "I was wondering about him. What do you mean, you don't know where he is?"

"His wife reported him missing this week," Quinn said. "He hasn't been seen since Saturday, October second, the weekend of the encampment up on George Whiting's land."

"But that's when the . . . when the guy in the woods must have been killed," another of the guys said. "You think it's related?"

"We don't know. That's why I wanted to talk to you. Do you all remember seeing him that weekend?"

"Yeah, sure. I was next to him during the demonstration," one of the guys said. Quinn took down his name.

"I had a talk with him Saturday night," another guy said. "We were all up around the fire that night and I chatted with him for a while. Just about this stuff." He gestured around at the encampment.

"Hey, you know what," one of the guys said, "You should talk to Chris. He knew Churchill better than we did. Hang on." He stepped away and yelled to another little group of men. "Hey, Chris. Come on over here."

A tall, youngish guy with thinning red hair and bad teeth that made him look even more authentically Colonial than he would have otherwise came over and was introduced to Quinn as Chris Wright.

"He hadn't been with us that long," he said when Quinn told him why he was there and asked him how well he'd known Churchill. "Just since last year. He loved the reenactments. His uniforms and weapons were always impeccable, and we liked having someone who was such an expert, you know, on account of him being a historian and writing books and everything. But he wasn't that sociable. He would do the battles, but then he wasn't around a lot, if you know what I mean. He seemed to kind of go his own way. Jeez, I hope he's okay."

"Did he ever mention the book he was working on?"

"Josiah Whiting?" Quinn nodded. "We all knew he was working on it. He talked about Whiting fairly frequently. I'm from Concord and so I knew a little bit about Whiting. Kenneth was so passionate about the book. He had written other books, but he said that he really thought this one was going to blow a hole in the existing scholarship. That was the way he said it."

Quinn leaned forward a little and lowered his voice. "He

had been spending a lot of time down here doing research. His wife said he stayed at the Minuteman Inn. Was that true?"

"I think so." But the guy seemed uncomfortable again.

Quinn asked, "Where else did he spend time down here? Where was he doing his research?"

"He'd been visiting graveyards a lot. I know a little bit about stonecutting techniques and the history of some of the cemeteries from the relevant era. So he and I had fun talking about that. I know he'd been spending a lot of time at the Minuteman Museum too. They have a fairly extensive collection of artifacts and historical documents." He glanced down at the ground and Quinn had the feeling that he was holding something back. He'd have to come back to it.

"Great," Quinn said. "Tell me everything you can about that weekend. How did he seem? Was he his usual self?"

The guy thought for a minute. "Yeah. He seemed fine. If anything, he seemed kind of hyped-up, happier than usual. He was going off to do some research and I assumed that's what it was. Maybe he'd found something."

"Okay, so when's the last time you remember talking to him that weekend?"

"Let's see. Saturday, of course, and then Sunday morning, I think. After the encampments, we have a big breakfast cooked over the communal fire. The women prepare it, make things the Minutemen would have eaten. I remember talking to him there and I think that was when he said he was going to stick around and do some research. He said he wanted to spend some more time in graveyards."

Quinn asked, "Did he say why he wanted to spend time in graveyards?"

"I guess he just wanted to look at Whiting's handiwork."

"So, what time was that when you last saw him? On Sunday?" Quinn was writing this all down furiously. This was great. This was the first person he'd talked to who had seen Churchill on Sunday.

"Well, I saw him getting ready to go around nine, I suppose. He said good-bye and we said we'd see each other the next weekend. And then a couple of hours later, I saw him heading out to his car. That was the strange thing, though, I just remembered . . ."

"Just remembered what?"

"Well, I was across the field and I saw him heading to the parking area and I waved at him. He was getting into his car. He'd changed out of his uniform but he still had his hat on. I think he saw me, because he waved back, but it was really weird." He looked up at Quinn. "God, I didn't think of it until just now. He seemed strange, not like himself." He looked stricken all of a sudden. "God, I didn't think of it. I would have . . . it's just that you know how people sometimes look like that when—" He paused and looked up at Quinn, his eyes wide. "When something awful has happened."

EIGHTEEN

SWEENEY HADN'T BEEN SURE WHAT TO DO WITH MEGAN AT first. After Quinn left them, Megan had started whimpering and Sweeney's attempts to soothe her proved fruitless. Finally, she undid the complicated harnesses that held her in the stroller and picked her up, holding her tightly and letting Megan play with her long hair.

When they came to a tent selling reproduction military uniforms, Sweeney left the stroller outside among the racks of coats and brought Megan in to look at the uniforms, running her fingers over the thick wool.

"That's the very best, double-weight wool," said a man's voice from behind her.

She turned around. "Oh, thanks. I was just having fun looking. Do you make them?"

"I do. I'm a tailor by trade. This is my passion, though." He stuck out a hand. "Bill Carver."

She shook it. "Sweeney St. George. Your stuff is beautiful. I'm kind of a vintage clothing nut and it's fun to see such skilled work."

"Well, let me know if you have any questions."

"I will." She looked through the clothes, admiring the fine tailoring, particularly on the British uniforms.

"What would a Concord Minuteman have worn?" Sweeney asked him. She was trying to picture Josiah Whiting and she figured it would help to know what his clothes would have looked like.

"Well, you have to remember that most of the Minutemen were farmers. At Lexington and Concord, they would have worn their regular clothes, usually a white tunic and dark-colored breeches and vest." He led her over to one of the racks and showed her a beige coat. "This would have been a fairly common overgarment for a Minuteman from this area."

"Do you make uniforms for all of the reenactors here?"

"No, God no. There wouldn't be enough time in the day. There are a few tailors around who make them. Lots of people on the Web. And some of the reenactors have learned to make their own."

"How much would a full uniform cost?"

"A couple of hundred dollars. More than that, depending on what you get. But the guys trade them around sometimes. If someone's moving away and can no longer be part of his regiment, he might give his uniform to a new member who's just starting out. Sometimes you can even find uniforms in thrift shops."

Sweeney hesitated before asking him, "The body in the woods—did anyone ask you about the uniform?" An image of the scarlet-clad body swam in front of her.

"Yeah. The police were around all morning. Showed me some pretty horrible pictures. It wasn't one of mine, though. I could tell right away."

"How?" Megan was squirming in Sweeney's arms, reaching for the clothes and Sweeney stepped back so she wouldn't pull anything off the racks.

"It wasn't very well made, for one thing. You could see that even in the photographs. And there were a few inaccuracies. The shape of the coat was wrong and there weren't enough buttons. The British uniform had brass buttons along the pockets. Things like that. My guess is that it was made by a reenactor. A lot of guys will design something and then have their wives sew it up. It's fine for a first uniform, but as they get more involved, they tend to like to have someone like me make their gear. A lot of those uniforms end up in dress-up boxes, thrift shops."

"It seems strange that nobody knows who he is, doesn't it? I mean, you're all a pretty tight-knit group and all of the reenactors are part of a regiment, right? Even if he came from somewhere far away from here, wouldn't the other members of his regiment know who he is?"

"That's just what I've been thinking," Bill Carver said. "It's like he, I don't know, came out of nowhere. Remember the Connecticut Yankee in King Arthur's Court? It's like that."

Sweeney laughed. "Except that his uniform's not right."

Bill Carver smiled. "Except that his uniform's not right."

"Thanks. It was great to see your things. And I'll take one of these." She held up a little Colonial bonnet made of flowered calico and handed over four dollars. She put it on Megan and tied it under her chin.

"Perfect," he said. "She looks like a proper Colonial lassie."

The sun had come up in the sky and it was quite warm out on the field. Sweeney checked her watch. It was almost one.

"Okay," she said to Megan. "Let's go find your dad."

He was standing in front of the surgeon's tent and Sweeney came up behind him. "Hey," she said.

He turned around and took Megan from her, kissing her on the side of her head and sniffing her diaper. "Hey." He laughed and held up a little bonnet identical to the one Sweeney had bought. "She'll have one to go with every outfit," he said.

The surgeon was giving a little demonstration for the group of people standing in front of his booth, and Sweeney and Quinn stepped in and watched him demonstrate the various tools that an eighteenth-century surgeon would have had at his disposal.

"This is a long saw," the man said. "It was used for battlefield amputations. Unfortunately, anesthetic hadn't been invented yet, so this is what doctors used to take the bite off the pain. No pun intended." He held up a short stick that was covered with bite marks. You would bite down on this and"—he raised the saw in the air—"off with your arm!" Sweeney flinched.

"How did things go?" she whispered.

"Okay," Quinn whispered back. "I'll tell you later."

The surgeon went on. "Then, of course there were other kinds of treatments. If someone had a fever, the belief was that it was a poisoning of the blood, and you had to let some of that blood out. Of course, you've heard of doctors using leeches, but they also bled people using little knives like this." He took out a small switchblade and held his wrist over a small white enamel bowl.

"So, you would just nick the vein, like this." He pretended to cut himself. "Did you know that George Washington actually died of blood loss? He'd been sick and they overbled him. It was . . ."

Sweeney looked up at Quinn. He had gone pale and he was staring at the man's wrist poised over the bowl.

"Let's go," she said suddenly, taking Megan from him and pulling him away from the small crowd of people. He stumbled, then stopped, and she said, "Tim," and tugged again, trying to hang on to Megan with the other arm. She had never called him Tim before and the name felt odd in her mouth, a taste she couldn't quite identify.

"It's okay," he said breathlessly.

"No, it's not. Let's just . . ." She tried to steer him away from the tent.

"Leave me alone," he shouted, pushing her hand off. "I'm okay. Just . . . just leave me alone." Sweeney, who had been standing too close, lost her balance and almost dropped Megan, who started to cry. A few of the people who had been watching the demonstration looked up at Quinn's raised voice.

Quinn strode over to the side of the field and leaned over for a moment as though he was going to be sick. Sweeney watched him dry heave, then sink down to the ground, where he put his head in his hands.

Megan had stopped crying and was watching her father

and whimpering, and Sweeney, not knowing what to do, tried to distract her with a little stuffed rabbit that was tied to the stroller. "It's okay, Megan," she told her. "It's okay."

It was a few minutes before Quinn came back, pale and worn-out-looking. He took Megan from Sweeney and put her in the stroller. Sweeney watched him buckle Megan in, the vein on his left temple quivering in the midday light.

"I'm sorry about that," he said when he stood up. He met her eyes for only a second and then looked away. "I didn't want to . . . I didn't mean to push you. It was the . . . the wrist."

"It's okay. I knew where it was coming from."

"It was . . . I don't know why that happened."

Sweeney didn't know what to say and settled for another "it's okay." She didn't want to look at him, didn't want to see his pain. His name still sat uncomfortably on her tongue. Without speaking, they walked back toward the main field, where some kind of battle was taking place.

They stopped and stood with a crowd of people watching a line of Redcoats approach from behind a stand of trees at the edge of the field, a blur of red and then a row of marching regulars, stepping in time to the drum beating out the minutes. The drummer boy's yellow coat seemed almost to reflect the brilliant gold of the trees around them. When they reached the center of the field, the men stopped and waited. It was very silent and the red-coated soldiers raised their muskets toward the sky.

The men marched onward and then she caught sight of the Minutemen, fanning out across the field, kneeling to shoot and then running on. It was odd, Sweeney thought, how *slow* war seemed. When it came down to it, it was just men marching over land, trying to own it. She thought about her conversation with Ian and felt guilty.

"I found someone who saw him on Sunday," Quinn said as they walked back toward the car. "Said he looked real upset."

"Did he have any idea why?"

"No, he said everything went just as usual at the reenactment. He didn't know of any argument Churchill had with anybody."

They were heading back toward the parking lot when a man's voice called out, "Hey, hey. Mr. Quinn."

Sweeney turned around to find a tall strawberry-blond-haired guy dressed in a Minuteman's breeches, coat, and tri-corner hat running toward them.

"Mr. Quinn. I wanted to talk to you because, well, there's something I think you should know. About Kenneth."

They stopped and the man went on breathlessly. "I wanted to tell you that I think Kenneth was seeing Cecily Whiting. The woman who runs the Minuteman Museum. I didn't say anything because of his wife, but if he's missing, maybe she can help." He breathed in hard and Sweeney saw his small, discolored teeth. "I think they were having an affair."

NINETEEN

LAUREN WHITING TURNED OFF THE BURNER BENEATH THE
teakettle and stood in front of the range for a moment, waiting for the knock. Cecily always insisted on knocking, even
though Pres knew he could just come right on in. But Lauren
had overheard her once, telling him that it was rude to walk
in without knocking because Daddy and Lauren might be
having "private time." Lauren had felt like strangling her for
the smarmy insinuation in her voice. What was poor Pres
supposed to make of his father and stepmother having "private time"?

She had been watching through the window for their ar-
rival. In the family room, she could hear Bruce playing with
Rory and Noah. Rory's high screech of delight made her
wince as she waited at the window. Cecily's Saab pulled up
in the driveway and Lauren watched her get out and help
Pres get his backpack from the trunk. He was walking
slowly and seemed weak today, and she felt her heart sink a
little. She loved their Saturday nights at home, just the five
of them, a real family. But if Pres was feeling sick, he
wouldn't want to play with the kids and Bruce would be
worried and distracted all night.

Well, if he was going to be distracted, anyway, she decided it wouldn't make things worse if Bruce finally talked
to Cecily about the shares.

There was a knock at the door and Lauren counted to ten

before going to open it. "Hi, Pres," she said brightly, reaching out to squeeze his shoulder. Cecily winced and she took her hand away. "Hi, Cecily. How are you?"

"Fine. And you?" As she always did, Cecily looked around her at their house as though she expected to find something nasty on the floor. Lauren supposed it wasn't up to Cecily's decorating standards, with the blue ruffled curtains, heart-shaped rag rugs, and the blueberries stenciled along the top of the wall, but Lauren liked it and that was all that mattered. Still, seeing Cecily always brought back the feelings she remembered from when she and Bruce had first gotten together. She got along great with George and Lillian now, but at first she'd known they all looked down on her and blamed her for the divorce. That she'd been pregnant when Bruce left hadn't helped any, but eventually things had gotten smoothed over. They usually did if you waited long enough.

"We're good," Lauren said, smiling, throwing in the "we" for good measure. Rory and Noah came running into the room, rushing Pres and wrapping themselves around his legs. "Pez. Cack. Oppon," Noah babbled.

"He wants you to open his chicken game," Lauren told Pres as Bruce came into the kitchen and gave his eldest son a bear hug.

"How ya feelin', Elvis?" Bruce liked to call Pres Elvis, even though his first name was Preston and not Presley. Lauren had once asked him how it had started and he'd told her that they had called him that when he was a baby because he had had a dark shock of hair that stood up on top of his head in a pompadour.

"Okay."

"He was tired today, but the doctor said his numbers are actually pretty good," Cecily said. "Make sure he gets a good night's sleep."

"We will," Lauren said, then turned to Pres. "Pres, honey, why don't you say good-bye to your mom and then the four of us can go play with the chicken game while your mom and your dad talk about something important."

Bruce glanced over at her with a puzzled expression on his face, then blushed when he realized what she was doing.

"What about?" Cecily asked Bruce, her eyes suddenly suspicious. She probably thought they were going to ask for more days a week.

"We'll talk in a sec," he said. "Pres, say good night to your mom." He mumbled something approximating "night" and followed Noah and Rory back into the family room. Lauren followed them and shut the pocket doors behind her. She got Noah's chicken game out and set it up for him on the floor. Pres immediately put a chicken on his head and made clucking noises. Noah and Rory laughed in delight, and seeing they were content, Lauren sat down on the floor near the door and pretended to be cleaning up toys while she listened for Bruce's and Cecily's voices.

Through the narrow space between the doors, she could see Cecily's long dark-colored skirt, her soft leather boots. When Lauren had first gone to work at Whiting Monuments, she had been in awe of Cecily and her outfits. Lauren had never seen her dressed in anything other than the absolutely perfect pair of pants or jacket or skirt for that day, that season, that occasion. Lauren had even tried to copy Cecily's style for a few weeks before she realized that she didn't have the right clothes. She liked her own way of dressing. It was right for her. And Bruce seemed to like it too.

". . . because of George's plans," Bruce was saying in a low voice. "He'll hang on to his shares and so if we want to do anything with the business once he's been phased out, we just . . . well, we'd just feel better if we could kind of get everything wrapped up, if you know what I mean. We want to pay you for them, of course."

"Bruce, you gave those shares to Pres. They're not mine to sell. It's so he'll have some security. In case something happens."

"Cecily, he's my son. I'll always take care of him."

"Well, you promised a lot of things to me that didn't quite pan out, didn't you?"

"Come on!"

There was silence.

"It's not up for discussion, Bruce. When Pres is eighteen, he can decide whether or not he wants to sell them to you. Until then, they're not mine to sell. Have Pres back on time tomorrow. He has school Monday." Lauren listened carefully and heard the sound of the front door shutting and then the car starting. She dumped all of the scattered toys into the kids' big toy box and smiled as he came in, then raised her eyebrows. Bruce raised them back and she felt a little surge of love and guilt. She shouldn't have pushed him to talk to Cecily, not with everything that was going on. She had loved Bruce Whiting from the moment she'd first seen him, the moment he'd opened his mouth to say, "Now, tell me why you want to work at a monument company." She loved being his wife, loved being the mother of his children, loved listening to him talk, and loved watching him when he was quiet. She stood up and kissed him on the cheek. "I'm sorry," she whispered into his ear, feeling him shiver at the touch of her breath. "I love you."

He grinned and gave her a hug. "All right, kids, who wants to play climb the mountain?"

Noah and Rory cheered and even Pres joined in, pretending to climb up Bruce's back as he did his best to shake off his children, who tumbled, laughing, onto the floor.

TWENTY

"I NEED TO TALK TO ANDY LYNCH," QUINN SAID. "IS HE around?"

"Who are you?" The woman sitting behind the front desk at the station looked at him suspiciously.

"Detective Tim Quinn. Cambridge police. He'll know who I am when you tell him."

"Well, he's busy right now."

"I think we should let him decide that," Quinn said. "If you would just tell him . . ."

The woman looked exasperated, but she picked up the phone and dialed. "There's a Detective Tim Quinn here to see Detective Lynch. Yes. No, I . . . Okay." She hung up the phone. "You can go in," she told Quinn. "It's the second door on the right."

Quinn was just about to knock on the closed door when it opened and Andy came out with a huge grin on his face. "Quinny!"

"Hey, Andy." He was just the same, with that spiky dark red hair and the off-center nose from some childhood fight or other. "It's great to see you."

"You too. You look just the same. Woulda known you anywhere."

"Yeah, just a little older, right? I would have known you too. Never got that nose fixed, huh?"

Andy grinned. "No, turns out the ladies like it."

"That's what they tell you, anyway."

They laughed and Quinn felt inordinately happy. Andy Lynch! He couldn't believe how good it was to see him.

Andy gestured for him to sit down on a folding chair across from the desk. "Sorry about this," he said, gesturing around at the room. "I'm setting up camp here for the investigation, but I don't have any of my own stuff. So, I couldn't believe it when they told me you were out here. What's this thing you're working on? Missing-persons case?"

Quinn updated him on Kenneth Churchill and told him about what he'd learned at the encampment about Cecily Whiting. "It seems like something must have happened at the reenactment. Something that disturbed Churchill, upset him. I just can't figure out what it was. I asked around and nobody could remember anything strange happening that weekend, like a fight or anything. But as you know, the reenactment wasn't far from where they found the body."

"You know when your guy died yet?"

"Saturday or Sunday. He'd been gone about a week or so."

"So that fits."

Andy looked up. "You think he had something to do with our guy?"

Quinn shrugged. "It's a question I gotta ask myself. I assume you still haven't identified him?"

"Nope. He seems to have dropped in from the eighteenth century. Seriously. No wallet, no watch, no jewelry, no tattoos, no signs of surgery. Nothing. The guy doesn't even have any unusual dental work. Nobody's asking about him, nobody knows anything."

"Any word on cause of death? I mentioned to Chief Tyler that Churchill had quite an arsenal in his house. And I found out today that he bought a new reproduction musket the weekend he disappeared, fitted with a bayonet. I got the specs on the bayonet for you." He handed over the paper. "Might narrow it down."

"That was you? Thanks. Yeah, it came back that he was stabbed nine or ten times with a blade about the same width and length as a bayonet. We didn't get a weapon at the scene, but if Churchill had something to do with it, he could have taken it with him. So, what do you want to do?"

"I can't get over the feeling that Churchill's still alive. It just seems like he would have shown up somewhere, you know? Now that we know there's a good chance he had an affair with Cecily Whiting, I think I want to talk to her. I'm out of my jurisdiction, though. I can interview her as part of my missing-persons thing, but it's beginning to look more and more like this is all connected. And I thought I should get you in on it."

"Well, I appreciate that. Any help I can get on this, I'm gonna take. Check this out." Andy took a *Boston Globe* off the filing cabinet and handed it to Quinn. MYSTERY BODY IN CONCORD BAFFLES POLICE, the headline read.

"You wouldn't believe the pressure I'm getting from the D.A.," Andy went on. "And practically every day I've got these crazy guys dressed up in Revolutionary War costumes coming into my office to tell me about how they spend their weekends. Jeez! Anyway, why don't you go ahead and talk to her. Don't say anything about the guy in the woods. Just say that you're looking into Churchill's disappearance. Tell her you know about the affair, but don't tell her how. See what she says. How did this guy know about it, anyway? Did Churchill tell him? I'm wondering how many people knew about it."

"Yeah, I'm wondering the same thing," Quinn said. "But I don't think Churchill was going around telling people. At least not in so many words. This guy, his friend from the reenactment, said it was the way he talked about her. He said he kind of went on and on about how wonderful she was, how smart she was, et cetera, and finally one day he asked if there was anything going on between them and Churchill kind of raised his eyebrows, but he didn't actually say yes."

"Okay, well, good luck. Let me know what happens. Where are you living these days?"

"Somerville. Not far from the old neighborhood, though it's a different place now. But I'm staying at the Minuteman Inn here in town for a bit. It was where Churchill stayed when he was out here. I interviewed the guy who owns the inn really briefly this morning. He didn't have too much to say, showed me the guest records. Churchill stayed at the inn six times over the last year. I'll have to sit down with him for longer. Oh, hey, I just realized I should tell you about kind of a weird coincidence. The woman who was with the kid when he found the body, well, I know her. She helped me out on a case once."

"There's something weird about that chick," Andy said. "I'm still not sure she's being totally honest with me. It just seems weird that she'd follow the kid into the woods, you know."

"I think she was just worried about him," Quinn said. "She's a pretty trustworthy person, Andy. Seriously."

"Yeah, well, she's probably off the hook, anyway. The guy was long dead before she and the kid got there."

As they were walking out, Andy grinned and said, "Hey, how's Maura?"

Quinn turned and stared at him. "I guess you hadn't heard," he said. "She . . . she passed away back in the spring."

Andy looked stricken. "Jeez, I'm sorry, Quinny. I didn't know. I'm not really in touch with folks in the old neighborhood so much anymore. Shit, that's awful."

Quinn forced his voice into cheerfulness. "Well, I'm doing okay. I've got the baby, so that helps. She's doing great, getting bigger."

"What's her name?"

"Megan."

"Like Megan Reardon, huh?"

Quinn laughed. "Yeah, I never thought about that. If I had, we probably wouldn't have named her Megan." Megan Reardon had been the older sister of one of their junior-high friends and the source of much of their adolescent sexual speculation.

"Good. Well, I'll see you." Andy watched him walk to his car and when Quinn turned around to wave, he remembered something he hadn't thought about in a long time, how he had been walking home from school once and a couple of older kids had started messing with him, pushing him and trying to make him lash out so they'd have an excuse to hit him. Quinn had been just on the verge of getting a beating when Andy had run by, screaming at the top of his lungs, "It's the fuckin' cops. Don't tell them where I went." The boys had stopped messing with Quinn and gone to see what Andy had done.

Quinn still remembered the way Andy had looked when he'd found him a few minutes later behind the corner deli. "They leave ya alone?" he'd asked, his crooked nose twisting with his smile. "I bet they did, didn't they?"

THE MINUTEMAN MUSEUM WAS NEARLY EMPTY AND QUINN found Cecily Whiting—looking exactly the way Sweeney had described her—washing the glass covers of a set of display boxes in one of the rear galleries. He had taken a quick look around as he'd come in, telling the elderly woman behind the ticket counter that he was there on business, and had actually found himself intrigued by the few displays he'd seen, biographical portraits of the various men who had made history at Lexington and Concord.

"Mrs. Whiting?" he asked, feeling awkward coming into the gallery where she was intent on her work.

"Yes?" She looked up and he thought he saw something wary in her eyes. He'd seen that look before in the eyes of people who were expecting bad news.

"I'm Detective Tim Quinn from the Cambridge Police Department. I was wondering if we could chat for a few minutes?"

"Of course," she said, dropping the bottle of Windex and her rag onto the floor and standing up. She was a pretty woman, but there was something cold and inaccessible about her. She crossed her arms protectively over her chest and then led him through a door behind one of the exhibits and into a small conference room with a movie screen and projector at one end of a long table. She sat down at the head of the table, and he chose a chair halfway down so he could look directly at her while they talked.

"Mrs. Whiting, I'm here today to ask you—"

"Ms.," she said.

"Excuse me?"

"It's Ms. Whiting. I'm not married anymore."

"Oh, okay. Ms. Whiting, as I said, I'm from the Cambridge Police Department. We got a call on Monday from a woman named Beverly Churchill. Her husband, Kenneth Churchill, is a historian. He was doing research in Concord for a book he was working on. I guess he spent a lot of time at the museum. Anyway, he never came home after a reenactment and research trip the weekend of October second. There was a little piece in the local paper this morning and I don't know if you saw it, but I was hoping to find out when the last time you saw him was."

Her reaction was not what he'd expected. She had been so self-contained, her crossed arms and precise posture holding her entire body in check, and it was as though the invisible web that had been holding her together just collapsed. "Oh," she said very loudly. "What . . . what do you mean?" Her arms flopped at her sides and her posture sagged.

"He seems to be missing. He hasn't contacted his wife or family. I'm trying to talk to anyone who may have seen him in the last couple of weeks. When was the last time you saw him?" He had decided not to reveal that he had any suspicions about an affair. He had, after all, a legitimate reason for questioning her. She had helped Churchill with his research and he had spent a lot of time at the museum. In Quinn's experience, it was much easier to get things out of people when they didn't know how much you knew.

"Has something happened to him? Is he dead?" She looked up at him with eyes full of tears, but he had a strange sense of déjà vu and it struck him suddenly that she had the same expression on her face that Beverly Churchill had had on hers—sweet relief.

"We don't know. That's what I'm trying to find out." She

was so open, so vulnerable, that he decided to go for the gold. "What was your relationship with Mr. Churchill?"

But she didn't answer him. Instead, she leaned back in her chair and seemed to go off into her own world, talking almost to herself. "I'm such a horrible person," she said. "All this time I've been so angry at him for not calling me back. And he may be hurt or dead. I don't know what's wrong with me."

Quinn waited. Sooner or later, he knew, it was all going to come out.

She had begun to cry and again he had the feeling that she was relieved. Finally she looked up at him. "We were seeing each other," she said, tears still hovering in her eyes. "It started in February. He was coming down to do research for his book and he spent a lot of time here. We just kind of . . . fell into it. I don't know how to explain it." She looked up, embarrassed.

"So you had a romantic relationship?"

Her eyes narrowed a bit. "Of course, what did you think I meant?"

He took a deep breath. "Why don't you tell me about it?"

She seemed to calm down a bit. "I knew he was married, but he said that it had been over for a while, they were just staying together for their son. It's such a cliché. My ex-husband had an affair before we divorced and I'm sure it's what he told his . . . his new wife. But I didn't care. I didn't feel guilty at all. My son . . . my son had just gotten sick and it just was . . . it was escape." She looked up at him as though she wanted him to agree with her that it was okay, that she hadn't done anything wrong, but then she seemed to remember who he was and she crossed her arms again and she tried to regain her composure.

Quinn waited a moment and said, "So, you'd been seeing each other since February? Did he ever say anything about going away, about leaving his wife?"

"Sometimes we would talk about what it would be like, but then we'd come to our senses. It wasn't just him. It was . . . well, with Pres sick, I . . . I felt like I was betraying him. Pres—that's my son—he needed me. So, we would talk about it sometimes, about being together, but it was, you know, just talk. I think we both knew what the limits were." But she didn't sound too convinced as she said it.

"So, he never talked about going away on his own?"

"No, never. I mean, he had responsibilities. His teaching and his family. And his book. I know he loved me, but he was never going to love me the way he loved his book. I used to think that one of the reasons he was attracted to me was that I have this connection by marriage to Josiah Whiting. He wouldn't have gone anywhere until the book was finished. No." Her eyes widened. "That means something must have happened to him."

"We don't know that. You'd be surprised at how many people just go off. Stay away for a few weeks to figure out whatever it is they need to figure out, then go home. They're usually amazed at how worried everyone was." He waited to see if she was going to say anything else, then said, "You said he didn't call you. When were you expecting him to get in touch?"

"He was down for an encampment that weekend. Usually we would meet after the encampments, but the Friday before I had called to tell him that I didn't think we should see each other anymore. I was feeling guilty about his wife, about Pres. I decided we had to end things. So I told him I wouldn't meet him. I told him not to call." She was silent, staring down at the table.

"But you thought he would?" Quinn finally prompted.

"It was how it always went!" she almost screamed at him. Her thin face looked suddenly haggard, older. "I'd tell him not to call, and he always did. When he didn't, I didn't know what to think. I thought maybe he'd finally decided to end things once and for all."

That was why she'd been relieved, Quinn realized. She'd thought he was breaking up with her. Would she be happier if something had happened to him? It was a good question, he realized. "Who else knew about your relationship?"

She looked up at him, confused. "Nobody. What do you mean?"

"I mean, did anyone know about the relationship? Other than the two of you?"

"I don't think so. We were pretty careful. He didn't care so much. He wanted to go out to dinner and things like that, but I felt funny about it. I didn't want it to get back to Pres or . . ." She stopped. "I don't think anyone knew."

"Not even his wife?"

"According to him, she had no idea. But I can't see how she didn't suspect something. I mean, he was gone for days on end." There was blame in her voice and Quinn wondered if she'd been similarly duped. He'd found that people were the quickest to condemn behavior or traits they despised in themselves.

"What about your ex-husband?"

"No. I don't think so." She gave an ugly, sarcastic grin that put Quinn on edge. "Not that he would care."

He studied her for a minute. He wanted to get out of there. There was something about her face when she'd talked about her ex-husband that made him feel ashamed. "Thanks for being so honest with me. I may get back in touch with you. In the meantime, if you hear from Mr. Churchill, please let me know." She nodded, though he wasn't at all convinced that she would.

He got up to leave, but she stayed in her chair, twisting a piece of her short hair above her ear and staring at the table. "Hey," he said. "I just thought of something. When you met up with him, where did you meet? Not at your house?"

"No. I was always afraid that Pres was going to come home and find us." She looked up at him and gave a little smile. "I'm embarrassed to tell you, but we met in the woods. Behind my ex-in-laws'. It's private and you can get to it from the road on the other side. There's this little . . . the clubhouse, they call it. My ex-husband built it when he was in high school and they've kept it up over the years. There's a couch and everything." The smile faded. "It was where my husband used to meet his mistress . . . his wife. I always liked the irony of that." He could see it dawning on her a second after it dawned on him. "Wait," she said, "I just realized. The body up in the woods. It was near the club-house." She stared at him and he could see her trying to process it, trying to figure out what Kenneth Churchill could have had to do with the body in the woods. "You don't think . . . ?"

The problem was that Quinn didn't know what to think.

TWENTY-ONE

SWEENEY WAS WATCHING CNN WHEN QUINN GOT BACK TO his room. She was stretched out on his bed, wearing his fleece jacket, which he'd left hanging over the desk chair, and he found himself annoyed suddenly that she'd made herself so at home, though he knew it was ridiculous. She had done him a huge favor.

"Thanks so much for taking care of her," he said quietly. Megan was sleeping in the Pack 'n Play, one hand shoved in her mouth. He felt his stomach contract with love as he looked at her. "I really appreciate it."

"No problem. She was good. We went for a walk downtown and then came back here and she fell asleep on the floor, so I put her in her playpen. I hope you don't mind—I borrowed your jacket. It was kind of cold and I didn't want to leave her."

"No, that's fine. She have a bottle?" He leaned over the side of the playpen and touched his daughter's hair.

"Yeah. Just before she went to sleep. So, what did you get from her?"

"They'd been seeing each other since the winter," he said after a moment, sitting down across from Sweeney in the desk chair. "The weekend he disappeared, she told him not to call her anymore. She was worried about her son. From what I can tell, she felt like it would have been a betrayal of her son to have another relationship." He glanced, quickly, at the sleeping Megan.

"But it seems like it was part of their routine," he continued. "They had ended things a few times before, either because of Pres or because he was feeling guilty about his wife and son. He always called, anyway and they always . . . saw each other." He felt himself blush. "But not this time. This time he didn't call. I'm almost a hundred percent she doesn't know where he is. She was too surprised. You can't fake that."

"Did anybody know about them?"

"She doesn't think so. She made an incredible effort to make sure Pres wouldn't know. She seemed really concerned about it."

"Why?" Sweeney asked him. "Why would she be so concerned? Lots of kids' parents date after they get divorced."

"He was married. She was probably ashamed of that." He was silent for a minute, then said, "I think I understand. It's like when you . . . when your kid is already dealing with something that's . . . really bad, like Maura, or like her son being sick, well, you feel like you have to make it up to them somehow. You have to be extra good. You have to give them all of you." He paused. "She's still in love with her ex-husband. It was really weird. She's so angry at him. But she clearly still loves him. It was kind of sad, actually."

"I wonder how he feels about her," Sweeney said.

"From what she said, he left her for someone else. So he must have fallen out of love with her."

"It's not usually that simple."

He looked up and found her looking troubled. "Yeah, well, I just wish I knew what Churchill was doing that weekend. Where did he go after he left the encampment?"

"He was doing research, right?" Sweeney said. "So he must have gone off to do something on Josiah Whiting."

"This guy who told me about the affair said he was going to look at graveyards."

She sat up. "But I don't understand what it was he was looking at. Okay, so I'm looking into his gravestones because I'm interested in the way his death's-head designs change. But Kenneth Churchill isn't an art historian. So, why was he interested in Whiting's designs?"

"I don't know," Quinn said. "You're the academic. But I'd imagine if you're studying someone's life and that someone was a gravestone maker, you'd want to study his gravestones."

"I suppose," Sweeney said. "Do you have any idea what his book was about?"

"Everybody I've talked to says that he was working on something that was going to 'change the scholarship,' something 'explosive.' "

"Well, in the context of academia, that can mean anything," Sweeney said. "In the art world, you can be explosive by asserting that someone was influenced by painter A rather than painter B. But it's interesting that he used those words. He must have been planning to prove that Josiah Whiting wasn't who we thought he was."

"And who was that?" Quinn asked.

She sat up on the bed and fluffed his pillows behind her. Again, he felt a flash of annoyance, that she'd taken some kind of liberty. "A Revolutionary hero. A stonecutter."

He stood up and went over to the window. It was dark outside and he stared back at his reflection. Even in the glass, he could see the bags under his eyes. "It's funny, isn't it? That Josiah Whiting disappeared and then Kenneth Churchill is writing about him and he disappears too?"

"Yeah. If we knew what he was working on, we might be able to, I don't know, kind of retrace his steps. See who he talked to. Did you ask the wife about any other research materials? Even if he has his laptop and all of his research materials with him, there's got to be something."

"Nothing. I searched his BU office and his home office pretty well, although . . ."

"Although what?"

"Well, it's just that most of the home office was pretty messy, newspapers and books and everything all over the place, but the desk wasn't. It looked like someone had cleaned it off."

"You think he took everything related to the book with him when he left."

"I don't know. Why would he do that?" Quinn rubbed his eyes. "Why would he take it all with him?"

"If he didn't want anyone to know what he'd found out?"

"But that's ridiculous. We're talking about someone who's been dead for two hundred and fifty years."

"I know," Sweeney said. "Listen, I'm working on this gravestone thing, anyway. I could just kind of . . . I don't know. Put myself in his shoes and try to figure out who he was talking to and what he found out."

"Would you do that? You don't know how much that would help me out."

"Sure. When I talked to George Whiting the other day, he said that Kenneth Churchill asked him about whether Josiah Whiting and John Baker could have been spies for the British. George Whiting was pretty pissed off about it, but there might be something there. I'll look into it a little bit more. Oh, hey, I was going to tell you, I was looking around in one of the tents that sells uniforms today and I asked the guy if he could tell me anything about the guy in the woods. From his uniform, I mean. He said that the uniform wasn't very well made, that it was probably made by a reenactor himself rather than by a real tailor. He described it as the kind of thing that ends up in a thrift shop. So, I was thinking, maybe you should ask around at all the thrift shops in the area. See if they sold the uniform to the guy in the woods."

"That's a good idea. Thank you." Christ, he was tired. He yawned and Sweeney yawned too, then smiled and got up, leaving a rumpled depression in the center of the bedspread. "Hey, I just remembered something. Kenneth Churchill's wife said he went to London back in May, to do research on the book."

"London? London, England?"

"That's what she said. I thought it might help you."

"That's weird." She yawned again. "I'm going to bed," she said, slipping his fleece jacket over her head and handing it to him.

"Thanks again for watching Megan." He was embarrassed suddenly. "Thanks for this afternoon too. The thing with the doctor guy."

"Oh, don't worry about it." She looked down at the floor and her hair fell in front of her face. "It was kind of awful. I could see him starting to do it and I . . . thought I should get you out of there."

He looked up at her, and when she met his eyes, he said, "It's funny how certain things bring it up. I cut myself on a piece of wire in the basement a couple of weeks ago. Gashed myself good. There was blood everywhere and I just flipped out. I was yelling and . . . and crying like a baby. Thank God Megan was taking her nap. I was embarrassed as hell about it."

He watched her, seeing something cross her face that he couldn't quite identify. Sadness. Pain. She almost winced and then she nodded. "For me," she said. "It's loud noises. Cars backfiring. That kind of thing. And the smell of, you know, gunpowder. Explosives." The room was very quiet, and all he could hear was Megan's even breathing from her playpen. Quinn was confused. What was she talking about? She must have seen it on his face because she went on, her head bowed, a few pieces of her red hair falling out of her ponytail and onto her cheek.

"Remember that night at that bar where they were having a session," she said after a minute. "When I told you that I was engaged to an Irish guy who played music?" He nodded. "Well, he died. In a bombing. Right in front of me. I probably should have died too. But I didn't."

He stared at her, not sure what to say.

"It was almost two years ago now. It gets better. It really does."

"I'm so sorry." He wanted to touch her, put an arm around her or something, but he wasn't sure how she'd take it, so he stayed where he was and watched her face.

She got up and went to the window. "So, you said you're doing okay, but how are you really doing?"

"I don't know, to tell you the truth. It's better now. Like I said, having Megan helps. I have to keep it together for her. Although these days, I'm not doing a very good job of balancing home and work." He told her about Havrilek's ultimatum. "So I gotta figure out what happened to this guy. I mean, I guess my job's on the line." He rubbed his eyes. "It seems so strange somehow. That he would just take off. I always heard about people taking off on their wives and kids. Even investigated a few of 'em myself. But now, after Maura, I just don't understand how you could do it. I guess I'm figuring this guy's got to be dead. But then the question is, Where is he?"

Sweeney stood up to go and as she closed the door behind her, he looked around at his room, at his sleeping daughter. And he whispered it again to himself, "Where the hell is he?"

TWENTY-TWO

WHEN SHE GOT BACK TO HER ROOM, SWEENEY SAT ON THE edge of the bed for a long time, thinking about what Quinn had told her. He had asked Cecily Whiting if anyone else knew about her relationship with Kenneth Churchill. She didn't think so, but did Pres know? She remembered being twelve. She had always known when her mother was seeing someone new. It was small things, extra attention paid to her perfect makeup, whispered phone conversations, a feeling sometimes in the middle of the night that there was someone else in the apartment. Children were amazingly astute observers of parental behavior and were able to pick up on things that adults didn't even know they were doing. What were the chances that Pres hadn't known? Pretty small, probably.

Sweeney suddenly remembered telling Pres she wanted to write something about Josiah Whiting. He'd hesitated, and thinking back on it, she was almost sure that he had been about to say something about Kenneth Churchill. She could ask him, but she didn't like the idea of bringing up such a painful subject.

She got ready for bed and dialed Ian's number, but he didn't answer and the voice mail picked up after four rings. She waited for a second after the beep, then said, "Hi. It's Sweeney. You must be out on the town. Anyway, I just wanted to say that I'm sorry about last night. I was tired and

I, well . . . I'm not as much of a raging patriot as I sounded. So, anyway . . . So, I miss you." She paused, about to hang up. "Hail, Brittania!"

She sat in the middle of the bed for another few minutes, holding the phone, feeling strangely bereft. He had as much right to be out as she did, but it was two in the morning in London, for God's sake. Where was he?

She scrolled through her phone book and when she reached Toby she pressed SEND.

"Hey," he said. "How's Concord?"

"Okay. Where are you?"

"At home. Why?"

"I don't know. I didn't want to bug you if you were out."

"It wouldn't be bugging me." She could hear the sound of his banging a door closed in the background.

"What are you doing?"

"Cleaning."

"Toby, why do you always clean when you're talking to me? You do it when I'm there and you do it on the phone too."

"I don't know."

"Can't you just sit and talk to me? Am I so boring that you have to do something else?"

"You're definitely not boring." She could hear the sound of water, the bathtub, she thought, and she could see him perfectly, wearing old sweatpants and a T-shirt, his unruly dark hair falling over his forehead, his glasses misted up from the water. She felt a sudden sense of longing for Toby. She missed him. They hadn't seen much of each other lately. He'd been on a writing jag and she'd been working hard.

"So, what's going on with you? How's the writing going?" she asked him.

"Really good. I had such a good day of writing. I think I'm pretty near to a rough draft. Are you talking to Ian while you're out there?"

"Why do you ask that?"

"Because I was thinking that you guys have been talking a lot lately and I was thinking that if you continued to talk even when you were away from home that it would really mean something. That it would be like your relationship translated, if you know what I mean."

"We don't have a relationship. We're phone buddies."

"Hmmm. Well, it's interesting to me, is all. What's going on with your stonecarver guy?"

Sweeney told him about what had been going on. When she was finished she said, "So, you should come out and visit. It's nice out here. We can have dinner at this inn I'm staying at."

"Okay. How about Wednesday?"

"Yeah. Good. That'll be fun." She listened to him scrubbing something and then said, "Hey, you never told me what happened with Lily."

"I didn't?"

"No. You just said things didn't work out."

"Oh, yeah, well. She said that I was still hung up on you. That until I wasn't hung up on you anymore, I wouldn't be able to really be there with her. Something like that. Sounded like psychobullshit to me."

Sweeney didn't say anything for a minute. Then she said, "But we didn't even . . ."

"No, we never did. Lily said that was the problem, that it just kind of hung out there, that we'd never resolved it one way or the other." There was a heavy silence on the phone and then he said, "God, my sink is really disgusting."

"Toby!" Sweeney didn't know what to say, so she listened to him scrubbing out the inside of the sink. Finally she lay down on her side, the phone still to her ear. "So, are you coming out on Wednesday?"

"Yeah," he said. "If I'm done with this floor by then."

She laughed and hung up on him.

Twenty-three

Sweeney and Pres were standing in the South Burying Ground, looking at George Whiting's list of likely Josiah Whiting gravestones.

"So, your grandfather says that he did that one, but I'm really not sure," Sweeney said. "See, the borders aren't the same. And look at the lettering. Josiah Whiting tended to use those rounded o's, and these ones are different. We'll keep it on a maybe list, but I'm not convinced."

"Why couldn't he just make them different one day?" Pres asked. "I write different sometimes. Like, I used to put smiley faces over my i's but then I realized that was stupid."

"Good point. Okay, we'll hang on to it."

They spent another thirty minutes checking stones against the list, and Sweeney put down three more stones as definite Josiah Whitings and another two as possibilities.

The definites, once she was able to focus on them, offered lots of possibility. She took photographs of the stones and sketched their shapes, noting the dimensions, as well as some of the more interesting features. She would have to make prints and lay all the photographs out to get a good sense of what was going on here, but even from photographing them, she had the distinct sense that Josiah Whiting's style had indeed evolved over time. The face on the Abner Fall stone started out as a fairly straightforward death's-head, the skull shaped like a lightbulb, the eyes round and hollow, similar to the other death's-heads you saw on eighteenth-century stones. But as with his stones in the Hill Cemetery, Josiah Whiting's skulls on these stones had changed. As time went on, the eyes became more expressive, the pupils larger and more finely carved, and the hair became wilder, more Medusa-like.

"This is really interesting," she told Pres, scrolling through the photographs in her digital camera. "Check this out. The first stone we have here was made for someone who died in 1762. It's pretty close to other death's-heads from the period. But then things start to change. His faces become much more expressive and more human."

"And crazier," Pres said.

"You're right, they get crazier. The question is why. Was it symbolic of his own mental state? Was he trying to say something about the political situation? Or was it a reflection of his own evolving theology?"

Pres gave a little shrug, then looked down at the ground as though he was embarrassed that he couldn't answer her question.

"Anyway, that was a good day's work," she said. "Do you want to go get some ice cream or something?"

He looked pleased at that. "Okay. Yeah, that would be good."

They walked back to Main Street and found a little café that served ice cream sundaes. Pres ordered a banana split and Sweeney got a strawberry concoction—strawberry ice cream, strawberry syrup, and strawberries and whipped cream. They found a table by the window and Pres shrugged out of his coat, then put down his ice cream. Sweeney saw his hands shake a little as he set it down, slopping whipped cream onto the table. He mopped it up with a napkin while Sweeney pretended to be unzipping her jacket.

"They never found out who that man was," Pres said after a minute, through a mouthful of ice cream. "I asked my mom to find out and she called the police and they still don't know."

Sweeney watched him for a moment. "Yeah. I was at the

encampment yesterday and they were asking around, but as far as I could tell, no one there knew him."

"Wouldn't his family miss him? Don't you think he has a family?"

"I don't know. Some people have lost touch with their families, or they don't want to see them. He could have been homeless."

"But why was he wearing that uniform?" Pres seemed troubled. "Why was he in the woods?"

"I don't know. I wish I knew, but I don't."

Pres looked down at the table for a minute. "But he . . ." Sweeney saw something very adult cross his face—caution, maybe. She was positive that what he said next was not what he'd been about to say. "He was in the woods. Why was he in the woods? What was he doing in my grandparents' woods?"

Sweeney put down her spoon and looked at him. "Pres, why do I feel like there's something you're not telling me?"

He looked up and she almost thought he was going to smile. But then he looked down and mumbled miserably, "There's not."

"Okay." They ate in silence for a few minutes and then Sweeney said, "Did your mom tell you I came by the museum?"

"Yeah. She said she told you about Josiah and April nineteenth."

"She did. What do you think happened to him that day?"

"I don't know. He probably got killed by the Redcoats. What else could have happened to him?"

That was the question, Sweeney told herself. What else could have happened to him?

Pres pushed away his ice cream and looked up at her. "Do you have a husband?"

Sweeney was slightly taken aback. "No. I'm not married."

"Well, are you going to get a husband?"

"I don't know," she said, trying not to smile. "Husbands aren't the kind of thing you go out and get."

"So, you don't even have a boyfriend?"

"Well, there's a guy, a man I know who's kind of my boyfriend, but I don't know if he really is. He lives in London, so it's kind of hard for him to be my boyfriend, but if anyone was, it would be him. I guess. I don't really know." She was babbling and Pres looked at her as though she'd disappointed him.

"Wouldn't you know if he was your boyfriend?" It was as though he had been looking forward to some kind of romantic certainty in his adult life and was horrified to discover that it might not exist.

"I don't know, Pres. It's complicated. I almost got married once, to a guy I really, really loved a lot. And then he died and it's kind of hard to feel like I'll ever want to get married now. But it's not this guy's fault, you know. And I like him too. It's just that . . . Does any of this make any sense to you?"

"That's how my mom is," Pres said sadly. "I think my dad was like that guy. She never really wanted to have any other husband."

"Did she ever have any other boyfriends?" Sweeney asked innocently. She couldn't come right out and ask Pres if he knew that his mother had been seeing Kenneth Churchill, but maybe this was a way to find out.

"Yeah, maybe," he said vaguely. "A couple of guys."

"What about you?" she asked.

"Me?" He looked up at her incredulously. "No way. All the girls at school think I'm weird. Because I'm sick and everything."

"Well, they're just stupid."

"Yeah." But he didn't sound convinced. "I went to this math camp last summer, before I got sick. And I met this girl there. She was really cool. We could just talk about stuff. That was the cool thing about her, you could just talk to her, like she wasn't even a girl or anything. And she liked the same stuff I like."

She flinched. That kind of pain was no less real because you were twelve. If anything, it was worse, she remembered. "That's the best," she said. "When you like the same stuff."

As they were walking out of the café, Pres said, "I was thinking that maybe people saw that man go into the woods. People who live around my grandparents' house. Maybe they would know why he went in there and why he . . . why he went in there."

"Maybe." Sweeney wasn't sure what he was getting at.

"Well, maybe we could go ask them, you know, like, interview them and find out. They probably wouldn't talk to me because I'm a kid, but they might talk to you, like, if you said that you're a professor."

Sweeney turned to look at him. "Pres, I know it was horrible finding that body, but you have to let the police do their job. I'm sure they've already asked everyone who lives nearby about what they saw around the time when the guy probably died. I don't think we should get involved."

"But they don't know . . ."

"What don't they know?"

It was a crisp, breezy fall day and out on the sidewalk, Sweeney's hair blew across her face. Blinded for a moment, she missed whatever expression it was that Pres's face held as he said, "Nothing. I'm walking home," and he turned and left her there, watching his retreating figure.

BACK AT THE INN, SHE FOUND WILL BAKER IN THE FOYER, ARranging red and white dahlias in a pewter pitcher. She had been standing there for a few seconds before he became aware of her presence and turned around to say, "Hello. How are you today?"

"I'm fine," Sweeney said. "Do you have a few minutes to talk?"

He was wary all of a sudden, but politeness won out. "Of course," he said, turning away from the half-finished flowers. "Is everything okay with your room?"

"Everything's fine. Actually, I was wondering if I could ask you about Josiah Whiting and your ancestor John Baker."

The effect of her words was quietly explosive. He had been holding five or six blooms in one hand and suddenly they fluttered to the carpeted floor. Sweeney bent down and picked them up, handing them back to him.

"S-S-Sorry about that," he stammered. "These gloves . . . What did you want to know about them?"

"Well, I think I told you that I'm doing some research on Josiah Whiting. I was talking to Cecily Whiting at the Minuteman Museum and she explained that everything we know about what happened to Josiah Whiting on April nineteenth comes from John Baker's account. So I was hoping you could tell me a little bit more about him."

"Of course. Yes. Why don't we sit down in the lounge. It should be fairly quiet this time of day." They sat down, Sweeney in one of the big, comfortable chairs by the fire and Will Baker on the couch across from her. He was wearing an open-necked oxford shirt, showing his skinny Ichabod Crane neck and oversize Adam's apple. Sweeney tried to put him at ease by smiling and relaxing in her chair. But he leaned forward and his hands played nervously with the sofa cushions.

"Why are you interested in Josiah Whiting again?" he asked.

"I've gotten really interested in his work, particularly his death masks. I was hoping to find out a little bit more about him, about his life, in order to figure out where the death masks came from. I kind of have this theory that they may correspond to his interest in politics, that in fact they may reflect the growth of democracy in the colonies."

"Interesting," Will Baker said. "I hadn't ever thought of it, but, of course, that's right, to some extent the gravestones must have reflected the personal lives of the men who made them."

"What do you know about him?"

"Probably the same sorts of things that Cecily told you. His family was from the Plymouth area and he moved up here with them when he was in his teens, I believe. His father was a stonecutter as well and he apprenticed until he was eighteen or so, when he began making his own stones. He knew my ancestor John Baker quite well, and of course everything we know about Whiting's heroism on April nineteenth comes from Baker's narrative. What are you looking for in particular?"

"I don't know exactly. How did Whiting get involved in Revolutionary politics?"

"Well, we don't know much about him, but we can infer a lot from what we know about John Baker. Baker was a member of a local Sons of Liberty group. Do you know about the Sons of Liberty?" Sweeney shook her head. "They were the men responsible for the Boston Tea Party. The British called them the Sons of Violence and they certainly were violent. They saw violence as the only way of overcoming the power of the British administration in Boston. My ancestor was one of the leaders of the local Sons of Liberty. He was also involved with the Boston group; he knew Sam Adams and Paul Revere and he was responsible for a lot of the planning for the local Minuteman companies.

"We know that Whiting was also involved in the Sons of Liberty because Baker wrote about their friendship later in his life, when he was reflecting on his own role in Lexington and Concord. But if his path progressed the way Baker's did, he would have started out being fairly apolitical and then gradually becoming politicized with the passage of the Intolerable Acts."

"Would it make sense to you that his newly radical political leanings started around, say, 1770?" Sweeney asked, checking her notes for the date when Whiting's stones really started to change.

"Yes, I would say that's about right."

"I got a lot of good information from George Whiting, and Cecily too," Sweeney said. "You must have known them most of your life, growing up here in Concord."

"That's right," Will Baker said, looking away. Sweeney glanced down at his hands again and found them furiously twisting the edge of the cushion. "Bruce and I are of an age. We went to high school together." He blushed slightly and Sweeney watched the Adam's apple bob quickly up and down.

"Did you go to Vietnam too?" Sweeney asked him.

"No, no, I didn't." He sat up straight in his chair. "Was there anything else you wanted to know about?"

Sweeney, ignoring his obvious desire to finish the conversation, said, "George told me that Kenneth Churchill was looking into Josiah Whiting's stones too. He was staying here. Did you ever talk to him about it?"

Baker stared at her levelly, but she saw him swallow hard a couple of times. "Yes, he stayed here quite frequently and so he did come talk to me. He interviewed me about John Baker and I knew him from the hobby, of course." She must have looked confused because he explained, "That's what those of us who are members of regiments and militia companies call it. I've never liked 'reenactor' myself. Kenneth joined the Concord Minuteman company last year."

"What did he want to know about?"

"Well, I remember he was very interested in Baker and in the account that he gave later of April nineteenth. It's one of the most well known accounts of the day, because he was literate, you see, so it's very well written. But Mr. Churchill was very interested in that account and in whether there were any other accounts that might give him some more information about Josiah Whiting's death."

"And are there?"

"Not that I know of. I have some family papers and I even looked through them for him, but I didn't find anything else that referenced Whiting."

"Well, thanks for all your help," Sweeney said. "I really appreciate it."

"You're very welcome." He stood up quickly.

"Oh, one other thing," Sweeney said. "When I was talking to George Whiting, he said that Kenneth Churchill seemed very interested in the possibility of there being an unknown spy in Concord. He even seemed to think it could be Whiting or Baker. Is this anything you've ever heard about?"

Will Baker turned to look at her and Sweeney saw that he was genuinely surprised. He had not been expecting the question.

"No," he said, looking strangely at her. "No, I never heard anything like that." He drew himself up and held the dahlias out as though they were a weapon. "But if you don't mind, I have to get back to my work."

TWENTY-FOUR

QUINN WAS BROWSING THROUGH VINTAGE PAJAMAS, TRYING to figure out how men could ever have worn such hideous things, as he tried to keep an eye on Megan, who was playing with a used teddy bear in the toy section of a thrift shop in a Lexington church basement.

He had woken up Sunday morning feeling stymied on the Kenneth Churchill front and figured that it might be worth following up on Sweeney's thrift-store idea. He didn't want to mention it to Andy until he knew there was anything in it, but if he got a lead on the uniform the guy in the woods had been wearing, he might be able to offer up a good clue. He'd be doing Andy a favor and it would probably get back to Havrilek too.

So he'd looked in the Yellow Pages and made a list of the thrift shops within a twenty-mile radius. A lot of them were closed on Sunday, but he'd found a few that weren't, including one in Lexington.

He looked through the rack of Halloween costumes, flipping through gorilla suits and old prom dresses and Cleopatra outfits, but there wasn't anything resembling a soldier's uniform.

"Do you ever get Revolutionary War uniforms?" Quinn asked the woman behind the counter. She looked up from the magazine she was reading—*News of the World*—with barely disguised contempt.

"Not that I've ever seen," she said, turning a page with a lime green fingernail, though Quinn wasn't entirely sure she would know what a Revolutionary War uniform looked like. She so clearly wanted him gone that he decided not to press the point.

"Okay, thanks."

He tried the next thrift shop, this one back in Concord and found an even more meager assortment of costumes, a few of those plastic kids' Halloween costumes you bought at the drugstore and, again, a rack of old prom dresses. One of them reminded him of a dress Maura had once had to buy as a bridesmaid. It had been an ugly dress, he remembered, a kind of peach color, with a big bow over one shoulder. She had tried it on for him before the wedding and they had laughed about it.

When he asked the kid behind the counter about Revolutionary War uniforms, though, the kid said, "Not Revolutionary War, but we had a sort of a Civil War uniform. This really scruffy-looking guy came in and bought it. I was never sure if it was because he had a thing for Civil War reenactments, or if it was just warm."

"Would you have any way of tracking down a customer, if you had sold something like a Revolutionary War–era uniform?"

"Not really. A lot of our customers pay cash, so we wouldn't really be able to find them. Sorry."

"That's okay. I was just curious. That's probably true of most thrift shops, right?"

"I'd say so. Unless you're talking high-end consignment shops."

Quinn got Megan buckled into her car seat and sat in the driver's seat for a minute, thinking. He hadn't been able to prove Sweeney's theory, probably wouldn't be able to, but he could suggest it to Andy. They'd been assuming all along that the man found in the uniform was a Revolutionary War reenactor, but Sweeney's idea about the thrift shops was a pretty good one. What if the guy was someone who had just bought the uniform at a thrift store because it was warm? If it was a homeless person, it might explain why there didn't seem to be any family looking for him. It might not turn into anything, but it seemed worth passing on.

Quinn stopped in at the station, and when he said he wanted to see Detective Lynch, the receptionist, her hair piled in an unlikely and unmovable beehive, glared and told him to wait. A few minutes later Chief Tyler came out into the waiting room. "You looking for Andy?"

"Yeah. I might have something for him on the uniform on the guy in the woods. Just an idea. You know where he is?"

Tyler looked around the waiting room and then said in a low voice, "Up where they found the body. Come on, I'll take you."

They parked on Monument Street and Tyler waited while Quinn wrestled Megan into her backpack carrier. "Normally, I wouldn't let you bring a kid to a crime scene," he said. "But if you keep her in that thing, it oughtta be okay."

They followed a well-trampled path into the woods and then hiked along an older, even more well trodden path. The woods were moderately thick, the taller trees shading the sun out so that it was dark and cool as they walked along. Quinn looked around and wondered what kind of trees they were and how long they had been there. It was the kind of thing he really ought to pay more attention to, he told himself. Someday pretty soon Megan was going to be asking him questions like that, and he didn't want to seem stupid.

After a few minutes he caught sight of a small wooden structure ahead through the trees. As they got closer, he saw that someone had put orange traffic cones around the house and there was yellow police tape strung around the perimeter. Andy Lynch was standing in front of the little house, staring at it with rapt concentration. "Hey," he called out. "How ya doin'?"

"Okay." Quinn introduced him to Megan. "This is the place, huh?"

"Yeah. The body was right about there." He pointed to an otherwise unremarkable spot on the ground at the side of the building, and they both stared at it for a few minutes. Quinn ignored Megan, who was leaning out of the backpack, wanting to be taken down. All he needed was for her to eat the dirt where the poor guy had breathed his last. "Hey," Andy said, "she can't understand what I'm saying, can she?"

"No. Don't worry about it." But Quinn wondered. Would Megan grow up with a horrible memory of the day her father took her to a murder scene?

"Yeah, so, look at this, Quinn. We got blood, his blood, here, here, and here." He pointed to spots on the ground twenty, fifteen, and ten feet from where the body had been found. "I've got other blood too, but not as much."

"The murderer got cut up a little in the process."

"That's what I'm thinking." Andy rubbed his crooked nose in a gesture Quinn remembered from a long time ago.

"What were you trying to figure out when we came up?" Quinn asked him. "You were pretty deep in thought."

"Yeah," Andy said. "I was just thinking that if you were standing over here, you wouldn't even have seen the guy. It's almost like he was hiding, you know?"

"Could be. The blood suggests that he was dragged or dragged himself. Maybe his killer went away and he tried to hide."

They stood for a minute and listened to the silence of the woods. It was a nice day, the trees were pretty, yellow, and that red color that you didn't see any other time of the year. It was hard to imagine how someone could have been killed there.

"So, what did you get from the girlfriend?" Andy asked after a minute.

"She says nobody else knew about them and I basically believe her, though she may be fooling herself. At least I believe that she believes it, if you know what I mean. They'd been seeing each other since February, kept saying that they shouldn't anymore, et cetera, but the really interesting thing is this: Guess where they had their little meetings?"

Andy looked interested.

"Right here," Quinn said. "Right here. The clubhouse,

she called it. She said that Bruce Whiting used to meet his mistress here too. I think she liked that. I think she thought it was kind of a 'screw you' to her ex."

"No shit?" Andy looked at the clubhouse. "So, how does it all fit? Maybe this guy, our John Doe, maybe he found them in the clubhouse going at it and maybe he threatened to tell his wife and Churchill killed him. How's that?" Andy looked proud of himself.

"Yeah, except she seemed genuinely surprised that he was missing." He thought back, remembering his impression that she had almost been relieved that something seemed to have happened, that it wasn't just that he didn't want her anymore. "I don't know. I don't think I buy it."

"Well, listen to this. We checked on the bayonet thing. You were right. A bayonet attachment of exactly that size almost definitely caused the wounds on our John Doe. The guy says he made about twenty-five similar ones, owned mostly by people who were also at the reenactment on George Whiting's land. So, it's not definitely down to Churchill, but it narrows it down a lot. Say we get a match on Churchill for the other blood at the scene, doesn't it look like Churchill killed this guy, got hurt in the process, and took off because he knew that his injuries would incriminate him?" Andy said.

"It's gotta be," Quinn said. "Of course, the other possibility, if it's his blood, is that someone else attacked both of them, but then where's Churchill? He couldn't have hauled his own body off."

"You're right."

"Hey, I was thinking. What about the ex-husband?"

"Bruce Whiting?" Tyler had been quiet up to now, listening to them. "Bruce is a good guy."

"Yeah, but what if he found out his ex-wife was getting it on with Churchill? How do you think he'd feel?"

Tyler said, "No way. He left her. His new wife is . . . well, let's just say she's a little bit younger than Cecily Whiting. He's a happy man."

Quinn looked over at him. He decided he liked John Tyler

just a bit less. "Still, maybe he found out and told Churchill that he'd . . . I don't know. Maybe he threatened him or something. I was thinking I should talk to him. Just about Churchill's disappearance. Get a sense of whether or not he knew."

"But how are you going to do that without telling him?" Andy asked. "If he doesn't know."

"Would it be the worst thing? I mean, it's got to come out sooner or later. The guy's missing. I'm going to have to tell his wife about it when I talk to her. I've got evidence of foul play and if he's not a suspect, then I have some pretty good reasons to suspect something bad happened to him. Whatever the guy wanted to keep hidden, he lost control of it when he didn't come home."

"Nah. Not yet. Let's see what happens with your guy. See if he shows up. We're working on the ID for our John Doe. There was a cleaned-up photo in the papers today. We'll see if anybody knows who he is, and our guys are trying to get us some more stuff from the scene too."

Quinn wanted to pursue his idea further, but Andy seemed to want to move on. "Andy, I had kind of an idea about your John Doe. I mean, we've been looking for a connection between the guy in the woods and Kenneth Churchill and maybe there isn't one. Maybe he was just a homeless guy or something. Maybe he found the costume at a thrift shop."

"But why would Kenneth Churchill kill him if he didn't know him?"

"I don't know, but sometimes people are killed by accident. Hang on . . ." Quinn's cell phone rang and he rummaged in his jacket pocket, losing the phone amid the teething rings and pacifiers. "Quinn here."

There was a raspy breath and he thought he heard a sob.

"Hello?" he said.

There was a long silence and then, "Detective Quinn?" He recognized the voice, though he couldn't place it. "It's Beverly Churchill."

"Mrs. Churchill." For some reason, her voice caught him

off guard. "I was just going to call you, to update you. Unfortunately, I haven't found any leads, but I'm out in Concord and I—"

"No, I . . . I'm calling because I just got a call from the credit card company. Kenneth used his card in Lexington yesterday. A McDonald's and gas station off Ninety-five."

Andy moved into action. "All right, get me her number and the credit card info and we'll get out there and see what we can find."

"Great," Quinn said. "If it was yesterday, then he might still be around. God, I wonder where he's staying? You want to ride with me?"

But Andy grinned at him.

"You kidding me, Quinn? You can't come out with us," Andy said. "We're going to be interviewing witnesses. You have the kid."

"But I can put her in a stroller. You won't even know she's there. Come on, this is it. We're going to bring him in." But even as he said it, he knew he couldn't bring her.

"Timmy, no can do. Sorry. I'll call you later and let you know what we get, okay?"

"Come on, Andy. I need this."

"If it turns out that Churchill killed our guy, you'll get credit for making the connection. Don't worry about that."

"But . . ."

"Nope. Get a babysitter and meet us up there. I'm sorry, Quinn."

But his face, which Quinn studied for a minute before he turned away, didn't look sorry at all.

Twenty-five

CECILY WHITING WAITED FOR A MOMENT BEFORE CROSSING the street at the crosswalk. She wasn't sure why, but she had experienced a quick moment of caution, maybe sensed that someone was watching her. But all she saw was the group of thirty or so high school kids who had just gotten off the bus in the parking lot at the Old North Bridge.

She walked along Monument Street, her head down, trying to avoid being recognized by anyone walking by. It wasn't that she was doing anything wrong, it was just that she didn't want to have to stop and have a conversation with anyone. She knew that Bruce and Lauren were taking the kids to some pumpkin festival, so she wasn't worried about seeing them.

She waited to cut into the woods until she was almost to George and Lillian's house. Through the woods ahead, she could see Bruce and Lauren's house on the second lot. At first, after the divorce, she had sometimes gone up to look at their house, hoping to catch a glimpse of them, she realized, hoping to see something that would indicate that Bruce was unhappy. That he might be coming back to her. But it was just a house. Sometimes she'd seen Lauren walking outside in her bathrobe in the morning; sometimes she saw Bruce getting into his car. None of it revealed much of anything.

She was at the clubhouse in a couple of minutes. She had half expected the police to be there, but it looked as though they were done. There were orange traffic cones and the yellow police tape was still wrapped around the clubhouse. She stopped and listened. It was very quiet. She had to strain to hear anything but the quiet.

This was where Pres had found the body. She had tried to talk to him about it again on Friday. Worried because he'd seemed withdrawn for a couple of days, she'd sat across from him at the breakfast table and said, "Pres, at some point we're going to have to talk about what you saw in the woods that morning. Would you like to go talk to someone about it? The doctors gave us the name of a therapist who's supposed to be really good with kids."

He had looked up at her with contempt. "Well, I don't really think of myself as a kid," he said cruelly. "And I don't need to talk about it because I'm okay with it. He was dead. Big deal. Lots of people are dead." Then he had delivered the final blow. "I'm probably going to be dead." She had barely been able to hold it together, and after he'd left for school she had gone upstairs and had a good cry before going to work.

She felt the tears start to come and she sat down on the ground by the side of the walking path. Kenneth. She wanted Kenneth, wanted the comforting feel of his tall strength that reminded her so much of Bruce's body. The tears flowed and she began to sob as she looked at the clubhouse. It had been a long time since she had cried about anything other than Pres's leukemia. It felt odd, this kind of self-indulgent emotion. Kenneth. Where was he? The police seemed to think he'd had something to do with this guy's death.

If he had killed this man, it must have been for her, because of her. She wasn't sure what she meant, really, but the fact that the man had been killed here had to mean something. What if Kenneth had come here to meet her as usual, thinking she would just show up, without his calling her. It had happened once before, she realized with a start. Why hadn't she remembered that when the cop was asking her questions? There was that time when he had ended it, saying that his son had gotten into trouble in school, something about bringing a hunting knife with him on a field trip, and he felt guilty because he was gone so much. He hadn't called that weekend, but then she had gone to the clubhouse and he had been there.

What if he had . . . ? What? That was the question. What had he done? Perhaps he had found the man, and the man knew her and had threatened to tell, and Kenneth had attacked him. He had a temper. She had seen it once, after the last time Pres had gone into the hospital, and she had told him she couldn't see him anymore, that it was taking too much of her energy away from Pres. He had slammed the wall next to her in the clubhouse and screamed that he needed her, that he was getting closer to leaving his wife and she couldn't do this to him, not now.

Thinking about it, she got angry. Of all the selfish, sonofabitch things to say to her. But then she remembered how he had cried and apologized and said that he loved her and that was what made him do these things. She had made love to him, told him it was okay.

Cecily stood up and walked out into the afternoon. The trees were on fire with red and yellows and golds. The air smelled of smoke.

The things people do for each other, she thought. It is terrible the things people do for those they love.

BOOK TWO

TWENTY-SIX

THE BELOITS LIVED IN A GIANT HOUSE OUT ON ONE OF THE
roads heading back toward Route 2 that Quinn had passed
one day when he'd gotten lost on the way back to the inn.
The street was thickly lined with houses that he assumed
were supposed to look old but were clearly new construc-
tion. The big three-car garages and horseshoe driveways
gave them away.

"Nice place," Andy said as he pulled into the driveway
and parked in the middle, right up against the path leading to
the house. "Isn't it funny how you'd think being a cop would
mean that you spend all your time with lowlifes and crimi-
nals? But I've been in more houses like this since I've been
working homicide than the rest of my life put together."

"I know what you mean," Quinn said. "I guess it goes to
show that the rich don't get to be immune from all the bad
stuff or something. Sounds like they must have had a pretty
fucked-up relationship with their son if they didn't even
know where he was."

"Yeah, seems weird to me too. Anyway, we'll get the ba-
sics and then you can ask if there was any relationship with
Churchill."

"Sounds good," Quinn said. He had been playing with
Megan when Andy called. "We're back from the gas station,
Quinn," he'd said, his voice excited as a kid's. "I'll tell you
all about it, but get this. A guy called this morning to say his

wife recognized the drawing in the newspaper of the man found in the woods as possibly being of their son." Andy explained that Don Beloit had identified his son's body and when they asked how long he'd been missing, he had said that he really needed to talk to someone, to explain the whole thing, he said. Andy had told Quinn that he could come along if he wanted, in case there was some connection between these people and Churchill.

Now Quinn pushed the doorbell next to the huge front door and they listened to a series of medieval-sounding gongs go off somewhere in the house. A few minutes later the door was opened by a small, neat woman with short, frosted blond hair wearing black pants, a green sweater, and a silk scarf patterned with what looked to Quinn like horse's bits and reins.

"Come in," she said without introducing herself or asking for identification. She led them into a large formal dining room and motioned for them to sit down at the table. As they sat, a heavy, middle-aged man in red corduroy pants and a blue sport jacket came into the room. He was almost completely bald, with a delicate fringe of close-cropped white hair making a half-inch circle around his head. It almost made him look like one of those monks you saw in old movies.

"I'm Don Beloit," he said. "This is my wife, Ann."

"Can I get you some coffee?" Ann Beloit asked, looking as though the last thing she wanted to do was actually get them some coffee. Quinn and Andy said no thanks.

"Could you tell us what led you to call the Concord police this morning?" Andy asked. It was a good question, open-ended, and it would probably elicit more information than something like "who do you think killed your son?"

"We'd been away, you see," Ann Beloit was saying. "That's why we didn't realize until yesterday, when we saw the paper. He didn't . . . call us very often, so we didn't know where he was living or anything."

"Your son's name was Tucker, Tucker Beloit?" Don Beloit nodded. "Date of birth?" Andy asked.

"Two-fourteen-seventy."

"Thank you. So when you saw this police sketch in the newspaper, you recognized your son?" Andy passed the folded newspaper, and Quinn glanced down at the line drawing of what the man's face would have looked like if it hadn't been eaten by whatever it was that had eaten it.

"Yes," Ann Beloit said, not looking at the picture. "Not right away, but the more I looked at it, the more it seemed sort of familiar, if you know what I mean. And then I . . ." Her voice broke. It was the first emotion she'd shown, and Quinn found himself surprised by it. "And then I showed it to Don and he agreed that we should call you."

"Thank you. And you last heard from Tucker, when?"

"I'd say January," Don Beloit said. "Right?" His wife nodded.

"So, it wasn't strange that you hadn't heard from him in a while?" Andy asked.

"No. We weren't in touch with him," Ann said.

As though she knew there was more to be said, she went on. "Tucker was mentally ill. We had tried to get him into treatment programs, tried to get him to take his medication. But he always ended up leaving, stopping the meds. So finally we just realized there wasn't anything more we could do. We had to just . . . let go. He got in touch with us sometimes, maybe every couple of months, but this time it had been much longer."

Quinn looked out the window over Andy's shoulder. Was it his imagination, or had the trees grown suddenly brighter since yesterday? That always happened in the fall. You weren't paying attention, and then suddenly it was over.

"So the last time you were in touch with him, where was he living?" Quinn asked.

"Duxbury. He had been homeless, then he'd been living in this awful apartment building. We gave him money, but we don't know what happened to it. He would just give it away."

Andy asked them, "He didn't tell you he was coming to see you?"

Don Beloit spoke up. "There weren't any messages on the answering machine, but we'd been away for two weeks, so it's possible he called and hung up when no one answered."

"Well, the body had been there for about a week and it's been another week now, so that's unlikely," Andy said quickly. Quinn winced. He didn't need to be quite so graphic.

"And the other thing," Ann Beloit said, "is that we're not entirely sure he knew where the house was. We only moved in two months ago and, of course, we hadn't heard from Tucker during that time. He knew we were moving to Concord and we left the new phone number at the old one, in case he called."

"But it seems like he must have been coming to see you. Unless there was some other reason for him to be in Concord," Quinn pointed out.

For the first time since she'd walked into the room, Ann Beloit looked upset. "Yes, that was the first thing I thought of when I saw the picture, that he must have been coming to see us. And that makes me feel awful. I . . ." She choked back a sob and Quinn and Andy waited for a moment before she reached into her purse for a pack of tissues. "I hope you don't think that we're heartless or . . . but when he was younger we really tried to make things better for him. We spent a lot of money and . . . none of it seemed to do any good, really."

Don Beloit looked embarrassed at his wife's show of emotion. "Darn right we did," he said.

"As you know, the body was found wearing a Revolutionary War–era British soldier's uniform," Andy said, looking down at the notes in front of him. "Was that something he owned, that you knew of?"

Ann and Don Beloit glanced at each other, and Quinn saw her nod imperceptibly at him.

"Tucker always liked things related to war and . . . soldiers," Don said finally. "When he was little, he didn't just play with toy soldiers, he would read about real battles and then re-create them in the basement. He was obsessed. All the books he got out of the library, well, they were all about war and weapons. We just thought he was precocious, but then when he was eighteen, he became very sick. We found, well . . . weapons. In his room. Grenades and things like that. He'd been buying them from army surplus stores, from dealers. We didn't know what to do. In retrospect, we should have gotten him help then, but it's so hard to know. Anyway, he joined the Marines. We thought it would be good for him. Give him some discipline."

Quinn sat up, paying attention now. The Marines. Why were the Marines ringing a bell?

"They allowed him to join up?" Andy asked. "With his history?"

Don Beloit nodded. "Well, we didn't know what was the matter with him. If we had known, we would have gotten him some help, and it would have been on his record. But he was so excited about joining and it seemed like it might be a good thing for him. Might make him grow up, you know."

"When was this?" Quinn asked. "How long ago?"

"Nineteen-ninety," Don Beloit said. "He was in the Marines for a while and it was a really good time for him, or it seemed to be, anyway. He liked the training. But then came the Gulf War."

That was it. Now he had it. Kenneth Churchill had been a Marine and he'd fought in the Gulf War. That had to be the connection. He thought about waiting until they were done, but there were questions they needed to ask the Beloits.

"Andy," Quinn said, leaning forward in his seat. "Churchill was a Marine. Gulf War vet too." He could feel his heart speed up.

"Who's Churchill?" Don Beloit asked, looking confused.

"There's another man who may be involved in your son's death," Andy said quickly, giving Quinn a look that said, *Not now*. "What else can you tell us about—"

"Did he kill Tucker?" Ann Beloit looked very sad all of a sudden, and Quinn was afraid she was going to start crying.

"We don't know anything at this point. What else can you

tell us about Tucker's time in the Gulf War. Where did he serve?"

"He was machine-gun specialist, something like that," Don Beloit said. "He was in Saudi Arabia and then Kuwait, and everything seemed to go okay for the first couple of months, but then things really went wrong. There was some kind of accident. We never got the details, really. He shot someone. Another Marine. It may have been an accident and it may not have been. There wasn't a court-martial or anything, but even if he hadn't meant to do it, he had been negligent, so they sent him home. He was dishonorably discharged and he came to live with us. But that was when things got really bad. He started talking about these guys we'd never heard of, Colonel this and Colonel that. Our daughter, Allison, she looked them up and said they were famous military men, but from the French and Indian War and the Crimean War and all these crazy things." He looked up at them and Quinn could see tears in his eyes. "He talked about them like they were real people, like they were his friends. That was the hardest thing for us to take."

"Who was the man he killed?" Quinn asked.

"I don't remember. We could find out."

"Okay," Andy said. "Did you know any of his friends? Was there anyone he talked about or stayed in touch with once he got back?"

"He talked about people, but with Tucker it was hard to know what was real and what wasn't."

"Does that name, Kenneth Churchill, does that sound familiar to you?" Andy asked them. Both Beloits shook their heads.

"Okay, thank you. That's all for now. We'll have more questions for you in the next couple of days. But for now we really appreciate your being willing to come in. And we're sorry for your loss."

Don Beloit showed them to the front door, and as they started to walk away, he called after them, "I don't know what you can do, but if there's any way you can keep this, you know, kind of quiet, I'd really appreciate it. We just moved out here and we haven't met a lot of people yet. I hope that doesn't sound bad. Of course we want to find out who did this, but Tucker was, well, the Tucker we know died a long time ago, if you know what I mean."

Quinn didn't know what to say. Andy just nodded. "We'll do our best," he said.

When they were pulling away from the house, Andy turned to Quinn and said, "You thought that guy was an asshole, didn't you?"

"It's his son. I mean, his son's dead and all he can think about is what his new pals at the country club will think? Yeah, I thought he was an asshole."

"Thousand people would be thinking the same thing he was thinking," Andy said. "They just wouldn't have said it. Anyway, you shitting me about Churchill?"

"No. He was in the Marines. He went to the Gulf."

They drove for a few minutes in silence and then Andy said, "Okay. I want you on this military thing. I'm going to keep following up on the credit card. I'll get clearance from my guys for you to help me out on this. Do you need me to get the okay from your lieutenant?"

"No," Quinn said. "It's okay. He sent me here to find out what happened to Churchill, so he oughtta be cool with it. Thanks, Andy. I really appreciate it, you know."

Andy grinned and took the turn into the driveway of the station a little too fast and Quinn heard tires screech against gravel. "We're going to get Kenneth Churchill and we're going to arrest him for the murder of Tucker Beloit and I want you to find out why he did it."

TWENTY-SEVEN

AFTER HER CONVERSATION WITH WILL BAKER, SWEENEY HAD gone straight to the Minuteman Museum. There were a few tourists around, and when she asked the elderly volunteer at the ticket desk if she could talk to Cecily, she was told that she had the day off.

So Sweeney bought a ticket and decided to see what more she could learn from the exhibit on the spies of the Revolution. As she had remembered, the exhibit featured profiles of a few of the more prominent spies operating in the colonies in the 1770s.

"There were many spies operating during the American Revolution," the text read. "Information about the size and strength of troops and the movements of the whereabouts of General Washington and other military leaders was always in demand, and as much as Revolutionary fervor had taken hold of the colonies, there were always people willing to betray the fledgling country for financial gain. There were also so-called loyalists who spied for the Americans.

"The first American traitor was Boston's own Dr. Benjamin Church, a prominent member of the Committee of Safety and a friend and fellow conspirator of Paul Revere, John Hancock, Samuel Adams, and Dr. Joseph Warren. In September of 1775, a young woman, Church's mistress, was found to be carrying letters from Church to General Gage. The letters were coded but upon further examination were found to contain information about the number and size of the provincial forces. Church claimed that he had been conducting a double cross, that he had grossly exaggerated the size of the American force in order to trick the British. But his story was not believed and Church was locked up in a Connecticut jail. He eventually sought release on the grounds of his poor health and sailed to the West Indies on a ship that disappeared without a trace."

Sweeney read through the text of a display on the most famous spy of them all, Benedict Arnold, about how the pompous, greedy hero of the battle for Fort Ticonderoga, only just court-martialed, sought a promotion to the command of West Point. Of course, all along Arnold was secretly planning on turning West Point over to the British and was stopped only because of the untimely capture of his intermediary, John André, who was caught carrying suspicious letters from Arnold in his boot. The letters were forwarded onto General Washington, who had just arrived at West Point to find the command in a state of disarray and Arnold nowhere to be found. Sweeney read about the poor, unfortunate André, who was hanged for his crime while Arnold escaped to Britain, where he lived out the rest of his life.

She read through the information about the women who had spied during the Revolution and the different kinds of codes that were used, but there wasn't anything new that she hadn't seen the other day when she'd been to the museum.

Of course, she hadn't expected that Josiah Whiting's name would magically appear, but she had hoped there would be some kind of a clue. But when it came right down to it, the exhibit was fairly basic, directed at schoolkids and people who were just learning about Revolutionary history.

She needed something much more in-depth. It was Sunday, so the Concord Public Library wouldn't be open, and she doubted they'd have an extensive enough collection, anyway. It would have to be the university library.

She was in Cambridge in under thirty minutes and she found what she needed and stopped by her favorite Thai place to get takeout. She was on her way back to Concord just as it was starting to get dark, and she rolled down the windows in the Rabbit and smelled the chill in the air.

Hungry now, Sweeney watched CNN while she ate her Pad Thai and then turned off the TV, put on her pajamas, and spread the books out across the bed.

The Spies of the Revolution gave her a more detailed account of Arnold's treachery, and she read a vivid account of André's hanging, penned by a young surgeon who was present for the event.

> *It was his earnest desire to be shot, as the mode of death most conformable to the feelings of a military man, and he had indulged the hope that his request would be granted. At the moment, therefore, when suddenly he came in view of the gallows, he involuntarily started backward and made a pause.*
>
> *"Why this emotion, sir?" said an officer by his side.*
>
> *Instantly recovering his composure, he said, "I am reconciled to my death, but I detest the mode."*

She flipped through the indexes of all of the books, checking references to "spies" or "spying" for names she recognized, but came up empty-handed.

But what was it that she was looking for, anyway? George Whiting hadn't told her who Kenneth Churchill suspected of being a spy. It could have been Whiting, or it could have been Baker or anyone in Concord. Maybe Whiting had suspected someone else of being a spy.

And then there was Will Baker's response. He had been really nervous when she'd told him she knew about Kenneth Churchill's work, but she was pretty sure that her question about spies had been a complete surprise to him.

If Baker and/or Whiting had been a spy, she assumed that they would have been retained by the British administration in Boston to inform about the activities of the local Sons of Liberty they were involved in and about the preparations of the country people and the Minuteman groups. After all, someone had told General Gage about the stores of munitions in Concord. It stood to reason that there were loyalists who were passing information back to Boston and that there were local people who were doing it too.

What would either man's motivation have been? Was it possible they were secret loyalists? Sweeney supposed so, but it would have been an elaborate hoax, to be involved with all of the Revolutionary causes they were involved in, to train as Minutemen, to actually fight on the bridge on April 19.

She took out her notebook and looked through the sketches she'd made of Whiting's gravestones. Were these the gravestones of a man who was betraying his country? She looked carefully at the increasingly manic-looking death's-heads. It was as good an explanation as any, she supposed. And if Whiting had been a spy, it provided a possible explanation for his body never having been found. What if the attack by the Redcoats was all a front and he had in fact been spirited away?

She was thinking about what to do next when she happened to catch sight of a blurb on the back of one of the books. "A tour de force. Henkels illuminates the lives of some of the most colorful characters of the American Revolution." The praise was credited to Henrietta Hall, an American history professor at the university whom Sweeney had gotten to know last spring after Brad Putnam was killed.

She got the number through Information and when Henrietta's precise, Brahmin-toned voice answered on the fourth ring, Sweeney identified herself and asked Henrietta how she was.

"Fine, I suppose. I need to have hip-replacement surgery and I'm dreading it, but I must count my blessings. For eighty, I'm quite spry, really. Now, what can I help you with, Sweeney?"

"I'm looking at the gravestones of a guy named Josiah Whiting," Sweeney told her. "He was kind of a hero in the Revolution and he fought at the bridge in Concord on April 19, 1775, and then he disappeared. The story I've gotten from his descendants and people around town is that he was killed by the Redcoats—there's an eyewitness to his being bayoneted—and must have dragged himself into a pond or into the woods to die. The eyewitness account comes from John Baker, who was a good friend of Whiting's. Anyway, the possibility has been mentioned that Baker or Whiting or someone around them was actually a spy. So I started thinking, what if Whiting had turned and what if he slipped away during the fighting? It would have been a good way to disguise the fact that he'd fled. Maybe, like Benedict Arnold, he even got out of the country altogether."

"Well, I guess the first place to start would be to find out a bit more about the family. Did they have any sudden change in fortune? What happened to them after he was gone?"

"Good point," Sweeney said. "I don't know why I didn't think of that."

"As far as the spies of the Revolution go," Henrietta went on. "It's hard to say how many there really were. And people spied on all different levels. It could be as organized as Benedict Arnold's deception and as simple as someone casually mentioning troop movements in the tavern. I've written a bit about some lesser-known spies, but I definitely haven't come across Whiting's name. I know about Baker, of course, but again the name hasn't come up in the context of anything other than heroism. As for other Concord spies, I can't think of any who traveled in those circles."

"How would you try to find out whether or not someone was a spy? If it wasn't someone who had been caught spectacularly like Church?"

Henrietta said, "It's difficult. Most of these meetings and arrangements were made secretively and so we don't have records of them, except in a few cases when British soldiers gave accounts of their service and mentioned this or that colonial spy. I have a friend at the University of London who's doing some work in that area. When he's finished, his work may be very revealing. But generally speaking, there's not much out there."

"What's your friend's name?" Sweeney asked. "Would it be okay if I got in touch with him?" She was thinking about

Kenneth Churchill's trip to London in May. Perhaps he'd had the same idea that Henrietta had.

"Certainly. His name is Hamish Jones. Let me look for his e-mail. Here it is." She gave Sweeney the address. "Can I help you with anything else?"

"Actually, Henrietta, I was just wondering. Do you know a guy named Kenneth Churchill? He's at BU?"

"Yes, of course."

But there was something snippy in her voice that made Sweeney ask, "What do you think of him? He's not a friend, so you can tell me what you really think."

"I respect him as a scholar and not as a person," Henrietta said. "I'll leave it at that."

Sweeney thanked her for her help and said she'd be in touch. She composed a quick e-mail to Hamish Jones and just as she was about to get ready for bed, her phone buzzed and she checked the display. It was Ian.

"Hello," she said. "I was hoping it was you."

"Good," he said, sounding pleased. "How are you?"

"I'm fine. And I'm sorry about the other night."

"I'm sorry too. It was stupid. I'm not a very political person, but there's something about talking about the victories of you uppity colonials that just gets our backs up."

"So we're made up then?"

"We're made up."

"It's kind of a historic thing, you know. Our first fight."

"That's true. It's also our first makeup."

"And wouldn't it be so much more fun to do it in person?"

Sweeney stood up and went over to the window. The moon was nearly full and she watched the patterns it made behind the swiftly moving clouds.

"Sweeney?"

"Yeah?"

"What do you think about, you know . . . a real visit. No more of this phone stuff. It's too easy to have misunderstandings."

Her room seemed cold. "You're right," she said. She felt

dizzy all of a sudden and she sat down in the desk chair. "You're right."

"But . . . ?"

"But nothing. You're right." But she forced herself to say it and she was sure he could hear it in her voice.

"Well, good." He sounded uncertain. "I'll look at my calendar and see what works. Maybe around the first?"

"Okay, I'll look too." She wanted to get off the phone. Her stomach was suddenly pitching around as though she were on a cruise ship.

After they had hung up, she lay down on her bed, feeling sick.

They had just pulled out another little block of wood.

TWENTY-EIGHT

WHEN QUINN GOT BACK TO THE INN, BEVERLY CHURCHILL was standing out front. There were two suitcases next to her and she was staring into the road, as though she thought someone was going to emerge from it. She was wearing jeans and a red sweater with a thick cowl neck, and the sweater seemed to swallow her up. Her skin seemed even paler next to the blood-red wool, and her light eyes stared out at nothing.

"Mrs. Churchill?" He was confused. When they'd talked on the phone, he had told her where he was staying and she had mentioned coming out to Concord if they found anything, but what was she doing here now?

"Oh, hello. I was just . . . Marcus and I just got here. I was going stir-crazy at home and I thought maybe we should come out and stay here for a few days, just until we figure out what's going on with Kenneth."

He wasn't sure what to do. He didn't love the idea of having Churchill's wife staying at the inn, but there wasn't a lot he could do about it.

"This will be better," she said firmly, then looked down the street again. "Marcus said he was going to go downtown and I was just . . . wondering why he would do that."

"It's been a hard time for all of you," Quinn said. "Can I help you with the bags?"

"No, no, I can do it. It's just the two." She suddenly noticed that he had a stroller with a baby in it. "Is this your daughter?" She leaned over and studied Megan carefully. "She's beautiful."

"Thanks."

"Have you found Kenneth yet?"

"No, but the state police went out to the gas station and they're interviewing all of the employees. We hope to have something soon."

"Is he here?"

"I don't know. You have to remember that it's possible the card was stolen."

"But if it was, wouldn't he have reported it?"

"Mrs. Churchill, at this point, we just don't know. You'll have to wait and see."

"I know," she said, allowing him to open the door for her. "I know that, but it's so difficult. I mean, the not knowing. I almost wish they would just find him, because then it would be all over." She looked up at him. "But there's a part of me that doesn't want him to be found. I just can't imagine what he . . ."

Quinn stood with her while she checked in and then walked her up to her room. At the door he said, "I should tell you that we've identified the man in the woods. His name is Tucker Beloit. Does that name ring a bell at all?"

"No. I don't think so." She seemed scared all of a sudden. "Why? Should it?"

"Not necessarily. But he did serve in the Gulf War around the same time as your husband."

"So, you're still thinking that Kenneth killed him?"

"We don't know anything. That's very, very premature. I'm going to look into Beloit's military service tomorrow, see if we can find a connection, but at this point we're just still looking into things."

Megan gave a loud squeal and Quinn shifted her to his hip. "I'd better get her to bed. Let me know if you need anything."

Beverly Churchill smiled and said, "You know, I really do appreciate how nice you're being to me, even if I don't seem very grateful. You're doing more than you need to and I'm very . . . well, thank you." The blue eyes were very clear and her dark hair fell against her white cheek.

He smiled at her. "It's okay. Just doing my job."

Megan went right to sleep. It was ten and he wasn't tired at all, so he sat up, plugged in the baby monitor, and took the receiver with him down the hallway.

Sweeney answered the door after his first knock. She was dressed in old gray sweatpants and a T-shirt that had the word BASEBALL emblazoned across the front, her hair up in a messy ponytail. She looked up at him and said, "Wanna come in?"

"Sure. I just put Megan down and . . ." He held up the baby monitor. "I can hear her if she cries. You sure I'm not bothering you?"

"No, I'm actually glad of the company. I just went down and got a bottle of wine from the tavern and I don't want to drink all of it myself. Really. Besides, you didn't get to tell me about the guy in the woods." It struck him that she meant it, that for some reason she was glad he had come by. She held up one of the glass tumblers from the bedside table and he nodded, watching as she poured a velvet stream of red into the glass. It was rich and fruity when he tasted it, and as he sipped, he let the liquid roll on his tongue. Just the taste relaxed him.

"So, who is he?" she asked, propping herself up on the bed.

"His name is Tucker Beloit. It looks as though he was mentally ill and he was coming out to see his parents. But here's the thing. He had a connection to Kenneth Churchill." He told her about both men's military service. "It may not come to anything, but if they knew each other, it's beginning to look more and more like Kenneth Churchill must have killed him and taken off." He told her about the credit card and Beverly Churchill's coming out and checking into the inn.

"I interrupt some real work there?" he asked, pointing at the books spread out on her desk.

"Not exactly." She told him about her conversation with Will Baker. "So, I'm trying to figure out where Kenneth Churchill could have gotten this idea from. It may just be something he was throwing out there, but on the other hand, it's a pretty serious allegation. I tend to think he must have had some reason to ask. If Josiah Whiting was a spy, maybe that's why his gravestones got so weird. You know, a man fighting against his own conscience. Maybe that's the meaning of the death's-heads."

She was excited, pacing back and forth across the room while she talked. "You mean, a spy, like James Bond or something?" Quinn sipped his wine and stretched out his legs. Suddenly he felt very content, pleasantly exhausted.

"Kind of. He was killed, or disappeared, in 1775, so in those early days, he must have been passing on information about the underground organizations, about the preparations of the militia, that kind of thing. If he was a spy at all. That's the thing. I have no idea if he was or not. And it could have been John Baker too." She told him about Will Baker's response when she'd asked him about it.

He watched her. She seemed hyped-up to him tonight, as though she'd had too much caffeine, and her eyes seemed worried. "You're positive that there weren't any more notes, nothing indicating what he was working on?" she asked him. "That trip to London seems strange to me. I talked to a friend of mine who said that she knows someone in London who is cataloging a series of letters from British officers during the Revolution. I just feel like there must be something indicating what direction he was going in."

Quinn shook his head, then said, "I'll ask his wife about it again, though." He picked up the baby monitor and checked to make sure the little light was on, then replaced it on the bedside table and sat down in her armchair. He was suddenly very, very tired. He wanted to go to sleep, he wanted to go back to his room and get into bed and go to sleep. But Megan would be getting up soon. She'd napped for hours. He'd have to change her, get her dressed, fix her a bottle, find something to eat.

He must have sighed because Sweeney said, "What's the matter?"

"Nothing. I'm just tired. So how long are you staying out here, anyway?"

"I don't know. I was thinking just for the week, but now that I'm into Josiah Whiting, I'm thinking I'll stick around until I figure out what happened to him."

Quinn raised his eyebrows. "And until we figure out what happened to Kenneth Churchill?"

"Why not? What's wrong with that?"

He laughed at the hurt expression on her face. "Nothing, it's just that you like playing detective. I can tell."

"Well, this stuff may just help you solve his murder," she said, looking proud of herself. "Then you won't be laughing at me."

"I'm not laughing at you."

"Okay." Through the baby monitor, they could hear Megan make little gurgling sounds, then snore loudly a couple of times before settling back into her even breathing. They listened to her for a few minutes.

"So, are they going to call you when they know anything about whether they find him?"

"Yeah. It's funny, actually. The state guy in charge of the investigation is an old buddy of mine. We grew up on the same street. Andy Lynch. I guess he interviewed you."

"Oh, yeah, he was kind of a jerk. He definitely thought there was something wrong with me. Did you go to school together?"

"I went to college and he joined the Marines. He was in Desert Storm and everything. If he'd stayed in, he'd probably be over there now. But he went to the police academy and he got promoted a bunch of times. They love the military in my line of work."

"Was it good to see him again?"

"Yeah. He lived down the street and his old man was a real asshole, so he used to come over and spend a lot of time at our house. My mother used to call him her honorary son. They got a real kick out of each other."

She was studying him intently and he suddenly wondered if his face had betrayed his sudden sadness. "Are your parents still alive?"

"No. My father died when I was in college. Heart attack. And my mother got cancer a few years ago, before Maura and I got married. She died quick. It was the bad kind, pancreatic."

"I'm sorry."

"Yeah, well . . ." He put his hands in the air, shrugged.

"Do you have siblings?"

He hesitated a moment and she felt she'd asked the wrong thing. "A brother, but he's . . . well, for one thing, he's a lot older. They—my parents, I mean—left Ireland in the early seventies, just before I was born. My father had gotten mixed up in some stuff over there and we had to get out, but my brother was pretty deep into it. He stayed. Ended up spending most of his twenties and thirties in prison. It just about broke my mother's heart. I never met him, if you can believe it. But he's out of prison now, he lives in Cork, has a family and all. I was thinking about taking Maura and Megan over to meet him sometime. Before."

"What kind of stuff was he mixed up in?"

He studied her for a minute, then looked away and said, "Oh, you know. Stuff. So, I never had a brother. But Andy Lynch was kind of like a brother to me. At least, until we were in high school. After that it was strange. I knew too much about him. He knew too much about me. Once he was in the military, we didn't have a lot to talk about. He became a soldier. He believed in what he was doing. I guess I had a hard time relating."

"It's funny, you know. We tend to think of the guys who fought in the Revolution as being somehow different from all these other guys who ever fought in wars. But it's all the same thing, isn't it? People dying for an idea."

"Except it's hard to know what the idea is anymore."

"They probably felt that way back then too," Sweeney said. "It was probably vague and strange to them too. Freedom. Liberty. What does it really mean?"

He was about to say something when Megan's voice, just a whimper at first and then a full-blown howl, came through the baby monitor. Sweeney started.

Quinn suddenly felt so tired that he could barely lift himself up out of the chair. He hesitated for a moment. Maybe she'd just go back to sleep. If he just waited . . . Her cries came even louder. He stood up and unplugged the monitor. "I'd better go," he said. "I'll see you later."

TWENTY-NINE

MARCUS CHURCHILL PULLED HIS WINDBREAKER MORE TIGHTLY around himself and walked into the wind. It had gotten really cold in the last hour since he'd been walking around, looking for something to do. He'd already gotten himself a cup of coffee and now he was just walking, trying to get his mother's face and voice out of his head, the way she'd looked when he left her at that stupid hotel and told her he was going downtown. It pissed him off, the way she looked all hurt, as though he was wounding her by wanting to get away from her, but now that he thought about it, he felt kind of sorry for her. She was pretty bummed out about his dad. Maybe "bummed out" wasn't quite right, maybe it was pissed. But it was a weird kind of pissed, like she was pissed at herself as well as at his dad and just for good measure she'd decided to be pissed at Marcus too.

And it was all his dad's fault. That was what he kept coming back to. If his dad hadn't done what he did, none of this would have happened. He was a bastard. That's what he was. A total bastard. It was a word Marcus had only ever heard adults say. Kids his age called people assholes or retards or something. But he liked the way the word felt in his mouth as he said it. *Bastard. Bastard.*

He was cutting through a parking lot behind a bunch of the cutesy little stores on Main Street when he saw the kids. They were about his age, maybe a little younger. He checked out their clothes. They looked kind of preppy, but it was worth a shot. He took a cigarette out of the pack in his back pocket and stood for a minute while he lit it, watching them to make sure he wasn't making a mistake. There were three girls and two boys. One of the girls was kind of cute, he decided. The boys were pushing each other, pretending to fight, showing off for the girls.

"Hey," he said, walking over to them. "Any of you guys interested in buying some weed off me?"

They looked around at one another as though someone had just told them they'd won the lottery. "Yeah," one of the boys said. "You got some?"

"I wouldn't have asked if you were interested if I didn't have some." A station wagon pulled into the parking lot, its headlights illuminating the kids' faces for a minute, then drove on. In the light, he could see that the boy he'd been talking to had really bad acne, stretching over his face like red lace. One of the girls bent down, hiding her face. "There anywhere we can go and smoke?"

"I don't know," the boy said.

Suddenly, the only thing Marcus wanted was the warm camaraderie of sitting around and getting high, the way people seemed to really like him then, the way he felt happy and easy and peaceful. "Come on. I won't even charge you for it."

The kid watched him. "You can come with us," he said finally. "I have a car and we have this place we go to out in the woods."

"All right," Marcus said, grinning. "You got a deal."

THIRTY

MONDAY, OCTOBER, 18

PUSHING THE STROLLER THROUGH THE LITTLE STONE PILLARS marking the entrance to the New Boston Cemetery in Lincoln, Sweeney wondered if she was doing permanent damage to Megan's sensibilities, bringing her on a tour of graveyards of eastern Massachusetts in her infancy. Would she remember anything of it when she was older, all this communing with the dead?

"Hey, Pres?" she said. He was walking behind her, carrying her backpack and the milk shakes they'd stopped for at McDonald's.

"Yeah?"

"Was it weird, growing up around all those monuments?" She stopped the stroller next to the path. "I mean, it must have been strange having friends over and stuff, right?"

"I don't know." He thought for a moment and she realized it was something she really liked about him, that he didn't just answer questions any old way. He always thought about it. "It was kind of strange when people would come to pick them out and be crying and everything. But it was just normal for me, really."

"I was worrying about bringing Megan to all these graveyards, but I suppose with a homicide detective for a father, chances are she's going to be pretty screwed-up, anyway," Sweeney said cheerily, taking Megan out of the stroller and putting her down on a blanket on the soft grass of the cemetery. Megan immediately crawled off the blanket and over to a slate stone with a beautiful carving of a death's-head and an hourglass. Sweeney supposed she couldn't do much damage to herself in the cemetery, so she blocked off the entrance with the stroller and set to work finding the six stones Whiting had carved in the Lincoln cemetery. George Whiting had listed them on his survey, and Sweeney wanted to add them to the Concord ones.

She was still waiting to hear from Hamish Jones about his spy information, but since she was taking care of Megan today, she'd decided to come out to the cemetery to document a few more stones mentioned on George Whiting's survey. With these, she'd have a fairly complete list of Whiting's stones in the area, with sketches and notes for each. She had thought it would be just her and Megan, but when she'd gone downstairs, Pres had been waiting for her in the lobby. "It's a teachers' meeting day today," he said. "But my mom said I could hang out with you. Otherwise, I have to go to my gramma's."

Sweeney said he was welcome to come along. Now, she looked at the little map George had drawn and found them easily. They were all in a row, and had been commissioned for members of the Hardy family. The dates ranged between 1765 and 1774, and just like the rest of Whiting's stones, they showcased the evolution of the death's-head over time. On the earliest stone, which belonged to Henry Hardy, the death's-head was fairly plain, but by the time it adorned the grave of young Liza Hardy, who had died at six years, two months in October of 1774, it had the wild hair and staring eyes Sweeney had come to know so well.

While they watched Megan crawling industriously around the graveyard, she and Pres photographed and sketched the stones and checked George Whiting's list to make sure she hadn't missed any. At the bottom of the page, she saw he had typed in "Stone for Mrs. Elizabeth Wheeler. Lincoln, 1776." It couldn't be a Whiting stone, because Josiah Whiting was dead by 1776. Or at least he wasn't making stones anymore, Sweeney told herself.

Cecily Whiting had told her that Whiting's son had taken

over the business. It must be that he had made the stone, and perhaps his early designs closely resembled those of his father's before he developed his own style. That had to be it. She found herself wondering about the son. What had he been like? What had he thought about his father's disappearance? She flipped back through her notebook to the notes she'd taken from her conversation with Cecily Whiting. Cecily hadn't been able to tell her very much about Josiah Whiting's family, but there were the copies of the family letters she had given Sweeney.

Sweeney retrieved Megan from a far corner of the cemetery and put her on the blanket with a selection of toys from her diaper bag. Then she and Pres sat down on the blanket next to her and drank their milk shakes.

"Pres, have you ever heard your mom or your grandfather talk about spies?"

"Spies? Like James Bond?"

"Well, Revolutionary War spies. Like Benedict Arnold and those guys."

"There's an exhibit at the museum about the spies during the Revolution," Pres said. "It's really cool. There's this whole thing about how they used these masks to send secret letters. My mom made me one that was shaped like a heart and she would write me these funny letters that I could only read if I held them up behind the mask."

"Yeah." She tried to think of a way to ask him about Josiah Whiting without bringing up Kenneth Churchill. "You don't think Josiah Whiting could have been a spy, do you?"

"I don't know, maybe. But why would he be a spy? I mean, it seems like he was pretty into the whole war thing. But I guess you would be if you were a spy, wouldn't you?"

"Maybe. Have you ever looked at the Whiting family gravestones?"

"Yeah. They're in the Hill Cemetery."

"You want to see them again?"

He looked over at her. "Sure," he said with a shrug. He was wearing a blue sweatshirt that seemed too tight on him,

and his face was puffy and pale. Sweeney felt a sudden flash
of concern for him. "I've got nothing better to do."

He led her right to them. The stones were situated near the
back of the cemetery, Rebecca Whiting's in the center and
her four children and their spouses buried nearby. Sweeney
had been half expecting some spectacular examples of
American stonecarving, but the stones were very plain. By
the early 1800s, gravestones had gotten a lot less interesting,
Puritan symbolism abandoned in favor of more secular designs, and the Whitings' stones were replete with willow
trees and urns, simple inscriptions, and not a single Medusa
head among them. It was almost disappointing.

She had read all of the other stones when she came to
Lucy Whiting's. It was at the far left of the row, a small,
child-size stone bearing the name and the dates of the child's
life, September 2, 1772, to August 30, 1774. She had been
only a few days shy of her second birthday. Infant and toddler deaths were exceedingly common in those days, and you
couldn't walk around an eighteenth-century cemetery very
long without stumbling over the graves of children. But
Sweeney always found them sad, and today she found Lucy
Whiting's grave sadder still. Maybe it was all the time she'd
been spending with Megan. Maybe it was that she felt as
though she'd come to know Josiah Whiting and his family.

"Do they always use little ones for kids?" Pres asked,
standing quietly by her side and reading the stone.

"Oftentimes." She knelt down and inspected the stone. It
featured a simple design at the top, scrolled shells inter-
twined with flowers and a pattern of starbursts traveling
down the sides, and as she stared at it, she realized there was
something familiar about the carving.

"Pres," she said. "I think Josiah Whiting made this stone.
Look, the starbursts are on a few of the other ones we've
seen and the way he carved the letters. I didn't notice it right
away, because there's no death's-head, but it's definitely one
of his." She turned to Pres, excited, but he was looking off
across the cemetery, lost in thought.

"You okay?" He seemed off today, more tired than usual.

"Did you ever think about what kind of gravestone you want to have?" Pres asked suddenly, tracing the outlines of one of the African-mask faces.

"Are you kidding? People always ask me that question when they find out what I do. For a long time, I hadn't thought about it, but now I have an answer I give, though I'm not sure it's what I'd choose anymore." Pres looked at her expectantly. "Okay, I have this idea for a really *big* gravestone, like four or five feet tall—that probably means I have a big ego or something—and it would have a giant soul's head on it, like that one over there, and it would just have my name and dates of my life and death. That's what I'd like. Now I think I want to be cremated, though, so it would just be a place people could come if they wanted." She wondered suddenly, Who would come? "Maybe they could put my ashes under it too."

Pres thought about that for a minute and then said, "I don't think I want to be cremated. I tried to tell my mom, but she started crying and she wouldn't really listen." He looked up at Sweeney. "Could you tell her . . . if . . . you know. You know her now, so she would listen to you."

Sweeney studied him for a moment. She weighed a thousand lame assurances and then, finally, just said, "Okay. I will."

Sweeney and Megan walked Pres home and then headed back to the inn. Megan fell asleep on her shoulder, so Sweeney ordered tea in the lounge and decided to learn a little bit more about the Whiting family.

She had looked at the copies of the family letters Cecily Whiting had given her, but hadn't seen much of anything relating to gravestones. Most of them were addressed to Whiting's wife, Rebecca, and seemed to be letters from her mother or sisters focusing on household goings-on. But there were three letters from Josiah Whiting to his wife, and Sweeney took them out and read them carefully. The first one, dated June 15, 1772, was written in a beautiful, flowing hand.

Dearest Becky,

    It has been a good long stretch of work, but I am tiring of being away from you and the children. How is John? I think of him often and wish that the fever passes and that his bad leg doesn't bother him too much. Tell him that his father is in much admiration of his bravery and wishes him the best. And tell the others that I will be home soon and I will tell them a new story about a monstrous beast who roams the woods of Acton.

I remain, yours,
Josiah

The second letter was dated May 1, 1773, and also seemed to have been written during a trip away.

Dearest Becky,

    I thought of you this morning when the innkeeper's wife showed me her lettuces and I thought they were not nearly as nice as yours. Things have been well here. I sold three stones and have taken five more orders, so we should have the money for John to see Dr. Hooper. I should start for Concord on Thursday and will see you then.

Yours,
Josiah

The final one wasn't dated and Sweeney read it through a couple of times, but it didn't make any sense to her.

Dearest Becky,

    I know that you did it very well and for John I would not suppose I love the pies that you make.

Josiah

Sweeney read through the letter a few more times, trying to figure out what it meant. It sounded as though they had some kind of fight or something and he was trying to make up to her. Or it may have been some kind of private joke between them. But in any case, there wasn't any more information about the family. She would have to keep looking.

THIRTY-ONE

QUINN DECIDED TO START BY CALLING TUCKER BELOIT'S commanding officer, a guy named Lieutenant James Hegman. He had gotten the name from Don and Ann Beloit, and while he knew he could probably get contact information from the Defense Department, he figured he'd try the easier path first. So he turned to the computer on the desk Andy had given him to use, Googled "Lt. James Hegman" "U.S. Marines," and came up with a whole list of hits. He tried the first one and found a personal website someone had made to commemorate a reunion of Marines who had fought under Lieutenant James Hegman in Kuwait. Bingo.

There was a picture from the reunion on the site and Quinn studied it carefully, trying to make out the faces. After scanning the caption, he was certain that neither Kenneth Churchill nor Tucker Beloit was in the picture. But one of the names was Lieutenant James Hegman and whoever had written the caption had helpfully added in "Plano, TX." Quinn popped that into the Internet White Pages and came up with a listing for James and Leeane Hegman in Plano and wrote down the number. He found a new notebook in the top drawer of the desk and dialed the number. A woman's voice, rich and mellow with Texas rhythms, answered after the third ring, and when Quinn said he wanted to talk to Lieutenant Hegman, she said, "He's at work, hon."

"Oh, could you leave him a message for me?"

"Course I could, hon. Or you could call him at the office. I can give you the number."

Quinn said that would be great and copied down the new number in his notebook, then dialed.

"Hegman here." He had the same Texas accent his wife did, rich and long.

"Lieutenant Hegman. My name is Detective Tim Quinn and I'm a cop out here in Massachusetts. I'm helping the Massachusetts State Police look into the murder of a man named Tucker Beloit, and according to his parents, he served under you in the Gulf War. Is that right?"

There was a long silence and then Hegman said, "Shit. I haven't heard anybody say his name in years. Tucker Beloit? Who murdered him?"

"Well, that's what we're trying to figure out. Can you tell me a little bit about him?"

There was a long silence. "Only thing you need to know about Tucker Beloit is that he was sick in the head. I don't mean to speak ill of the dead, but he was. He wasn't all there, and they never should have let him join up in the first place." There was another long silence. "But they did, and I had to deal with it."

"When did you first meet him?"

"Boot camp. This was before the war started. He joined up in November, I think, and I got to know him pretty well. He was real gung-ho. You know the type. He was always talking about how proud he was to be a Marine. He was a strong recruit, but he wasn't much of a team player. That was the first thing I noticed. It wasn't that he didn't want to work with the other guys, but it was like he just didn't have it in him. He thought of everything in terms of how he could get some personal glory out of it. I took him down a few pegs, really broke him down and built him back up again, and he was a lot better then, but I still always felt like I had to keep an eye on him, you know?

"The ground war started in February and we went right in at the front. We were a reinforced artillery regiment, and mostly what they wanted us for was to conduct these night-

time raids on the Kuwaiti border. We would get coordinates
and we would head in and fire on a couple of targets and
then get out before they could fire on us. It was like that
night after night. Tucker seemed like he was doing okay. You
know, he was really into what we were doing, just . . . gung-
ho is really the word. But the thing is that in a wartime situation, that's what you want. So I was very willing to let it
go." He paused then, and Quinn had the feeling that he was
thinking about what to say. "You go over there? To the
Gulf?" he asked finally.

"No, sir," Quinn said. "I've got a buddy here working on
the case with me, though, who did."

"Well, I only asked because I'm trying to figure out how
to explain why I didn't do something about him before . . .
well, before what happened. See, there's something about
being out in the desert. It just plays with your sense of
things. There's so much of it and it all looks the same, and
you kind of forget. Well, you forget stuff that you might remember if you were back home.

"Anyway, we were doing some reconnaissance and before we left camp, Tucker took me aside and told me that he
hadn't wanted to say anything but that he thought Hank
Giordano might be talking to the enemy. It was kind of a
weird thing to say because there wasn't any enemy around.
It was just us out in the middle of a huge desert, and sometimes we ran across civilians or our guys, and sometimes we
had to, you know, kind of take guys down because we
weren't sure who they were, but it wasn't like there were
Iraqi soldiers hanging around camp or anything.

"So, we went out on the mission and as we were creeping
along in the desert, I suddenly heard someone say something. I pulled them up and went back and it was Tucker and
he was fighting with Giordano. We were in the middle of a
mission and I couldn't afford to work it out then and there,
so I told them to go back to camp and we continued on."
Quinn heard him take a deep breath. "When we got back to
camp that night, I went to find them so we could figure out
what was going on. This was pretty serious stuff. They'd put

the mission in jeopardy, not to mention completely disobeying orders. I was pissed and I called for them. Tucker came kind of slinking around one of the tents and he came over and he looked me in the eye and he said, 'Lieutenant Hegman, sir. You can find Corporal Giordano's body in tent number five, sir.' And then he saluted me. It was the creepiest thing, that salute. I said, 'Excuse me?' and he just kept on looking at me with those cold eyes and I knew, I knew. Damn it! He didn't even have to tell me. But he said, 'I told you sir, he was trying to talk to the enemy, sir. He was a spy. I executed him. I did my duty, sir.'" There was a long pause and then Hegman went on. "They sent him home and I never heard anything more about it. I swear to God. I thought there might be a court-martial or something. I even thought my head might be on the chopping block. But nothing. At some point I realized they'd just hushed up the whole thing. I don't know what they told Giordano's family. Probably accidental discharge or friendly fire or something. I wrote 'em a letter later, just telling 'em what a good guy he was, but I tell you, to this day I don't know if they know what happened."

"Did you ever hear anything about a guy named Kenneth Churchill?" Quinn asked him.

"Churchill? That rings a bell for some reason. Maybe." But he didn't sound convinced.

"He was a Marine. Fought in the Gulf too."

"That could be it. I could have come across him at some point."

"Could you think about it? It seems like he may have something to do with Beloit's death and we're just trying to track down any connection between the two of them. Like, say, that he was friends with Corporal Giordano or something."

"Yeah, yeah, of course. Let me do some looking through my things. I kept a journal when I was over there. Might be something in there."

"That would be a big help," Quinn said.

"I tell you. I didn't know what to think. You hear about these things, you know. In Vietnam, guys would kind of go off. The pressure got to be too much. But this was the Gulf War. I mean, we hardly lost any guys. It was supposed to be in and out. That's what everybody said.

"The thing about war that I didn't know about before I went over there is how many people die because of things that have nothing to do with fighting. You know what I mean? Hell, we lost more guys in car accidents and stuff like that than we did to the enemy. Anyway, I'll look through that journal and get back to you if I find anything."

Once Quinn was off the phone, he sat and thought about the conversation for a minute. Hegman might have heard of Churchill, but maybe he should try to come at it from the opposite angle. Not did Tucker Beloit know Kenneth Churchill, but did Kenneth Churchill know Tucker Beloit?

He called the main number at the inn and asked to be connected to Beverly Churchill's room. When he told her who it was, she said, "Did you find him? You found him." He could hear her breathing hard, the fear evident in her voice.

"No, no. I'm sorry. There's no news. I was just wondering if you could tell me a little bit more about your husband's service in the Marines. When was he deployed during the war?"

"'Ninety-one to 'ninety-two," she said. "I don't remember the exact dates, but he went back in right after the invasion."

"Where was he stationed?"

"I don't remember exactly. He talked about being on the Kuwaiti border. That's all I remember."

"Do you remember what his company was called?"

"No, but I can find out for you. It'll be at home somewhere."

"Thank you. I was also wondering if you knew who any of your husband's Marine buddies were. Was there anyone who he stayed in touch with after he got back?"

"Oh. There were a couple of guys. One who came and stayed with us once. Bob something. I could probably find it for you. He was from Colorado or Montana or something.

He was kind of a hillbilly type, really, different from Kenneth, though Kenneth had grown up like that and I think he felt comfortable with him. But after he came and stayed with us, he and Kenneth didn't really stay in touch anymore. I think that he saw how we lived and that Kenneth had a good job, and maybe he realized they didn't have as much in common anymore.

"Anyway, there was also a guy who lives around Leominster somewhere, Athol, I think. He and Kenneth used to get together a lot. Not so much in the last few years, but Kenneth really liked him."

"Do you remember his name?"

"Yeah, it was kind of a funny name. I think he must have gotten made fun of a lot as a kid. Francis Pebbles. Frank, Kenneth called him."

"Can't be too many Francis Pebbles in Athol, can there?"

She laughed, and for a second he imagined her face, the blue eyes turning up in amusement. "No," she said. "I bet you can get it from Information."

But as it turned out, Information had no record of a Francis Pebbles. Quinn sat there, trying to figure out what to do, then got the number for Athol Town Hall and asked the woman who answered if she knew of a Francis Pebbles. He was an old friend from the Marines, he said, and he happened to remember that Frank had lived in Athol. Would she know where he could find him?

"Frank? Oh, it's probably listed under Laurie's name. Laurie Ferrano. That's his sister. Hang on, I've got a phone book here, let me see if I can find it." He could hear her flipping through pages and then she came back on and gave him the number. "Good luck," she said kindly before hanging up.

Frank Pebbles wasn't home, but Quinn left a message on the answering machine and was typing up his notes from the conversations when Andy came in, looking downcast. "You find anything?" he asked Quinn.

"Nothing great," Quinn told him as he sat down. "But I got the story on Beloit. He went crazy while he was over there, started accusing one of the guys he served with of being a spy for the Iraqis and then he killed him. Shot him dead one night while the rest of the unit was out on patrol."

"Jesus," Andy said.

"The commander said that he got sent home and the whole thing was kept pretty quiet. He's not sure the family even knew what really happened, which was backed up by our conversation with the Beloits. It looks like he and Churchill were both deployed on the Kuwaiti border around the same time, but that doesn't tell us a whole lot. Hegman didn't think he knew Churchill, but the name rang a bell for him. He said he's not sure why, but he's going to think about it and get back to me. So, it looks like there may be a connection. I'm not counting on it, though. It's a common enough name."

Andy sat on the edge of the desk and turned to look through the window. "I knew a couple of guys who went crazy over there. It just got to them, the sun and the sand. They couldn't hack it. The way I look at it, it's tough on everybody, you know. You just have to deal with it and do your duty."

"How about you? Anything on the credit card?"

"Yeah, we found an employee who said she's eighty-seven percent sure—I swear, that's really what she said, eighty-seven percent—that she remembers the credit card. Her mother's maiden name was Churchill and she remembered wondering if they were related when she ran the card through. A miracle, really, when you think about how many cards they run through. But she says it was a young kid who used it."

"So, it was stolen, or he gave it to someone."

"Yeah, which means he could be anywhere right now."

"I know."

"It's weird, I didn't know how much stock to put in the girl's story. I don't know about this thing with the mother's maiden name. But she remembered that he had a little penguin earring in one of his ears. He was—"

"Wait a second, did you say he was wearing a penguin earring?"

"Yeah. Why?"

Quinn was up before Andy had finished talking. "Because Kenneth Churchill's teenage son has a penguin earring too. I saw it the first day I went to talk to Mrs. Churchill."

Andy's eyes were wide. "You sure about that? A penguin? Like Chilly Willy, or whatever that cartoon is?"

"Yeah. Like Chilly Willy," Quinn said, grinning. "We can get him in here and you can see it for yourself."

THIRTY-TWO

MARCUS CHURCHILL SAT ACROSS FROM THEM, HIS LONG, grubby-looking white rugby shirt untucked and hanging over his baggy jeans, which, as he'd walked into the inter-view room, had threatened to fall down around his ankles with every step.

"Do you know where your father is, Marcus?" Andy started, and the look the kid gave them told them that either he didn't know or he had a future on the stage.

"What? No. Of course not."

"So how come you have his credit card?"

"He gave it to me. For stuff for school." Marcus reached up to fiddle with the little penguin earring. Quinn noticed that it was inlaid with tiny pieces of turquoise.

"How come your mom didn't know about it, then?"

"He doesn't tell her every time he gives me something."

"But don't you think he would have told her if he'd given you his credit card?"

Marcus just shrugged, then scratched his chin and looked around the room as though he were appraising the furniture.

"When did he give you the credit card?" Quinn asked.

Marcus narrowed his eyes and Quinn suddenly felt the same chill he'd felt when he passed the boy at Beverly Churchill's house. "I don't know. A couple of weeks ago."

"Well, he's been missing for two weeks now, so it must

have been longer than that, unless you've seen him since then."

"I haven't seen him," Marcus said defensively. "It was probably like a month ago, then."

Quinn went for some detail. You usually tripped up people on the details. "Did he tell you to keep it, or did he want it back right away?"

"I don't know. He just gave it to me, okay?" He was playing with a piece of thread hanging off the shirttail hem of his rugby shirt.

"What did you need to buy that made him hand over the credit card?"

"Books."

"What books?"

He gave a sardonic little grin. "Schoolbooks."

Andy was pissed. "We know schoolbooks. What were the titles of the books?"

Quinn could see the kid making it up. "*War and Peace*," he said finally. "And *Madame Bovary*."

"Let's assume you're telling the truth," Quinn said. "Why were you out buying gas at a Mobil station out on Ninety-five? According to your mother, you don't even have a car."

"I was with a friend," Marcus said. "In his car."

"What's your friend's name?"

Marcus folded his arms across his stomach. "I forget."

"Wasn't a very good friend, was he?"

"No," Marcus said. "He's kind of an asshole."

Andy stood up, glaring at the boy. "Marcus, I get the feeling you're not being entirely honest with us here. Is there anything else you want to tell us? Now would be a good time."

But there wasn't and when it came right down to it, there wasn't anything they could hold him for. He was in possession of a credit card that, after all, had his own last name on it. There wasn't anyone to say that his father hadn't given it to him. Quinn's instinct told him Marcus was either lying or holding back, but there wasn't a damn thing he could do about it.

Beverly Churchill was waiting for them outside. "What's going on?" she asked Quinn when she saw him. "Should I get a lawyer? I don't understand what Kenneth's credit card has to do with—"

"You don't need to get a lawyer," Quinn told her, gesturing for her to follow him into the hallway, where they could talk privately. "Marcus hasn't done anything. He claims that his father gave him the credit card to buy books. Is that possible?"

"I don't know." She put her face in her hands for a minute. "I don't know anything anymore about what Kenneth would or wouldn't do. Why would Marcus be at a gas station out here?"

"He says he was driving around with a friend, but he wouldn't tell us who it was."

"I don't know what to do with him," Beverly Churchill said, and Quinn recognized the look on her face. He'd seen it so many times on the faces of the parents of kids he'd arrested for drugs or assault or even murder. "It's not my fault," the parents' faces seemed to say. "Please don't think I made him like this." And was it their fault? It was hard to say. He thought of Megan. What was he doing to screw her up? He didn't even want to think about it.

"Well, we'll let you know if anything else comes up. If he seems willing to talk, try to get him to talk to you."

"Thank you." They were standing very close together in the small hallway and Quinn looked down at her, into those odd ice-blue eyes. He blushed.

"You're welcome. It's no problem."

Her eyes were so light, they almost seemed like they couldn't belong to a human. And her lips were very lightly moist. He felt himself leaning toward her very slightly and then he stepped suddenly away, afraid that he had been about to kiss her.

Shaking, he said good-bye and went back to find Andy.

THIRTY-THREE

SWEENEY GOT THE E-MAIL WHEN SHE GOT UP THAT MORN-
ing. "Ms. St. George," it went.

> Thank you for writing to me about your very interesting
> project. I myself have done some work on British soldiers
> who turned during the war. I have an idea about how I can
> help you. I am currently sorting through a series of letters
> written to the Earl of Sandwich during the war by British
> officers. Some have been indexed, but many have not.
> There is much new material here. I estimate that it will
> take me another six months to properly catalog everything.
> I am looking for funding right now, but I'm not optimistic
> about getting it this year. I would allow you to look
> through the documents, if there's a chance you could come
> to London. Let me know if this suits and I can help you
> make the necessary arrangements. As for your question
> about Mr. Churchill, it is very interesting that you should
> ask. I knew of his work, of course, and he contacted me
> around April. He didn't tell me what he was working on,
> though, just that he was coming to London and might be
> interested in taking a look at the collection. He took a
> quick look through, but didn't seem to find what he
> wanted. I hope that helps. If you know Mr. Churchill, you
> can tell him that he is still welcome to come and look at the
> letters again.

Yours,
Hamish Jones

Sweeney logged off and sat at the desk, thinking about his offer. If Churchill had taken a "quick look through" and hadn't found anything supporting his theory about Whiting being a spy, then it was unlikely that Sweeney would either. But on the other hand, maybe he had found something and just didn't want Jones to know.

It might be worthwhile, but she really had no idea whether she would find anything. And what if she did find proof that Josiah Whiting was a spy for the British? It would be an interesting footnote to her study of Whiting's gravestones, and it might even explain the evolution of his stones, but she wasn't a historian.

Besides, she felt a responsibility to stay in Concord and help Quinn as much as she could. As soon as she acknowledged that she felt a responsibility to him and to Megan, she found she was annoyed. She didn't mind helping him out, but he had barely said thank you. Why did he think she was just available to him anytime he needed her? Was it because she had been there when he'd found his wife, and he knew she felt sorry for him?

She checked the clock. It was 8 A.M. in Massachusetts, which meant it was noon in London. She dialed Ian's cell phone number and sat down, her stomach nervous as she heard his voice.

"A daytime phone call," he answered. "To what do I owe this honor?"

"Hi," she said.

"Hi. Is everything okay?"

"Yeah," she said. "I was just thinking about you. I'm sorry if I sounded strange the other night."

"Hang on. I'm just going to head back to my office." She could hear his footsteps and then a door shutting. "I felt like I was pressuring you," he said.

"No, no, you weren't. I'm just . . . I want to see you. I'm glad you're coming to visit."

"Good." But he didn't sound convinced.

"Anyway," she said. "I was also wondering if you could do me a favor." She told him about Hamish Jones and the collection of letters. "I don't think it would take more than an hour or so to just skim through them, see if you see the words 'Whiting' or 'Concord.' I would completely understand if you don't want to. It's just that I think there may be something in there that would prove this theory one way or the other."

"Of course I'll do it," he said. "It may have to be this evening, though. Will that be all right?"

"Yeah, I'll just tell him. Thank you so much. You don't know how much I appreciate this."

"What you have to understand, Sweeney," he said with a touch of humor in his voice, "is that I'd do anything for you."

She was preparing for her class when Quinn came by with Megan and what Sweeney had started referring to as her accoutrements. "I put a couple of bottles in there, and there are Cheerios and a couple of bananas. We'll just be downstairs and I should be done by two or so and I'll come get her then."

"Okay."

He studied her for a minute. "You know how much I appreciate this, right? I don't know how I'll ever make it up to you, but I really, really appreciate everything you've done for us."

"It's okay," Sweeney said. But she knew that the annoyance she'd felt earlier was showing on her face.

Quinn stood in the doorway for a moment. "I know I need to find a better day-care solution," he said. "I think I need a nanny or something. Maura's sister offered to do it, but there's so much baggage there. I think I just need to hire someone who can come every day and who won't care if I'm late sometimes. But I don't even know if there's anyone like that. I don't know how I'm going to. . . ." Sweeney watched his face. For a second she thought he was going to cry. His face softened and she saw how tired he was, not tired like tired from the past week, but tired from the past year.

"You're doing okay," she said. "You really are. I don't know how you're even doing as well as you are. I would be a total mess. But Megan's doing fine, and once this is over, you'll be back to a schedule." It sounded lame even to her ears.

"You're right," he said. "I'm sorry."

"It's okay," Sweeney told him. "Now go talk to your Marine."

THIRTY-FOUR

QUINN AND ANDY HAD DECIDED TO MEET WITH FRANK PEB-
bles at the tavern at the Minuteman Inn. Andy said he was
hoping that a more relaxed atmosphere would loosen up
Frank Pebbles's tongue, but when Quinn suggested that
Andy just wanted a beer with his lunch, Andy grinned and
said maybe he did.

Pebbles was early and when Quinn and Andy came in at
11:30, he was sitting at the bar with a pint of Guinness, reading the bar's copy of *USA Today*. Quinn would have known
it was him even if he wasn't the only person in the tavern.
He was a big guy, wearing a leather jacket that had the Marine Corps insignia embroidered across the back, and when
he turned around to greet them, he looked the way Quinn
had expected him to from his gruff voice on the phone when
he'd called back. He had a worn, abused-looking face
pocked with old acne scars and a permanent sunburn, and
his smile was broad when he shook Quinn's hand.

"As Detective Quinn told you on the phone," Andy said,
"Kenneth Churchill has disappeared. We don't know what's
happened to him, but we suspect that his disappearance may
be connected to the death of a man named Tucker Beloit,
whose body was found here in Concord a little over a week
ago. Tucker Beloit also served in the Marines and we're trying to figure out if they could have known each other. Does
the name ring a bell?"

"Yeah, maybe," Frank Pebbles said. "At least, I think so. But then I met a lot of guys over there. It was a long time ago now. And my memory isn't so good." He put a hand to his head and Quinn watched him for a second as something passed across his face. "I got this Gulf War syndrome thing, headaches, joint problems. I been doing better lately, though."

"Tell us about Churchill," Quinn said. "How did you get to know him?"

"We served together," Pebbles said simply. "Best way to get to know a guy there is. We were two of the older guys in our unit. Most of the others were nineteen, twenty, just kids who didn't know their ass from their elbow and had joined up because if they didn't, they probably would have been in jail the next year. Ken and me, for us it was about something else. He had been in when he was younger and the Corps had put him through school and when old Saddam Hussein got busy over there, he felt like it was his duty to go back in when they needed him. For me, it was more that I just needed something, and joining up gave me that something. Call it structure, purpose, whatever. I didn't have any idea what I was getting into, of course. War isn't something you should get into because you don't know what else to do."

"What was Churchill's time over there like?" Quinn asked him. "Tucker Beloit was dishonorably discharged for his role in the shooting death of a fellow Marine. Hank Giordano. Was Churchill involved in anything like that? Do you think he knew about it?"

"I would have known about it if he had. No, Ken was an exemplary soldier, in every way," Pebbles said. "I really mean that. He believed in what he was doing over there and he saw it as his duty. Not like some of us."

"Can I ask you something?" Quinn said. "Would it surprise you to know that he was unfaithful to his wife in the months before he disappeared?"

"Nah. Kenneth was kind of a whaddyacallit, ladies' man. Yeah, he was always like that. Ever since I'd known him. We never talked about his marriage, but I kind of had the sense that it wasn't so great. He mentioned women sometimes, students a few times, which seemed to me to be skating on pretty thin ice. But no, it wouldn't surprise me."

"Thank you," Quinn said. "What did you mean when you said he believed it was his duty, 'not like some of us.' "

"Oh, I got pretty cynical about the whole thing pretty quick after I got over there. I don't know if you know what's it's like, but you get there and it's like something out of *Star Wars,* I swear to God. The desert and these crazy people who you don't understand and they don't understand you and you're there to help them, but you kind of feel like nobody told 'em that. I started feeling like there was nothing I could do to change anybody's situation, you know?"

Andy was looking pissed and he said, "That's why there's a chain of command. You don't know what your part of the whole thing is, but your leaders do. You have to follow commands."

"You serve over there?"

"U.S. Army, 105th Field Artillery Division," Andy said proudly.

"Well, I admire you, I really do. Just like I admired Kenneth. I wanted to keep the faith, but I just couldn't. There was this one night when we were coming into a village way out in the middle of the desert and I remember as I walked in I felt like I was going to my death. I wanted to take off, but that damn desert was all around me. I think that was the first time in my life I knew that the desert could drive you crazy. All that sand and loneliness.

"There was weird shit that happened over there," he went on. "We heard about this one guy who was court-martialed because he was giving information to the Iraqis. What would make somebody do that?"

"And why didn't you stay in touch in the last couple of years?" Andy asked him. "Churchill's wife said you'd been good friends and then you just kind of lost touch."

Pebbles looked up at them. "I don't know," he said. "Life gets busy, you know."

"Well, we thank you for coming all the way out here,"

Quinn said. "Is there anything you can think of that we should know?"

"If he did kill that guy, it's the Marines' fault, you know," Pebbles said suddenly. "What they do is they make you into a killing machine. That sounds terrible, but it's true. You're a controlled killing machine. They give you a switch, and the thing is, you never know what or who's going to flip it. That movie, *The Manchurian Candidate,* you ever see that? It's not as crazy as you might think. It's not like they put the chip in your brain, but it might as well be."

He finished his beer in a long gulp. "Maybe that's what happened to Kenneth."

THIRTY-FIVE

AFTER QUINN PICKED MEGAN UP, SWEENEY WENT DOWN TO the lounge for a drink in front of the fire before dinner. She was sipping a cognac when her cell phone vibrated in her bag. It was Ian.

"Hey," she said, taking the phone outside and sitting down on the porch swing to talk.

"Hello," he said. There was something cheerful in his voice.

"You found something?"

"I certainly did."

"You're serious?"

"Yes. It was kind of fun, actually, looking through all these old letters. A lot of them were very pompous stuff about how well this lieutenant or that lieutenant was managing his command. Anyway, your friend was very accommodating and helped me find the ones that had been written right around April of 1775. There weren't many, really, and it didn't take me that long to sort through them. A lot of them were letters written when ships arrived in Boston or Plymouth, letting his lordship know that all was well, that sort of thing. Then I found one talking about April nineteenth. It's funny. He doesn't even mention what happened at Lexington. He just writes that the troops went out to Concord to confiscate munitions and were 'successful in that task.' But then he goes on about what happened afterward. That's when things get interesting.

> 'The Rebels' treachery knows no bounds. As the grenadiers and Light Infantry returned to Boston, the Rebels hid themselves behind stone walls and inside houses so as to have the advantage. They killed a number of our men, but so many of ours as might be expected. The cowards wou'd not attack in the open.
>
> 'The most treacherous act I saw that day, tho, was of one Rebel upon another. On the return journey, while under enemy fire, I and a young lieutenant went into one of the houses along the road to slake our thirst. It had been a good many hours since we had access to water. We meant no harm to the good woman of the house, but immediately upon entering, two of the Rebels also entered and forced the lady to go to the cellar of the house.
>
> 'Martin called the man by name, "Whiting" it was, and spoke a few words to him, and the coward turned and with a great cry, he bayoneted Martin through the heart, killing him instantly so I was never able to discover what was the nature of the acquaintance between them. But the most extraordinary thing I saw that day was yet to follow. The other Rebel who had entered the house suddenly turned on this Whiting and the two of them took off in a great rush. I followed and observed them mounting their horses and one taking off in pursuit of the other. The one in the lead, the killer of Lt. Martin, had a lead as his fellow Rebel's horse had wandered some distance off and I had to wait for him to pursue unnoticed.
>
> 'I followed, seeing it my duty to track and kill the killer of Lt. Martin, and so I followed in pursuit until we entered a wood, near the bridge where the Rebels fired at us only that morning. I followed behind silently so they would not see me, and watched as the second man caught up to the first in a small clearing. I was too far away to hear what they were saying, but there were many loud exclamations and at once, the second man took his musket in hand and put the bayonet through the chest of young Martin's cold-blooded killer. I watched as he stood over the body and then made to hide the body in a bush by the side of the bridal path. I watched until I was certain that poor Martin's killer had been dispatched and then returned to the melee.

'These Rebels must be put down, your lordship. They are savages, willing to kill even one of their own in cold blood.'"

"Holy shit! Baker lied!" Sweeney said. "That proves that Baker lied. You are amazing! I can't believe you found it."

"It wasn't very hard," Ian said modestly. "Is it what you were looking for?"

"I think so," she said. "Although I don't know exactly what it means. It proves Baker lied and that he killed Whiting, but the question is why?"

"It sounds like it was something that was said in the conversation between Whiting and Martin."

"Yeah, which would support the idea of Whiting being a spy. Maybe he and this Martin had met before and Martin was referencing it. Anyway, thank you so much. I can't tell you how much I appreciate this."

"Don't give it a thought, Sweeney," he said. "I have a late client dinner, so I should go, but I'll talk to you later tonight or tomorrow. Okay?"

"Okay."

She threw on a jacket and walked along Lexington Road to the Minuteman Museum. It was six, so she might have missed Cecily Whiting, but she figured it was worth a shot and was rewarded when she saw the slim, brown-clad figure locking the front door and heading toward her car.

"Cecily," Sweeney called out. "Can I talk to you for a second?" Cecily turned around, and Sweeney saw annoyance pass across her face before she smiled.

"What's up?" she called back. Sweeney walked over to the blue Honda. Cecily got into the driver's seat and rolled down the window. "What can I help you with?"

"I know you probably want to get home, but really quickly, I just wanted to know if Kenneth Churchill ever mentioned anything to you about Josiah Whiting's possibly having spied for the British and John Baker's having lied about what happened to Josiah Whiting on April nineteenth."

The look of surprise that Sweeney had expected wasn't

there. Instead, Cecily smiled sarcastically and said, "He asked me about that. It was ridiculous, of course. I don't know where he got the idea. There wasn't any evidence to suggest it. It was just an idea he had. I think he thought it would have made a better book."

Sweeney hesitated, not sure if she should tell Cecily about the British officer's letter.

But Cecily decided for her. "Was that all? I need to get home to Pres." She started the car.

Sweeney smiled. "Oh, yes. Thanks." She watched Cecily drive away, then walked back to the inn and sat down on the porch swing, thinking about what she had learned. The most crucial point was that Baker had lied in his deposition, so everything that historians thought they knew about him and Whiting was based on a falsehood. Baker had also killed Whiting. She turned and saw Will Baker through the window, speaking to a guest. What would he say if he knew that his beloved ancestor had murdered his best friend?

She planted her feet on the floor and pushed herself back and forth a few times on the swing, feeling like she'd lost control of her project. It had seemed like such a good idea, a simple paper on the evolution of an eighteenth-century stonecutter's designs. But it had gotten all mixed up with people, with Pres and Quinn and Cecily Whiting. It was a mess. She was planning to head into Boston tomorrow to try to find some of the probate records for Josiah Whiting's stone, and she found she was looking forward to getting out of town. And Toby was going to come out for dinner tomorrow night. It would be good to see Toby. Then she would finish up her research and head home to write the paper.

Maybe she would just pretend she'd never heard anything about Josiah Whiting's being a spy.

THIRTY-SIX

WEDNESDAY, OCTOBER 20

QUINN LAY ON THE BED IN HIS ROOM, LISTENING TO MEGAN sleep. It was late afternoon and he was exhausted, though he didn't have much to show for it. He'd told Andy he needed to spend the day with Megan and had taken her to a pumpkin farm in Lincoln, then to a playground he spotted on the way back, and then out for lunch. Now she was sleeping and he was exhausted.

It struck him that this was how Maura had felt all the time. Was that why she had killed herself? The shrink that Havrilek had made him see once before going back to work told him that many spouses of suicide victims never really know why they had done what they'd done. "You have to come to accept that you may never know why. You have to come to accept the action itself."

That was bullshit. Quinn hadn't accepted it. He didn't want to accept it. It had been fucking selfish, is what it had been. To go and leave him with Megan. He loved Megan—of course, he loved Megan—but Jesus Christ. He could feel himself spiraling down into the anger that he knew was there. What had she been thinking? She couldn't have loved him. Couldn't have loved Megan, to do what she did.

Megan made one of the small whimpering sounds she made in her sleep, and Quinn got up to make sure she was warm enough.

Stop it, Quinny, he told himself, lying back down on the bed. Think about the case. Just think about the case.

He took a deep breath.

The last known sighting of Churchill, the last one without doubt, had been Chris Wright's sighting on the Sunday morning after the encampment. That was all they knew for sure. He looked back at his notes on the interview with Cecily Whiting. She had expected him to call that weekend of the encampment, but he hadn't. His wife had expected him to come home after the weekend, but he hadn't. He was supposed to show up to teach his classes, and he hadn't. But no one had assumed at first that anything had happened to him. They had all assumed he was just off on his own. It struck Quinn that Kenneth Churchill was an extremely unreliable person. He didn't seem to do what he was supposed to do, ever. This seemed an important detail.

He lay back on the bed and closed his eyes, thinking about Beverly Churchill. He still hadn't figured her out, and while he couldn't see how she had had anything to do with her husband's disappearance, he also was pretty sure that she was lying to him about something.

He closed his eyes. Just for a minute, he'd nap for just a minute, and then he'd wake Megan up so she would go down tonight. He lay there, conscious of his even breathing.

He was thinking about Josiah Whiting and then suddenly he was on a battlefield, a musket under his arm and a row of Redcoats approaching him across the field. He hoisted the musket up to his shoulder, but it wasn't like any gun he'd ever used and he didn't know how to load it. He pulled the trigger and nothing happened, and then the gun was heavy, so heavy he could barely lift it, and he sank to the ground, knowing the Redcoats were coming at him.

He slept on, and an image of Beverly Churchill's face came to him unbidden. He had noticed her breasts beneath her thin sweater the last time he'd seen her. They were full and her nipples had been tantalizing shadows beneath the fabric.

Suddenly they were standing in a field and he was mov-

ing toward her. Her blouse fell away and she took his hand
and put it on her breast. He held it and leaned in to kiss her.
Her tongue was warm and wet in his mouth. . . . Then he
looked up, and over her shoulder he saw Marcus Churchill,
watching them. He tried to get away, but she clung to him
and he kissed her again, her mouth melting into his. . . .

He started awake, sweating and aroused, and he jumped
up from the bed and rushed into the bathroom, where he
splashed cold water on his face and looked at himself in the
mirror. What was with him? It was dark outside, and back in
the bedroom he checked the clock. It was almost seven.
They'd slept for three hours. He'd never get Megan to go
down tonight. He leaned over the playpen and shook her
awake. She screamed and he picked her up and walked her
around the room, soothing her.

"Are you hungry, little girl? You want to go out to dinner
with your daddy? Huh?"

Megan just cried.

"That's no way to accept a dinner invitation," he said.
"Come on now."

Downstairs, the dining room was full and Will Baker
found a high chair and seated them at a table near the window. Quinn gave Megan some Cheerios and asked Baker to
bring her some mashed potatoes immediately. "I'll order in
a minute," he said.

As he bowed his head to look at the menu, he saw Beverly
Churchill coming into the dining room out of the corner of
his eye. Embarrassed about his dream, he kept his head
down, but she saw him and came over to the table. "Hi," she
said. "Do you mind if I join you?"

"Of course not." He stood up and pulled out the chair for
her.

She smiled and sat down. "Marcus decided to 'go out.' I
don't know where he went. It's not like he knows anybody
here. I tried to force him to have dinner with me and at some
point, it's just, like, do you really want to wrestle with a
fifteen-year-old boy? Who's twice as strong as you are? He's
hardly ever home anymore, so I shouldn't be surprised ex-

actly. You're lucky. When they're that age, they don't have any option but to do what you want." She leaned over and smiled at Megan in her high chair.

"Well, I don't know about that exactly." He leaned over and smiled at Megan. "You pretty much do what you want, don't you?"

"Are you a single parent?" she asked after they had ordered their food. "I ask because it seems like you always have your daughter with you."

"Yeah." He took a long drink of his water. "My wife passed away."

She looked horrified. "I'm so sorry. It must be very hard for you. Taking care of her on your own."

"We do fine." He picked up the bottle of wine that Will Baker had brought and topped off her glass.

She took a sip and said thoughtfully, "When I think about it, I've been a single parent for a long time now. That's the thing that . . . if Kenneth comes back, I feel like I finally see things for what they really are. I'll probably leave him."

Quinn was suddenly uncomfortable. "Well, you'll have to see how you feel when the time comes."

"No," she said, a little too loudly. "It was having to tell you about it that did it for me. I mean, normal husbands don't just go off for weeks at a time. Somehow he was always able to convince me that there was a good reason for it. But when I saw the look on your face, I knew how crazy it sounded. And I said to myself, 'I'm not going to take this anymore.' "

Quinn didn't know what to say. At some point, he was going to have to tell her about Cecily Whiting, but he wasn't sure how to do it.

Their food came and for the next ten minutes they ate, Quinn feeding Megan mashed potatoes and mashed-up pieces of his cod. They talked a little bit about the inn, and Quinn told Beverly what he knew about its history. She finished her glass of wine quickly and poured herself another.

"Kenneth always said he stayed at some mediocre place when he came out here," she said with a falsely cheery laugh. "What a liar! I'm sure he didn't tell me how nice it is so I wouldn't want to come with him."

Quinn decided that if she was going to get drunk, he'd better get drunk too. He had another glass of wine, finishing off the bottle as they finished their meal. When Will Baker asked them about dessert, Beverly said she'd like a piece of cheesecake and Quinn had to wait while she finished it. He was intensely uncomfortable without being exactly sure why, and when she had finished and Will Baker brought the bill for them to sign to their rooms, he stood up gratefully, extricating Megan from the high chair.

They were leaving the dining room when he saw Sweeney sitting at a table near the fireplace. Across the table from her was a man with dark, curly hair. Sweeney saw him before he could slip by, and she waved him over. Beverly Churchill followed.

"Hi." She stood up. "Tim Quinn, this is my friend Toby DiMarco. Toby came out for dinner," she said, as though she needed to explain something to Quinn. He realized he hadn't seen her dressed up before. She was wearing a sleeveless black dress made of some kind of old-looking velvet and her arms were skinnier than he'd thought they would be. Her hair was pulled up on top of her head with just a few curly pieces coming down, and it made her seem older and more serious.

"It's so nice to meet you," Toby said. He seemed like a nice enough guy, but there was something about him that put Quinn off. He was wearing a leather jacket that looked like it probably cost as much as Quinn's car, and he seemed a little too friendly. Quinn wondered if Sweeney had told him about Maura. "Oh," he said, uncomfortable, "and this is Mrs. . . . Beverly Churchill."

Sweeney's eyes were wide for a minute and then she recovered and said, "It's very nice to meet you. Sweeney St. George." Beverly Churchill shook her hand.

"Well, enjoy your dinner," Quinn said. He felt hot and flushed all of a sudden. He wasn't used to drinking anymore, and the wine had been a bit too much.

Out in the lobby, he turned to Beverly Churchill. "I think I'm going to take Megan for a little walk," he said. "She took a three hour nap this afternoon and I have a feeling that it's going to be hard to get her down. The cool air helps."

She hesitated for a minute, then said, "Do you mind if I come with you? Marcus is still out and I hate being alone in hotel rooms."

He tried to think of a way out of it and couldn't. "No, of course not."

She held the door open for him to push the stroller through and they walked out into the night.

"I love the fall," she said. "I love the way it smells." He heard her take a deep breath and, just for the hell of it, he did the same. The air was cold and damp and smelled of mold and something sweet—apples, maybe. He found a sweater in Megan's diaper bag and wriggled her into it.

"It will be winter soon," Beverly Churchill said. "It seems like it was just winter, and here it is winter again." They walked in silence for a minute and then she said, "So, is Sweeney a friend of yours?"

"In a way. She's an art historian. I got to know her through another case I was working on. Then it turned out that she's writing something about Josiah Whiting. Different from what your husband was doing, though. She's looking at his gravestones. Hey," he said after a minute, "there's something I've been wondering about. I didn't find anything related to his work in his office that day. But it looked like the desk had been cleaned off. Did Kenneth do that? Do you think he might have put the notes somewhere else?"

She didn't say anything, and he had the distinct sense that she was buying time. "I don't know," she said. "I'll look around."

They came to Monument Square and Beverly Churchill said, "Look at that. She went to sleep."

Quinn checked and, sure enough, Megan was asleep. "I should probably wake her up," he said. "But I can't quite bring myself to do it."

"I remember worrying so much about Marcus sleeping

and at some point I realized that I should just let him sleep when he wanted to sleep. Eventually they get used to a sleep rhythm."

Quinn sat down on a bench in the square and she joined him. They were silent for a few minutes and then Quinn got up his nerve. "That day that I interviewed you at your house," he said. "I asked you if your husband was having an affair. You seemed like you were just about to say something and then your son came in and you didn't. Was there anything you were going to say to me?"

To his surprise, Beverly Churchill laughed. "Of course he was having an affair. He'd been having affairs for years. You're right that I didn't want my son to know, though. And I didn't think it would matter since he'd done it so many times before and he'd never gone off with any of them. I didn't think that could have anything to do with it."

Quinn was silent and she said, "Ah, but you know who it is, don't you? You were trying to figure out a way of telling me?"

He nodded and she laughed again. It was an ugly laugh and he didn't like it. It made him nervous, put him on edge. "Who was she?"

"She owns a museum down here, where he was doing his research."

She turned to look at him, her eyes wide. "Not Cecily Whiting?"

"You know her?"

"That bastard."

"I'm sorry, do you know her?"

She turned to look at him, and in the light from the streetlights, he could see that she was crying.

"He talked about her. He told me about her son being sick and about how her husband left her for someone else. I didn't think that . . . I didn't think he would . . ." She reached up to wipe the tears away from her cheeks.

In his hesitation, she could hear his question. "I know it sounds crazy, but all of the . . . all of the other women were just people he met. Waitresses, graduate students. He never talked about them. But he talked about her." She was sobbing now, and Quinn knew he had lost control of the situation. "He *talked* about her. What did he think, that he could just talk about her that way and then . . ." She slumped against him, sobbing nonsense words, and he lamely put his arm around her. She moved closer, her body shaking. "I don't even care anymore," she said. "I'll tell you what I did. I don't care. I'll tell you."

Quinn had once been calmly interviewing a murder suspect when the kid had started crying and admitted his crime while Quinn held him like a baby. He had a sense of déjà vu, but instead of telling him that she'd killed her husband and hidden him in a closet, she sat up suddenly and straightened her sweater, taking a Kleenex from the pocket of her coat and wiping her eyes.

"I'm so sorry," she said. "I don't know what came over me."

"It's okay," he said. "You've been through a lot. What were you going to tell me?"

"Oh." She stood up and in a second, she was gone. He watched her light-colored coat float across the green, across the road, and up into the cemetery. Struggling, he pushed Megan to the top of the hill and left the stroller anchored by a tree before following the ghostly glow of the coat among the trees. He was angry now, and when he reached her, he took her arm and turned her to face him. "What's going on? What were you going to tell me?"

She looked up at him, scared, and he grasped her arm more tightly before he said, "Did you kill him? Is that what you were going to tell me? Tell me." He knew he was hurting her from the look on her face, but he didn't care. He could feel his heart beating and he felt suddenly seized with rage. He wanted to punch her, kick her, hit her. It was the same rage he'd felt earlier, thinking about Maura. It scared him, but he didn't let go of her.

"I . . . no. I destroyed his book. Burned it, everything. That's what I meant. I was embarrassed. I didn't want to tell you, but I destroyed his book. When he didn't come home. I thought it was appropriate. He gave up his family for that goddamned book. I thought he deserved to have it destroyed."

"You didn't kill him?"

"No. I just . . . I burned his book. The copy in his office. His notes, everything. In the fireplace." He was still gripping her arm. Instead of feeling the anger seeping away, he felt it build and he held her so she couldn't move. She was looking up at him and suddenly he remembered his dream from the afternoon. He was standing so close to her that he could smell her shampoo, something fruity and sweet. She looked up at him and her eyes reminded him of his own. After he turned away, he realized how close he had come to kissing her, and it was this realization that made him flee.

In the light from the street, he could see that she was crying again, but he ignored her and stumbled out of the cemetery, not looking back as he got the stroller and nearly ran back to the inn.

THIRTY-SEVEN

"THIS IS VERY NICE," TOBY SAID WHEN THEY GOT BACK TO her room after dinner. "No suffering on the job for you."

"Yeah, well, I haven't had a vacation in a while, so I figured why not live it up a little."

"Good thinking." He walked around the room, looking at the art, and then sat down in the upholstered armchair by the window.

"Want a glass of wine?" She pulled a bottle out of the closet and got two glass tumblers from the bathroom.

He nodded, then said, "I thought you weren't drinking for a while."

"I didn't drink for a while. I had to show myself that I could not drink and I didn't drink for five whole months. Now I can again."

"Okay," Toby said, taking the glass from her. "But just one. I have to drive home."

"Fine. So, that was the cop who was working on the Brad Putnam thing. The one whose wife killed herself." At dinner, she had told him about Pres and Kenneth Churchill and the body in the woods.

"Poor guy. Who was the woman?"

"That was Kenneth Churchill's wife. It was weird, though, didn't you pick up a kind of energy between them? I don't know, it was either that they were mad at each other, or some kind of sexual tension, maybe. But it was really strange."

"I didn't pick up on anything. But I was pretty much focusing on my prime rib. Now, you have to finish telling me about Ian. You had just started when they came over and you never told me what's going on."

"I don't know. He wants to come visit. It really freaked me out. Why is that so crazy? I mean, we talk on the phone almost every night. It's not like I don't know him. But I have this feeling that it will ruin things. If we actually see each other."

Toby took his shoes off and stretched his legs out in front of him. "Or maybe it would be really great."

"Yeah, maybe," she said doubtfully. "I don't know what to do."

"Why don't you just see what happens? It's not like he asked you to marry him."

"But he's serious. I can tell. I'm worried I'll, I don't know, hurt him or something. Anyway, he asked about you. He said to say hi, but I think he was really trying to figure out if anything's going on between us."

"Between us?"

"Yeah, he was kind of suspicious the whole time we were in Vermont."

Toby looked away. She knew he was thinking of Rosemary, whom he might have fallen in love with, and of Sweeney's pronouncement of love and his own angry response to it. He was thinking of the long uncertainty of their friendship.

"Toby?" Sweeney asked quietly.

"Yeah?"

"What you said the other night, about Lily. Do you think it's true?"

"Do I think what's true?" He looked embarrassed and she knew he was stalling.

"About being hung up on me?"

"I don't think there's any secret there," he said, and gave a sarcastic little grin.

"So, what do we do about it?" She met his eyes from across the room. It wasn't the first time they'd had this conversation.

"I don't know that there's anything we can do about it. I mean, we've both kind of moved on, I think. You've got this thing going with Ian, and I'm sure I'll meet a nice girl. Either that or I'll die alone. But it's all good." Sweeney threw a pillow at him from the bed. He caught it and put it behind his head.

"I don't know what I have going with Ian. Should I let him visit?" she asked him. "There's a part of me that's excited about it and a part of me that wants to tell him not to come."

"Is it Colm?" He knew her so well, Sweeney thought, he knew exactly what it was.

"Of course. It feels like I'm cheating on him. That's the problem."

"Yeah. I don't know what to tell you. What about the cop?"

She looked up at him. "Quinn? What do you mean?"

"I don't know. It just seems like you're getting awfully pally with him."

"I'm his babysitter, is what I am. What are you talking about? You think I . . . No way. He's not my type at all."

Toby just shrugged. "Okay. You know best."

"Maybe I don't." She felt like crying all of a sudden. "I don't seem to know anything about myself these days."

"Oh, Swee." Toby got up and went over to the bed. He lay down next to Sweeney and she rolled into his arms, putting her head on his chest and wrapping an arm around his waist.

"Can you stay?" she asked him. She didn't want to be alone tonight.

"Of course," he said. "Don't worry. You'll be okay." And lying there, for just a minute, she felt as though she might.

BOOK THREE

THIRTY-EIGHT

QUINN GOT THE CALL AT 7 A.M. HE HAD BEEN AWAKE SINCE five, and he and Megan had already gone for a walk and had breakfast, a bottle and some oatmeal for her and pancakes and four cups of coffee for him.

When his cell phone rang, he checked the display and saw that it was Andy's number. "Hey," he said, answering it. "You're up early."

"Yeah. Well, a bunch of high school kids out drinking last night found your guy. He's been in the trunk of his car for a while. Pretty nasty stuff."

"Seriously?" Quinn sat up and Megan, who was playing with a cardboard toilet-paper tube on the floor, looked up at him, alarmed, and started to cry.

"Yeah, hey, listen, if you can find yourself a babysitter, why don't you get down here and you can be in on it. We're out on Monument Street. Fairfield Farms. You'll see the cars." Quinn jotted it down on the notepad on the bedside table. Monument Street, he thought. So it wasn't too far from where the first body had been found. How had it stayed hidden for nearly two weeks now?

"You got it," he said. "I'll be down as soon as I can."

It was 7:45 by the time he knocked on Sweeney's door. He'd given Megan a quick bath, dressed her, and put together a bag full of her things. He knocked and smiled at her, sitting in her stroller and playing with the cardboard tube.

When the first knock didn't bring any answer, he tried again, a little bit louder in case she was sleeping. He heard footsteps and then the door was opened by the guy from the dining room the night before. He was wearing boxer shorts, and when he opened the door, Quinn could see through into the room. Sweeney was sitting up in bed and when she saw him, she looked embarrassed and pulled the covers up over her chest.

"I'm so sorry," he said, unsure of what to do. "I was just checking to see if you could watch Megan for a few hours. But I'll figure something out, it's okay. Don't worry about it." He turned to go, but Sweeney, in a T-shirt and sweatpants, got out of bed and came to the door. "What happened?" she asked him, and he could see that her eyes were still swollen from sleep, could smell the wine on her. "Did they find him?"

"Yeah," he said. "I need to go down there."

"I'll watch her," she said. "It's okay. Where is he? Where has he been?"

"No," he said. "He's not . . . He's dead."

It took him ten minutes to get down to Fairfield Farms. It was about half a mile past the Whitings' house, a large yellow farmhouse surrounded by fields that Quinn was sure must be worth a fortune. You could put about twenty huge houses on so much land. There was a big sign out front saying FAIRFIELD FARMS. ORGANIC VEGETABLES. FARMSTAND OPEN MAY THROUGH OCTOBER. The farmstand, a little yellow barn with a rooster weather vane on the roof, had rows of fat orange pumpkins out front.

Quinn showed his ID to the state cop guarding the long driveway. "Andy Lynch said he'd let you know I was coming," he said. The cop waved him through, and he parked next to the mobile crime lab van. Andy was talking to a couple of plainclothes guys when Quinn wandered up.

". . . says they didn't notice anything. One of the seasonal workers said when they found the car, it was pretty well hidden," one of the guys was saying. "They're not down in the fields a lot this time of year, so that's probably how they missed it. Anyway, we'll get them in again, make sure there isn't anything they're holding back, but my instinct tells me no."

"Hi, Quinny," Andy greeted him. "We got him. Similar stab wounds to the other body. We'll have to get forensics on it, but there are some leaves and debris in the trunk that may match what we found at the Tucker Beloit scene. He's been dead about three weeks."

"So that puts us right back at the encampment."

"Yeah, we're thinking he was killed that Saturday or Sunday, just about the same time Tucker Beloit was killed. So, we're probably looking at a double homicide. And goddamn it, we're way behind, thinking he was on the run all this time. We don't even have alibis for anybody."

"How'd you ID him?" Quinn asked.

Andy said, "Dentals you gave us. We didn't need 'em, though. It's his car. We checked the registration. And despite the fact that his face is falling apart, it sure as hell looks like him. Looks like he's been in the trunk the whole time. No animal damage like the other guy. You gotta tell the wife."

"Why me?" Quinn felt his stomach drop.

Andy looked surprised. "Because he was yours before he was ours. She knows you. You've got all the background. And you said you needed to be part of this. So, whaddya think? How does this change things?"

Quinn wasn't sure, but he thought there was a hint of sarcasm in Andy's voice. "I don't know. We probably have to discount Churchill as the murderer." He thought for a minute. "It still doesn't make any sense. Where was he going when he left the encampment in his car?"

"Maybe here," Andy said.

"But then how is it connected to Beloit?"

"I don't know. Let's just think about Churchill for a minute. I like his kid for it."

"Yeah, that sounds good. Kid kills his father, steals the credit card, thinking he's gonna take off somewhere."

"Okay, I'll pull him in. We gotta talk to him again."

"Wait until the wife knows, so she can tell him, though, will ya? If he didn't do it, it's gonna be a big shock that he's dead."

"Yeah, yeah," Andy said, without promising. "Give me some scenarios."

Quinn thought for a minute. "We have the witness saying that Kenneth Churchill was heading back to his car Sunday morning, looking like something was very wrong. So, maybe it doesn't discount Churchill as the murderer. Or maybe Kenneth Churchill saw Tucker Beloit being killed. So he's scared and he takes off. But the murderer, whoever it is, tracked him down and killed him, and put him in the trunk of the car, then left the car at Fairfield Farms."

"That's pretty good, Quinn," Andy said. "I like that. The problem is, we don't have a hard tie between Beloit and Churchill yet. So we've got to focus on Churchill. What do you think about his wife? He was having an affair. Could she have wanted to kill him?"

"Maybe," Quinn said.

"Okay, so I want you to find out about her alibi around the time Churchill was last seen. What about the mistress?"

"Cecily Whiting? She was pissed, but I don't think I buy it. I've been thinking some more about the ex-husband, though. Maybe he was still in love with her, and he wanted Churchill out of the way so they could reconcile. I'd like to take a shot at him."

"You got it," Andy said. "Who else?"

"Well, here's the thing. He was working on this book about this Revolutionary War stonecutter guy. When he was out there, it seemed kind of crazy, but I've been wondering if there's anything there that might have led someone to want to kill him. You find anything in the car? Notes, laptop, anything like that?"

"Yeah to both," Andy said. "You want to take a look?"

"Yeah," Quinn said, thinking of Sweeney. "Beyond that, I don't know who might have wanted him killed. Except that . . ." He thought for a minute. "His wife told me that he'd had lots of affairs. With graduate students, waitresses. Lots of women. What if there's some connection there?"

"Sounds good to me. I want you to do the ex-husband, the mistress, and the wife. The rest of that family while you're at it. See how they respond to the news. Are they surprised? Get some alibis we can check out. You know the drill."

"Yeah," Quinn said, picturing Beverly Churchill's tear-stained face in the darkness of the cemetery. "Got it."

He headed back up to his car and made his way past the line of gawkers who had parked along the road, hoping for a glimpse of the grisly discovery.

He was back at the inn in under five minutes and he went straight up to her room, knocking on the door and steeling himself. He realized that his fists were clenched and he made an effort to unclench them, taking a deep breath and trying to slow his racing heart.

"Hi," she said when she answered the door, and he felt his stomach pitch when he realized she was happy to see him. "I'm so sorry about last night. I've been wanting to apologize for the way I acted. . . . I . . ."

Quinn broke in. "Is Marcus here?"

"No, why?"

"I have some bad news. Can we go in and sit down?"

"Of course. Is it about Kenneth?" She didn't seem afraid. She stood there almost defiantly, bravely, waiting to hear whatever it was.

"Please. Sit down." He couldn't say her name.

"No, I want to know."

There was no other way to do it. "Your husband's car was found this morning. His body was in the trunk. He's been dead for three weeks."

"Three weeks? You mean, he didn't disappear? All that time, he was dead?"

"It looks that way. Is there anyone I can call for you? Do you want someone else to be here when you tell your son? I can arrange for someone to stay here with you."

"No," she said. "I just want to be alone."

"Mrs. Churchill."

"Oh, please don't call me Mrs. Churchill. Besides, I'm not Mrs. Churchill anymore. Just leave me alone. I'll tell my son on my own." She was pacing back and forth, working furiously at the cuticles on her right fingers.

"I'll have to ask you some questions, but we can do that later. Are you sure you don't want me to—?"

"Oh, for Christ's sake! Just go."

He left her alone, shutting the door quietly behind him.

He told himself he should stop and see how Sweeney and Megan were doing, but he wanted to see Bruce and Cecily Whiting as soon as possible, so he settled for dialing her cell phone number as soon as he was in the car. "Everything okay?" he asked when she answered.

"Yeah, she's been great. We went for a walk and now she's playing with a shoebox."

"A woman of simple tastes, my daughter."

"So, what's going on?"

"It was him. He's been dead three weeks, so we've got what looks like a double homicide. I'm going to talk to some people now but I just wanted to make sure everything was okay. I'm sorry about dropping her on you. And I'm sorry about this morning. . . . I didn't know that . . ."

She hesitated for a moment before she said, "Don't worry about it. Toby's just a friend. And I'll forgive you for dropping her on me if you promise to tell me everything when you get back."

"Okay," he said. "It's a deal. I've got something else for you as well. They found a laptop and notebooks. If I can get hold of them, can you look through and see if there's anything there? Anything related to his book on Josiah Whiting that might have caused someone to want to kill him?"

"You got it," she said.

He was at Whiting Monuments in a few minutes. A bell on the front door jingled as he entered, and he found himself in a little waiting room, complete with a couple of couches and a coffee table covered with magazines and, he saw when he leaned down to read the titles, catalogs of tombstones.

At the other end of the room, a tall, dark-haired man was showing a young couple a series of little square blocks of stone. "Had you thought at all about what you want the monument to say?" He looked up quickly, his face fixed in annoyance. "Can I help you?" he called out a little rudely.

"I'm sorry, I just wanted to talk to you for a few minutes. I'll wait until you're done." To show his willingness to wait, Quinn sat down on the couch and held up a magazine. Bruce Whiting still looked annoyed, but he went back to the couple.

"We were thinking her name and something like 'beloved daughter,' " the woman said. "Will that look nice?"

"That will look beautiful," Bruce Whiting said soothingly.

Quinn leafed through a couple of catalogs of tombstones. He still hadn't picked one out for Maura. Her remains— "cremains," the funeral home director had called them— were still in a square box in the hall closet. He'd have to do something, but he didn't like the look of these stones, big and boxy and plain.

Bruce Whiting finished up with the couple and came over to Quinn.

"I'm really sorry to barge in on you like this," Quinn said before Bruce Whiting could get a word out. "I'm Detective Tim Quinn and I just wanted to ask you a few questions."

Whiting looked at the badge and said, "Sorry about that back there. Their two-year-old daughter died. We usually try to let them come in on their own."

"I'm sorry," Quinn said, feeling awful. "I had no idea."

"Of course not. Are you here about the body in the woods? I told the Concord police the same thing I'll tell you. I have no idea who he is." It sounded rehearsed, with a subtext of minor annoyance.

"Actually," Quinn said. "It's about Kenneth Churchill."

Bruce Whiting looked perplexed, then said, "Who?"

"Kenneth Churchill. He's a historian from Cambridge. He was writing a book about your ancestor Josiah Whiting."

"Oh, him. My father and I talked to him a few times. Gave him some information about the family."

"But you never met him?"

"No." Whiting picked up a pencil and doodled a few little designs on a piece of paper lying on the desk. Quinn was pretty sure he was lying.

"Did you know that he was married and that he'd been seeing your ex-wife since February?"

Genuine surprise. "What? Shit, no. Jeez, poor Cecily. Makes sense, though." He reached up to stroke his beard and he looked suddenly thoughtful. "Did she know he was married?"

"Yes. She did."

"Would he have left his wife for her?" There was something hopeful in his voice that caught Quinn's attention.

"I don't know. What's your relationship with your ex-wife like?"

"It's okay. We have a son who's very sick. We've tried to make the best of things for him." Bruce Whiting cleared some catalogs off one of the chairs across from the couch and sat down. Quinn noticed that he kept looking nervously over his shoulder, as though he was waiting for someone to show up.

"Your ex-wife was sleeping with this man. Were you jealous of him?"

"Detective Quinn, you have to understand. I left Cecily for another woman, for a woman Cecily knew, a woman who worked for us. I was dishonest with her, I broke her heart. The worst thing I've ever had to do in my life was to tell her that I was in love with Lauren and that she was pregnant. I have been paying for it in ways big and small ever since." He raised his eyebrows in a self-deprecating little smirk. "It's something I will always have to live with."

Quinn was about to follow up on that when an older man came out of the back of the building. He looked so much like an older version of Bruce Whiting that Quinn knew this had to be George Whiting.

"Bruce?" he asked, looking from Quinn to his son.

"It's okay, Dad." He said to Quinn, "This is my father, George Whiting."

"Tim Quinn. I'm a police officer from Cambridge." Quinn stood up and shook the man's hand. He was sure he saw something there, a flash of nervousness or fear.

"What's he doing here?" George Whiting asked.

"I need to know where you were on Sunday, October third, Mr. Whiting."

"Why are you asking me this?"

"Because some local kids found Kenneth Churchill's body this morning. Not far from your house. And we're asking anybody who had any connection to him about what they were doing that weekend, in case they saw something that might help with the investigation."

"You found . . . Where?" Bruce Whiting seemed angry somehow, though Quinn would be damned if he hadn't been surprised too.

"At Fairfield Farms."

"Does Cecily know yet?"

"No. I'm going to tell her as soon as I leave here. Sunday the third?"

George Whiting had been listening to them and now he said, "Kenneth? Kenneth is dead?"

"Yes. I'm sorry."

Bruce Whiting had gotten up and gone over to a little calendar hanging on the wall. "The third? I think I came into the office that morning and then I spent the rest of the day with my family. My wife can tell you when I got home. She has a good mind for numbers."

"Was anybody else here on Sunday morning? Were you, Mr. Whiting?" Quinn looked up at the older man, who was staring at him with a look of fear on his face.

Bruce Whiting prompted him. "That was the weekend of the encampment, Dad. You were here in the morning and then you went back up there in the afternoon. Right?"

"Yes, yes," George Whiting said. "That's right." But he didn't sound convinced.

Quinn studied him. "Are you sure, Mr. Whiting? We'll need to check on it."

George Whiting nodded. "Yes, that's right. I was here and then I went up to the encampment."

Quinn stood up. He wanted to talk with George Whiting again. He'd had the sense his son had been covering for him. "Okay. Thank you," he told them. "We'll be in touch."

Bruce Whiting walked him outside. "Listen," he said, shaking Quinn's hand. "When you tell Cecily, do it . . . I don't know, gently," he said. "She's sensitive. She's going through a lot right now."

Quinn watched his face. He hadn't been sleeping. Quinn knew the signs. Bruce Whiting's eyes were shot through with red veins and his skin had a gray, washed-out pallor. He seemed about to say something and then knotted his hands together in front of him.

"Are you okay, Mr. Whiting?"

Whiting looked up quickly. "Yes, I'm fine. I'm just . . . with my son being sick, I haven't been sleeping."

Across the street, Quinn saw a redheaded woman walking out of a bagel shop. She looked just like Sweeney and he raised a hand to wave before he realized it wasn't her, just someone with the same curly scarlet hair. It gave him an idea. Chris Wright thought he had seen Kenneth Churchill across the field at the reenactment, but what if it hadn't been Kenneth Churchill at all?

"I'm sorry," Quinn said simply. "I guess that's it, but if you think of anything that might help us, please let us know." Bruce Whiting looked sad for a minute, and on impulse, Quinn said, "What did you mean when you said that it made sense Cecily would choose a married man?"

He looked back toward the building. They could both see George Whiting watching them out the window. "Well, it was like she was getting back at me, wasn't it? You don't have to be fucking Freud to figure that out."

Quinn drove up the Whitings' driveway, past George and Lillian Whiting's house and back to the log cabin where Bruce and Lauren Whiting lived. He'd called ahead, so he knew that Lauren Whiting was there.

He knocked and she answered the door in a pink sweat-suit and showed him into a kitchen painted with blueberries. There was a nice warm feeling about the room, kids' drawings on the refrigerator, a big bowl of fruit on the counter, and Quinn found that he wanted to stay there. It was the way he always wanted his house to feel, the way it felt once every six months when he cleaned up and remembered to go shopping and built a fire in the fireplace and Megan was dry and happy. It usually lasted for about an hour.

He accepted her offer of a cup of coffee, hoping to stamp out the last vestiges of his hangover from the night before, and they sat down at the kitchen table.

"Did your husband tell you that we found Kenneth Churchill's body?"

"Yes, of course. He called to tell me that you were down at the showroom and that you talked to him and George." Damn. Quinn had been hoping to get to her before she talked to her husband. "It's terrible. I feel really badly for his wife and son. And, of course, for Cecily."

"Can you tell me what you and your family were doing the weekend of October second and third?"

"Is that when you think he was killed? Let me check." She strode over to the kitchen and took down a calendar magneted to the refrigerator. It had pictures of babies sitting in flowerpots on it.

"We had Pres that weekend. Oh, that was the picnic. Let's see, we had this church picnic on Saturday. Pres came with us. We came home later that afternoon and I think Bruce went over to the showroom and worked for a while. Then we all watched a movie and had dinner and went to bed."

"What about Sunday morning?"

"Pres went home early because Cecily had something she wanted him to do. I don't remember what it was. She sometimes makes things up so that we can't have him the whole weekend. She called Saturday night and said she needed him to come home. So Bruce took him home and then went to the showroom and then came back here."

"What time was he back here?"

"Oh, I'd say around eleven or twelve."

"And you were here with your children all morning?"

"Yes, well, not with the children, actually. They were up with Lillian."

"Okay." He took a long sip of his coffee, then looked

down at his notebook, trying to figure out what to ask her next.

But she beat him to it. "I just want to say that if you think Bruce had anything to do with it, you're completely missing the point. My husband left Cecily because he fell in love with me. For the past four years, we've been slaves to her pain. I don't know what possible motive you think he could have for wanting anything to happen to her new boyfriend. He was happy about it!" When he looked up at her, her face was slightly flushed, nearly the color of her pink sweatsuit, and she was looking almost triumphant.

Quinn sat up. "Wait a second. He knew they were sleeping together?"

She looked suddenly nervous. "He told you that, right?"

"He said he didn't know."

"Well, he probably just didn't want to confuse things. He'd seen them together, by accident. He was really embarrassed about it."

"When was this?"

"Oh, a few months ago, I guess."

"Did he ever confront Churchill about it?"

"No. He didn't even know what his name was. He'd been at the showroom a few times and interviewed George, but it wasn't until this whole thing with the body in the woods that he put it together that that's who it was. Besides, why would he confront him? He was happy about it. Why can't I get that through to you?"

Quinn had to admit that it made sense. "All right. Thanks for your help," he said. "I may be in touch again."

Lauren Whiting walked him to the door and held it open until he was safely outside. "I'm sure you will," she said. "I'm sure you will."

Cecily Whiting's house was a little split-level ranch on a cul-de-sac behind the Hill cemetery. It was painted yellow and the green shutters set off the carefully landscaped yard, flower beds encircling the house, two half barrels filled with yellow chrysanthemums flanking the front steps.

He knocked on the front door and waited. She must have been watching from the window, because the door opened immediately and he could see she had been crying. She was wearing panty hose, nice shoes, and a dark skirt that looked as though it was part of a set, but on the top, she had on an old Boston Red Sox T-shirt. It was as though she'd been half dressed when she'd gotten the news.

"I know," she said. "One of my neighbors told me. I know already, so if you're here to tell me, don't bother."

Shit. Now he wouldn't be able to see her face when she found out. But he had to be sure. "You know that Kenneth Churchill's body was found early this morning? He was murdered."

"Yes. I told you. I know."

"Okay. Do you have any idea who might have wanted to kill him?"

"No." She put her head in her hands and a new wave of grief—or something—swept over her as she cried in front of Quinn. It struck him how different her reaction was from Beverly Churchill's. "How could I possibly . . . ? Of course not."

"Ms. Whiting." This time he remembered. "Were you angry with Kenneth Churchill for not leaving his wife? Had you thought he was going to leave her?"

"Oh." She sank back against the couch. "You don't understand. How can I make you understand? He wanted to leave his wife. I didn't want him to. What would I have done with him? What, was he going to move down here and marry me? I can't explain it to you! My husband is the only man I've ever loved. Kenneth was just . . ." She was crying and she choked out the next word. "Revenge!"

He gave her a minute to compose herself again. And then he asked her, "Do you remember what you were doing the weekend of October second and third? I need to ask everyone."

She gave him a look he couldn't quite identify and got up to go over to the dining room table. She took a silver PalmPilot out of her handbag and scrolled down. "Pres was at his father's, so I was here alone on Saturday night, and then on

Sunday I went for a walk by myself in the morning and then I came back here by noon, when they dropped Pres off."

"So you were alone all morning? Where did you go for a walk?"

"I didn't go up to the clubhouse, if that's what you mean. I just walked around town, and then I had coffee and read the paper, and then I came home."

"Can I ask you something?" Quinn put his notebook down and studied her face. "What was he like? Kenneth?"

She looked up, her large brown eyes surprised. "He was brilliant. That was the first thing you noticed about him. He wasn't exactly what you'd call a handsome man, maybe, but there was something about him. People were attracted to him. He was one of those people who everything they do, they do it to the tenth degree, you know? When he got into the reenactments, he got into it all the way. He was obsessed. He was obsessed with his book. For a while, anyway, I think he was obsessed with me."

"So, why didn't you return his feelings? He sounds like he was a good catch."

She looked thoughtful. "I told you, I thought of him as revenge. If I'm honest, I'm still in love with my ex-husband. But maybe there was more to it. Kenneth had this way of looking at you. It was like he was a child. He could be taunting. I don't know how else to describe it. It was like he sometimes took pleasure in other people's discomfort. I remember one time when I was feeling guilty about spending so much time with him and I was telling him that I didn't think we should see each other anymore, I looked up at him and I could see that on some level he was enjoying it, enjoying my anguish. I don't know why. There are people who get off on other people's emotion that way, you know."

She took a sip of coffee and sat back, playing with the hem of the T-shirt. "I wouldn't be surprised if that was why he got killed. It was the way he looked at you. Like he couldn't imagine anything he'd rather be doing than enjoying your discomfort."

THIRTY-NINE

TOBY HAD BREAKFAST WITH SWEENEY AND MEGAN AND THEN left for Cambridge about eleven. Once he was gone, Sweeney put Megan in her stroller and went in search of Will Baker. She found him in the lounge, changing the magazines on the coffee table for new ones.

"Hi," she said, watching as he carefully fanned out the magazines, *Architectural Digest* on top, then a few *New Yorker*s and *Boston*s and some others she couldn't see.

He jumped. "Oh, hello. I'm sorry, you surprised me." He was wearing a green wool vest over his white broadcloth shirt, and it actually suited him, made him look vaguely outdoorsy. "Is there something I can help you with?"

"There is," Sweeney said. "Remember when I asked you about Kenneth Churchill, about whether he'd ever said anything to you about Whiting or Baker being a spy?"

He stood up suddenly, blinking at her, and didn't answer.

"Well, I think that Kenneth Churchill told you he'd seen a letter written by a British officer documenting the murder of Josiah Whiting by John Baker. Am I right?"

Will Baker stared at her for another few minutes, then sat down on the couch. Sweeney sat down across from him.

"He told me he had proof that John Baker had killed Josiah Whiting, proof that directly contradicted Baker's famous account of April nineteenth. I couldn't imagine what it could be.

I mean, it didn't make any sense. They were best friends and I had never heard anything about this, I mean even remotely. It was crazy. He didn't tell me about the spy charge, though. I was surprised when you asked me about that."

"Were you worried he was going to tell people about it?"

"Yes, I . . . I got worried about what would happen to my business if people knew. I mean, part of the reason people come to stay at the inn is that there's a long history here, and John Baker is part of that history. But he said he wouldn't be publishing the book for a while and he needed to verify that the letter was legitimate. So, I thought I had some time. I even thought maybe he'd forgotten and it was over. You, you're not going to . . . ?"

"I don't think so," Sweeney said. "Not unless it's absolutely necessary. Besides, we don't even know why he killed Whiting. Maybe there was a good reason."

"Maybe," Will Baker said. But he looked upset, and Sweeney felt guilty leaving him there.

She was carrying Megan and the stroller down the front steps when she saw Pres coming toward them. He was wearing khaki pants, a blue sweatshirt, and the Red Sox hat and was looking down at the ground. He seemed troubled, and when Sweeney called his name and he looked up at her, she knew he'd heard about Kenneth Churchill.

"You okay?" she asked him.

"They found another man," he said, looking up at her, his giant, sad eyes shadowed by the brim of his hat. "Did you know?"

"Yeah. I did." She wasn't sure what to say. Did Pres know that Kenneth Churchill had been his mother's lover? She still wasn't sure.

But he solved the problem for her. "Can we go for a walk?" he asked her. "I want to tell you something."

Sweeney nodded. "Do you mind if Megan comes?" He shook his head. "Where do you want to go?"

He looked into her eyes, and as though it was the most obvious thing in the world, he said, "Up to the woods."

* * *

They walked slowly up Monument Street. Pres seemed more tired than usual, and Sweeney pushed the stroller along, enjoying the feel of the light autumn sun on her head. Megan fell asleep and they were silent as they walked, as if they'd agreed not to say anything until they'd reached the woods. She remembered the first day she'd met Pres and how she'd followed him along this very route, into the trees. A police car passed them, going too fast, and she saw him flinch.

They turned off the sidewalk into the woods, and Sweeney remembered the feeling of peace she'd had that first day. The leafing trees gently shaded the path and the wind moved through them, whispering. The colors were so vibrant, she suddenly had the feeling that they couldn't get any more beautiful, that this was it, this was the brightest these colors could be.

"Okay, Pres," she said gently. "What's going on?"

He didn't say anything for a minute, and then started with, "You know that day, when we found that man?" Sweeney nodded. "Well, you're right. I did do something before you got there. But it wasn't anything bad. When I found that man, I didn't want to tell the police, because I was afraid they would go in the clubhouse." They were almost there and Sweeney had the feeling that he wanted to wait until they had arrived to go on, so she let him walk along in silence.

"There was a key," he said when they'd reached the little structure. "We kept it under that rock over there. There didn't used to be a key, but then some of the high school kids started coming down here to do bad stuff, so my grandfather had to get a lock because he was worried that if something happened it would be his fault.

"When I saw the man, I got worried that maybe he'd gone inside, so I went to check the door and it was open and the key was in it." He looked up at her. "I know you're not supposed to move things when someone gets killed, but all I did was lock the door again and take the key out. I didn't know that man and I didn't know why he would open the door. How did he know where the key was?"

It was a good question. As he talked, Sweeney started to see a little glimmer of light. She knew Pres didn't see it, but it was the only way the whole thing made any sense.

"Pres," she said. "Who knew where the key was?"

"Just my grandpa and my dad and my mom and maybe Lauren." And Kenneth Churchill, Sweeney thought. Quinn had said that Kenneth Churchill had gone with Cecily to the clubhouse. Kenneth Churchill must have known.

"Pres, remember when we were talking about how it feels when your parents start dating other people and I asked you about your mom and you said maybe she'd dated a man. Who was it? Can you tell me who it was?"

Pres looked very embarrassed. "I'm not sure," he said. "But I think maybe Mr. Baker."

"Mr. Baker, who owns the inn?"

"Yeah." He blushed and she felt terrible for causing him so much embarrassment. "I think so. One time I came home from being at Dad and Lauren's and he was over and she seemed real nervous. And then another time I saw him waiting for her at the museum."

"Okay," Sweeney said. She hadn't expected him to say Will Baker. "But the thing I don't understand is why you didn't want the police to go in the clubhouse."

"Well," Pres said. "It's because of the General."

"What?" Sweeney's mind swam. The General? Was there some ghost of a Revolutionary War general haunting the woods? Hadn't Pres said something about local kids believing in a spirit who screamed as if in pain?

"Maybe he's . . . Let me show you." Pres fumbled in the pocket of his jeans for a minute and came out with a key. He strode over to the clubhouse, moved aside the sagging yellow police tape, and opened the door, holding it for Sweeney. She left Megan and the stroller just outside the door and followed him inside. The clubhouse was dark, with brown-and-orange curtains at the windows, and she could just barely make out a low couch, a coffee table, and some boxes in one corner.

There was a not-unpleasant smell of mustiness, like an old attic full of treasures. It took her eyes a minute to adjust and when they did, she saw Pres go over to the couch and lean over. And then she saw a small black kitten stand up and arch its back, stretching against Pres's hand. He mewled once, an oddly dignified mewl for such a small cat.

"That's the General," Pres said. "I named him that because he has medals on his shoulder. See?" He picked the kitten up and held him up so Sweeney could see the three small medal-shaped patches of white on his jet-black fur.

"But, Pres, why didn't you just take him home?" The kitten was stretched out in Pres's arms, purring as though his life depended on it.

"My mom won't let me because she said it could make me sick because of my immune system. And Lauren's allergic and my grandma already has three cats and they're mean to each other, so I think they'd be mean to the General. Maybe you could take care of him? Just until I get better and my mom lets me have him."

"Pres, I'm staying in a hotel at the moment and I don't even . . . Look, he's probably fine here for a while. The police have been in and out and they haven't found him so far. Where did he come from?"

"I was walking home through the woods a month ago and he came out of the bushes. Someone must have left him here. I was walking toward the clubhouse and he went up to the door like he wanted to go in. So I let him in and he jumped up on the couch and stretched out like he wanted to stay. The next day I brought him some food and water and I left the window open a little so he could go out to go to the bathroom. So, then I just started coming by every day to feed him. He's really nice. You would like him. And he's very clean. I haven't had to clean up after him once." The General looked up from Pres's arms as if to say, "It's all true. Every word of it."

"Oh God, Pres. Let's leave him here for now and see what happens, okay?" Seeing the look of disappointment on his face, she added, "I'll think about it, okay?"

"Okay." He seemed happier as he locked up the clubhouse and they started back toward town. In front of the inn, Sweeney said she was going to take Megan in and put her down and Pres said he was walking back to his mom's house.

"Thanks," she said, "for telling me all that stuff."

"It's okay," he said. Sweeney watched his face for a minute. He was very pale and there was something in his eyes that spoke of weariness, but he seemed happy.

"Do you want me to drive you back?"

"No," he said. "I'll just go slow." And then, with a strange little nod of his head, he turned and walked away.

It was 10:30 by the time Quinn got back, and when she heard him knock, Sweeney opened the door and pushed him out into the hallway, shutting the door behind her. "Megan's sleeping," she said. "But listen to this. When Pres got there and found Tucker Beloit's body, the door to the clubhouse was open. So, someone had been in there, someone who knew where the key was. Pres didn't want the police to go inside, so he locked it again, but someone was in there before Tucker Beloit was killed."

Quinn looked confused. "Okay," he said. "Someone was in there."

"Where was Kenneth Churchill killed?" Sweeney asked him. "Have you figured that out yet? Is there any chance he was killed by the clubhouse too?"

"Who knew where the key was?" Quinn asked. Sweeney could see his mind working around it, trying to put it all into place.

"George Whiting, probably his wife too, Bruce Whiting, I imagine Lauren, Cecily Whiting, and Pres Whiting. But here's the thing. We know that Cecily Whiting took Kenneth Churchill to the clubhouse, so he must have known where the key was. But isn't it likely that she took other lovers there too? If it was a revenge thing, that's what she would do. I just found out that at one time, Cecily Whiting was probably seeing Will Baker, so it's pretty likely that Will Baker knew where the key was too."

Quinn thought about that for a minute. "Okay," he said. "But what about Tucker Beloit?"

"You know what?" Sweeney said. "I've been thinking about it and I don't think Tucker Beloit was meant to die. I think that someone was in the clubhouse and Kenneth Churchill came along and there was a fight and Kenneth Churchill was killed. And I think Tucker Beloit saw it happen. I don't think Tucker Beloit had anything to do with it. I think he was just in the wrong place at the wrong time."

"So Kenneth Churchill was the intended victim?"

"It looks that way, don't you think?"

"Maybe." He rubbed his eyes. "Look, I'm so tired, I can't even begin to sort this all out. Let me take Megan off your hands and we'll talk about this in the morning." He was holding a manila envelope and he handed it over. "This is the stuff that was found in Churchill's car. If you could take a look through it and see if there's anything new on his research, that would be great."

"Sure," Sweeney said, feeling deflated. "I'll take a look."

FORTY

SWEENEY COULDN'T SLEEP. SHE HAD SLEPT FOR ALMOST THREE hours on the couch with Megan, but then Quinn had come by and now she couldn't sleep at all. So, she got out of bed, took the padded mailer off the table by the window, and popped the CD into her laptop.

Kenneth Churchill's hard drive had contained the kind of stuff any college professor's computer would: student e-mails and papers, class curricula. He also had lots of photos of himself in his Minuteman uniform and a folder titled "Josiah Whiting research."

Bingo. Sweeney opened it and found twelve documents that seemed to correspond to chapters for the eventual book. It seemed that Churchill had chosen the most logical structure for a biography, a chapter on Whiting's early life, his apprenticeship with his father, and his early involvement with the militia.

Sweeney scanned through the notes. While he had all kinds of wonderful details he'd gleaned from searches of probate records and historical documents, the bare facts stuck to the lines of the story as she knew it.

She read through the rest of the chapters. He followed Whiting through the buildup to April 19 and then devoted three chapters to the actual day. Much of the early material was the stuff she knew already, and Churchill had obviously relied heavily on Baker's account of the day. At the bottom of the document, though, she found a transcription of the letter Ian had found in Hamish Jones's collection. She knew from Will Baker that Churchill was aware of the contents of the letter, but here was proof that he'd seen the same document Ian had.

She turned to the handwritten notes. From the photocopies, she was able to tell that they had been copied from a ruled notebook. The notes looked a lot like her own research notes, with scrawled titles like "Concord Trip 9/1" and "notes from George Whiting interview 6/21." Sweeney read through them and found some notes that Churchill had taken during an interview with Cecily Whiting in January, before they had started seeing each other, she realized. "No proof of what happened," he had written in his messy hand. "But she thinks killed and dragged himself into pond. Only explanation. She says, 'People here in Concord knew him. His family would have been looking for him. I think he would have been found if he died in the woods.'"

It was a good point. The woods had certainly been thicker in the eighteenth century, but they had been well traveled and it just didn't make sense that someone wouldn't have found his body. Had Baker buried him, or had he just been lucky?

She read all the way through the notebook but didn't find anything more of interest. She thought for a moment. One of the questions she'd had all along was why Kenneth Churchill had been so interested in Whiting's gravestones. She felt she'd missed something, so she flipped back through the notebook and looked for references to Whiting's gravestones.

Kenneth Churchill had obviously been interested in the death masks because he'd drawn a few little sketches of some of the later very strange ones and written, "Unusual?" next to them in the margin. He had also, Sweeney realized, gotten interested in the shapes of Whiting's headstones. There were lots of little sketches of the tops of the stone. She scanned across his messy writing and read the notes he'd made next to them. "Tops uniform until 1774," he'd written, and Sweeney congratulated him for noticing how the shapes had changed in 1774. The tops had indeed gotten thinner. "Mask?" he had scrawled next to one of sketches. He was wondering why the death masks had changed too.

"Well, Kenneth Churchill," she said as she put the disks and the photocopied pages back in their envelope. "I'm going to sleep."

FORTY-ONE

MARCUS CHURCHILL HAD BEEN CRYING. IT WAS OBVIOUS from his red eyes and the way he wouldn't look at Quinn and Andy when he came into the room. But when Quinn said, "I'm so sorry, Marcus," and tried to touch him on the shoulder, Marcus stepped back as though Quinn had tried to stab him with a red-hot poker.

"We need to know how you got hold of your dad's credit card," Andy said gently. "I know you want to help us clear this up."

Marcus didn't say anything. They had called Beverly Churchill that morning and asked her to bring him in that afternoon. They had arrived dutifully, Marcus dressed in jeans and a ratty sweatshirt, a tiny sad patch of stubble on his chin.

"Marcus," Quinn said. "We need to know if you had anything to do with your dad's death."

He looked up at them, his eyes wide. "I didn't . . . I didn't *do* anything," he said.

"What do you mean?"

"I didn't do anything to him. . . . Wait, you think I . . . ?" Quinn watched him carefully; he couldn't be sure it wasn't an act. There was a kind of dullness to the kid's protestations.

"What are we supposed to think? You use your dad's credit card and you won't tell us how you got it, and then your dad is found dead."

Marcus stood up and lunged toward them and Quinn watched Andy reach instinctively for his holster. He jumped up and took Marcus by the shoulders. "Marcus, you need to sit down," he said. "We want to keep this calm and low-key, right?"

"But . . ." Marcus's eyes filled with tears, and Quinn waited. "Okay, I stole it from him, okay? I stole it from him."

"Why didn't you tell us that before?"

"Because I didn't want my mom to know, okay?"

"Okay," Quinn said. "When did you steal it?"

He looked away. "A month or so ago. At the end of the summer."

"Why? Did you need money for something?"

Marcus mumbled something unintelligible.

"What, Marcus?"

"No. I was pissed at him, so I thought it would be cool if I charged a bunch of stuff on his card and if he got mad I could just . . . He wouldn't be able to punish me."

"Why were you pissed at him?"

Silence.

"Why were you pissed at him?"

Marcus stared out the window.

"Because he had a girlfriend. Out here."

Quinn looked at Andy. "How did you find out, Marcus?"

He was silent for a long time, then said, "Because I followed him out here and I saw him with her, okay?" He looked up and his eyes were full of tears again. "I saw them in the woods."

Quinn looked up. "What do you mean, you followed him here?"

"I got this guy from school to drive me out one of the weekends there was a reenactment and I watched. It was really weird. He'd been going to them for a year, but I didn't really know what he did, you know? But I watched him pretending to fight and then after it was over, I hung around and I saw him walk up the road and kind of duck into the woods. So I followed him."

"He went to the clubhouse?"

"It was some kind of little house in the woods, and when he got there, this lady came outside and they started kissing. Then they went in and I waited for a while but they didn't come out."

"When was this, Marcus?"

"In May."

"And you didn't come out here again?"

"No. I knew where he was after that, though." Marcus Churchill's eyes welled up with tears again and he tried to wipe them away with the back of his hands. "He was a bastard," he said suddenly, and started to sob. "He was such a bastard."

"I don't know. Either he's a really good liar or he's telling the truth," Andy said once Marcus had gone.

"I think he's telling the truth. We'll have to check with the friend who he says drove him out here, and we want to check his alibi for the third. But my instinct tells me it's not him."

"Yeah? I'm not so sure. What else have we got at this point?"

Quinn thought for a second. "I don't know. We haven't been able to find any connection between him and Beloit. So, I think we have to consider the possibility that maybe Beloit wasn't connected to it at all. Maybe he was kind of a casualty, an accident. So, then we're left with the question of why someone would want to kill Kenneth Churchill, and I keep thinking that this book he was writing must have had something to do with it. I mean, in a way this whole thing with Cecily Whiting just kind of obscured that."

"You think he got killed because of this guy who died what? Like two hundred years ago? I don't see it, Quinny."

"Well, it was why he was out here, right? That's why he was going around and talking to all these people. What if he found out something that people didn't like?"

"I don't know." Andy looked at his watch. "I'm wrecked. You want to go grab a beer?" He grinned. "For old time's sake?"

Quinn checked his watch. It was almost nine. Sweeney had had Megan all day. But another hour probably wouldn't matter. She'd seemed pretty cool about it that morning. "Sure," he said. "For old time's sake."

They went to the tavern at the Minuteman, and Andy pointed Quinn to a booth and went up to the bar to order two pints. He brought them back and sat down across the table. "So how about this, huh? The Somerville boys on the case. Remember how we always played detectives when we were kids?"

"Jeez. I'd forgotten all about that." Quinn took a long sip of his beer. "We were nosy little bastards, weren't we? Remember when we decided that old Mrs. Mahoney had killed her husband and we tried digging up her backyard?"

"She was so pissed at us. I thought she was going to kill us. What happened to the husband, anyway? Did we ever find out?"

"I don't remember. I think maybe he just had a heart attack. But there must have been something that made us suspicious."

"I don't know. Kids are always suspicious." They laughed and worked on their beers for a few minutes. Quinn looked around the tavern. It was nice to be out like this, like a regular person. It had been a long time since he'd gone to a bar.

"So, what about you, Andy? You got a girlfriend? You never said."

Andy looked uncomfortable for a minute, then said, "Nah. Nobody special at the moment, though I can have my share if I want it. It's the damn job. I had a girl I lived with back last year, but she got tired of me never being around, and that was that. I don't know how you did it with a wife and kid."

"Well, I don't think I did it very well. It's funny, I always thought you'd end up with what's-her-name, Heather. Didn't you date her all through high school?" Quinn found himself embarrassed all of a sudden. He had reminded them both that they had lost touch in high school, that Quinn didn't really know whom Andy had dated.

"Yeah, mostly." Andy looked embarrassed too. "But she went off to California after school. She had an aunt out there who was going to set her up with a job. I never heard what happened to her. Probably married with a whole bunch of kids by now." He seemed sad, and Quinn found that he wanted to cheer him up.

"Well, you've made a nice little career for yourself, anyway. Can I expect to hear about your promotion one of these days?"

"We'll see, we'll see."

Andy drained his glass and motioned toward the bar. "You want another one?"

Quinn checked his watch. "Nah. I better get upstairs. Thanks, though. I'll get you next time."

Their eyes met and neither of them had anything to say for a second. Andy looked away and Quinn said, "You know, Andy, there's something I always meant to say to you. About that time, with your dad. I always felt bad I didn't do anything about it. I should have called the police or something."

As he said the words, Quinn felt as though it had happened yesterday rather than fifteen years ago. He had gone to pick up Andy on a Saturday night. They were going out somewhere, to a party or something, and he'd knocked on the door, but nobody had answered, so he'd gone around to the back door, which was standing open in the summer air.

Andy's dad had been a big guy, an ex-boxer who had worked, for as long as Quinn knew him, on the docks, and he had the beefy forearms to prove it. When Quinn opened the back door, Andy's dad had been taking a swing at Andy's head. Andy, a skinny teenager, had his hands up in front of his face and Quinn heard him pleading, "Dad, don't. Come on, don't," but he'd heard Mr. Lynch's fist connect with Andy's face and he'd seen the blood spurt out of Andy's nose. At that moment, Mr. Lynch had looked up and seen Quinn standing there.

Quinn hadn't know what to do, so he'd just stood there and said slowly, "I came to get Andy." Andy had stared at him, but Quinn wasn't sure what he was trying to say, and

Mr. Lynch had turned around and given Quinn the scariest look he had ever seen on an adult's face.

"Get the fuck out of my house!" he'd screamed. "Andy's not going out tonight."

And Quinn had slunk away like a cat.

Now Andy looked up and something came down over his eyes, like a shade had been pulled. He looked away. On the other side of the bar, someone laughed loudly. "I forgot all about that," he said. "Seriously. You still thinking about all that old stuff?"

"Nah, I just . . . I always felt bad about it."

"Well, don't." His voice was cold. "I'm gonna hang out and have one more. I'll see you tomorrow, right?"

"Yeah. Night." On the stairs, Quinn turned around and watched Andy's solitary figure sit there for a minute before getting up to go to the bar for one more.

FORTY-TWO

BEVERLY CHURCHILL DROVE STRAIGHT PAST MONUMENT Square and the inn, straight out Lexington Road, past houses and barns and expanses of field. It was dark and the lights inside the houses along the road flashed past like the trails of Fourth of July sparklers. She wasn't sure where she was going, so she just kept driving. Beside her, Marcus was silent, staring out the window, and she had the feeling that he wanted her to keep driving too. She turned onto a residential road, then onto another and another, the big houses set back from the road hulking in the night. She kept driving until she was sure they were lost and then she pulled the car over and turned it off. She hadn't smoked for going on fifteen years now, but she wanted a cigarette so bad that she could feel the smoke in her mouth.

"What are you doing?" Marcus asked her.

She turned to find him slumped in his seat, staring out the window.

"I wanted to talk to you. I didn't know where else to go."

"Nice houses out here," he said, still looking out the window. She looked past him at the roof of a big white house rising above a tall hedge.

"Yeah. They are nice. Remember when we moved into our house? I didn't think I'd ever seen a nicer one. But then there's always a house that's nicer or bigger than yours. Always someone who makes you feel bad about what you've got. Remember that. You have to feel good about who you are, no matter where you are or who you're with."

He looked over at her, confused, and she bumbled on. "Marcus, your father is dead."

He stared at her for a minute and then said, "You think I don't know that? Why was I just interrogated for two hours?"

She undid her seat belt and turned around all the way, so she could look him in the eye. "No, listen to me. Your father is dead and we have to learn to do better for each other now. You're all I have, Marcus. You're my only child, and I'm the only mother you have, and we have to figure out how we're going to be now. We haven't been doing very well for each other lately."

As she said the words, she felt a sudden sense of lightness. Her headlights illuminated the trees alongside the road, gave each of them a little halo of light so that they looked almost like they were covered with snow. She loved it when the trees were covered with snow. It would be winter soon; soon it would snow. And they would be okay. She knew it with sudden certainty.

"I know you had nothing to do with your father's death. I don't even need you to tell me that, and you know what? Even if you had, I would still love you and I would find you a lawyer and we would go forward together. Even if you had killed him. Because you're my son and I will never love anyone as much as I love you." She was able to say the words very calmly and when she was done, she looked over at him.

He was staring out the window at the haloed trees, and though he said nothing, she felt a sense of peace coming from him. As they sat there in the now dying autumn, they listened to the sounds of the car cooling down, the little knocks and whines it made. Beverly reached over and put a hand on his arm.

Marcus didn't push it away.

FORTY-THREE

BRUCE WHITING LOOKED OVER THE FIGURES ONE MORE TIME.
He had been staring at them for hours, and they didn't make
any more sense than they had when he'd first looked at them.
Up until January, everything looked okay, but once you got
into the new year, there was something strange going on. He
took out the calculator and entered all the figures in the "paid
out" column, but even after doing it three times, it didn't
match the total George had put at the bottom. They were a
good $10,000 short.

And then when he went to the "paid in" numbers, there
were huge discrepancies between the monthly totals and the
numbers Bruce got when he added them up himself. What
the hell was going on?

It was Lauren who had alerted him to the fact that something might be wrong. "Hon," she'd said that afternoon, "see
if you can get your dad to show you the accounting. The
bank called and there have been a few problems with our deposits lately. They think there might be some checks missing."

So Bruce had gone down to the showroom. But George
wasn't there and he knew that if he asked to see the books,
George would come up with some excuse about why he
couldn't show them to him. So Bruce had gotten a screw-
driver from the workshop and busted the lock on George's
desk drawer and got the books out.

He looked up at the clock. It was Friday night, his mother's women's group meeting down at the church. She was usually gone until ten or so, so he ought to be okay. He didn't want her home when he confronted George about this. He put the books into a paper bag he found in the workroom and locked up the showroom. As he drove up Monument Street, he tried to think of a possible explanation for the books, but he couldn't come up with anything that made sense.

The house was dark, and Bruce parked next to the Whiting Monuments van and walked up the drive. The front door was open and he flipped on the hall lights and called out, "Dad? You home?"

One of Lillian's cats came stalking out of the kitchen, meowing aggressively. Bruce followed it back into the kitchen, and in the light from the outside fixture, he saw George sitting at the patio table, staring out across the backyard toward the woods.

The details of the kitchen were so familiar to him that he could have listed them with his eyes closed, the braided ceramic fruit bowl on the table, the chicken-and-rooster salt and pepper shakers, the red curtains with little cherries on them, but in the near darkness, the room seemed almost sinister, everything in shadow.

The sliding glass door squeaked as he slid it open, but George didn't look up.

"Dad?" Bruce said again. "What are you doing out here? It's freezing cold."

"I'm all right," George said, looking up at him. He was wearing trousers and a flannel shirt. No coat. "Nothing wrong with a little fresh air."

"But what are you doing? Just sitting here, thinking?" Bruce sat down on the other side of the table. The metal chair was like ice against his legs. He shivered.

"I guess. I . . . I wanted to see the leaves, but it's too dark. I'm not sure I really saw the leaves this year." His eyes seemed strange to Bruce, distant. He felt something, a little warning, deep in his stomach.

"Dad, I came because I had to look through the books to-day and there's a lot of money missing. What's going on? Have you been taking money from the accounts?"

George turned to look at him, incredulous. "You think I . . . how could you say that, son?"

"Well, there isn't any other explanation. You do all the books, you do all the deposits, and there's something really wrong here." He dropped the bag on the table and took out the books. "Do you want me to show you where the problem is?"

"I knew something was wrong," George said, staring out at the trees again. "I knew it, but I couldn't figure out what it was. I think that . . . I think I . . ." He stopped and turned around, and Bruce could see tears in his eyes. "My memory, Bruce. It isn't as good as it used to be. I think I forgot to put some things in there." His hand played idly with a pebble on the table.

Bruce was concerned now. "How long has this been going on?"

"Since last year, but it's worse lately. Your mother has noticed it in the last few months. I don't know what's wrong with me. It's like I can't . . . get at things the way I used to. I know they're there, but I can't find them. And I don't remember where I was or what I was doing. It's like there are these . . . these gaps in time. If you ask me what I was doing on a particular day, just a few weeks ago, I couldn't tell you, even if I looked at a calendar. And I've been having nightmares, Bruce, bad ones."

"Nightmares? What about?"

As his father started to speak, Bruce thought about how the things you didn't know were always worse than the things you did know. The night was very cold, but suddenly he couldn't feel it. He listened to his father.

"Bruce," George said, quietly at first, his voice gaining strength as he went on. "I did something bad, something very bad." And then he told him.

FORTY-FOUR

SATURDAY, OCTOBER 23

WHEN QUINN GOT TO THE STATION THE NEXT MORNING, Andy was already there, sitting at Quinn's desk and talking on the phone. "Yup," he was saying. "I really appreciate it. Okay, that's great. If you think of anything else, give us a call."

He hung up the phone, jotted down a few notes, and looked triumphantly up at Quinn. "That was Frank Pebbles. He remembered why the name Tucker Beloit sounded familiar. He met him over in the Gulf. At a military hospital. He was there for heatstroke and Beloit was there because of some problem with his foot. He said he didn't get to know him very well, but he definitely remembers the name."

"So, did Churchill know him too?" Quinn hung up his jacket and sat down at Andy's desk.

"He's not sure, but we've just closed the circle a lot, don't you think, Quinny? If there's a connection between Pebbles and Beloit, then there's gotta be a connection between Beloit and Churchill."

"Maybe," Quinn said, sounding skeptical. "But I think we've also got to consider the possibility that there isn't any connection between Beloit and Churchill."

Andy looked over at him, his eyes narrow. "It doesn't make any sense. What were Churchill and Beloit doing together in the woods?"

"Maybe they weren't together. Maybe Churchill was

meeting someone at the clubhouse and Beloit showed up and, I don't know, got in the way. And that's why he was killed. I think we have to think about everyone who knew about the clubhouse and had a reason for wanting Kenneth Churchill dead. I've got some information that Churchill was working on something that would have been offensive to at least two of the people around here, George Whiting and Will Baker, who owns the inn. Then there's Cecily Whiting, who we know was angry at Churchill for pressuring her to continue their relationship, as well as his wife and son. I think we should be looking at those people."

"I don't think so," Andy said condescendingly. "Listen, I've been patient on this, Quinny, but we need a connection between Beloit and Churchill. We need to know why they were killed. I don't think it had anything to do with anybody around here, I think it was someone they met over in the Gulf, someone who's the missing link in all this."

Quinn felt his face get hot. "You've been patient?"

"Yeah, I knew you needed this for your job. I was happy to give you a piece of the action. For old time's sake and because of your wife. But now my job's on the line too and the D.A.'s giving me shit about not having anything yet. I'm sorry, but I think I better use my guys." He crumpled up a piece of paper on the desktop and shot a basket into the metal garbage can. "Besides, this thing with your kid is getting old. I mean, half the time you bring your kid with you on the job. Not very professional, Quinn."

But Quinn was suddenly so angry that he could barely see. "A piece of the action? You've had me doing all your grunt work."

"If that's how you want to think of it, Quinn."

"That's exactly how I want to think of it, and don't bring my daughter into this." He realized he had raised his fist. If he hadn't been standing in a police station, he knew he would have thrown the punch.

"Whatever."

"Fuck you, Andy."

Andy's face was little-boy petulant and suddenly Quinn

remembered him as an eighth-grader. Quinn had gotten a new glove from his father for Christmas, and somehow Andy had talked him into betting for it. Quinn couldn't remember what the bet was, something stupid that he should've known better about. But when Andy had won, he had given Quinn the same look he gave him now.

"Too bad, Quinny," he said before he turned away. "You win some, you lose some."

Quinn was so angry that he drove right past the inn and down Lexington Road. So, that was it, then? After all his work, Andy was going to freeze him out and take all the credit if and when he solved this thing. Quinn would go back to Cambridge with his tail between his legs. Who knew what Andy would put out there about why he and Quinn had parted company. Havrilek would likely have his job, and he'd have to go figure out what he was going to do with the rest of his life.

He pulled off the road onto a little cul-de-sac and got out of the car. Jeez, he was pissed. He slammed the car door and then went over and kicked a tree by the side of the road. It hurt but he didn't even care and he stood there, breathing hard for a few minutes, feeling the cold autumn air in his lungs, thinking about all of it, about Andy screwing him and taking the credit for himself.

But what if Andy couldn't solve this thing? Quinn was pretty sure that Andy was off on the wrong track. He was pretty sure that Kenneth Churchill's killer was someone who knew him not from a far-off desert, but from somewhere a lot closer to home. He'd already talked to most of the people who had access to the clubhouse. He wasn't sure about Cecily Whiting and he had been almost positive that George Whiting had been lying about his alibi, but the one person he hadn't talked to yet was Will Baker. He got back in the car and headed toward the inn.

Will Baker was in the kitchen. Quinn had asked for him at the front desk, and the woman behind the desk in the lobby said he was talking to the chef about dinner. "Can I help you with something?" she asked Quinn.

"No. I really need to talk to him. I'll just go back and find him." Quinn headed back toward the dining room before she could stop him. He pushed through the swinging doors and found Baker talking to a young guy in a white chef's smock.

"Can we help you?" Baker asked, looking annoyed.

"Yeah, I was just hoping to chat with you for a few minutes."

"Well, I'm in the middle of something here. Can it wait until later?"

Quinn leaned against the countertop and crossed his arms. "I suppose so. I was just interested in talking to you about Cecily Whiting."

The effect was exactly what Quinn had been hoping for. Baker blushed and stood up suddenly, knocking a spatula off the butcher block. "Harry, I'll be right back," he said. The guy in the chef's smock nodded.

Without looking at Quinn, Baker led the way back through the dining room and into a little office off the lounge. He shut the door carefully behind them and sat down behind the desk. He didn't offer Quinn a chair, so Quinn stood.

"What is it you want to know?" he asked, straightening a few pieces of paper on his desk and refusing to look at Quinn.

"When you and Cecily Whiting were seeing each other, did you meet at the clubhouse?"

Baker continued straightening papers. "I don't see how that's any of your business," he said.

"It's my business because I'm a police detective and there was a murder right next to the clubhouse." Two murders, he said to himself. "And we need to know about everyone who spent time at the clubhouse, anyone who knew about it."

"I don't see how it could possibly help you, but if you must know, yes. We went there sometimes."

"When were you seeing her?"

"It was a year or so after her divorce. For maybe a year, off and on."

"How did you get to know her?"

"I didn't have to get to know her. Bruce and I went to high school together. We were friends. So I had become friends with both of them. And she was very lonely after the divorce and it just . . . started."

"Did Bruce know?"

"No. And I don't want him to. I don't think he would have any right to protest, but he's my friend and I didn't particularly want him to know. Cecily wanted to tell him. That was what made me realize that she was just using me to get back at him."

"And did you break things off because of it?"

"I'm ashamed to say that I didn't. I loved her and I thought that maybe, after some time, it would stop being about revenge and we could . . . well, she would be with me for a different reason." He stood up. "If that's all."

"It's not," Quinn said. For some reason, Will Baker was pissing him off. "Why did you break up?"

"I guess she decided that she didn't want to see me anymore." Even as he said the words, Quinn could see he was reliving the hurt of it.

"When was this?"

"Beginning of the year."

Right about the time she started seeing Kenneth Churchill. Quinn could feel his heart speed up. "She didn't give you a reason?"

"No." He was lying. Quinn was sure of it.

"How well did you know Kenneth Churchill?"

"I told you before. He stayed here at the inn when he came to town. We were members of the same Minuteman company. I knew him casually."

"Did you know that he started seeing Cecily Whiting?"

Baker looked up at Quinn, afraid. He didn't say anything.

"How did you know? Did you follow them? Did you see them together?" Quinn was standing over the desk now, in Baker's face, letting him know that he wasn't going to give up. All the anger he felt at Andy was right there, right on the other side of his fist, and he felt as though he would like to start hitting Will Baker and not stop until he was good and satisfied.

"No, no. I didn't follow them." Baker looked scared, as though he could sense what was in Quinn's mind. "He told me."

"Kenneth Churchill told you?"

"Yeah. We were talking one day at a reenactment and he said, 'By the way, I'm not just spending time down here because of the reenactments and my book.' Something like that. I asked him what he meant and he told me about Cecily. I realized that he was probably the reason she broke up with me."

"Did you say anything?"

"No. What was I going to say? Besides, he was . . . I don't know how to describe it. It was like he was smirking. I think he could tell that I was uncomfortable. I don't know. Maybe he knew about Cecily and me. Anyway, I had the distinct feeling he was enjoying it." He looked up at Quinn. "And I know what you're going to ask. Yes, I hated him enough to kill him." He looked away. "But I didn't."

By the time he got upstairs, Quinn was exhausted. He knocked on Sweeney's door and when she didn't answer, he tried the door again. It was propped open very slightly, and he pushed it in and found Sweeney talking on the phone. She waved him in, a concerned look on her face. "What floor?" she asked the person on the other end. "Okay."

Quinn lifted Megan out of the Pack 'n Play and collapsed it to bring back to his room. "Hi, little girl," he said. "How are you?"

"Okay, I'll see you soon," Sweeney said. "Good-bye." She hung up the phone and turned to look at Quinn. Instinctively, he stepped closer and put a hand on her arm. She looked stricken.

"What's the matter?" he asked her.

"It's Pres. He's in the hospital."

FORTY-FIVE

"I DIDN'T WANT TO ASK HOW SICK HE IS," SHE TOLD IAN when she got back from the hospital later that night. "I think I was afraid to find out how far the leukemia's gone."

"I'm so sorry," he said quietly. "I'm really, really sorry."

"It's funny," she said. "I haven't known him very long, but I feel as though I won't be able to stand it if he dies. It's so damned unfair. He's twelve years old."

"It's awful," he said. "It's really awful."

She felt the tears coming and at first she tried to stop them, but then she couldn't and she cried, letting him hear her, letting him hear every sob. He listened to her.

"I wish you were here," she said when she had stopped. And at once, she knew she meant it. She did. She wanted him there, she wanted to find out what they were. Suddenly she wanted it more than anything.

"Sweeney," Ian said. "I have to tell you something."

"What?"

"I wasn't entirely honest when I said that I could come for a visit. Look, the thing is, we'd been thinking of opening a Boston branch of the auction house for years now, even before I met you. It means I would be over there for six months or so, getting things up and running and, well, I didn't want to tell you because I wasn't sure how you would feel about it. But I realized that I need to just put my cards on the table and tell you that I want to try to see what's here.

"Listen, I hope you don't think that this is really presumptuous. I can—"

"No, no. You're right," Sweeney said. "I want you to come. I think you're right that we need to, you know . . . find out what's here. I think it will be a good thing."

"Really?"

"Really."

His voice was warm over the phone lines. "Good."

Spent and nervous, she poured herself a glass of wine after they hung up, and took out all of her notes on Josiah Whiting to try to figure out what she could possibly write about him. She didn't have absolute proof that Whiting had been a spy, so she couldn't put his evolving designs down to that. She could just write about the designs. It might not be very intellectually honest, but she was too exhausted for intellectual honesty.

The copies of Churchill's notebook were lying on the desk and she paged through them again, looking for anything she'd missed. What insights had Churchill gained into the gravestones? Maybe that was a good place to start. She came to his sketches of the stones and read his little question to himself in the margin.

She'd been assuming that he was referring to the death's-head designs as masks—it was an alternate term, as in "death masks," but *mask* had another meaning too. Hadn't Pres been telling her about how his mother had made a mask for him, one in the shape of a heart through which he could read coded letters? During the Revolution, some spies had used masks to send coded messages. They were nothing more complicated than a shape cut out of a piece of paper to form a window. You held the letter up behind the mask, and the real message would be revealed. But it didn't seem to have any relevance here. She didn't have any letters Josiah Whiting had written to the British administration. She had never even heard that such letters existed, and as far as she knew, no one had ever found anything even vaguely resembling a mask among his belongings.

No, the only letters she'd ever heard of in connection with Josiah Whiting were the family letters. Her heart sank. She'd never be able to prove that Whiting had been a spy and she'd never be able to assert that the evolution in his death's-head designs was related to his betrayal of the cause. And Quinn would never be able to prove that Kenneth Churchill's work on Whiting had anything to do with his death.

She took out the family letters and looked through them again, stopping to re-read the undated letter from Whiting to his wife. It hadn't made any sense to her when she'd read it before, and it still didn't. It seemed an odd sort of letter for a man to write to his wife, and it reminded her of something. She flipped through her notebooks and came to the notes she'd taken during her visit to the Minuteman Museum, realizing what it was. Josiah Whiting's letter reminded her of a letter Cecily Whiting had on display at the museum. It had been written by a Boston shoemaker who had done some low-level spying for the British. Sweeney hadn't written down the exact words, but she remembered that the letter was fairly nonsensical until you placed it behind the mask—she had been fascinated to see that it was in the shape of a shoemaker's mold viewed from above, a form readily accessible to that particular spy.

It was an ingenious method. Even if the letter fell into the wrong hands and it was noticed that the letter read strangely, it would be impossible to understand its true meaning without the particular mask that went with it. The mask could be destroyed as soon as the letter was read, keeping it safe from prying eyes.

She flipped through her notes again. She'd found the idea of masks so interesting that she had jotted some sketches of the various forms described in the exhibit, and now she looked at them, not sure why they seemed so familiar. It wasn't until she flipped ahead and caught sight of one her gravestone sketches that she saw the similarity between the masks and the ornately carved gravestones made by Josiah Whiting.

Could it be . . . ? It was an interesting idea. The shoemaker had used the form best known to him. Didn't it follow
that a gravestone maker would do the same? Josiah Whiting
would have the dimensions for his stones committed to
memory. What could be easier than writing a letter that
could be read only when viewed behind the mask of a gravestone?

She took out the letter and spread it out on the desk.

*Dearest Becky, I know that you did it very well and for John I would
not suppose I love the pies that you make.*

                                                        Josiah

It didn't seem very likely that there was important secret
information contained in the letter—there didn't seem to be
enough words, for one thing—but maybe Josiah Whiting had
written a personal letter to his wife, a personal letter he
didn't want anyone else to read. Maybe, before he was killed
by Baker, he had found the time to write this short letter and
put it somewhere she would be sure to find it. Sweeney
couldn't begin to imagine how he would have pulled it off,
but perhaps he had.

Now her task was to figure out which gravestone had been
used as the mask. She could take the letter to all the cemeteries she'd visited, but that would take forever. She looked
over her sketches of the gravestones. Which one would he
have chosen? It would have to be one that was familiar to his
wife and one that was near to hand. He couldn't have expected her to travel to Lincoln or Lexington to read the letter.
So it was one of the Concord ones, then. But which one?

She looked through her sketches, and the answer came to
her quickly. Of course, that had to be it. Sweeney folded the
copy of the letter, tucked it safely into the pocket of her
jeans, and found a flashlight in her backpack. Then she put
on her warmest coat and wrapped her scarf around her neck.

It was dark outside and the sidewalks were nearly empty,
only a few pedestrians walking back from dinner. Sweeney
walked along Lexington Road and looked both ways before

crossing into the Hill Cemetery. There wasn't anything wrong with it, but people might find it suspicious that she was going into the graveyard at this time of night.

She turned on the flashlight and climbed the hill, making her way between the stones to the Whiting family plot and fixing the flashlight's beam on the stone of Josiah Whiting's dead daughter.

Of course it was Lucy's stone. It was the one that Becky Whiting knew best, the one she visited, the one she had touched and prayed and wept over. Sweeney took out the letter and unfolded it, smoothing out the wrinkles and placing it carefully behind the stone.

The words were right there, had been there all along. *I did it for John. I love you.* John? Who was John? There was John Baker, of course, but then she remembered another John. She picked up the other letters. Of course. Whiting had a son named John, a son who was sickly, who had a bad leg. That must be it! He had mentioned treatment. How would he have paid for treatment? He must have gotten money in exchange for spying. Hadn't Henrietta Hall said that Sweeney should look into whether the family's fortunes had changed?

Sweeney replaced the letter in her pocket and shone the light on Rebecca Whiting's gravestone. Had she known to come here to read her husband's letter? Had the letter even reached her? Had she known what it was? Sweeney might never know.

She walked back to the inn and knocked on Quinn's door.

"Hey," he said. "Megan's asleep and I don't want to wake her up. Come in, but we should whisper." She followed him in and sat down on the bed.

"I'm sorry," she said. "I know it's late. It's just that I was so excited and I needed to tell someone." She held up the letter and told him about the gravestone mask. "I was looking for proof that he was a spy, and I think this it," she said. "He was explaining to his wife why he did it, but he coded it in case it fell into someone else's hands. He did it for is son, because he needed the money to help his son."

"He spied for money? That's all it was about? Somehow that's kind of disappointing," Quinn said.

Sweeney looked down at the letter in her hand. "I know, but it wasn't just for the money. It was for his son, to try to heal his son. The money was just a way to do that. I think that when it came down to it, he was probably pretty idealistic. I think he believed in all that stuff he was fighting for, but when it came down to it, his son was just more important."

Quinn was staring at her, and when she met his eyes, she blushed and looked away. There was something there that she couldn't read.

"Sweeney," he said.

"Yeah?" What was wrong with him? He just kept staring at her. And then he grabbed his coat from the desk chair and put it on.

"I need you to watch Megan," he said. "I think I've figured this out."

"But, where are you . . . ? What do you mean?"

"I realized," he said. "That it's all about fathers and sons. That's the whole thing. It's as simple as that."

And then he was gone. Confused, Sweeney sat on the bed and turned on the TV. She tried halfheartedly to watch an old movie about two sisters on a cruise, but she was too distracted and kept staring at the letter. What had Quinn seen that had made him take off? What did he mean by "fathers and sons"? And where was he going?

She read the letter through again. *I did it for John. I love you.* What could that possibly have suggested to him? Sweeney wasn't sure. Josiah Whiting had betrayed his principles for his son. That was what the letter meant, didn't it? Reading the letter, she felt a sympathy for Whiting that she hadn't felt before. He had done it because his child was sick. He had needed the money so badly that he had been willing to betray the cause to which he had pledged his life, to which he had seemed willing to give his life on April 19. But you couldn't blame him, could you? People who had children would do anything for their children. Sweeney looked over at Megan, sleeping in the playpen. Quinn would do anything for her. Sweeney had seen that the day he had raced up the stairs to get Megan before he was even sure whether Maura was dead. She had seen on his face that raw protectiveness that Sweeney had seen on his face since then, that she had seen on Cecily Whiting's face and on Bruce Whiting's face too.

Sweeney sat up. She had an image in her head now, an image she couldn't get rid of, and she used Quinn's room phone to dial Toby's number. "Toby," she said when he answered. "I need you to come out to Concord. Right now. It's a huge favor, but I wouldn't ask if I didn't really need you to do it."

"What's going on?" he asked her. "Are you okay?"

"Yes, I'm fine."

"So why do you need me to come out to Concord?"

"I need you to babysit."

FORTY-SIX

WHEN HE LEFT THE INN, HE'D KNOWN WHERE HE WAS GOING, but once he got in the car, Quinn was suddenly unsure how to handle it. He knew he ought to call for backup, but he wasn't sure he was right and he didn't like the idea of calling out Andy and half the state troopers in the county on a hunch. So he just drove for a good ten minutes, out Monument Street and then back and out Lowell Road, planning it out.

He had been thinking he would go to the house, but as he drove by the monument company, he saw that there was a light on somewhere in the back. He pulled in, found his service revolver in the glove compartment, and tucked it into his waistband, then turned off the car and got out, striding up to the main door. It was locked, so he went around to the side and found one of the loading entrances open. He could hear the sound of machinery from inside, and he walked in and tried to get his bearings, following the noise around a corner. He tried the side door and, finding it unlocked, slipped in, one hand on his back in case he needed the gun.

It took him a minute to adjust to the bright light in the workroom and he didn't see the figure, dressed in a leather smock and wearing safety glasses, until the figure had seen him. The loud buzz of some kind of sander halted and the figure tipped the goggles up onto his head.

He had been engraving a tall black granite stone. It had a

delicate scallop shape at the top and Quinn was struck by how beautiful it was, how Sweeney was right that gravestones could be works of art.

"What do you want?" Bruce Whiting asked angrily. "It's very late, Detective Quinn, and my son went into the hospital today."

"It's Pres I wanted to talk about," Quinn said. "I wanted to talk to you about what you did for him."

"And what was that?" Whiting was suddenly wary, and Quinn watched him put down the sanding tool and inch his hand along the top of the workbench. He was going for something, and Quinn pulled out his gun and trained it on him. Whiting blinked and dropped both of his hands in front of him.

"I think you know," Quinn said. "I think you know exactly what I'm talking about."

"I have no idea what you're talking about. Are you crazy, coming in here and pointing a gun at me? You can't do that. I'm going to call Chief Tyler and see what he has to say about it."

But he didn't move and Quinn just kept the gun on him.

"I think I know how you must have felt," he said. "You found out that your ex-wife and Kenneth Churchill were seeing each other. You weren't jealous for yourself. You didn't have any feelings for your ex-wife anymore, but you were jealous on behalf of your son. I think I understand. You wanted the best for him. You knew about Churchill. You told me you didn't, but your wife told me that you had found out by accident. I wondered why you'd lied about it."

Whiting laughed. "I saw him one day when I was dropping off Pres. We were early and he was just leaving the house, but I didn't know who he was. Then a couple of weeks later, I went to Cecily's to pick up Pres and there was this car waiting at the end of the road. It was weird. As I drove away, it started up and pulled into her driveway. I watched it in my rearview mirror and I remembered the car and what the guy looked like. And then as I was driving away, I figured out who he was. He'd been in to interview me a couple of months before. Said he was writing a book about Josiah Whiting and he wanted to ask me some questions. The thing was, he had this little grin the whole time, like he knew something about me, or he had some kind of little secret, and at the time I didn't get it, but later, when I figured out who it was, I was pissed off. And I knew he did the reenactments with my dad."

"Tell me what happened. The day Kenneth Churchill and Tucker Beloit were killed."

Bruce Whiting looked at the gun and at Quinn. "I don't think you're allowed to force confessions like that, Detective Quinn."

"Tell me." Quinn let his hand shake a little, just for good measure.

"Okay, okay. That was in the papers, wasn't it? That his name was Tucker Beloit. Homeless, they said. I didn't know that, of course. He was just there . . . I saw him, watching us, and I couldn't let him go and tell. I couldn't do that to Pres."

"Tell me what happened." Quinn tried to keep his voice very quiet, very steady, very soothing. "How did you run into Churchill?"

"He was at the clubhouse. I was out in the woods, just walking, you know. It was Sunday morning and I was here, like I told you, though my dad wasn't. I don't know where he was. I left a little earlier than I told you. It was a beautiful day, and so on my way home, I stopped at the bridge and I decided I'd walk up through the woods. And I thought I'd go to the old clubhouse. It had been ages since I'd gone to see it. And when I got there, he was there. He must have heard my footsteps because he called out, 'Cecily?' and then he came out and saw me.

" 'This is awkward,' he said when he saw who it was, but he had this grin on his face, like he was glad he'd gotten caught. He was all dressed up in his stupid costume and he had this musket with him, with a bayonet on it, and I remember wondering if it was real.

"I asked him if he and Cecily were still seeing each other, and he smiled and said he thought they were. I told him that her son was very sick, that he needed her right now, and that he was a distraction I didn't want her to have. He just looked at me. I can't explain it, it was like he saw through me or something, and he said, 'I don't think you have any right to talk to Cecily about distractions. She is an excellent mother, with no help from you, and she's also an adult and she has the right to make her own decisions.' He was so . . . he was so fucking proud of it. I said, 'Don't you know my son is very sick? Don't you know he might die?' And he just looked at me and he said he loved Cecily and he was going to leave his wife for her and he would help her get through this thing with Pres. 'This thing with Pres!' Like he was already dead! He said he loved her. He said he would do anything for her."

"Why couldn't she be in love?"

"Because I know what it's like. I know what it is to be in love. That's what happened with Lauren. I couldn't . . . I just couldn't stop thinking about her. And I neglected Pres and Cecily. Pres didn't . . ." He was distraught now, his hands shaking. "Cecily always said that it was the reason he got sick. That it was my fault. And maybe she's right. So, you see, I couldn't let that man take her away from him too. The only reason I even felt okay about leaving them was because I knew that she'd take care of him. But he was going to take her away too."

"So what happened?"

"I told him to stay away from her, to let her be Pres's mother while she still could. But he kind of laughed and said I couldn't stop love. 'The heart wants what the heart wants,' he said. He laughed at me. He said something about how it wasn't enough for me to be happy, I wanted Cecily to be unhappy. I don't know what happened. I just . . . I went for him. I thought I'd beat him up, but he came after me with his musket, with the bayonet. I don't really remember this part. I took it from him and I stuck it in him. Something took over in me, something from a long time ago. I didn't know I still had the ability to kill someone, but I did. Self-preservation, or whatever you want to call it. It just kicked in. It was awful.

I didn't mean to, but one minute he was standing there and the next he was lying on the ground and he was bleeding. And that was when I looked up and saw that guy, that other guy, watching us. He was wearing a uniform too, and I assumed he was from the reenactment. He'd seen the whole thing. I could tell from his eyes. And the only thing I could think of was that I had to stop him from telling because Pres couldn't know. He couldn't find out, he just couldn't. So I chased him down and I . . . I killed him too. It was so surreal. He was standing there in this British uniform and he was just staring at me. He wouldn't stop staring at me. It was easy that time, you know. It just all came back, combat, killing quickly, efficiently.

"I didn't know what to do after that. They were lying there, and I knew someone would find them and I might have been seen going into the woods, so I knew I had to move the bodies. But then I realized that Cecily might be coming to the clubhouse, so I hid and waited for an hour just to make sure, but she never turned up. Then I remembered about the reenactment and figured Churchill's car must still be up in the field, so I found the keys in his pocket."

"What about the hat? Did you take it off Churchill's body?"

"How did you know about the hat?"

"That was what gave me the idea," Quinn said. "I was thinking about how people can look similar from a distance. Someone said he saw Kenneth Churchill walking back to his car on Sunday morning, but he didn't see Kenneth Churchill, he saw someone who looked like him, wearing his tricorner hat. You, your father, and Will Baker all resemble Churchill in a superficial way. You're all tall men. But it wasn't one of them, it was you."

Whiting said, "It had fallen off during the struggle. I was afraid someone would see me getting the car, so I put it on. I didn't think anyone would notice, but there were some guys around and they saw me getting into his car and they waved at me from far off, so I waved back. I drove his car as far up the path as I could.

"Then I dragged Churchill's body over and got it in the trunk. I was going to put both of them in there and take the car somewhere. But by the time I got back, the other guy was gone. I didn't know what to do. I swear to God, I was so out of it, I thought maybe I'd dreamed the whole thing with the other guy, so I drove Churchill in his car up to the farm and left him there. I walked home and waited for them to come arrest me. It was weird, waiting and not hearing anything, and then when they found the body, I realized that the guy must have dragged himself around by the clubhouse and died there. There wasn't anything to tie him to me. Everyone thought he was a reenactor. I felt like I'd been spared." He looked at Quinn as though he wanted sympathy. "But I wasn't."

He was silent for a minute and Quinn thought he was finished, but he wasn't. "That's the thing about war," he said in a very quiet voice. "You think it's over, but it never is. It comes back to get you; sometimes I think everything about my life has been punishment for what I did over there in the jungle. Take my father. He's a rah-rah soldier, patriotic as they come, and what does he tell me the other night but that he helped kill a guy when he was in Italy, all those years ago. It was someone who was helping the Allies, but he drank too much and he'd become a liability, and George and another guy had to kill him. Smothered him while he slept, just like that. He's been living with it all these years."

He started walking toward Quinn. "You think you can get away from it," he said in a low voice. "But you can't."

FORTY-SEVEN

SWEENEY DROVE STRAIGHT TO THE SHOWROOM, AND WHEN she saw Quinn's car parked in the lot, she pulled in next to it and waited for a minute. No one came out, so she got out, put the flashlight and her cell phone in the pocket of her jacket, and approached the door to the showroom. It was dark inside and the door was locked, so she went around the side of the building and found a door. Through the glass she could hear voices and she got down low and listened as best as she could through the door.

"I told him to stay away from her, to let her be Pres's mother while she still could," Bruce Whiting was saying. "But he kind of laughed and said I couldn't stop love. 'The heart wants what the heart wants,' he said. He laughed at me. He said something about how it wasn't enough for me to be happy, I wanted Cecily to be unhappy. I don't know what happened. I just . . . I went for him. I thought I'd beat him up, but he came after me with his musket, with the bayonet. I don't really remember this part. I took it from him and I stuck it in him."

Sweeney crawled around the corner of the building so that they wouldn't see her through the window. She wasn't sure where she was going, but she thought there had to be another door and, sure enough, as she rounded the corner by the driveway, the voices got louder again and she found herself standing in front of an open garage door. From their voices, she could tell that they were in the next room over, so she inched her way inside and kept herself pressed against the wall. Finally, she found herself in a doorway and she had a good view into the workroom. At one end of the room, Bruce Whiting was standing, wearing a leather apron and talking, and at the other end, Quinn was standing stock-still, pointing a gun at Whiting.

"I'm going to have to take you in, Bruce," Quinn said finally. "You know that, don't you?"

"You can't. Pres is in the hospital. I'm not going to let you do that. I'm not going to let you wreck things. He was a bastard. He was married, did you know that? He was cheating on his wife with Cecily. He deserved to die."

"I have to. Let's go get in my car and I'll—"

"No!" Bruce Whiting yelled. Sweeney, watching, knew what he was going to do before he did it. He picked up a crowbar from the workbench next to him and swung it over his head at Quinn. But Quinn had been expecting it and he ducked and put a hand up to block the crowbar, knocking Bruce Whiting on to the ground. He kept the gun trained on the other man.

"You don't want to add assaulting a police officer to everything else," Quinn said good-naturedly. "Come on, Bruce. It's time to go. You know I'm right." Sweeney watched him plant his feet.

"Just leave me alone. Can't you just do that? Just leave me alone, let me be with my son. Why can't you do that?"

Sweeney, not sure what to do, eased the cell phone out of her pocket and held it up so she could see the keypad. Carefully, she held the phone out in front of her and dialed 911. She pressed it to her ear and when a voice answered, she whispered her name and where she was, then pressed END. But as she was replacing the phone in her pocket, she dropped it and it clattered on the concrete floor.

"What was that?" Bruce Whiting turned and saw her, and in the same instant Quinn saw her too and the look on his face told her what he was thinking.

"Where's Megan?" he called out to her.

"It's okay. She's safe. She's not here."

His face relaxed, but in the moment he had been distracted, Whiting made his move. He rushed across the room, so fast that Sweeney barely saw him, and the crowbar came down hard on Quinn's right shoulder. The gun went skittering across the floor, under a workbench. He groaned with pain, and Sweeney saw blood run down the torn white cloth of his shirt. Even from across the room, she could see that Whiting had opened a gash the size of Sweeney's fist on Quinn's bicep. She saw him reach for the arm, and realize what had happened.

Then Whiting came at Quinn from below, grabbing him around the waist and knocking him to the ground. He got a couple of good punches in, and Sweeney heard Quinn groan and saw blood flow from his nose. He rolled Bruce Whiting over and punched him once, then tried to get Bruce's hands behind his back, but his arm was nearly useless and he couldn't hold him.

Whiting rolled over and got on top of him. Sweeney could hear the crunch of bone and cartilage as Whiting punched Quinn's face over and over. He was going to kill him.

"I called the police," Sweeney said. "They'll be here any minute. Stop it." The look of shock on Bruce Whiting's face was so great that she thought maybe he just might do it, but instead, he came at her so quickly that she barely had time to scream, and before she knew it, he was holding her against him, her arms pinned painfully behind her back. She could smell sweat and something tinny that she knew was blood.

Quinn staggered to his feet. "Let her go, Whiting," he said.

"No." He looked wildly around the room. "I'm taking both of you out of here before the police get here." He picked up the crowbar and held it over Sweeney's head. She could smell him, the sweat from his body, and feel his heart beating fast.

"Let her go," Quinn said. "I'm warning you. Let her go." She met his eyes and they stared at each other for a long moment before Quinn put his hands up in the air and started walking toward them. Blood from his arm drip-dropped onto the floor. "Come on, Whiting, I'm going to let you go. I'm giving you a head start. Just let her go first."

Whiting tightened his grip on Sweeney's arms, and she heard herself groan. "No," Whiting said. "She said she already called the police. I need her to get out of here."

"I was lying," Sweeney whispered. "I just said that to get you to stop hitting him. I dropped my keys back there. Look, I don't even have a cell phone. You can search me."

Whiting hesitated. "Are you sure?"

"Search her," Quinn said, meeting Sweeney's eyes again. She held his gaze, and suddenly it was as though she knew exactly what he was going to do. Whiting let her arms go and reached into one jacket pocket and then the other, and then there was a loud scream and she was knocked to the ground, and when she opened her eyes she saw Quinn catch Whiting from behind. Whiting didn't lose his balance, but Quinn got him around the middle and for a second they looked like lovers embracing. And then she saw the stack of granite headstones leaning against the far wall, and she saw Quinn see them at the same moment she did.

"Come on, Whiting. Let it go," he said as he slowly, carefully backed him across the room. His face was glistening with sweat and his shirt was nearly red with his blood. "Come on. You know it's over."

And as Whiting swung for Quinn's face, Sweeney watched Quinn take his face in his hands and snap his whole head back against the granite. The sound was like a gunshot, and Whiting's face held a look of innocent surprise as he slid to the ground, blissfully unconscious.

Sweeney crawled over to Quinn. He was lying against Whiting, his arm flopped onto the floor, and she pulled him into her lap, taking off her sweater and tying it tight around his lower arm as a tourniquet.

"Is he . . . ?" Quinn whispered.

"I think you knocked him out," she said. "But I don't think he's dead."

Quinn relaxed against her and she felt the weight of him, his back and arms and head. She wasn't even sure if he was conscious, so she just held him like that until she heard the sirens and Andy Lynch was rushing in.

FORTY-EIGHT

MONDAY, OCTOBER 25

THE HOSPITAL WAS QUIET SUNDAY MORNING, AND SWEENEY found Cecily Whiting sitting by her son's bed, holding his hand, not talking. She looked up and smiled when Sweeney came in, and stood up to greet her. They went out into the hall.

"He'll be glad you're here," she said. "He's alert, but very, very tired. He keeps asking for Bruce and I don't know what to say."

"Are they still going to let him visit?"

"Yes, later today. They're not going to tell Pres anything. Why don't you go in with him. I'm going to go get something to eat and I'll be back in an hour."

Sweeney went into the room. He was lying in the middle of the hospital bed and seemed so small, so fragile against the blue sheets, an IV snaking out of his arm, oxygen whispering in his nose. The room was painted to look like a giant aquarium, with tropical fishes scattered across the blue walls. She sat down and took his hand, and he opened his eyes for a moment, then closed them again.

"How are you?" she asked him.

He opened his eyes again and gave her a funny little smile, as if to say, "How do you think I am?"

"I went and checked on the General," she said. "This morning. He's fine. He has lots of food and water. I'll keep checking on him until you can do it again."

"You take him," Pres whispered. "You take him home."

Sweeney squeezed his hand. "Let's see, Pres. You're going to be out of here soon, and maybe your mom will change her mind. It's you he loves." She was speaking just a little too fast and she was conscious of the tightness of her throat, of how it was suddenly hard to breathe. Another second and she was blinking back tears.

"No," he said. "I won't. Please. Please take him."

It took her a moment to get control of her voice, but she did it and squeezed his hand again. "Okay," she said. "I'll take him."

"Good." He gave a faint smile.

"Now," she said, "do you want to hear about Scherezade?"

He nodded and she began to read to him about the king and his brother, and the death sentence on Scherezade, how she called for her sister and asked her to request a story so that she might entice the king to spare her life, for one night at least.

"'The Fisherman and the Jinni,'" she read. "'It hath reached me, O auspicious King, that there was a fisherman well stricken in years who had a wife and three children, and withal was of poor condition. Now it was his custom to cast his net every day four times, and no more. On a day he went forth about noontide to the seashore, where he laid down his basket and, tucking up his shirt and plunging into the water, made a cast with his net and waited till it settled to the bottom.'"

Pres smiled and she read until he slept, until his breathing was a soft, even hush, and then she closed the book and left it there for when he woke up.

FORTY-NINE

IT HAD BEEN HARD WITH HIS RIGHT ARM IN A SLING, BUT
Quinn had cleaned the house and even gotten some roses at
the supermarket, red ones with white inside, and he'd
arranged them on the mantel in a crystal vase that he and
Maura had gotten as a wedding present. He'd given Megan a
bath and she was wearing a little yellow dress he'd bought,
with matching yellow-and-white tights and her white patent-
leather shoes. He wasn't sure why he'd dressed her up. He
guessed he wanted to make a good impression.

Looking around at the house, he was happy with how it
looked, as though a real family lived there, Megan's toys
stacked neatly in one corner of the room, some magazines
on the coffee table. He was going to try to keep things nice,
he decided, for Megan. So Megan would have a real home.

He'd called Debbie as soon as he got out of the hospital.
"I really appreciate everything you've done for us, Deb, I really do. And you'll always be an important part of Megan's
life because you're her only aunt, but I think I've gotta figure
out the child-care thing on my own, you know?" She had
taken it okay, considering, said maybe she'd look for a new
job, something at a day-care center. Quinn had told her she'd
be great. Then he'd called the agency.

"She's excellent," the woman said. "Nothing but the very
best references from her previous employers. And she has a
lot of experience with young children. I should warn you,

though, that she was, well, in some difficulty back in her country, back in Africa. She was attacked. I don't know much about it. There was a civil war. But the scar can be disturbing if you're not prepared."

He heard the taxi pull up in front of the house, and he picked up Megan and went out to find her getting out of the cab.

"Patience?" he called out.

"Yes. Mr. Quinn?" She spoke in precise English accented with French. She was very tall, and her cornrowed hair fell to her shoulders like water. "I can tell the taxi to wait?"

"No, that's okay. I can drive you home after the interview." He could see her studying him, studying them. When she turned, he could see the scar running down one side of her face. *Will they be good to me?* he saw her thinking. He could see her studying him, his black eye and his nose, still taped and stuffed with cotton. It wasn't a pretty picture, but he thought Megan helped. He could see her wondering, *Is this what I am meant to do, to be the nanny for this child?*

He wanted to tell her that there wasn't any way of knowing, that you didn't know anything about anything before it happened, that you just had to go ahead and . . . live.

"Okay," she said. He saw her lean in to pay the driver, and then she turned and came toward them, smiling shyly.

"This is my daughter, Megan," he said, smiling back at her. "Do you want to come inside?"

ACKNOWLEDGMENTS

I should first of all like to thank the town of Concord, Massachusetts, for being such a wonderful place to be forced to take research trips. And I apologize for littering its lovely, peaceful woods with dead bodies.

A number of books were helpful to me in my study of Colonial stonecarvers and the beginnings of the Revolutionary War in Concord and Lexington. Among them are: *Lexington and Concord: The Beginning of the War of the American Revolution* by Arthur B. Tourtellot; *Rebels and Redcoats: The American Revolution Through the Eyes of Those Who Fought and Lived It* by George F. Scheer and Hugh F. Rankin; *The Minutemen: The First Fight: Myths and Realities of the American Revolution* by John R. Galvin; *Gravestone Chronicles* by Ted Chase and Lauren Gabel; *Graven Images: New England Stonecarving and Its Symbols, 1650–1815* by Allan I. Ludwig; *Memorials for Children of Change: The Art of Early New England Stonecarving* by Dickran and Ann Tashjian; *Early American Gravestone Art in Photographs* by Francis Y. Duval; *The Masks of Orthodoxy: Folk Gravestone Carving in Plymouth County, Massachusetts 1689–1805* by Peter Benes; *Early New England Gravestone Rubbings* by Edmund Vincent Gillon. I'm also appreciative of the Revolutionary War enthusiasts who shared their time and expertise with me.

Thanks, especially, to Roger Fuller of HM 40th Regiment of Foot.

As always, a huge bucket of thanks to the terrific folks at St. Martin's Minotaur. There isn't a better editor than Kelley Ragland, and I am thankful for the sharp eye of Stephen Lamont, the assistance of Carly Einstein, and the amazing abilities of Linda McFall. So many, many thanks to my terrific agent Lynn Whittaker for her enthusiasm and friendship. And last but not least, I am so grateful for my wonderful family—Susan, David, and Tom Taylor—and to Vicki Kuskowski, Josh, Michelle, Jamison and Logan Dunne, and of course, to Matt Dunne, my best critic and best fan.

Keep reading for an excerpt from
Sarah Stewart Taylor's next Sweeney St. George mystery

STILL as DEATH

COMING SOON IN HARDCOVER FROM ST. MARTIN'S MINOTAUR

1979

The room was as silent as a crypt.

Karen Philips laid the jewelry out on her work table and
reflected on the aptness of the metaphor. The items spread
out before her had, of course, come from crypts, or more ac-
curately, tombs of Ancient Egyptians who had been well
outfitted for their passage to the afterlife. Under the bright
fluorescent bulbs, the faience, glass and metal amulets, the
beaded necklaces and collars lost some of their appeal. But
she knew that they would look beautiful in a display cabinet,
their colors revealed under perfect, golden light.

She felt a little charge of excitement. She had seen wonderful pieces of gold and bead jewelry in Cairo and in New
York and Washington, D.C., but this was the first time she
had actually handled jewelry from an ancient Egyptian tomb.
The collection was part of a recent donation to the university
museum made by a wealthy alumnus with an interest in
Egyptian antiquities and everyone, including Karen, was riding the wave of excitement generated by the announcement.

The donation was the result of a carefully planned friendship between Willem Keane, the museum's curator of ancient Egyptian art, and Arthur Maloof, a financier with a
huge personal fortune. Willem had convinced him to hand
over a number of items from his excellent collections and he
was most excited about the donation of a stunning sheet gold
mummy mask that would make the museum's collection of

antiquities the envy of most museums in the world. Because of laws forbidding antiquities from leaving Egypt, it was rare that important pieces like the mask came on the market anymore, Karen knew.

There were some other items of interest in the Maloof collection, canopic jars that had held the organs of a mummified king; game boxes and a large number of little shabti figures that had acted as stand-ins for the dead in the next world, meant to do any work they might be called on to do. The jewelry had been kind of an afterthought. There weren't any especially rare or valuable pieces in the cache and she assumed that Maloof wasn't interested in storing them anymore and had decided to let Willem have them along with the mask.

Willem hadn't been particularly excited about the jewelry, but when Karen had asked him if she could inspect it, he'd readily agreed. She was writing her thesis on women's funeral jewelry and thought she might find some additional material amongst the new acquisitions. In any case, she was probably the first scholar to really study them and that gave her a little thrill.

She looked over the files to get some background before inspecting the pieces themselves. First were a series of little amulets in the shapes of animals and deities that had held various meanings for the ancient Egyptians. There were a huge number of scarabs and eyes of Horus, a few crocodiles, vultures and baboons. The little charms had likely been found amongst the linen wrappings on a mummy, meant to protect the dead in the tomb. The amulets were common and Karen had seen them before. There was no need to pay them much attention. Next were a series of simple beaded bracelets and necklaces, made of gold and glass beads. She was able to date them pretty reliably to the New Kingdom and she took some notes before moving on to the last piece, a beaded falcon collar featuring rows of gold and faience beads interspersed with amulets of many different kinds of stones. The falcon heads at either end of the thick necklace were made of gold, with accents of lapis and carnelian.

Karen sat up a little straighter in her chair. It was a beautiful collar and she hadn't expected to find it. The file on it said it was eighteenth dynasty, from a tomb in Giza, but she didn't think that could be right. It looked vaguely familiar to her. Not the necklace itself, but the style. She jotted some notes on a piece of paper and was about to go back to the files when she started at the sound of voices out in the basement gallery. It was against security regulations, but she had left the door to the study room propped open just a bit, to let some fresh air in. She couldn't hear what they were saying, but she assumed they were looking at the displays of Egyptian antiquities, Willem's two sarcophagi and the exhibits of statuary and other items from the collection.

She turned back to the collar, knowing she was lucky that Willem had given her access to it before he'd even had a chance to look through the pieces himself. She was very, very fortunate. *Don't forget it, Karen. Don't let yourself forget how lucky you are.*

Willem's recommendation would look good when she applied to graduate school, and experience with the jewelry would be helpful if she became a curator. *When,* she reminded herself, remembering what the speaker at the last meeting of the campus women's group had said about undermining one's own possibilities. *When* she became a curator.

She sifted through the papers in the file folder, trying to find a document that mentioned the beaded collar. According to the paperwork, the jewelry had been excavated in the Valley of the Kings in 1930 on a dig sponsored by a British collector named Harold Markham. The Markham collection was well known and much of it had gone to places like the Metropolitan Museum and the British Museum, so that was in order.

But she couldn't shake the feeling that the collar wasn't eighteenth dynasty. In any case, it was so well preserved it was hard to believe that it was three thousand years old. It was what she loved about Egyptology, the vibrancy of the works of art, the way they seemed so relevant, so modern so

many years later. What it must have been like to be one of
the first archaeologists to uncover the entrance to a king's
tomb, to stand there under the hot Egyptian sun, to hear the
men shout suddenly that they had found something, a staircase! She had relived Howard Carter's discovery of the
tomb of Tutankhamun so many times that she almost felt as
though she'd been there.

Ever since she had seen the Tutankhamun exhibit at the
Metropolitan Museum in New York on a school trip four
years ago, she had known that this was what she wanted to
do. She had begun learning about Egypt, about the strange
burial customs, and the cult of the afterlife that had so obsessed the ancient Egyptians. She had loved memorizing the
names of the gods and goddesses, the strange sounding
words, and then the hieroglyphs, the secret code that unlocked the secrets of that ancient world. She had done research into which colleges and universities were the best for
studying Egyptology and then she had decided that she
wanted to study here. After that, everything she had done
was for the purpose of attaining this goal. It had been easy to
keep her grades up, knowing that the prize for doing so was
realizing her dream.

After she'd gotten to the university, the dream had become Egypt itself, and during her junior summer, she had finally been able to go, joining a dig at Giza for three months
with an expedition from the Hapner Museum that included
Willem Keane and some other faculty members, along with
a number of graduate students.

She had been disillusioned, of course. There was no way
she wouldn't have been disappointed by the reality of Egypt,
the hot, dirty poverty of the cities obscuring the fantasy
she'd created, the endless sand and drudgery of work on the
dig. She had known enough about archaeology at that point
to know that she wanted to be an art historian and not an ar-
chaeologist, that it wasn't all uncovering intact tombs and
treasures, but still she'd been surprised that it had been so
different from her expectations. They were digging for tiny
pieces of ancient history now, shards and fragments instead

of golden statues and alabaster unguent vases, all the things of Karen's dreams.

It had been a sort of relief to return to the university and the museum, with its lovely pieces of antiquity, already cleaned of dust and dirt and grime, already in place behind glass. But then she'd realized that the darkness she'd found in Egypt had followed her home.

It was while she was away that she'd begun to question whether those beautiful things should be behind glass in an American museum at all. She'd met a young Egyptian graduate student working on the dig, who had told her that Egypt's history had been looted by rich white men, nothing more than "pirates," he'd said, who had stolen his country's most valuable assets, leaving nothing behind but empty graves. "Why is it," he asked, "that I should have to come to American or Britain, to see the art of my own country? You Americans wouldn't stand for it, you'd buy it back or find a way to take it, just as you take everything you want. The white men are nothing more than rapists, taking what they wanted by force when they couldn't seduce my countrymen into giving it willingly."

Since coming home, she'd been different, too. It was as though she'd awakened from a fog, she thought. She saw things so differently now. Everything she'd once taken or granted was now as uncertain as the history of the beaded collar.

As she was putting the collar into its box she heard the voices again, out in the gallery. This time, there was something about them that made her pay attention, something about the urgent low tones. It was two men and they seemed to be arguing.

"You're not doing it right," she heard one say. "Like this." *Museum goers*, she told herself. *Looking for the sarcophagi.* And then there was a loud crack from outside the door, a violent sound, and then another one. She jumped up, surprised, overturning the metal stool she'd been sitting on, and she heard one of the voices say, "What the fuck?," and then the men were'at the door, two of them, dressed in raincoats and carrying hatchets. She saw the hatchets before she took in the details of their plain, almost pleasant faces, and she must have screamed because the shorter of the men yelled, "Shut up!," and crossed the room to her, clapping a hand over her mouth and pushing her to the ground, grinding her face into the musty smelling industrial carpet that lined the floor of the study room. Sitting on her back, she had her arm twisted behind her. Her shoulder throbbed. She struggled to breathe against the carpet, gasping and choking, and tasted stomach acid in her mouth.

"Who the fuck are you?" the man near the door asked in a low, hissing whisper. Karen could hear her own breathing, ragged and uneven. She felt as though she'd run twenty miles. "You weren't supposed to be here, you bitch."

"Give me the tape," the one on top of her said in a similarly low voice. *They're afraid of someone hearing,* she told herself. *They think someone can hear.*

There was a slapping sound and then the ripping sound of tape being pulled from a roll. "No one said anything about someone being down here," the guy near the door said.

She felt herself being turned over, saw the man take a strip of silver duct tape from the roll and sever it with his teeth, then slap it over her mouth. She felt her lungs panic, forced herself to slow down and breathe through her nose.

He looked at her then and she knew, from the look on his masklike face, from the almost dreamy fixated look in his eyes, what he meant to do. She shook her head. *No, No,* knowing her fear would only excite him. His eyes were green, and somehow dead. She could smell his breath, peppermint masking stale beer, and he was sweating. She could smell that too.

"Do her hands and feet," the other guy said.

"Why don't you get the stuff out and I'll be right there." He was still looking into her eyes.

"No, you asshole. Tape up her hands and feet and get out of here."

She saw the dreamy look leave his eyes and then she felt

herself turned over again, and her shoulder screamed as he wrapped the tape 'round and 'round her wrists and ankles.

"Be good," he said, giving her a strange little pat, almost reassuring, as he stood, taking the duct tape with him.

"Okay. Let's go. We have to hurry now," the other one said, and she craned her neck around, trying to get a look at them, trying to burn those plain, very average faces on her brain. The guy near the door had eyes that were too close together. The other guy had a weak chin, a slight underbite.

She watched them flip the light switch and open the door and before it swung shut, she saw the Plexiglas display cabinet, which must have been split with the hatchet, the statuary inside tipped over, their long noble faces lying face down, in mockery of her own confinement.

The museum is being robbed, she said to herself before the door clicked shut and the storeroom fell dark. *That's what they're doing. They're robbing the museum.*

* * *

SWEENEY ST. GEORGE AWAKENED SLOWLY, AWARE ONLY OF A sense of breathlessness, as though something was interfering with the air getting into her mouth and down into her lungs. She opened her eyes to darkness, darkness, she realized, of a specific texture, composed of individual strands of darkness, soft, and smelling faintly of . . . fish.

She rolled over and sat up, displacing the large black cat that had been sleeping nestled up next to her face, her prolific red, curly hair a comfy cat bed. The cat, now sitting up in the dignified iconic pose of his species, blinked a few times and looked indignantly at her as if to say, "I had just gotten comfortable, thank you very much."

Sweeney gently pushed him off the bed and he stretched as he landed gracefully on the floor, then turned and sprang onto the windowsill and out the slightly open bedroom window on to the fire escape. He turned back, gave her a farewell glance through the window and was gone.

"What?" asked the other inhabitant of the bed sleepily.

"What's wrong?"

Sweeney curled herself against the long back and whispered into warm skin, faintly scented by the dark brown ovals of soap sent every month from London. "Nothing, just the General. It's okay. Go back to sleep."

She lay there for a few minutes, listening to his deep, even breathing, then got out of bed, slipped into the silk robe on the rocking chair in front of the window and went into the kitchen. It was nearly six and the sun was rising above the Somerville skyline, giving everything a clean and optimistic aspect that Sweeney appreciated. She got the coffee maker going and broke two eggs into a frying pan, flipping them out on to a plate when they were just barely set. Two pieces of buttered toast and an orange completed her breakfast and she sat happily munching as she watched her next-door neighbors enjoy their own breakfast on their second story balcony. It was late August and al fresco dining offered a respite from the current heat wave. Through the open kitchen window, Sweeney felt a slight breeze and turned toward it for a moment. As she finished eating and got up to rinse her dishes in the sink, she heard a whoosh and turned to find the General sitting on the kitchen windowsill, watching her.

"What are you doing back here?" she asked him. "I thought you'd gone for the day." The cat, who had been living with Sweeney for ten months now, tended to leave through one of the windows in her apartment early in the morning and return at night for dinner and bed. What he did during the day she had no idea, but the arrangement suited them both.

When she had first brought him home the previous fall, she had tried to get him to use a litter box and be a proper indoor cat, but he had hated using the box as much as she had hated cleaning it and when she accidentally left the bedroom window open one day, they both discovered a routine that suited them. She hadn't wanted a cat in the first place and so she did not want to fuss over him too much. He in turn, did not like being fussed over.

He looked meaningfully at her plate, still smeared with egg yolk, and she set it on the counter for him. In a few seconds, the plate was clean and shiny and the General used one huge paw to wash his whiskers before disappearing again out the window. "Have a nice day," Sweeney called after him.

Once she'd washed up, put on jeans and a linen blouse and tied her hair up and out of her face against the heat, she leaned over the bed and brushed its occupant's dark fall of hair away from his forehead. "Ian?" she whispered. "I'm heading out to the museum. It's seven. I'll see you tonight, okay?"

He opened his eyes and looked up at her, squinting into the sunlight. His glasses were on the bedside table and she knew he saw only the most vague outline of her face. "But it's early," he said. Ian didn't usually get to his office until nine or ten.

"I know, but the exhibition opens in three weeks and I still have so much to do. The catalogs are done and I have all this text to write. They're still painting the galleries and I need to make sure all the framing is right. I told Fred and Willem I'd get in early."

"Okay, okay, I can take a hint. However . . ." He reached up and pulled her back into bed. "I assert that I ought to be allowed to have a small memento of your existence, since I shall have to do without you all day."

"But I have so much to do . . ." She ran her hands over his bare chest, trying to decide if she wanted to be seduced. His skin was as warm as sun-baked stone, his arms around her sure and familiar. It had been almost six months since he'd arrived in the States to open a Boston office of his London auction house and Sweeney often found herself surprised at how quickly they'd settled into domesticity. They had known each other for nearly two years now, she supposed, so even though they'd only been in the same city since January, it made sense that there had been no need for prelude. But still . . . Sometimes when she came home at night and found him reading the papers on her couch or cooking dinner wrapped in his navy blue, monogrammed bathrobe, she had the sense of having entered someone else's house. She sometimes thought to herself, "Who is this man?" for a moment before she remembered, "Oh, it's Ian."

In any case, she thought, looking at him, he was a very handsome man and a very kind one and at the moment, a very sexy one.

"Just one thing you have to do here, though," he murmured, unbuttoning her blouse. She thought about protesting, then relaxed into his arms.

"Okay," she whispered into his ear. "But only because you're so persuasive."

Forty minutes later she was walking through the front door of the Hapner Museum of Art, holding a cardboard cup of takeaway coffee. The Hapner was arguably among the most distinguished college or university art museums in the country and like most art museums connected with institutions of higher learning, the Hapner had a strange and eclectic variety of collections, largely dependent as it was on original holdings and gifts by alumni or benefactors. In addition to works of American, European and Near-Eastern art, the Hapner housed the university's well-rounded collections of ancient Egyptian antiquities—thanks to the interest of its director and Egyptologist Willem Keane and the proliferation of wealthy and well-connected alumni associated with the university through the years.

The grand, gray stone façade of the museum presented a paternal and imposing aspect to passersby and, Sweeney had always thought, seemed singularly uninviting. She stopped for a moment to look up at the banner over the main entrance. "Still as Death: The Art of the End of Life," it read, announcing Sweeney's exhibition of funerary art from the museums collections. It panicked her to see the words up there when she hadn't even finished putting everything in place.

"Hi, Denny," she called out as she climbed the ten stone steps to the main foyer. In contrast to the outside of the museum, the foyer was surprisingly welcoming, bathed in sunlight from the soaring skylights high above the marble floor. The antiquities were housed on the basement and main floors, with the European and American galleries on the second, third and fourth levels. The museum was constructed around a central courtyard, open all the way to the ceiling, with wraparound balconies on each floor that led into the galleries. Standing in the courtyard, you could look all the way up to the balconies of the fourth floor high above you.

The security guard raised a hand and answered, "Hey, Mizz St. George." She had tried to get him to call her by her first name long ago, but Denny Keefe, who had been working at the museum for thirty years and apparently using the formal address for all that time, wouldn't budge. "Hot day, huh?"

"Yeah. Again." She smiled at him, glad, as she always was, that the museum administration hadn't let Denny go for someone younger and spryer, but rather supplemented his presence with a revolving collection of imposing looking twenty-year-old body builders to safeguard the collection. Denny himself wasn't a very convincing security guard, but he was a cheerful presence and Sweeney liked him. He had always reminded her a little of a frog, with his large, egg-shaped eyes and his longish white hair, which he kept smoothed to his head with applications of a slippery substance that smelled vaguely of sandalwood. His uniform had never fit him properly and the loose green fabric added to the effect. Sweeney wasn't sure what he would do if he were actually faced with a determined art thief, but she liked the idea that he might just put out his tongue and . . .

She headed up to the third floor, where a series of connected galleries would soon house her exhibition. It had long been a dream of Sweeney's to plan an exhibit of the things she studied: tombstones and mourning jewelry, death masks and Victorian post-mortem photographs and Egyptian burial items from the museum's collection.

The pieces had all been chosen and the previous year had been spent working with museum staff to create installations and displays for the items. As she walked into the first of the linked galleries, she saw that one of the Egyptian sarcophagi had already been carried up. Tomorrow they would be bringing up other Egyptian burial equipment from the basement galleries. Though they could no longer display the museum's mummy, they could display many of the items that would have been buried with it. The elaborate preparations of the bodies of the Ancient Egyptians—first the nobility, but eventually those on other levels of society as well—was great evidence for the overriding assertion of Sweeney's exhibition: that death and speculation about the afterlife were the motivating factor for much of the great art of the world. By choosing representative pieces of funerary art from different eras, she hoped to show the diversity of responses to human mortality.

Today she had to choose a piece of Egyptian funeral jewelry to replace one that the conservation department had determined wasn't in good enough shape to be displayed. The catalog was already completed of course, but she and Willem had decided that they should just choose another piece. She hadn't found exactly what she wanted among the displayed items, so she went down to the storage areas located beneath the museum to browse the files.

The art and antiquities displayed in the Hapner's galleries represented only a tiny percentage of the museum's holdings. The rest of the items were stored in five large rooms beneath the museum. Banks of file cabinets flanked the large workspace where Harriet Tyler, the collections manager, had her office and controlled access to the rooms of priceless and not-so-priceless treasures.

Every piece in the museum's collection, no matter when it had been acquired or donated, nor how insignificant it might be, had a file containing information about its history and connection to other pieces owned by the museum, and Sweeney went to the "E's" and found the files kept on examples of ancient Egyptian jewelry.

Her choices were very nearly endless. The museum had huge numbers of Egyptian antiquities, most of them unimportant pieces that had been gifted to the university long ago. They were used for research, brought out for special exhibitions, or loaned to other museums, but for the most part, they remained in storage. Attacking the row of files, Sweeney felt a bit like a prospective dog owner at the pound. Who would the lucky antiquity be?

She had already included the more obvious examples of Egyptian funerary art, the sarcophagi and the canopic chests and jars that had held the internal organs of entombed ancient Egyptians. What she didn't have was an example of the elaborate jewelry that had been buried with the mummies, the amulets and collars and pectorals that archaeologists often found amongst the layers of linen wrapping the prepared bodies. Some jewelry from ancient Egypt would be a nice counterpoint to the Victorian mourning jewelry she was also including in the exhibition.

There were scores of insignificant pieces, scarab rings and gold hoop earrings that had been donated years ago and weren't seen by anyone but students anymore. Sweeney remembered coming down to the museum as a graduate student and looking at some New Kingdom amulets for a paper she was writing about funerary mythology.

Now she found listings for a number of amulets in the shape of various animals and flowers that had special meanings for the Ancient Egyptians, hippos and flies and vultures and lotuses and fish. She put them aside, thinking it might be interesting to include a few, but quickly forgot about them when she opened the file folder labeled "Beaded Collar. 18th Dynasty." On the outside was a little grid with a name and date scrawled in it. Sweeney assumed it was a record-keeping device to track everyone who had taken the piece out of storage. It appeared that the last person had been someone named Karen Philips.